GW00657827

Tony Marturano was born in the UK in 1969 and has written several plays (thrillers and family dramas), many of which were staged throughout Cambridgeshire.

It took Tony three years to write his first novel, Nimbus, juggling the writing in between his full time job and any spare time he could lay his hands on!

To find out more visit www.tmproductions.co.uk

NIMBUS

By Tony Marturano

GLACYK

www.glacyk.co.uk

Published in Canada by Trafford Publishing. 2001
ISBN 155212568-8

Published in the United Kingdom by **Glacyk** Publishing. 2001
ISBN 0-9540137-0-0

© Tony Marturano 2001

The right of Tony Marturano to be identified as the author of this work has been asserted.

Typeset, printed and bound in the UK by
Antony Rowe Ltd, Chippenham, Wiltshire SN14 6LH

For Bella, without whom…

Acknowledgements

Tony Marturano would like to thank (in no particular order) the following people for their help during the writing of this novel:

Dr Ed Uthman, MD (For all the grisly details)

Derek Hardy, UK Met Office. (For the hard time you gave me in the name of realism!)

Gareth Bates, UK Environment Agency. (For Blake.)

Chris Sawyer, Authors Aid. (For all the constructive criticism.)

Nimbus Focus Group: Marina Coleman, Glenys Shaw, and Bill Ratcliffe. (For help in orientation.)

Bella Coleman. (Without you, there wouldn't be a Nimbus. You are and always will be my inspiration.)

Trafford Publishing. (For all their help in bringing this book to print!)

You, the reader. (If you are reading this page, it is probably because you bought this book. Without you, all my work would be worthless. Thank you.)

Prologue

Icelandic Coast – 100 km Southwest of Reykjavik

After ten minutes of flying over Iceland's barren region, the helicopter was approaching the glacial perimeter. Erupting geysers and bubbling mud lakes cooled into a winter wonderland of snow capped mountains, gurgling brooks and green valleys. The sky was a steely blue ceiling from which hung large black cumulonimbus clouds.

Stefán laughed politely as the pilot made a joke then he turned to look at the ground speeding by beneath him. He smiled, the more he thought of his wife and what she had told him over the breakfast table that morning, the more his heart filled with joy. He had waited a long time for this day and finally it had arrived; he was going to be a father.

He blinked back tears as another snow-capped hill erupted from the horizon. The pilot gunned the engine and the chopper climbed upward.

Beyond the hill, the Glacyk Chemico complex nestled inside the valley like an absconding armadillo. The three square miles of white hexagonal buildings, satellite dishes, radio masts, and giant chimneys all encased in a twelve-foot high electrified fence, resembled a moon base.

The pilot spoke into his mouthpiece, identified himself and requested authorisation to land at one of the four giant helipads that marked each corner of the complex. A few minutes later the helicopter dipped and began its descent over a concrete platform, marked H North.

Stefán unbuckled his seatbelt, thanked the pilot and stepped out of the craft, stooping to avoid the whirring blades.

He sucked in deep lungs full of air as he took in his surroundings: The valley all around was dusted with snow in stark contrast to the sky that was dark and atmospheric. He made this journey every morning but it had never looked so beautiful as it did today. He was the happiest man in the world.

He cheerfully greeted the driver of the waiting jeep and climbed into the passenger seat. Behind them, the whirring of the helicopter's engine grew louder as it climbed back into the gathering gloom.

The jeep pulled up alongside a flight of steps. At the top, two armed guards, in black duffel coats, stood to attention outside a set of giant double doors.

Stefan climbed the steps and said, happily, "Morning."

"Morning," one of the two replied. Then, noticing the smile on his face, added. "You seem pretty happy this morning."

"I am," Stefán said, holding up a bar-coded identity card to the close circuit camera above the doors. The lens zoomed in and a laser scanned him, the image, and the code.

"Oh yes? Is there something we should know?" the guard asked curiously as the doors swung open.

"Yes, there is," Stefán beamed at them both as he entered the building, "but I am not going to tell you."

Specialising in the production of pharmaceuticals, ChemiCo was one of the leading producers of antidepressants. Currently, its most important project was the development of a revolutionary drug, which promised to be a breakthrough in the treatment of mental disorders. The details remained highly classified. Indeed, Glacyk ChemiCo, a fraction of the size of its sister plants, had been awarded the research and development contract for this potentially very lucrative drug because of its remote and secret location.

The main reception area was large and lavishly furnished with dark grey marbled floors and walls to match. The décor, in striking contrast to its glacial location, captured an essence of the desert in the form of two huge cacti with roots imbedded in what looked like ocean pebbles. They stood, like giant pillars at an ancient coliseum, on either side of the room.

Stefán nodded at the guards who sat behind a rosewood reception desk, their caps pulled down tightly over their foreheads, concealing their eyes. As one of them greeted visitors the other sat like a bird of prey, eyes glued to the bank of monitors in front of him.

At the row of elevators at the back of the lobby, Stefán swiped his card through the reader. The doors opened instantly. As the lift descended into the bowels of the complex, he found himself thinking of his wife again and her smile. Oh God how he loved her smile.

He stepped out of the lift and hummed as his footsteps echoed around a dimly lit tunnel. He stopped when he came to a pair of doors upon which a card read: *"TURBINE 3000. AUTHORISED PERSONNEL ONLY."*

Turbine 3000 was, effectively, a power plant inside ChemiCo. Because of its remote location, Glacyk ChemiCo could not benefit from conventional forms of electricity and needed to manufacture its own power. This it did very efficiently. The T3000 was unique. Designed by ChemiCo's own engineers, it could generate enough electricity to power a major town.

He placed his right hand on a small glowing red panel and after a few seconds, it beeped and turned green. Then, with another swipe of his card, the doors opened. He squinted; it was very bright in here compared to the gloom of the corridor.

There was a murmur of voices and somewhere a telephone rang and was answered. The walls in this room were jammed packed with various electronic monitors and gauges of all sizes. There were computers on desktops behind which sat men in white overalls, each of them gazing into monitors; their faces blue from the filtered glow. A wall clock read 8:00am.

Hinrik, a young man in his late twenties, wearing a grey overall, looked up from a computer printout and smiled. "Morning."

"Morning," Stefán replied. "Anything exciting happen?"

Hinrik mulled the question and then, without taking his eyes off the report in front of him, he offered, "No, not really. We had a minor problem with B in the early hours but nothing serious."

"What happened?" Stefán asked.

Here we go. "Nothing much, thought we had an alarm in one of the coolers but it stopped before we could even trace it."

"Did you run diagnostics on it?"

"What for? There wasn't a fault."

Stefán forced an incredulous laugh. "Hinrik, it's procedure. There could be other faults in the system."

And you would know, of course. Just because he's been here a few months longer than me he thinks he can tell me how to do my job."

Hinrik breathed deeply, stood up, handed the printout to Stefán and said, apathetically, "Well, my shift is over now so what you do on your shift is entirely your own business."

Running the diagnostics programme would mean shutting off one of the generators and running the plant at half power for a minimum of five hours. Management hated these delays, as they meant many activities would have to be halted. A few hours delay for them could mean a massive advantage for their competitors.

Across the room Tómas, a young technician, was sitting in front of a bank of green lights and digital displays taking notes. Suddenly, he heard a beeping sound and looked up to see that one of the green lights had turned yellow. Instantly, the matrix printer to his left started churning out data. He had never seen anything like this before.

He looked round. Across the room, his managers seemed deep in conversation. Ignoring the urge to shout out to them, he read the report the printer was spewing out.

The words ***"ERROR 99"*** headed it, after that came a jumble of numerical data that meant absolutely nothing to him. Panicked, he called to Hinrik.

"Hold on a minute," his manager replied, distractedly as he proceeded to argue his case

"But Sir…"

"I said hold on a bloody minute!" Hinrik barked. *Mr know it all* had decided to make him look stupid by suggesting that they run diagnostics now. That would mean filing a report detailing exactly how and when the error originally occurred and that was during his shift.

"If management promoted me to shift manager they did so for a reason. They did so because they think I am up to the job, so who are you to say I'm not?" he continued.

"I didn't say you weren't up to the job, Hinrik. I am just…"

Stefán stopped in mid sentence as he locked eyes with Tómas. The boy was sweating and there was no need for them to exchange words. Ignoring Hinrik, who was still talking, he logged into a terminal. The yellow light had turned red and the beeping was now a loud shrill. Oblivious to a panicked Tómas peering over his shoulders, Stefán began to work the keyboard.

Hinrik joined them. "What the hell's going on?"

There was silence, except for the clicking of the keyboard and the alarm buzzer.

"Are you going to answer me?"

"I don't know yet," Stefán replied calmly. "Looks like there's something wrong with one of the coolers."

"What do you mean?" Hinrik asked, snatching up the report from the printer. His heart skipped a beat when he noticed the same error he had experienced earlier. Only this time, it was constant. He contemplated on whether or not he should tell but decided against it.

By now, the others were aware of the commotion. They watched as Stefán proceeded to key in various command strings. His fingers worked fast and efficiently, his face calm and composed.

The computer's screen scrolled data in response to his keyboard interrogation. Pausing momentarily, Stefán took in the information then said, flatly, "We need to shut down the turbine. Call Williamson and tell him what we are going to do." His words were not pointed at anyone in particular but Tómas would be very pleased to carry out his instructions.

"We can't call him, he's not here," Hinrik said.

"Then we'll have to shut it down anyway."

"Hang on a minute," Hinrik interjected, playing down the seriousness of the situation. "You can't just shut down the system without authorisation."

"Watch me," Stefán replied as more lights changed from green to yellow and the room filled with a cacophony of alarm shrills and buzzers. He looked at a bunch of keys hooked to Hinrik's belt.

Their eyes met. "Give me those keys, Hinrik."

Hinrik shook his head, "Oh no." Suddenly, he was filled with dread. Things were getting too serious. "I can't let you do it."

"Don't be a fool," Stefán said coaxingly.

Nevertheless, Hinrik shook his head. It was apparent that he had made a serious error of judgement. If Williamson learned of this he would most certainly be fired and then what would he do? Jobs like this, around here, were a once in a lifetime opportunity.

"Hinrik!" Stefán shouted, as if to awake the young man from a trance. Then gently, he continued, "This is serious Hinrik. I need those keys right now."

Behind them, Tómas and the others were watching the battle of wills, each silently urging Hinrik to hand over the keys.

As if he had heard them, Hinrik reluctantly unhooked the keys from his belt and threw them at Stefán who caught them with his right hand and then fell to his knees and used them to unlock a small metal cabinet situated underneath one of the desks. A yellow sticker with a bolt of lightening and the words *"Authorised Personnel Only"* branded the door. He opened it, revealing a panel of colour coded push buttons and one black handle.

In that moment, the lights dipped and a loud siren sounded, a red beacon at the centre of the ceiling flashed and a recorded female voice played over the public address system: *"Attention, this is an emergency. All personnel to evacuate the building immediately. Attention, This is an emergency."* The voice repeated itself like a demented robot.

"Oh my…" Hinrik breathed, "We're going into meltdown!"

Tómas, frozen with fear, watched his colleagues kicking and clawing at each other as they scrambled for the exit whilst, on the floor in front of him, his managers grappled for exclusive access to the cabinet. "Shut it off!" Shut it off!" Hinrik shouted.

The siren blared, the red beacon flashed, and somewhere, someone was screaming in agony. Tómas put his hands over his ears in an effort to block out the noise and his terror. He crouched underneath one of the desks, drew his knees up to his chest and began rocking himself gently.

Hinrik lashed out and hooked Stefán in the jaw sending him reeling backward. Then, reaching into the cabinet, he clasped the black handle and began to pull it down.

"NO! Off first… Hinrik, close the circuit first or you'll blow us sky high!" Stefán shrieked, tugging at the man's shoulder. However, Hinrik was determined and pulled the black lever down as far as it would go. That is when Tómas closed his eyes and prayed the lord to forgive his sins.

The wolf watched with unblinking eyes as the humans ran screaming from the building but it was too late. The first explosion ripped through the entrance lobby, propelling the double doors outward, mowing down the security guards on the steps.

The next one erupted upward, catapulting flames and debris into the air. Flames shot out of cavities like fire from a dragon's mouth, incinerating anything and anyone within its reach. A satellite dish on one of the nearby buildings whistled like a firework as it was blasted thirty feet into the air, it returned to earth crushing a man in a white coat and dyeing the snow crimson.

Before long, the valley was ablaze and all that remained of Glacyk ChemiCo was a pile of rubble, fire and smoke.
The wolf whimpered as the sun was eclipsed by great clouds of green tinted smoke that raced towards the sky, seeking and merging with the smog high above the troposphere.

One

Widemouth Bay, Cornwall, England 07:59 am

His trainers splashed the salty water as he ran the perimeter of the shingled beach. His heart pounded as the perspiration that had dampened his short black hair washed onto his forehead. "Just a little further..." he thought. " A little further and I'll be there…"

"… More than a thousand people have died in an explosion at a chemical plant in Iceland. The authorities believe that a massive

power surge caused the fire from which there were no survivors. The investigation continues. My name is Elena Parker for Southwest Radio and now with today's weather: Andrew Jarvis."

"Thanks Elena. Well, pretty easy forecasting today, It's going to be a warm sunny day for most of Great Britain. Indeed, I have been told that it is going to be one of the warmest May days recorded since 1932. But make the most of it because it looks like bad weather is on the way. Meteorologists have picked up a large band of cloud over the Atlantic Ocean and it is heading our way....

"Thanks Andrew. The time is now 08:00; time for a sports update with..."

Blake pulled the earphones off as he reached the Landrover Discovery. He threw the personal radio onto the passenger seat. Then, moving to the rear of the vehicle, he opened the boot. It was crammed with his everyday working tools. The inventory was essential and always the same:

1 electronic D.O.M (Dissolved Oxygen Metre)
1 ammonia Test Kit, 2 Eye wash bottles
1 pair of Wellington Boots
1 pair of Gloves
1 life Jacket
2 crates of small sample bottles (with colour coded caps)
2 wooden stakes
1 inflatable oil boom
2 bales of writing pads
1 slasher (A scythe with blunt blade)
1 hard black case (containing scientific equipment, a strapped down Stanley knife, and a pack of PH sticks).

On top of the case were a face-towel and a pair of clean trainers. He wiped his hair and face with the towel and changed into the trainers. As he bent down to tie up his laces, he paused, catching sight of the bay. It was cradled between two huge, rugged cliff tops on which nested several colonies of seagulls. Occasionally a group of them swooped down onto the aquamarine sea.

He watched, mesmerised, as the waves pounded the shingled

beach and the sun shone brightly in a pale blue sky. No wonder so many artists came here, he marvelled to himself. He breathed deeply, enjoying the fresh sea air. Oh, how he loved living here.

At thirty years of age, Blake Hudson had achieved much but still wanted more from life. He had been employed by the council as an Environment Officer not long after graduating from Cambridge. After six years, he had applied for and won a position with the Environment Agency.

It was when he was assigned to investigate the mercury water scare in Camelford that he had discovered his love for Cornwall. Within weeks, he had sold his Cambridge apartment and moved to the Southwest, into a converted lighthouse at Stony Point.

His parents, both retired, lived in a modest Georgian house in Stowe. They were very proud of their only son and although Giles Hudson's dream of Blake graduating in politics, and following in his footsteps as an MP, was not realised, he was not disappointed. Indeed, Giles took every opportunity to praise his son's achievements and cherished the bond between them.

Perhaps, influenced by his father's public role, Blake took great pride in his physical appearance. He weight trained regularly and, since moving to the Cornish coast, he had derived much pleasure in running at least five miles every morning. His hard work paid off, for Blake was a paragon of health; he had a muscular body, dark brown eyes, and a strong, chiselled jaw line.

He rounded a bend in one of the many narrow roads that snaked through the Cornish countryside and saw, ahead of him, the lighthouse. It stood in a regal position, nestled into a rocky cliff side.

The interior of the building was cool in contrast to the early May sun. Despite its circular architecture, the lighthouse was very spacious. The ground floor was partitioned into two areas; one area was the entrance lobby and the other a utility room from which an archway led to an extended area that was the lounge.

In here, dark, modern furniture was set off nicely against the virgin white walls upon which hung various colourful paintings. A door at the opposite end of the room led to a kitchen/ diner and a downstairs toilet with a tiny window offering an appetising view of the rocky shore.

A spiral stairwell led to the bedroom on the first floor. A custom made bed sat to one side of the room and a fitted wardrobe ran across the opposite wall. Next to the bed, a door led to a small bathroom, which was awash with daylight streaming in through small windows.

Blake's office was on the second floor; the thick glass that once ran right around the sides of this room had been replaced with double-glazing windows in a PVC frame. A sliding glass door led out onto the balcony that ran around the circumference and afforded spectacular views of the coast.

The conversion had taken place within the last year and was a success. The walls, in keeping with the rest of the building, were bright white. On them, hung mahogany picture frames displaying diplomas in various subjects. An oval desk, still in mahogany, was situated to one side of the room, on it stood a state of the art multimedia personal computer. On the opposite side of the room sat a leather sofa. Next to that, a telescope peered out of the balcony doors.

In his bedroom, Blake stripped, pressed play on the stereo and showered as the thumping sounds of club hits echoed throughout the building.

Two

Plymouth College, Plymouth, England. 11:00 am

Blake, now dressed in a dark blue suit, glanced discreetly at his watch. He was half an hour into the lecture and wondered if any of the students had taken in anything of what he had said. In that moment, a hand fluttered up at the back of the classroom, it revealed a thin young man with glasses.

"Yes?" Blake asked.

"May I ask a question?"

"Of course, I was going to take questions at the end of the lecture anyway."

"A moment ago you talked about the effects of acid rain in northern Europe and said that we were responsible for a large amount of it. I'm not sure I understand why."

Blake smiled and moved to the front of the desk, leaned back on it and proceeded to explain, "Well, most of you, I'm sure, are aware of the infamous smog that smothered the whole of London in the early 50s. For those of you that aren't, in the winter of 1952 London was plunged into what seemed to be a permanent fog, only it wasn't. It was a chronic smog caused by the over burning of fossil fuels such as…"

"Coal!" An excited blonde girl interrupted from the front row.

"Coal, that's right," Blake agreed.

The girl smiled sweetly and blushed. She was obviously attracted to Blake and he had been aware of this ever since he had started giving seminars here two months ago.

"And what else?" He offered the question to the rest of the class.

The blonde girl, Clare, jumped in again, " Discharge from power stations."

"Correct. It became just as bad as any other major epidemic. Four thousand people died whilst thousands of others were hospitalised. It took the appalling death toll from the killer fogs of 1952 and a great deal more to bring about legislation to clean up the air over London. So finally, in 1956, the Clean Air Act put an end to smog by banning the use of coal for domestic heating purposes within London. It didn't, however, ban other damaging pollutants. Chimneys were simply built taller. Therefore, for the past forty years much of the pollution that would have mimicked the smog of 1952 is being dumped further a field, over the rest of western and northern Europe."

"This still doesn't explain how it gets there in the first place," the boy said. "I mean, this so called smog ends up in the atmosphere, this we already know, but how does it manage to get all the way to Northern and Western Europe? Does it hitch hike a ride with a 747?"

A ripple of laughter ran through the class and the acne riddled young man grinned, proud of his quip.

Blake made a conscious effort to laugh with them. It was moments like these when he wondered why he had agreed to lecture here once a week. He had enough work to do without having to drive two hours across country to lecture this lot.

"That's very funny," Blake said. "But in answer to your question, no. You see, many different gasses combine in the earth's atmosphere to produce a cocktail of damaging acid. The most dangerous of these being SO2, Sulphur Dioxide and N0X, Nitrous Dioxide. These amalgamate with the moisture of clouds to form such things as rain, snow, fog, mist, cloud, and even flakes. Acid air is more of an accurate way of describing it. This acid air can fall as precipitation hundreds, sometimes thousands of kilometres away.

"And that's where it gets the name of acid rain," Clare added, knowingly.

Another hand went up; this time it was that of a thin young girl in a flowered dress and wearing spectacles.

"Yes?" Blake asked.

"How does acid rain affect humans? I mean, earlier you said that thousands of people died and others were hospitalised. What were they suffering from?"

"Many cases showed a variety of symptoms. As I explained earlier, acid air is made up from a combination of chemicals from our industry being dumped into the atmosphere. Each of these affects the echo system and us in different ways. Mercury and lead attack the central nervous system bringing on many psychological disorders, whilst nickel and beryllium damage the lungs. Antimony can lead to heart disease and cadmium causes liver damage. Yet, despite all this, we humans release over 450,000 tonnes of these deadly metals into the atmosphere each year. Over half of them come from a single source: vehicle exhausts. It's not only inhaling lead that is dangerous; airborne lead settles on food which we eat. You see, like acid rain, lead travels thousands of kilometres before descending to earth. Traces of lead and other pollutants originating in cities have been found in the snows of the polar ice caps. In Iceland the situation is so bad that officials believe that only with martial law will they be able to enforce any effective anti-pollution measures. In fact, over the last decade, Iceland has climbed the cancer charts and is now believed to be number one!"

Blake paused as he noticed the look of concentration on the faces of his pupils. He had lectured here for over two months and never before had he caught their attention as he had now. Some of them looked horrified by what they had just heard. He felt compelled to lighten the mood. Therefore, smiling broadly, he said, " Don't get me wrong, I wouldn't give up my Land Rover for anyone. Where I live, I couldn't survive without it."

There was another faint ripple of laughter.

"Where do you live, Sir?" Clare asked.

" I live in a converted lighthouse near Bude."

"Wow! A converted light house sounds really cool."

"It is," Blake replied. "Anyway, as I was saying, many countries have committed themselves to cleaning up their act but there are still many more that are yet to truly understand the gravity of the situation. Take Mexico City for example, numerous chemical companies move there in order to take advantage of their lax laws against pollution. Airborne toxins created by industry, cars, aerosols, burning forests or domestic fires are a controllable phenomenon. It is theoretically possible to repair the damage caused by these pollutants. Ambitious experiments are being conducted every day to stem the acidification of Scandinavian and Canadian lakes, for example, liming the lakes with aluminium, calcium and other neutralising agents. Such cures are not however, very satisfactory. In addition to the astronomical costs, there is the fact that these technical fixes do not actually solve the problem, and as long as we keep pumping acid into the air it will be necessary to keep liming the lakes and who knows, the agents counteracting the acid rain might themselves produce a new generation of environmental problems.

Now conscious and inspired by the class's full attention, Blake was slowly pacing up and down in front of his desk. For the next hour, he continued to explain about the environmental damage the earth was sustaining.

As he did this, Clare hung on his every word.

Blake chose to ignore the girl's obvious stare.

The bell sounded, signalling the end of the lecture. The class almost immediately rose from their seats, creating a scraping cacophony.

As Blake shuffled papers into his briefcase, the class emptied of its occupants, all with exception of Clare. As he turned to leave, he found her standing directly behind him. "Clare! You startled me."

"I'm sorry, Sir. I didn't mean to." She flashed a smile at him.

"Is there something I can help you with?"

Oh yes. " I... I just wanted to tell you how much I enjoyed the lecture today."

"Great, thank you very much." There followed an uncomfortable few moments where Clare would not move out of Blake's way nor would she offer anything more to the conversation. Blake broke the silence by saying, "Well, if you'll excuse me I need to get going."

"Oh, sorry." The girl obliged moving out of his way.

"Thank you, I'll see you next week," he said, picking up his briefcase.

"Yes, I look forward to it." Clare replied, smiling a sickly sweet smile.

With that, Blake left the classroom and although he did not look back, he could still feel Clare's gaze on him.

He hurried down the corridor and was relieved to exit the building and feel the sun on his face. Slipping on his sunglasses, he made his way to the football pitch at the rear of the college where, at the stalls, he sat next to a man in a blue tracksuit who was furiously blowing a whistle and shouting abuse at the players on the pitch. The rest of the benches were empty except for a couple of academic spectators.

PE Teacher Matt Allen was Blake's closest friend. He lived in Bude and looked nothing like a PE teacher; with short, dark wavy hair, a goatee beard and an earring in his right ear he looked more like a pop star than a teacher.

"How's it going?" Blake asked, taking a seat next to him.

"Could be better," he replied. Then, he shouting to a player on the field, "Wakey, wakey, Dave! Try passing that bloody ball!" Then he said to Blake, without turning, "I tell you, I'd get a better game from a bunch of twelve year olds. Anyway how was it with your little lot?"

"Good. They managed to remain conscious throughout the whole of the lecture today," Blake said, looking out at the players on the pitch.

"There you go, told you things would get better." They exchanged glances and he smiled. "So, how's your favourite pupil?"

"The same, " Blake replied indifferently.

"Maybe you should just give her one and have done with it."

"Thanks Matt, that is very responsible, encouraging me to have an affair with one of my pupils. Any other good suggestions on how to get myself sacked?"

Matt grinned. "I didn't say have an affair with her, man." He was obviously teasing and this made Blake smile to himself as his friend proceeded to bark some more instructions at his football team.

"Christ! Are they thick or what? I tell you, if united play anything like this lot next week we won't stand a fucking chance," Matt cursed, shaking his head in a hopeless gesture. Then snapping back to his happy-go-lucky self, "Are we hitting the town tonight or what?"

"Sure, where do you fancy?"

"Anywhere we can get wrecked."

"That is understood. Shall we drive down to Torquay?"

"Yeah, why not." Then, shouting out to the field again, "I saw that Jason! You do that once more and you're out…. I mean it!"

"I'll leave you to it then," Blake said, standing up.

"Cool, I'll see you tonight. What time are you picking me up?"

"What? It's your turn to drive."

"Oh, Come on, Blakey. You know I can't enjoy myself unless I have a few." Matt pulled a downtrodden face.

"I have a better idea. Let's check into a B&B whilst we are there. Never know, you might get lucky; I might let you have some of my cast offs." Blake said with a grin.

Matt playfully punched him. "Yeah, right. Just get the hell out of here. Some of us have work to do."

No sooner had Blake left and Matt was back to the football game in hand, shouting and gesturing at the players.

Blake walked back to the Land Rover, climbed behind the steering wheel and drove out, off the school grounds and into the busy Plymouth traffic, oblivious to the pair of green eyes that watched him until he was no longer in sight.

Three

The atmosphere 500 miles West of Heathrow Airport England. 21:00 Local time.

The Boeing 757 lurched eastwards through the atmosphere with the grace of a pterodactyl. Ahead, the sky was a clear mixture of evening colours: dark red with wisps of white cloud, whilst the northeast sky was a dark discoloration on the horizon.

Adam had not been a flight navigator for long, at least not for such a major airline. This was his first flight out to Orlando.

Up ahead, he noticed some flashes of light and asked, "What

was that, Captain?"

"What was what?" Captain Richard Ormond replied, without turning around.

"I don't know, looked like some flashes of light up ahead."

Peering out of the window, co-pilot Geoff Harrison said, " I can't see anything."

"I'm sure I saw a light," Adam added, frowning.

"Probably just a solar flare," Geoff suggested.

"No, it was more than…there!" Adam exclaimed, pointing to the horizon as another flash manifested itself.

"Did you see that?" Richard asked.

"Yeah," came Geoff's perturbed reply. "What do you think it is?"

"I am not sure. If it's a storm, we haven't been notified."

Flicking a switch, Richard spoke into the microphone that hung in front of his mouth. "This is Heathrow 101. Please come in."

There was a brief blare of static and then a metallic voice came through the cabin speaker.

"Go ahead 101."

"Yes, we have a visual on what seems to be electrical activity ahead. Please advise."

"Standby 101"

"Do you think it's a tropical?" Geoff asked.

"I don't know what it is," Richard replied as another flash appeared.

The passenger cabin was quiet except for the snoring of an elderly man in seat B42; most of the passengers were asleep.

At the rear of the cabin, the flight attendants, Jane and Amanda, were talking in whispers.

In Seat C36 Tracy sat next to a newly wed couple. They had spent most of the flight canoodling. No wonder they now sat with their heads lolling backward and their mouths wide open as they slept. They had worn each other out. *Some people just don't have any manners. Surely, they could refrain from those noisy, slobbering kisses whilst a complete stranger sitting in the passenger seat next to them!*

Tracy sighed. Was it the noisy kisses that irked her or simply the fact that she was jealous of them? She had decided on this trip to get away from the pain and the heartache she had felt and was still feeling. She could be the one celebrating her honeymoon. A tear trickled down her pale cheek as, once again, she imagined the wedding, the dress, her family, friends and the photographers. As she looked out of her passenger window, she could see the flashing of cameras up ahead as the plane dipped its wings and began to turn.

"If we head south-east we should be able to avoid the worst of it," Richard said, gripping the cloche and changing their course.

"Why didn't they advise us of the storm earlier?"

"They say it wasn't anywhere near our trajectory."

"They should still have notified us," Geoff moaned.

"Have you got that new reading yet, Adam?"

"Yes Sir, we should only have to deviate by 20 kilometres."

As the plane advanced on its course, the storm grew closer. Now, the crew and the few passengers that were awake could clearly see the huge mass of cumulonimbus cloud. The glow of the sun had disappeared, swallowed up by the darkness.

Condensation began to form on the windscreen of the cockpit. The flashing that had once been a small torchlight in the distance was now a menacing blanket of lightning.

"Should we warn the passengers?" Geoff asked.

Richard pondered on the question and then he very confidently answered, "No, what is the point? Most of them are asleep anyway." Then, speaking into his mouthpiece again, " This is Heathrow 101, please come in"

There was a pause, more static, then the familiar metallic voice once again, *" 101, you have now entered..."* Another blast of static and then the radio went dead.

"Heathrow, this is 101, please come in."

Static...

"Heathrow, this is flight 101 please come in."

More static...

"What's happened?" Adam asked. His eyes were wide with apprehension.

"It seems the storm is interfering with our radio," Geoff offered.

"It shouldn't do that, should it?" Adam asked.

Before Richard could answer, the plane dipped slightly, jolting the cockpit crew forward.

"What the hell was that?"

"Calm down, Adam. It's only turbulence."

The plane lurched forward again.

"Tighten your seat belts," Richard instructed. Almost in unison, both pilots proceeded to flick various switches.

The cabin door opened and a pale-faced Amanda walked in. "What's going…." Her sentence cut short as the plane dipped yet again.

"Wake up the passengers and tell them to fasten their seatbelts!" Richard ordered.

Without comment, Amanda left the cockpit, closing the door behind her.

Geoff flicked another switch on the panel above him, a bell sounded and the *"Fasten Seat belts"* light came on. Then, as Richard had before him, he attempted to establish radio contact with, at this stage, any who could hear them.

"Adam, I thought you'd plotted our course around the storm," Richard demanded.

"I did!" Adam panicked. "Look for yourself!" he shouted, thrusting the map at Richard.

Ignoring the young man's outburst, Richard said, "I do not need that, you do. Now, get back to those readings and check for any discrepancies."

Outside, the condensation had turned into rain and was hammering on the windshield.

Inside, the once dormant passenger cabin was now a bustle of voices. Amanda and Jane were rushing up and down the aisle responding to many demanding and frightened passengers.

The old man in seat 46 had awoken from his slumber and was now swigging from a bottle of duty free scotch. Tracy, in seat C36, glanced across at the newly wed couple who only moments earlier had been snoring in a perfect symphony. She no longer envied them as they huddled into each other. Oh, how pathetic they looked now. She wondered if it really came to the crunch and they had to choose between life and each other, what would they choose?

"Excuse me.... Miss?   Miss?"

Tracy looked up to see a blonde flight attendant peering down at her.

"Yes?"

"Could you please fasten your seat belt?"

"Of course." She complied, although she could not really give a shit about her seatbelt. Her mind was wandering again. She was thinking of Mark. What was he doing now? Was he with her? She felt a surge of anger and watched as the weather outside sympathised with her by flashing angrily and spitting rain at the window.

At the other end of the plane, Amanda joined Clare. "Jesus! The whole bloody plane's in a panic and that stupid cow was just sitting there, smiling out of the window."

"Probably under shock," Jane replied calmly.

"Well you seem laid back. Shit!" Amanda cried as the plane shook again, hurtling her forward. She managed to steady herself by grabbing hold of the nearby toilet door handle.

"I've flown through loads of storms worse than this one," Jane carried on, ignoring her colleague's near mishap.

"Yeah, well I haven't and I'm starting to feel sick," Amanda retorted.

Inside the cockpit, the atmosphere had become tense. It seemed that instead of flying around the storm, the Boeing 757 had flown straight into it. Captain Richard Ormond had begun to sweat profusely as hail stones charged at the windshield.

"We have to climb above it, Geoff. Help me with this!" Richard shouted, pulling back on the cloche. The engines laboured loudly as the plane began to climb against the storm.

Fork lightning flashed and thunder boomed nearby.

Grunting under the strain Richard began to say, "If we don't get out of this thing soon we are going to..." his words were cut short as fork lightning struck and the right wing exploded into a fireball of flames. The plane shuddered and the crew ducked instinctively as a shower of debris whizzed toward them, hammering on the fuselage.

"Oh my God…" Adam breathed.

"We've lost engine one!" Geoff said, quickly.

"Shut it off! We're going to have to try and level out."

Geoff flicked several switches above him waited anxiously for a reaction, but nothing happened. He flicked the switches on and off again but still nothing.

"What the fuck is going on?" Richard shouted, reading the gauges in front of him, "Talk to me Geoff!"

"I can't shut number one down; it's not responding!"

"Try manual!"

"It's not working!"

"If that fuel ignites we are…" Richard's sentence was cut short as a massive explosion ripped through half of the right wing sending the craft into a vertical dive, spiralling out of control as flames licked at the windows.

The whole passenger cabin was now a dissonance of terrified screams as they fell forward, following the motion of the craft. Amanda and Jane were thrust onto the aisle floor as the old man in seat 46 lost his bottle of Scotch and in an almost bizarre reaction to everything that was happening around him groped on the floor, trying to find it.

Tracy revelled in the terror of the couple next to her for she cared no longer about her own life; without Mark, it was not worth living anyway.

Looking out of the window, she marvelled at the colour of the lightening. It was unlike anything she had seen before. It blinked an eerie colour of green or was it yellow? She could not quite make it out; it seemed different every time. Were these the colours of imminent death?

In the cockpit, Richard and Geoff were battling against the determination of the aircraft. However, with half a wing missing, there was not much either of them could do to regain control.

Behind them, Adam was sitting with his hands over his eyes. He had ignored their cries for assistance and instead, he froze there, weeping hysterically as he contemplated the watery grave that awaited him.

"Mayday! Mayday!" Richard bellowed into his mouthpiece. "This is Heathrow 101...Mayday! Mayday!   Can anyone hear us?   We are going down! I repeat we are going down!"

The weather hammered the damaged Boeing 747 with hailstones and gale force winds as it dived vertically toward the icy waters of the Atlantic Ocean

Four

A Road, 2 miles south of Bodmin Moor, England 10:30am

Dr. Sky McPherson flicked off the car radio and put Bob Dylan out of his misery. She had unconsciously sung along with him for half the song before she remembered she could not stand him, or any of that *we love you, peace man* music. In fact, she loathed all the Swinging Sixties sentimentality that had become so popular of late. For at 30 years of age and having been trapped in a sixties time warp for most of her life, Sky was definitely a woman of the nineties.

As always, Dylan had evoked thoughts of her parents. Sky was their only child but she never felt as if she had a special place in their hearts because she had always had to share her parents with every good cause known to man. Pride of place in the caravan they called home was a black and white picture of Sky, age two, sitting in a pushchair holding a banner, which read PEACE FOR ALL - BAN THE BOMB. The picture had made front page of the national press and it was if they had discovered that their child could save the world.

Of course, she loved her parents but she had made it her life's ambition not to be like them. Sky was sensible and at school she studied hard to achieve her goal. Now she had the money to afford all the material things that she had been denied as a teenager, and it felt good.

Although unaware of it, Sky was a true beauty; her smooth black hair enhanced her stunning violet eyes and she kept in good shape by jogging every morning, whatever the weather.

After living in London for so many years, she felt she would never get used to the winding narrow roads of Devon and Cornwall. However, she had grown very fond of the rugged countryside.

Her relatively new job as forensic pathologist with Exeter Coroners' office was very demanding and often stressful, but she loved it. She had become a fully-fledged forensic pathologist eight months back. Joining the Exeter office in a senior position was the fulfilment of many years of hard work and sacrifice.

The farm was one mile west of Trevan, a picturesque village just off Bodmin Moor. The whole population was no more than a couple of hundred.

She swung the car right, off the main road and began the bumpy ride up the dirt track.

There was a police panda car parked in front of the weather beaten farmhouse. Outside, a uniformed policewoman talked to a nervous looking postman. The pale faced young man chattered on as the officer took notes.

Sky pulled up next to a Royal Mail van. As she left the car, she noticed a heavy set, middle-aged man with a moustache and dressed in a rumpled dogtooth suit, emerge from the house.

She was opening the boot to the BMW and taking out her briefcase when he asked "Dr McPherson?"

"Yes," she replied, slamming the boot door shut.

"I'm Detective Inspector Morrison," he said, in a very strong Cornish accent.

"Oh Hello. It's nice to meet you," Sky said, shaking his hand.

"Likewise. You found it okay, then?"

"Just about."

"Sorry to trouble you on your day off. This shouldn't take long."

"It's no problem. What have you got?"

They started toward the front door.

"Elderly woman. He found her," Morrison said, nodding toward the postman, "when he tried to deliver a parcel this morning."

They stepped inside the house. A strong musty odour hung in the air. Faded wallpaper adorned the walls. It was gloomy inside, despite the lights. They walked through a very short corridor, passing various paintings in cheap gold frames and one large sepia photograph of a smiling young couple. Sky stopped and looked at the picture.

"I think that's her husband," Morrison offered.

"Where's he now?" she asked.

"Dead. A long time ago."

Sky nodded. "What about children?"

"A son, in Australia, I think."

"I see." Sky wondered how long it had been since she had last seen her son.

"She's through here," Morrison said, interrupting her thoughts and waving her into the nearby doorway.

The kitchen curtains were still drawn when they entered the room. A single beam of sunlight shone through them, casting an eerie spotlight over the dead body.

The old woman was slumped over the kitchen table with her arms folded in front of her. Her grey hair was in plaits and it gleamed under the invading sun.

"We think she passed away in her sleep," Morrison said as Sky pulled on a pair of surgical gloves.

Sky nodded. "So, what's a detective inspector doing out here?" she asked, casually as she opened her briefcase and took out a dictaphone.

Morrison smiled. "I was in the area. Not much happens around here so we tend to muck in wherever we can."

"I see," Sky replied. Then, moving over to the body she began her preliminary examination.

She bent over and closely examined the old woman's face. Her eyes were sunken and her mouth was wide open. Sky spoke into the dictaphone, "Elderly lady, mid eighties. Well nourished." She touched the old woman's face delicately.

"Probably been dead for um..." she looked at her watch. "Twelve hours or so; no apparent cause of distress." She tried to push the body up in order to examine the woman's front but grunted when it resisted.

Morrison came over and helped her push the corpse into a sitting position. Sky examined the old woman's hands, the rest of her body and her neck. Then, speaking into the dictaphone again, "Preliminary examination suggests death by natural causes. The time is now…" She looked at her watch "8:33 am."

"It was her birthday last week," Morrison said.

"Really?" Sky replied, looking up at him. "How old?"

"Eighty-four. That is why the postman was here. He was delivering a parcel."

"From her son?"

"Looked like it"

"Any other relatives?" Sky asked, moving over to him and pulling off her gloves.

"I don't think so."

"Poor women," she said, looking over at the body. "She probably never even had the pleasure of seeing her grandchildren."

They emerged from the house, squinting in the glaring sunshine. Morrison gestured to the police officer who was still talking to the young postman. The PC nodded in acknowledgement and spoke into her radio.

"We'll get her moved from here then if you could…."

"I'll get a report to you later on this morning," Sky anticipated.

"Thank you."

"So, how long are you going to be with us?"

"Well, I've agreed to a trial period of six months."

"Where are you staying?"

"Parkview, Exeter."

Morison's eyes widened. "Nice," he said, appreciatively

"Yes, it is," Sky agreed.

"Think you will miss the hustle and bustle of London?"

"I don't know. Maybe," she said thoughtfully. Then, looking around at the green rolling hills that surrounded them, she added, "This morning, driving through Bodmin Moor, I discovered the real beauty of this county."

"And you fell it love with it."

Sky smiled.

"Happens all the time, you're smitten. You won't be able to leave us now," Morrison said decisively.

Sky laughed, slipped into the driver's seat of her car and added, "We'll see." She slammed the door shut, started the engine and drove off.

Morrison watched the black BWM leave the dirt track and join the main road.

That is when a gigantic shadow smothered the surrounding countryside. He looked up: a huge, black cloud had covered the sun.

Five

"Sea Emperor" Fishing Trawler, 20 miles Northwest of Bude, Cornwall, England. 12:00

The sun was hot as Arthur McElvoy stood on the deck of the

twelve-foot fishing trawler. Shading his eyes with his hands, he looked across the waters to the black clouds on the horizon. It did not look good. They really should be heading back, he thought as a fresh breeze blew up around him, bringing with it the smell of rain.

The thunder rumbled loudly, it had been doing so for the past hour and it seemed to be getting closer with every moan.

Arthur moved aft and joined the other three crewmembers who were busy deploying fishing nets with the help of a large hydraulic arm.

"I think we should head on back home," he said, seriously, scratching his beard.

"Why? Asked one of the heavier men, "We've only just got here."

"Because that storm's getting closer, Bill, and it ain't looking too good."

"You worry too much, old man." This time it was Glen, a skinny young man with a pasty complexion.

The sun disappeared behind a dark cloud.

"I thought you said we were going to miss the storm," said, an overweight man in his fifties, named Trevor.

"We were but now the winds gone and changed, hasn't it. I'm telling you, they wouldn't have issued a warning if it weren't serious." Arthur was feeling nervous now. Not only was the storm getting closer but the gale preceding it was growing stronger and was now sickly rocking the vessel.

"Look," it was Bill speaking again. He paused as more thunder cracked nearby. "I ain't leaving all these fish to those Spanish bastards. As it is, the fucking government's cut our fishing allowance. I've got a family to feed."

"Bill's right, Arthur," Trevor agreed.

"I certainly don't want to go home. I need the money," said Glen, nodding his head.

"All we have to do is wait a couple of hours until those nets are full and then we can go home," Trevor began. Then, in a more coaxing tone, he added, "I mean, come on Arthur, you've been a fisherman ever since you could walk. You, of all people, should appreciate how we feel."

Arthur sighed, "I know how you feel, Trevor but we're not even supposed to be here. It ain't right."

"It ain't right!" Bill echoed, losing his patience. "How can it not be right? We were born here. My dad came fishing out here with your dad. These are our waters. We should have first catch not some garlic smelling Spaniard who's ruined the crop in his fucking waters and has come over here to nick ours."

The others mumbled their approval as more thunder cracked and heavy black rain clouds drifted ominously over the fishing trawler.

"It's the law, Trevor," Arthur stated calmly.

"Fuck the law!" Glen spat.

"I don't understand you. Don't you care about what's happening to our fishing industry?" Bill asked.

"Of course I care…" Arthur began.

"I don't think you do," Bill interrupted. "The fish along this coast are getting less and less each day. There isn't enough for us let alone a bunch of foreigners!"

"Yeah," Glen piped up again, "Why should we let a bunch of wankers at the government decide where, when and who should fish in these waters. Just because they have gone Euro fucking mad, it doesn't mean the rest of us have!"

Arthur spoke but his voice was drowned in a massive thunderclap. The sky was now a blanket of blackness and the atmosphere was charged with electricity.

Lightening flashed as the men contemplated the weather and what had just been said.

"Let's get inside, have a brew," Trevor suggested.

All three men walked toward the cabin leaving Arthur standing there. Trevor stopped at the cabin entrance and shouted to him, "Are you coming?"

Arthur did not reply. He looked out to sea; the storm was nearly upon them. Only a few minutes ago the sun had been shining in a blue sky and now, day had turned into night.

Arthur watched the wall of rain as it swept across the ocean toward him. Within seconds, he was drenched.

Six

Environment Agency, Bristol. 15:00

Riding the elevator to the fifth floor, Blake wondered how long the meeting was going to last today. He knew once Hamilton got talking, there was nothing that could stop him; man loved the sound of his own voice.

The bell sounded and the elevator doors opened. Blake made his way down the corridor, passing various environmental posters. One of them was a picture of a world globe in flames. Underneath it, a caption read: "Act Now!"

Rounding the corner, he came to a reception desk. Behind it, a blonde girl, in her twenties was keying information into a computer.

"Hello Melissa," he said, smiling. "Is he in there?"

The girl looked up and returned the smile, "Hello Blake. They're all in there and you're late."

"Traffic," he said, and then walked across the hall to the conference room.

He did not knock he just entered.

Inside the spacious room was a large, oval boardroom table; all fifteen chairs that sat around it were taken, bar one. Behind them, large rectangular windows offered a stunning view of the city.

"You're late," said a spindly man with spectacles who was sitting at the far end of the table. He was Hamilton and he was Blake's boss.

"Sorry, traffic," Blake apologised, shrugging his shoulders and slipping into a free chair. He nodded to various people as they smiled at him.

"Right," Hamilton said, decisively. "Let's, finally, get this meeting to a start." He glanced at some papers on the table in front of him. "The Prime Minister has a bee in his bonnet about this power station in Derbyshire. He has received more complaints about the place, more cases of leukaemia. Now, what the hell is going on, David?" Hamilton was looking very expectantly at a blonde thirty-year-old man, three seats down on his right. "Have the six months you've spent investigating this place been a waste of time?"

"No, of course not," David replied.

"Is there any truth to these rumours?"

"No. We've done tests and the place is safe. Those reports about leukaemia are just the findings of a bunch of over zealous doctors."

"Well the PM doesn't seem to think so. Nor does the press."

"I'm telling you, it's old news," David said, waving his hand apathetically.

"Hey!" Hamilton snapped, leaning forward in his chair, his eyes narrowing menacingly. "It obviously isn't old news because if it were, I wouldn't be mentioning it to you today, would I?"

An awkward silence fell over the room.

"Would I, David?" Hamilton prompted with all the air of a condescending schoolteacher.

"No," David acknowledged in the tone of a small boy who had been spanked for misbehaviour.

"Maybe we should re-open the investigation." suggested a statuesque brunette, named Jackie.

"And risk looking incompetent in the eyes of the press?" answered an older man next to her.

"It's no worse than those doctors forcing the issue and bringing the whole mess out in the open again. That would solicit the media's interest. It would also give them an angle: not doing our job properly and therefore making our office look inept."

Hamilton smiled, proudly.

"I agree with Jackie," It was David speaking up. He straightened in his chair as if to encourage himself to speak. "It's my investigation. I would like to re-open it," he said, knowing that this was exactly what Hamilton wanted; the man just expected him to say it, thereby acknowledging that he had not done his job properly in the first place.

"Good," Hamilton replied, smiling wryly. I want a preliminary report by the beginning of next month."

David nodded in agreement.

Then, flipping to a cheerful mood again, Hamilton continued, "So, what's next?" He looked around the table. To his left, first seat down, sat Terry, a burly thirty-year-old man with curly black hair; he was holding up his hand.

"Oh yes, Terry," Hamilton nodded, knowingly. "You wanted to discuss something."

"Yes, it's reference a call I received from one of my contacts at the Met office. He told me about this mass of cloud." He produced two sheets of paper from a folder and handed them to Hamilton. One sheet was a black and white satellite photograph of a swirling cloud. The other was a printout containing meteorological information.

Hamilton Studied both sheets whilst Terry continued, "You will see from the printout that this cloud contains an unusually high content of Nitrous Dioxide, lead, and a high level of an, as of yet, unidentified toxin."

Hamilton nodded.

"Well, my contact has been tracking it and he says that it originates from somewhere in Northern Europe."

Hamilton looked up. "And?" he asked, expectantly.

"Well, I thought it might be a good idea to continue monitoring it for precipitation and, if necessary, obtain some samples and have the lab run tests.

"What for?"

"Well, for content. If those figures are accurate the rain from this cloud could be extremely toxic."

"Killer rain?" Hamilton asked, smirking.

"Possibly. Paul, my contact, said that this cumulous nimbus could well have formed over Iceland…"

"…Yes, thank you Terry," Hamilton Interrupted.

"If so, that recent explosion at the chemical plant could have…"

"I said, thank you. That will be all, Terry," Hamilton said firmly. Then, smiling sweetly, he added, "We really do need to press on. Can we discuss this in more detail after the meeting?"

"Of course," Terry said, reluctantly.

"Good. So what's next?" Hamilton asked, consulting his notes, "Ah, yes, Jackie, Fibredome Ltd and the river pollution."

For the next two and half hours, the team discussed various environmental issues, from flooding to toxic waste. Because of the ever-growing concern with world pollution, strict guidelines on toxic disposal had been issued and it was the Agency's job to ensure that they were adhered to.

In an almost dream like state Blake looked at his watch: it was five thirty and Hamilton was still droning in the background.

Then, the droning stopped. "Are we keeping you, Blake?" Hamilton asked.

"What?" Blake snapped out of his daze.

"Never mind," Said Hamilton. "I think that'll be all for today. Terry, don't forget that analysis report. I need it by the end of the week. Oh, and by the way…." He stood up, gesturing for Terry to follow him to the other side of the room.

Blake stood up from his swivel chair and grabbed the suit jacket he had draped over the backrest earlier. The whole place was a medley of shuffling papers, clunking brief cases and voices as the agents made their way to the exit.

Blake looked over at Hamilton who was now standing in the corner of the room with Terry.

"See you later," he called out to them.

However, he received no reply. For both men were deep in conversation and whatever Hamilton was saying, Terry was finding it difficult to comprehend.

The drive home was a hot and humid one. There was a tailback on the motorway due to a jack-knifed lorry. The Police and what seemed to be all of the emergency services were at the scene.

As a grim faced officer, wearing a fluorescent jacket, ushered the Land Rover slowly along. Blake saw the mangled tin can that was the Ford Fiesta. On the road, ten yards away, lay the body of the driver; ambulance men were huddled around it. Further on, he could see two bundles on the floor, covered with black plastic sheets.

Blake inhaled with relief as he, eventually, drove away from the scene. He switched the radio on and pushed the accelerator pedal down, eager to get back to the west coast.

"...*The Cornish Coast Guard has started the search for a missing fishing trawler. The Sea Emperor lost radio contact some time late this afternoon. Stephen Norton has the details...*"

Seven

Coastguard speed cruiser: sixty miles south of the Cornish coast. 21:00

The speed cruiser moved slowly through the eerily calm waters of the Atlantic Ocean. The searchlight on the bow probed the darkness as both men, subconsciously, leant forward from their position in the cabin, as if by doing so they would be able to see further into the night.

"Where the hell is she?" Gary, the heavier of the two men asked, breaking the ten-minute silence.

Mike, his colleague, glanced at the digital locator on the panel in front of him. It was lifeless. "God knows. According to these coordinates, we should be right on top of her."

There was a few minutes silence.

"At least the weather's calmed down," said Gary.

"Yeah, one minute there is a storm and the next..." Mike left the sentence unfinished but he was referring to the calm of the

Atlantic waters. Something about it unsettled him.

"Do you think they've gone under?" Gary asked.

"I don't know," Mike answered as the radar beeped to life. He smiled. "Here she is."

"Hold your horses. It might not be them."

"Of course it's them," he stated, grinning at his friend. "How much do you want to bet?"

"Let's just wait and see."

Gary pushed the throttle and the boat leapt forth, speeding toward the unidentified object on their radar screen.

Five minutes later, the white fishing trawler appeared like a phantom out of the darkness. "Told you!" Mike said, happily, as they drew closer to the boat and the words *Sea Emperor*, hand painted onto the bow, became legible.

Something about Mike's complacency irritated Gary. Finding this boat was good but altogether too easy.

"Shall I radio base and tell them that we've found her?"

"No, not yet," came Gary's swift reply. "Let's have a look on board first."

"You're the boss," Mike complied, still grinning, as if the whole affair was one of his practical jokes.

Gary killed the engines. Both men remained silent as the cruiser drifted toward the ghostly vessel. The whole world was quiet. The only sound was that of rippling water as the boat drifted forward.

The cruiser's searchlight licked over the boat. It did not appear to have sustained damage. So why did Gary have this dreadful feeling that something was wrong. *Marie Celeste*. He shivered.

The trawler was about 12 feet long. Years of early morning fishing expeditions on the Atlantic Ocean had taken their toll; the white paint had now turned into a dull grey, and the green trim had starting to fade. A small cabin with re-enforced, salt-stained glass windows sat in the middle of the vessel like a mini lighthouse.

"Hello there!" Mike shouted, breaking the silence and obviously startling Gary, much to his amusement. He grinned his childish grin.

No reply.

"Probably all stoned," He added, throwing a rope over to the craft.

"Is there anyone on board?" Mike shouted again.

Still no reply.

As Gary fastened the rope joining the two boats, Mike disappeared into the cruiser's cabin and reappeared moments later, carrying two torches. He handed one to Gary and then, with a deep sigh, he climbed off the rescue boat and onto the *Sea Emperor*.

There was no sign of anything irregular. Quite the opposite, Gary thought. Everything seemed very much in order, right up to the gleaming surfaces of the deck.

The deathly silence continued to cocoon them both and the nervousness that taunted Gary had now spread to Mike. "Enough to give you the creeps, isn't it?" he said, shining his torch around the deck.

"You're not kidding. Hello!" He called out.

His voice was swallowed by the expanse that surrounded them but no other sound was forthcoming.

"What about inside the cabin?" Mike suggested as the beam of light from his torch, revealed the door cavity.

Both men entered the cabin. Their flashlights forcing back the darkness.

"Doesn't look like much has been going on here," Mike said.

"Hello," Gary shouted impatiently, ignoring Mike's obvious statement. *Where the hell is everybody? Could they have fallen overboard during the storm? All of them?* "Is there anybody on board?"

"Let's take a look down there," Gary said, shining his torch down the wooden steps that led into the bowels of the vessel.

The room was small: twin bunk beds, a couple of battered lockers, and a small table surrounded by four wooden chairs. In the corner, stood a small gas stove, probably only used to boil water for coffee and to heat up the occasional stew, lovingly prepared by one of the fishermen's wives. Otherwise there was nothing unusual. "Looks like they just decided to abandon ship," Mike said.

"Yeah, but they thought they'd leave the place nice and clean for when we got here."

"What do you mean?"

"Didn't you notice the deck? It was practically shining."

Mike looked puzzled. "What are you trying to say? That they decided to clean up the boat and then dive overboard?"

"I'm not quite sure what I'm trying to say but everything just looks too…" The words escaped him.

"Let's just tow her back to shore. Let the police deal with it." Gary started up the wooden steps but stopped abruptly when Mike grabbed his arm.

"What the…" He stopped in mid-sentence as he turned to see Mike with a hushing finger to his mouth. That same finger moved and pointed across the room, at one of the lockers.

Mike had heard something. He was not quite sure what it was but the noise was definitely coming from within one of those lockers.

Gary descended the two steps quietly.

As if guided by telepathic communication, the two men moved in synchronisation. Neither of them knew what exactly they were going to find in the locker but both made their approach a cautious one.

As they drew nearer: *Rattle,* one of the lockers was shaking.

At least Mike was not imagining it.

The rattling continued approximately every thirty seconds; there was definitely something inside it.

Now, both men flanked the metal closet

Gary held up five fingers and mouthed the numbers in ascending order as he closed each one.

Five…

Mike glanced at him nervously, then at the locker again.

Four…

Another Rattle.

Three…

The boat groaned as a gale blew up outside.

Two…

Rattle…

One!

Gary yanked the locker door open and stared, open mouthed, at the naked man crouched inside.

What was left of the old man's balding grey hair was matted to his head. His knees were drawn up close to his face and his hands were clasped tightly together on top of them. He was shivering, his face was pale white and his lips had turned blue. He did not react when the locker door was opened. He just sat motionless; eyes wide open but unseeing.

"Jesus Christ…" Mike whispered.

"Get a blanket from one of those bunk beds," Gary ordered. He knelt down next to the man who must have been in his late sixties.

"Its all right. We're not going to hurt you," Gary said, reassuringly. He waited a few seconds then asked, "Can you tell me your name?"

No reply was forthcoming and he was not surprised. The man was obviously in shock.

Mike returned with the blanket and handed it to Gary who slowly placed it over the fragile frame of the shivering man.

"Can you tell us what happened here, Sir?" Mike asked in a raised voice as if the man were deaf.

"He's in shock. We better get him to the boat," Gary said.

"Good idea."

The old man stood up without the slightest resistance. There was a loud clanging sound; both coast guards stared at the fishhook the old man had dropped. They exchanged glances but said nothing and started up the wooden steps.

The gale that had now blown up outside whipped around the three men as they came out of the cabin. The Hessian blanket flapped wildly around the old man's bare ankles as they crossed him over to the cruiser.

On board, Mike, immediately disappeared inside the cabin and returned with what looked like a large sheet of tin foil and a flask. He wrapped the aluminium blanket around the man whose face remained expressionless throughout. "Sir?" Gary tried again. "Sir, I'm sorry but can you tell us what happened to the rest of the crew? Sir…?"

Nothing.

"What are we going to do?" Mike asked.

"We're gonna' have to get him back to shore."

"What about the others?"

"I don't know, Gary said, frustrated. "Maybe we'll be able to get some sense out of him back at base."

"What about his boat?"

"We'll radio back the coordinates, get search and rescue out here and we'll tow it back with us now."

"Okay."

Mike moved astern of the cruiser and pulled hard on a towing line. The cable made a whizzing sound as it unravelled from the cog. Once he had pulled enough slack to reach the *Sea Emperor*, he climbed on board and fastened it.

"Okay!" He shouted.

"Fine. Let's get going."

Mike had started to climb back onto the cruiser when he realised that the fishing nets were still deployed. "The nets are still out!" he shouted.

Gary was helping the man into the cabin of the cruiser. "Bring them in but make it snappy," he shouted back, without looking around.

"Okay." Mike complied.

He moved aft of the trawler and was relieved to find that the nets were deployed electronically. He pulled the lever; there was a whirring sound and a big metallic arm started upward, lifting a net with it. They had obviously caught a lot fish for the motor groaned loudly under the strain.

At first, Mike thought he was hallucinating. However, as the net surfaced from the water, the image became clearer yet remained incredible to him. He opened his mouth to scream but no sound emerged. He just stood, transfixed by what he saw.

Then, the whirring of the motor stopped, the net had been lifted out of the water, the arm swung in, automatically, heading for the very spot Mike occupied as he finally found his feet. However, he slipped on the wet surface and, with arms flailing, he fell heavily onto his back.

He lay there, eyes shut for a few moments, waiting for the pain to subside but then came the real horror: He opened his eyes just in time to see the contents of the fishing net spill out, pinning him to the deck.

The weight crushed the wind out of his body. He lay, frozen with horror unable to move as the smell of dead flesh and the deep permeated his nostrils.

He could barely see as his face was crawling with an assortment of sea urchins and seaweed. His right eyeball searched frantically around the boat for any sign of Gary but he was nowhere in sight. He opened his mouth to call for help but gagged as one of the sea urchins scrambled inside. He coughed and spluttered, tasting salt water and involuntarily crunching down on the unwelcome guest. A ball of bile rose in the back of his throat as the weight on his body eased suddenly. He looked up. Gary was standing over him with an incredulous expression on his face. He was shouting something but Mike's terror stricken brain refused to hear it.

What was happening? What was the weight on top of him? It could not be what he thought it was, that would be just too horrifying.

Gary yanked him to his feet. "Mike! Mike! Are you all right? Mike?"

However, Mike just stumbled away from his partner, coughing out the sushi from his mouth and spattering the deck with vomit.

It took a few minutes for Gary to take in the scene before him: it was a mound of death. Naked corpses with their legs and arms entwined in what looked like a macabre sexual orgy. He was looking at the grey sunken eyes of the rest of the *Sea Emperor's* crew. They lay, some with gaping wounds in their necks, others with limbs and genitals removed and mouths stuffed open with metal fishing hooks.

They stared up with dead eyes as if crying to him, imploring him for mercy on a horror bestowed upon them erstwhile.

It started to spit rain as Gary stood on the deck of the *Sea Emperor* and wept.

Eight

Bodmin Police Station. 22:03

When Detective Inspector Morrison entered the interview room, he winced; the smell of seaweed and a medley of other odours hung heavily in air.

The old man was sitting behind a battered wooden table in the centre of the dingy interview room. His eyes remained sunken and expressionless just as they had been when he arrived.

Morrison glanced at the wall mirror, almost looking for reassurance. He knew that a group of police officers were watching his every move from behind it.

He sat in a chair opposite the old man who continued to ignore his visitor and seemed to have adopted an obsessive interest in the invisible patterns on the table.

The room was silent but for the shallow breathing of the old man.

"Hello." Morrison said, tentatively

No reply.

"I'm detective Inspector Morrison. What's your name?"

Nothing.

At forty years of age and having been in the force for over twenty years, Morrison knew that a suspect as quiet as this one was not to be trusted. He continued questioning the old man but the silence continued.

From behind the two-way mirror, PC Baxter, a twenty-two-year-old ginger headed man known as "Ginger" to his friends, watched Morrison trying to coax the bearded man into talking to him.

Twenty minutes or more had ticked by but the old man had not even blinked. What happened next was so fast, it was a blur: through the tinted glass, Ginger saw the ineffectual old man leap over the desk and, with the speed and strength of a striking panther, grab Morrison by the throat.

Within seconds, Ginger and two other officers were scrambling out of the surveillance room and storming into the interview room

The attack was fast; Morrison did not stand a chance. Before he knew what was happening, he was falling backward on his chair, crashing to the floor with his assailant on top of him.

Now the once mute was screaming incoherent words as his hands clamped around the inspector's throat in a vice-like grip.

It was not long before Morison's head started pounding as his blood screamed for oxygen. The inspector kicked and clawed but the vice grip on his throat was relentless. Seconds were like minutes; voices were like echoes as his mind clouded and a zillion thoughts streamed through it: his wife, his children and their home.

The neon light above his head darkened as hollow voices called to him.

"Morrison! Inspector!"

Two more police officers ran into the room and all five men tried to pull the frenzied old man off their commanding officer but he had insurmountable strength.

"Get him off!" Ginger screamed.

As they tried to pull the demented man away, he dragged Morrison with him, hands still clamped around the inspector's throat.

Then, the grip released and a fist swung out at Ginger, hitting him on the chin and sending him reeling backward, over the table.

"You bastard!" Ginger yelled as he picked himself up and lunged forward.

The room was a conglomeration of shouting from the police officers and wailing from the old man. Meantime, Morrison crawled to his knees and was now spluttering and coughing as he tried to catch his breath.

All five police officers tried to restrain the man as, with one last inhuman shrug, he freed himself and started toward the door but he buckled over and fell to the floor; legs and arms thrashing about as he convulsed like a malfunctioning humanoid. They watched as his eyes rolled around in their sockets until only the whites remained.

"Get a doctor!" Ginger shouted at one of his colleagues who promptly scurried out of the room, being careful not to step on *the thing* on the floor.

Then, as unexpectedly as it had all started, it stopped. No more thrashing or screaming, just silence. The old man lay motionless on the floor with white eyes staring at the ceiling.

All four police officers simply stood and watched, aghast.

Nine

Plymouth College, Plymouth, England.

The smell of trainers, disinfectant and a medley of other school odours punched Sky as she entered the building, transporting her back to her own school days.

Her footsteps echoed loudly as she walked down the long corridor, passing various students loitering near lockers.

Somebody wolf whistled her and she turned and smiled sweetly at a trio of eighteen-year-old boys, dressed in jeans and identical Adidas T shirts.

She rounded a corner and collided with a young man wearing glasses. The impact knocked the briefcase out of her hand. The boy just recomposed himself and resumed his journey.

"Hey!" Somebody shouted from further down the corridor.

The boy stopped instantly.

"What the hell do you think you're doing?" Matt Allen shouted. He walked up to the young lad, passing Sky, and proceeded to reprimand him, "Andrew, how many times have I got to tell you not to run in the corridor?"

"There's no damage done, honestly," Sky interjected.

"No, he has got to realise that…" he stopped in mid sentence as he turned around. She was stunning with her blue eyes and her gleaming black hair cascading over her shoulders. "You…you didn't even apologise," Matt stuttered, not taking his eyes off her.

There's no need, really," Sky smiled.

Matt ignored her, turned to the boy and asked, "Well, what have you got to say for yourself?"

"I'm sorry, miss," the boy grunted.

"I'm sorry," Matt mimicked. "Oh go on, get out of here," he added, jerking a thumb down the corridor.

The boy scampered off.

"And stop bloody running!" He shouted after him. Then, holding out a hand to Sky he said, sweetly, "Hello, I'm Matt Allen, PT instructor."

"Never have guessed," Sky said, knowingly.

"Oh, right," Matt smiled, looking down at his tracksuit bottoms.

"I'm Sky, Sky McPherson," she said, shaking his hand.

"Sky…what a great name. "

"Thank you."

"So, you a new teacher here?"

She laughed…

"Please tell me you are," he said in mock imploration.

"No, I'm afraid not. Actually, I am looking for the principal's office."

"Well, you're on course," he said pointing to the end of the corridor. "It's just down there, turn left and carry on until the end. Actually, I'm going that way. I'll walk with you."

"Sure, it's no trouble?"

"It would be my pleasure."

"Okay."

They started down the corridor.

"So, are you from around here?" Matt asked.

"Well, I am now. I'm on a six month placement in Exeter."

"So, you are a teacher," Matt said, excitedly.

"No. I'm a forensic pathologist."

"A pathologist," Matt echoed, incredulously.

"Yes, I know, not very glamorous," she added.

"Oh no, it's not that. Just, I would never have guessed."

They walked a few more steps in silence.

"So, what brings you to our school?" he asked.

" I need to talk to one of the girls here. Her uncle was in an accident last night."

"Oh right. That would be Clare."

"I dropped by her house but was told that she had come into school today."

"Yes, I know. It's amazing. Although, to see her you would never think she's just suffered a such a great loss."

"Why do you say that?"

"Well, as you say, her uncle died last night but the girl is strutting around college today like she hasn't got a care in the world."

"Was she close to her uncle?"

"I think she was. He brought her up after her parents died."

They stopped outside a door, marked *Administration – Please Knock*. "Well, here we are," Matt said.

 "Thanks for everything… Matt."

"Oh, you're welcome. Please, get lost again soon"

They laughed.

He was cute but she was running late. "I'd better get in there," she said.

"Right, okay…well nice meeting you."

"And you," she offered, then turned and knocked on the door.

Outside, the sky was blue and a spring breeze rustled through nearby trees. On the football pitch, the blue and white teams were running around, each trying to take control of the ball.

As Blake watched them through the window of the empty classroom, he wondered what exactly many men and women found so addictive about the game. He did not like football very much but he was looking forward to going to the final next week.

It was when the white team scored a goal that Blake felt the presence. Someone had entered the classroom and was standing behind him. He turned around to see Clare McElvoy watching him.

"Clare…." he said, surprised.

"Hello, Mr Hudson, " she said, clutching a handful of books to her chest.

"We weren't expecting to see you here today," he said, staring at the books.

The girl shrugged and said, "Why not? I am a pupil here." She followed that with a sickly sweet smile and Blake thought he had seen a mischievous twinkle in her eyes. Didn't she know about her uncle? Surely, the police must have visited her by now.

"It's just, you have suffered a great loss…" Blake let the words hang deliberately so that he could gauge her reaction.

When the girl's eyebrows lifted, inquisitively, he felt that he had to justify himself. "Didn't the Police come to see you?"

"Yes. But they've gone now," she said, casually. "They came around in the early hours. I think it was about 04:00." She shook her head, "It took me ages to get back to sleep." Her eyes widened. "I was nearly late for class!" Then, her smile faded and she cocked her head to one side as if she were a bird. "What are *you* doing here? It's Tuesday. You don't have class until Friday."

The girl's question was so unexpected that Blake actually found himself replying, "I've just dropped by to pick Mr Allen up. His car's in the garage." Why was he explaining himself to this girl? She was the one who should not be here, the one that should be at home grieving the death of her uncle.

It was an instinctive gesture. He stepped forward and held both of the girl's arms lightly. Then, in a soothing voice he said, "Clare, I don't think you should be here"

The girl said nothing. Instead, she just closed her eyes, breathed deeply and said, breathlessly, "I've been waiting for this for a long time."

And, before Blake could even think about what the girl had said, he was tugged forward and kissed, full on the lips. Her embrace was strong and demanding. Blake's refusal was equally so. Pushing her away he cried, "What do you think you're doing?" He wiped his mouth with the back of his hand as if by doing so he could erase what had just transpired.

"I was kissing you," she replied casually.

Blake's brain froze, so many thoughts and no answers. He did not know what to do or say to this girl. Her uncle had died last night and today she appeared to be indifferent and as if that was not bad enough she was making a pass at he tutor!

He started forward, "I think we should get you home," he said, walking past her.

"Great," she squealed with delight. "Are you taking me?"

He stopped in his tracks and turned around, trying not to make eye contact with the girl. "No. I'll get the staff nurse to take you."

"You needn't trouble yourself." She said, losing her smile. "I've got a lecture to go to."

"Clare." he began, forcing himself to stay calm. What he really wanted to do was slap her face. Instead, he continued, "You can't stay here"

"Why not?"

Blake struggled to find the words. His mind was reeling. *What if someone saw what had just happened?* "Because it isn't healthy," he blurted out.

"Who says so?"

"I say so"

"Why?"

"Because it isn't"

"Why isn't it?"

"It just isn't, okay." He took a few seconds to compose himself. It dawned on him that the girl was actually unsettling him so he forced a smile and said, "I'd better get down to Mr Allen or he is going to think I've forgotten about him."

He was eager to get out of the room and away from her. On his way, he would stop by principal Truman's office.

"I saw you," she said, stopping him in his tracks.

"I'm sorry?" he asked.

" I saw you at The Pit with Mr Allen."

Blake turned to face her. Her eyes had that mischievous sparkle in them again.

"You were there with those two girls," she continued in reprimanding tone.

This conversation was insane.

"I don't know what you're talking about," he said decisively, although he remembered Friday night very clearly. He could not remember exactly how many drinks Matt and he had knocked back but what he did remember was picking up Leticia and Marie and ending up at the nightclub, famously known as The Pit.

Clare continued, as if reading his thoughts, "I know them; they're a right pair of slags." Her statement was expressionless.

"Really?" came Blake's feeble response.

"You really shouldn't hang around with girls like that. You'll be getting a reputation."

"Well, thank you, Clare. I'll be sure to bear that in mind next time I'm out socialising." Blake was tiring of this game.

"You should meet up with Tracy and me. We go to the Pit every Friday night. Will you be there this week?"

"No, I don't think so," he said firmly. He was not about to discuss his social life with a pupil.

"Why not?"

"It's just not my scene."

"It looked like it was your scene last week."

"Well, we were just sussing the place out."

"You didn't seem to be paying much attention to the establishment."

"Where were you? I didn't see you," he said, changing the line of conversation.

"Oh we were there," she said as a faint smile parted her lips.

A few seconds ticked by.

"Well, I'd better get down to Mr Allen." Blake turned to leave again.

"Matt," she said after him.

Blake stopped, "What?"

"His name is Matt, isn't it?"

"That's right Clare. His name is Matt," he said impatiently and added, "but to you or any other pupil in this college, his name is Mr Allen."

"That isn't what he asked me to call him the other night."

"I'm sorry?" Blake asked, irritated.

"That's right. He told me not to call him Mr Allen the night he took me for a drive in his car."

For a moment, Blake could not reply. A million thoughts raced through his brain. *What is she talking about?* Was she implying that Matt had had sex with her?

"What are you saying?" he asked, tentatively, for he was afraid of he answer.

The girl did not reply immediately. She deliberately kept him in suspense for a few seconds and then she blurted out, "I'm saying that Mr Allen showed me a good time."

"You mean he took you out."

She laughed, "I mean he showed me a good time. Come on, you must know what I am talking about, Mr Hudson. Or can I call you Blake?"

"It's Mr Hudson," Blake retorted.

Clare just smirked off his coldness. "He took me out to this isolated beach he knows."

Blake's heart skipped a beat. Indeed, he did know of an isolated beach that Matt boasted was a good place to take girls. Had Matt, his best friend, compromised himself and his career for a quickie?

The words stuck in his throat but he had to ask, "Clare… are you implying that you and Mr Allen had a sexual…"

"Oh, no I am not implying anything," she said and paused.

Blake breathed with relief.

"I know it," she added.

"I don't believe you."

"Why don't you ask him?" she suggested, nodding toward the door.

"Ask me what?"

Blake spun around. Matt was standing in the doorway.

"Matt…" Blake murmured.

"Ask me what?" Matt repeated.

Blake turned to look at Clare. She stood defiantly. She wanted this. She wanted Blake to question Matt in front of her.

"Ask you if… if…" he glanced at her and then back at his friend.

"What?" Matt asked.

"…If you were bloody ready. I've been waiting ages," Blake said.

He could almost hear Clare's disappointed groan.

"Sorry. You know what that lot are like. A bunch of soft tarts whining over a few scrapes on their knees."

"They ought to try playing a couple of games of Rugby," Blake said, forcing a smile. He turned to look at Clare. The mischievous twinkle had disappeared from her eyes and now it was Blake's turn to smile smugly.

Matt followed Blake's gaze. "Did I interrupt something?"

"Oh no, Mr Allen" Clare sparked to life once more. "Mr Hudson and I have made our arrangements," she said cheerfully. Almost skipping by Blake, she made for the door but before leaving the room she stopped and said, "I'll see you Friday, Blake." Then, after flashing a quick smile at Matt she left the room, whistling down the corridor as she went.

"Blake?" Matt asked, walking up to his friend. "That's a bit familiar, don't you think."

Blake was stunned by Clare McElvoy's words. He wanted to ask his friend if what she had just said was true. Had he really had a relationship with that girl? However, although they had been friends for years, he could not ask him, not now.

"You all right?" Matt asked, "You look like you've just seen a ghost or something. There was a pause and then Matt grinned, "You're not...?" He did not finish the sentence.

"Don't even joke about it," Blake said, sighing heavily. Did you know she was at the Pit the other night."

"Is that right? I didn't see her there," Matt said, sitting on a desk.

"Nor did I."

"She probably followed us there."

"It wouldn't surprise me." There was tension in Blake's voice.

"Steady on, mate. I was joking."

"No, I'm telling you, there's something not quite right with that girl."

Matt laughed, "There's nothing wrong with her, Blake. She has a crush on her teacher. She is not the first and she certainly wont be the last. I get it all the time. What is she doing here today anyway?"

"Good question."

"Have you heard any more about her uncle?"

"No. Have you?"

"Well," Matt began, excitedly.

"What?"

"Oh man," he shook his head incredulously as he replayed images in his mind. "I met the sexiest piece of skirt in the corridor. She was wearing this black trouser suit and she was..." He did not finish the words; instead, he closed his eyes and groaned, dreaming of her. "But get this..." He was back again, "I'm thinking she's like... you know, some classy governess or something and it turns out she's a bloody pathologist! Can you believe it?"

"Hello again." It was a female voice. Matt recognised it instantly and turned around. Sky McPherson was standing in the doorway.

Matt shook his head and said profoundly, "Now this is the part where the ground opens up to swallow me," His face was ablaze with embarrassment.

"Sky?" Blake breathed, incredulously.

"Blake?" Sky uttered, trying to contain the butterflies flapping in her stomach. "Oh my God, I don't believe it."

"Nor do I." Blake replied.

Before Matt had time to realise what the hell was going on, Blake and the gorgeous women from the corridor were in each other's arms.

"What are you doing here?" It was Sky asking the question.

"I work here," he explained with an incredulous smile.

"You do?"

"Yes."

"But the last I heard you'd become an environmentalist."

"Well, not exactly an environmentalist as in the real meaning of the word but as in I work for the Environment Agency."

"So what are you doing here?"

"I lecture here once a week."

"You're kidding me."

"No."

"Blake Hudson, a lecturer," Sky said, as if the impossible had just happened.

The sound of Matt deliberately clearing his throat caught their attention and Blake turned to see his friend looking at him expectantly.

"Oh, of course," Blake put an arm around his friend's shoulder. "This is my friend..."

"... Matt, um... Allen, isn't it?" she interrupted.

"The very same." He then explained to Blake, "I met Dr McPherson earlier, in the corridor."

"Doctor McPherson?" Blake asked.

Sky nodded, beaming a smile.

"I can't believe it, you made it!" he said, amazed.

Sky smiled; he was impressed, she liked that.

"Didn't you know?" asked Matt, as if this were old news. "Dr McPherson is a forensic pathologist."

"Good for you," Blake said as a whirlwind of memories whizzed around his mind.

Blake Hudson, son of Giles Hudson, the politician and Sky

McPherson, daughter of Alan McPherson, a new age traveller, had studied at Cambridge together. During those five years, the pair had been inseparable. Blake's looks made him the most eligible man, and Sky the most envied girl on Campus. He was hooked on her beauty and intelligence; she was hooked on his wit and his charisma.

However, their ambitions differed. Blake wanted to marry and have children; Sky wanted to become a doctor and then travel. He believed they could have both; she believed they could not. This, coupled with the ever-present social divide between them, led to a breakdown in their relationship.

Sky had told him that she had made plans and that they no longer included him. For the first time in his life, Blake had suffered a broken heart.

She vowed never to return to Cambridge; he vowed never to love again.

" So, what brings you here?" he asked.

"I'm looking for a pupil of yours."

"Really?" Blake said, smiling, still incredulous that Sky McPherson was actually standing in front of him. "And who might that be?"

"Clare McElvoy?"

Blake lost his smile and the room fell silent.

Ten

The Lookout café - Plymouth, England   15:59

Half an hour later, they were sitting in one of the many Plymouth cafés, overlooking the harbour. They had invited Matt to join them for coffee but he had tactfully declined saying he was late for an appointment. The real reason was that he imagined that the two of them had a lot of catching up to do.

As they drove from the school to the café Sky filled Blake in on some of the details of her investigation and why she wanted to see Clare McElvoy. They shared the same bewilderment as to why the teenager had decided to show up at college today.

The café was empty except for a young couple sitting at a corner table across the room. It was late afternoon and the evening rush had not yet started.

They ordered tea and scones and then sat at a small table by the window. Outside, a busy main road carried a steady stream of afternoon traffic whilst beyond that the sun was starting to set on Plymouth Harbour.

The waiter, a young man who could not have been much older than sixteen, casually strode over carrying a tray with their order.

After he deposited the tray on the table Sky thanked him. The boy grumbled an acknowledgement and disappeared back into the kitchen.

"So," Blake began, "any ideas on what actually killed Mr McElvoy?" He laughed, shaking his head.

"What?" she asked, smiling with him.

"I'm sorry. I just can't get over the fact that you, Sky McPherson, actually carried out the autopsy on this guy."

"Why?" She asked, still smiling.

" Well...." Blake struggled to find the right words." No particular reason, it's just, well, the last time I saw you, you were only dreaming of a being a doctor. Now, ten years later, you are a pathologist. It takes some getting used to."

"It just goes to show; dreams can come true."

"Why pathology anyway? Of all things, cutting up dead bodies." Blake shuddered.

Sky smiled and leaned forward. "You see, it's not the cutting up of bodies, it's the discovery, the investigation, the search into someone's past. Unravelling the mystery of how or why someone died can reveal so much about how the person lived: eating habits, etc. On the other hand, for someone who died violently, an autopsy can often provide clues as to the cause of death. So, it's not just about dead bodies but the piecing together of a fantastic jigsaw puzzle in the hope of finding that missing piece."

Blake was captivated. "Oh God, you make it sound like such fun, how do I sign up?" He grinned roguishly.

Sky shook her head, smiling, and sipped coffee. "You can tease all you like but I love my work. Anyway, what about you? Ten years ago, you were very anti-establishment and denounced anything to do with the government. You were determined to break your father's heart," she teased in revenge. " Now, you work for them."

"Well, not exactly," Blake said, buttering his scone.

"What do you mean, not exactly? You work for the environment agency, don't you?"

"Well, yes."

"They're a government body aren't they?"

"No, they're not actually. Anyway, I was not anti-establishment. My father was a politician and at the time I was going through my teenage rebellion phase but I never said I wasn't..."

"You fibber!" Sky cried, smearing blackcurrant jam over her scone. "You used to hate politics and politicians, if I remember correctly. That's why you and my mum got on so well."

Blake smiled, defeated. Sky was right. "Your mum. How is she?"

Sky fell silent and her eyes fixed on the tiny jam jar on the table in front of her.

"What?" he asked, concerned.

Sky spoke without taking her eyes off the 'County's Pride' jar, "They're dead."

"No," Blake uttered in genuine disappointment.

"They died four years ago. They were killed in a plane crash over Brazil."

"Oh my God, Sky." Blake was shocked. He felt an overwhelming desire to reach over the table and hold her.

Sky looked up at him, her eyes brimming with sorrow. She forced a courageous smile. "They didn't even get to see me graduate medical school."

Blake groped for words and then rushed, "I don't know what to say. I am so sorry, I didn't know."

"It's okay. It's been quite a while now. You know what they say: time heals."

Blake was not sure he agreed with this saying.

She swallowed hard and added, "Eventually," as if she had read his thoughts, and then said, "How are yours? How's life treating them?"

Sensing she wanted to change the subject, he replied, "Very well, thank you."

"Do they still live in that big house in Cambridgeshire?"

Sky's question was pointed and Blake wondered what she meant exactly but replied, "Oh no, they've moved from there. Retired to the Cotswolds"

"Nice," she said, raising her eyebrows and taking a sip from her cup.

Although Blake and Sky had not talked about it that often, the wealth contrariety between the two families had been, and Sky thought always would be, a contentious issue. Maybe, although she would never admit it, Sky was jealous of Blake. She was jealous that he had both the financial and emotional support to be whatever he wanted to be as an adult. She had never enjoyed such privileges. Sky's parents would have been much happier if she had decided to join Greenpeace.

Now, ten years later, she wondered what her parents would have thought of her success. Her mother never did understand her ambition to become someone who dissected dead bodies for a living.

"Sky?"

Blake brought her back to the present as Sky had gone into a trance and was staring past him.

"Oh, I'm sorry," she said, shrugging herself and smiling apologetically. "I was just remembering college," she lied.

"All the good times, I hope."

"Of course."

"You were telling me about Mr McElvoy," Blake reminded her.

"Off the record, he suffered some kind of aneurysm. What we don't know is what brought it on."

"It wasn't just a natural death, though, was it?" Blake asked, curiously.

"What makes you ask that?" Sky said, surprised. She wondered if Blake already knew something.

"Well, the police haven't released any details yet. They must suspect something."

"Well they have to weigh all the evidence. Most of the evidence, in a case like this, is supplied by the post mortem, and I'm still waiting for the lab results."

"But what's your preliminary prognosis?"

Sky shifted in her seat. He was making her feel as if she were giving evidence at an inquest. "Are you sure you're an environment officer and not a lawyer or a journalist for that matter?" she asked.

"I'm sure," he laughed. "It's just, well not much really happens around here and now my pupil's uncle has died in suspicious circumstances and my ex..."He corrected himself, "and one of my friends is conducting the post mortem into his death. It's pretty exciting stuff."

"Well, I'll tell you what. How about I ask you some questions?

Seeing that I am not supposed to be discussing this stuff with you anyway."

Accepting her request, Blake leaned back in his chair. "Fire away."

"This girl, the niece…"

"Clare."

"Yes. Clare. Have you ever met her uncle?"

"No, I don't think I have"

"And Clare's never mentioned anything about him to you. You know, habits, vices, things like that."

"No. But then again why should she?"

"Well, you never know, people talk. Maybe he'd been acting strange lately."

"No. What did she tell you?"

"Nothing. I haven't spoken to her."

"I thought you said you came to the college to talk to her"

"I did, but she said she was in a hurry. Had to meet a teacher for lunch or something."

"A teacher?" Blake's eyes widened but he said nothing.

"What?"

"Are you sure she said she was meeting a teacher?"

"I'm positive. Why?"

"Oh, no reason," Blake replied, thoughtfully.

"Oh, come on, Hudson. What's troubling you?"

It was obvious that Blake had suddenly become very concerned about something.

Blake looked into her eyes. He mused for a few moments. His gaze was so intense that it unsettled Sky. "What?" She asked, looking at herself, wondering if she had spilt jam over her white blouse.

"It's just…" He broke off in mid-sentence as he caught the attention of the waiter and ordered another two coffees. Then, he settled himself into his chair and said quietly, as if the café were rigged with invisible microphones, "This is strictly confidential."

"Likewise," Sky said, almost affronted that he should feel the need to say something like that to her after everything she had already shared with him about her investigation.

Over the next fifteen minutes, Blake told Sky all about Clare McElvoy and her strange behaviour. He included everything. Oddly enough, he felt much better for it. It felt good, finally being able to share his fears with somebody other than Matt. An added bonus was that the person in question was Sky.

She had listened to him without interrupting once and he had concluded that she had not changed at all. She was the same intelligent, sensitive woman he had known all those years ago. Somehow, although he could not explain it, by sharing this story he felt that he had re-established some kind of a mooring line with the girl he had once thought of marrying. Of course, things were not the same now. They had both grown up and moved on in their lives, but he felt good around her just like he had many years before.

Sky's gaze had turned to the harbour and beyond. The sun had disappeared behind a blanket of black clouds. It was obvious that rain was on its way.

"What are you going to do?" Sky asked, turning her attention to Blake once more.

"I don't know what to do for the best. If I go to Truman, I'm going to find myself in the middle of a bloody enquiry. If I don't, then God only knows what rumours she's going to spread about us both."

"What about Matt? Do you think he is having a relationship with this girl?"

Blake hesitated and then said, "I don't really know."

"Maybe you should tell Truman. You know, cover yourself."

"What, tell him about Matt?"

"No, I mean tell him about the way this teenager has been behaving around you. But, now that you've mentioned it, maybe you should tell him about Matt too."

"Tell him what exactly? I don't even know if what Clare said is true. I mean, look at the way she's been behaving around me. It could all just be a figment of her imagination."

"What if it isn't?"

Blake paused. "Then it isn't my place to go ratting on a mate."

"Maybe you're right," Sky said. She looked at him. He clearly was concerned about this affair and by the way he had blurted the whole thing out, it seemed to her as though he really needed a friend or confidant. The irony of the situation was not lost on Sky. She had always felt that his friends, and there had been many in those days, were more important to him than she was. Well, where were they now?

She scolded herself inwardly for being so cynical. After all, the breakdown of their relationship could not be blamed entirely on Blake. With hindsight, it was easy for Sky to examine her youth and realise that most of the problems in their liaison stemmed from the fact that she was an insecure teenager. She was a poor girl dating one of the wealthiest and most handsome boys in their school, it was only natural that she should feel intimidated by everything that interfered with that.

Her gaze fell back on Blake. He was deep in thought. His brow was creased into a frown.

"Anyway," she said, breaking the thought-processing interlude, "That's what I think you should do, but talk to Matt first. See what he says."

"You're right," Blake smiled.

"That's better," she said. "This whole thing really has you worried."

"Yeah. I don't know if it's for myself or because of what I might find out about Matt. Don't get me wrong, I'm not a prude. For Christ sake, if he is having it off with this girl, it wouldn't be a major ordeal for the simple reason that she isn't exactly under age, is she." The words were more of a statement than a question. "It's just, well rules are rules and if the College Principle found out, Matt would definitely be suspended. And if he lost his job, well, he'd be crushed."

"As you say, we don't even know if it's true. I mean, after everything you said it sounds to me as if this girl has some serious issues. She may be having the same fantasies about Matt as she is about you."

Blake nodded, "Thanks"

"What for?"

"For listening to me. With haven't been together for more than a couple of hours, after all this time, and I'm already telling you my problems."

"No, don't be silly. I actually enjoyed listening to you. Everybody enjoys a bit of a scandal and I don't get much of that where I work. My clients are very tight-lipped."

"I can imagine," Blake said, smiling.

A rumble of thunder intruded on their conversation. It came from deep within the dark clouds that were approaching rapidly.

"Looks like rain," Sky said, looking out of the window.

"Yes, thank God," Blake said, following her gaze. "We need some rain fall if we're going to get through the summer without a serious water shortage."

"It's probably the same rain that McElvoy got caught in yesterday."

"I wonder what did happen on that boat," Blake said. The question held an eerie twang to it.

He Smiled at Sky who knew exactly where he was going and, sighing, she asked, "Can you keep a secret?"

"Of course" he replied, excitedly.

Sky glanced around the room: it was empty. Then, leaning forward, she proceeded in a lowered tone, "It's believed that McElvoy mutilated and murdered all of his crew members." She leaned back in her chair again as if she had unburdened herself by sharing this information.

Blake's eyes widened. "Why?" he asked, his voice a whisper.

"We don't know why, but I think it may be a result of the embolism. You know what an embolism is?"

"Yes, a blood clot."

"That's right. A blood clot that forms somewhere at the back of the brain. Normally these blood clots are caused by a ruptured artery, fragments of a diseased organ or even a small mass of bacteria carried through the blood stream. Eventually the fragments," Sky began to gesticulate, "plug a major artery and that's when the problems start."

It was then that Blake really noticed her eyes. In the fading daylight, they were like fireflies, burning in the darkness. He wanted to kiss her. He didn't know why, he just felt compelled to lean across the table and…

"…When I did the post-mortem," she continued, " I noticed that there was a large haematoma at the back of McElvoy's brain. This was, obviously, what killed him. The convulsions he suffered prior to seizure could also explain his strength," Sky said, as if thinking aloud.

"His strength?" Blake had that same inquisitive look on his face.

"When McElvoy was brought in, the police said they had a very hard time restraining him. Apparently, he manifested incredible force. It took more than five policemen to subdue him. Well, I say that but they did not actually subdue him at all, he collapsed because of this embolism. However, I'll know more when I get the lab results."

Thunder rumbled once again. It was getting closer.

Sky glanced at her watch; it was 4.30pm. "I think we'd better get going," she said.

"Right," Blake replied. Her sudden statement had surprised him.

Sky reached into the inside pocket of her jacket and brought out a small wallet.

"Oh no," Blake said, as he saw the leather purse. "I'm getting this"

"I don't think so," Sky said. "I offered coffee, remember?"

There was determination on Sky's face and Blake knew better than to argue with her. He would pay next time.

"How about tonight?" Blake found himself asking as they made their way to the till.

"Sorry?"

"How about dinner tonight?"

Sky smiled as the freckle-faced boy emerged from the kitchen doors. Unlike their previous encounter, the boy now seemed to notice Sky and smiled at her, eyeing up the rest of her body in the process.

When she eventually got change from her ten pound note, they made for the exit.

Outside, the air was close and humid. It was the classical quiet before the storm.

They were silent as they crossed the busy street and walked toward the car until Blake said, " You didn't answer my question"

"What question?"

Their eyes met. Sky smiled, " Only joking. Yes, that would be nice."

"Great!" Blake said, brimming with enthusiasm.

"Where are you taking me?"

"I'll surprise you," he said.

Eleven

Stony Point - The West Coast.   18:00

It had been a great afternoon. Blake wasn't sure how he felt about Sky, he just knew he enjoyed being with her. It was hard to believe that ten years had gone by since they had sat by the embankment and planned their marriage. It is amazing how things can change. One minute you have made plans for the future and then next...

Blake thought about this as he drove back to Stony Point. The bad weather had not yet reached this part of the region but it was on its way. The sound of groaning thunder could be heard in the distance; the promise of a visit was confirmed.

Blake had given Sky directions to Stony Point where they would meet at eight thirty before moving on to the restaurant.

He parked the Land Rover Discovery and sat motionless in the vehicle. Was he expecting more form this encounter with Sky? Was he expecting everything to be the same as it was then? Of course not, he had just rediscovered a very close friend, nothing more.

He opened the car door and looked out to sea: the surface was calm. The air was thick and still. As if God had closed the door, locking out all the turbulence of the world. It was something Blake could not remember experiencing before. He stood there, vehicle door ajar, unmoving, savouring, experiencing this strange moment.

He could hear the soft lapping of the waves on the shore and, in the distance, the roll of thunder, quickly followed by a bolt of fork lightning.

He shut the car door and made for the house, whistling as he went.

Inside, Blake ascended the stairs, still whistling. Outside, the elements rumbled loudly as the black clouds drifted closer and closer.

Twelve

Greenacres - A farm, approximately 8 miles east of Bude. 19:00

They glided over the hill like giant UFOs, slowly and ominously blocking out most of the remaining daylight as they neared. Greenacres was a tiny farm situated in the heart of Rocky Valley, only a few minutes walk from the sea.

"Ouch!" Joyce cried as thunder cracked overhead. It sounded as if it was coming from inside the loft. She shook her finger, sucked the tip of it and then sat, staring at the small puncture wound.

"Bloody weather," She cursed.

Thunder had made her nervous ever since she had been stuck in a panoramic lift with Su Shin Yang, an Asian businessman hell bent on convincing her into moving to his Hong Kong branch. That night, there was an 80-mile an hour wind shaking the lift violently. Then, there was the lightening, oh God, how Joyce hated fork lightening.

The calling started up again, hurtling down the stairs with the insistence of a hungry baby. It brought her crashing back from an evening that had closed one and opened another very important chapter in her life.

She looked out of the window: the rain was close. A few small droplets splattered against the glass as darkness enveloped the surrounding countryside.

"Joyce! Joyce!" The rattling, throaty voiced called again.

"All right!" Joyce yelled back at the ceiling. She looked down at her masterpiece. The earless embroidery of a black and white cat stared back as her heart sank. She had so desperately wanted to get a black and white cat now that they lived in the countryside but her Mother had complained that cats made her feel ill.

"Joyce! I am going to wet myself!"

"I'm coming, Mother!"

Sticking her needle into one of the eyes of her embroidered creation, she set it aside and then heaved her heavy bulk out of the armchair.

Shuffling over to a nearby window, she peered out into the darkness. Lightning flashed. As it did so, it illuminated Joyce's reflection in the glass, giving her a snap shot of herself: white bloated cheeks with straggly brown hair falling over her shoulders. She wanted to cry. What had she become?

It was then that she saw them, flying around the yard like white phantasms. Her eyes widened in alarm.

"Oh no!" She cried and hurried to the door. She grabbed an anorak from a nearby coat stand, slipped into it and, ignoring more calls from the old woman upstairs, she launched herself into the storm.

The wind tore at her anorak as droplets of rain spat at her. She frantically searched the yard. It was getting very dark out here but she could just about discern her white blouse flapping about on the gravelled drive.

Clutching the lapels of her anorak and battling against the wind, she made for it and grunted in frustration as each time she tried snatch up the garment, it was blown away from her.

More thunder boomed overhead and she could not decide what to do first, try to apprehend her runaway blouse or shield her ears from the sound.

Then the rain arrived, it was sudden and in torrents. The water drenched her instantly. It was absorbed through her scalp into her blood stream, and as it did so, she smiled.

More thunder.

Joyce no longer felt the apprehension of a few moments ago. Now the rain had come and with it came a sedative. A drug more powerful than any other she had tried in her life. She could feel it. It was inside her, throbbing, rushing, and probing her mind with warm tentacles. It beckoned her back to the person she used to be: a smart successful woman, half the weight she was now and with a salary most men could only dream of.

As the water fell, Joyce Masters wept with joy. She was free, no more fetching and serving, cleaning and wiping. Like a supreme being, the rain had come to take her away. And, as if it were a supreme being, if not God himself, Joyce fell to her knees, thrust her arms to the heavens and allowed the water to baptise her as her friend, the thunder, roared and her companion, the lightening, struck the farm killing all the lights inside.

Joyce sniggered to herself. Things were going to change around here, tonight, now.

In the gloom of the room, the old women lay, shivering, under the covers.

It felt as if she had been calling for hours with no reply. Her throat was sore and now she was lying in her own urine again. Where the hell was that girl when she needed her.

On cue, in a scene worthy of any Hammer House horror, lightning flashed and the bedroom door swung open.

Dolores squinted through the darkness but she could not recognize who was standing, motionless, in the doorway.

"Joyce?"

No reply.

"Joyce, is that you?"

Still nothing.

"Joyce, I think the storm has knocked the meter out. And, I am afraid that it has happened again. I did call you but you took so long. What was I supposed to do? You know I can't move by myself otherwise I would." The old women's voice rattled on in the darkness but still no reply was forthcoming.

More lightning; more thunder.

Now Dolores saw. It was Joyce; the gleam of light outlined her heavy frame.

Almost with relief, the old women asked, "Why didn't you answer me? I've been calling you for over ten minutes now. Where have you been? Joyce…?"

Nothing.

"Joyce!" The old women whined in a frustrated guttural sound, "Why won't you answer me?"

The room was silent except for the drumming of the rain on the roof and the gurgle of the drains. Then, for a few seconds, the room was illuminated once again by the verdant shine of lightning. It was long enough for Dolores to see that her daughter had moved from her position in the doorway and was now standing next to her bed. She was holding something in her hand and it glinted in the darkness.

Thirteen

Stony Point   20:05

Outside, the rain fell heavily. Inside, the dulcet tones of Sade's *No Ordinary Love* filtered down from the first floor as Sky admired the pastel paintings that adorned the walls of the living room.

She was drawn to one particular charcoal sketch of children. Their faces were blurred, emphasising the look of pity in their eyes. Sky was intrigued by the artwork.

"La Petite Morte"

She looked up from the picture. Blake, now dressed in jeans and black polo neck, had entered the room. His short black hair was still shower wet. Her stomach turned over again, just as it had when they met earlier in the day. He looked good.

"Sorry?" she uttered.

"That's the name of the painting," he said, casually.

"Oh, right."

"It means…"

"The small dead," she interrupted…

Blake smiled, "That's right. It was a present from my mother."

"Nice," she said.

Thunder rumbled overhead.

"My God, isn't this weather ever going to let up?" Sky asked, looking upward.

"It shouldn't last much longer," Blake said, as if he were a weatherman. "Would you like a drink? He asked, moving over to the drinks cabinet. "Actually, I'm on call. Coffee would be nice."

"No rest for the wicked. Does that mean that there is a good chance of you deserting me mid dinner?"

"I'm afraid so. However, I don't think you've got much to worry about," Sky said, raising her voice for Blake had now disappeared into the kitchen.

"What makes you so sure?" Came his muffled reply.

" Well... I don't know," Sky struggled to find the words. "Its fairly quiet around here."

"Yes, that's what I like about the place."

There was an interlude of a few minutes, the only sound was that of the rain, which, as Blake had predicted, seemed to be dying down, and the occasional tinkering of coffee cups from the kitchen.

Sky admired the room. Blake had done well for himself. She wondered if he had decorated the interior personally or if Mummy had had something to do with it.

Alicia Hudson enjoyed controlling her son's life. It would not have surprised Sky to hear that Blake had moved all the way down here just to escape the controlling clutches of his mother. The memories streamed back and Sky was amazed to discover that the hurtful things that were said all those years ago, still affected her.

"I didn't bother with sugar," Blake said, as he entered the room, carrying a small tray. "I assumed you were sweet enough." He set the tray down on the coffee table and sat on a nearby armchair.

Accepting his waved invitation, Sky joined him. "Am I that transparent?" she asked.

"Well... not transparent as such. More like..."

"Predictable?"

"No, not at all I."

"One," she interrupted.

"Sorry?"

"I take one sugar in my coffee."

"Oh right," Blake replied. "I'll just go and get some."

"Thank you," she said smiling.   As a matter of fact Sky McPherson enjoyed her coffee black without but she was not going to let Blake get away with drawing assumptions.

"I'm sorry," Blake said, as he returned a few seconds later, carrying a sugar bowl.

"No, that's fine, honestly" she said, smiling. However childish, she relished the moment.

They drank in silence.

"I think you were right. The weather has calmed down a bit, "Sky said, breaking the quiet. Now you are going to tell me that predicting the weather is one of your favourite pastimes."

"Nothing so imaginative, I'm afraid. I do have a PC upstairs and it does have access to Met office data.

"Really?"

"Yes. It's for work of course."

"Oh, of course," she said, nodding.

"What?" he asked. He couldn't explain it but it felt as though Sky were toying with him.

"Well, you know what they say about boys with toys."

"It's not a toy," he laughed.

"Must be pretty smart, having your own weather forecast at the touch of a button."

"Helps plan days out. Would you like to see it in action?"

"Sure."

They ascended the stairs in silence.

"What's through there?" Sky asked, passing a door on the first floor.

"That's my bedroom."

"Oh..." She said, nodding. "Aren't you going to show me around?"

"It would be my pleasure, later," he said, looking back briefly.

Even in the dimness of the stairwell, Sky could have sworn he was grinning.

When they reached the second floor the rain sounded much louder and a gale could be heard rattling at the windows as if begging for shelter from the rain.

Blake flipped on the light, illuminating the circular room that was his study. Sky moved over to the balcony windows and stared at the reflection of herself in the glass.

"You must have the most spectacular views," she said, unconsciously fixing her hair and noticing that Blake was now seated in front of the computer.

"They are pretty wild, yes," he agreed.

The computer's screensaver was of a star simulation. It disappeared when Blake typed in a password, revealing a spinning world globe.

Sky joined him by the desk and as she stood looking over his shoulders, she could smell his aftershave and breathed in deeply; it was a musky, wooden aroma and smelt delicious.

After a few clicks of the mouse, the globe stopped spinning and a flashing rectangular frame appeared in the centre of the screen.

"Where would you like to go?" Blake asked casually as his finger hovered over the left mouse button.

"Oh, I don't know. Where can I go?" she asked, laying her hands on his shoulders.

Blake was pleasantly surprised by her touch but did not show it.

"You can go anywhere in the world."

"Really? Oh well… " She pondered like a game show contestant unable to decide on which prize envelope. "England, I suppose," she said, finally.

"England it is," he complied, cheerfully.

As Blake moved the mouse, the rectangle moved, roaming the world. When he stopped, a small magnifying glass appeared. Then he clicked and almost instantly, a map of the United Kingdom appeared.

"Wow," Sky breathed, obviously impressed.

"The pictures you are about to see are coming live from the Met Office's central computer"

"Are these satellite pictures?"

"Aha." Blake confirmed, nodding his head.

Then the mouse was moving again, the small rectangular shape hovered over the south of England. A few clicks and they could see London and the surrounding area. The map was very similar to that on a weather report but parts of London seemed obscured by a thin grey haze.

"What's that?" Sky asked, pointing to the grey blur on the screen.

"That's cloud."

"Cloud?"

"Yes, you see here," he said, pointing to the digital map. "Most of the picture is clear. That means that there is hardly any cloud in the troposphere, which means good weather. And you see here," he said, pointing to hazy London, "that means cloud."

"Rain?"

"No, not necessarily, it's probably just smog. You know that kind of blanket grey cloud you can get on some days?" he asked, turning his head slightly around.

"Yes."

"Well that's most probably what that is."

"My God, you can tell all that from here?" she asked, incredulous.

"Well, I'm not a meteorologist but that's more or less accurate."

"It's amazing," she said, moving from behind him to lean on the desk where she could get a closer view.

"Thanks to satellites, there is so much more we can see and do in the world today."

"You're not kidding," Sky said, still impressed.

"I wasn't," Blake replied flatly. He then turned and smiled at her.

"What about Cornwall? Let's look at Cornwall!" she squeaked with all the excitement of a five year old on Christmas morning.

"Okay."

Blake clicked his mouse again and the picture of London and the southeast metamorphosed into a map of England.

Several clicks later and the south west of England was displayed on the screen. The image was a complete contrast to the one they had seen earlier. This time a black and white haze blotched out most of the area, leaving only a few clear spots.

Directly over the Stony Point region, there was a chequered image of black and clear skies.

"Wow, is that what's looming over us right now?" Sky asked, her face green, from the glow of the monitor.

"Yep."

"How far can you zoom in with this thing?" she asked.

"As far as you like, really. Look."

Blake clicked the mouse over Stony Point and the area was magnified on the screen. Another click, and they were zooming through the black layer and peering down on what looked like the ground from inside an airborne plane.

A few clicks later, Sky's mouth dropped open. The image was dark green, very similar to one seen through night vision goggles. It was a picture of Sky's car, parked outside Blake house.

"Oh… My… God…" she whispered, incredulously. "I can't believe it. Is this live?" "Actually, this is a photo. They're taken at 30-minute intervals as the satellite passes overhead and the image is updated each time. This kind of technology is still very expensive and only a few top government agencies are allowed access to live pictures."

"It's amazing. How come you have access to this?"

"Well, officially I don't. But because I work for the E A and I have connections at the Met Office, I can dial straight into their mainframe and receive all the latest images."

"I am really impressed."

"Thought you would be," He replied, grinning.

Sky smiled and shook her head in disbelief. "I suppose it won't be long before this kind of thing will become standard in most of our homes," she said.

"It already is."

"Oh?"

"Yes, road atlas programs that allow users this kind of functionality already exist."

"I must admit, all this big brother stuff really does give me the creeps," she admitted.

"Why? It's technology. It's the future."

She eyed him seriously. "You sound like an advert for a stereo system."

He chuckled.

"So, what kind of weather can we expect for the game on Friday?" she asked, looking back at the monitor.

" I thought you didn't like football," he commented, moving the mouse.

"I didn't. But I fell out with rugby a long time ago."

Blake looked at her. However, either Sky was hypnotised by the image on the screen or she was trying to avoid eye contact.

After a few more clicks of the mouse and taps on the keyboard, the map redrew itself. This time a grid appeared over the whole of the United Kingdom whilst the foot of the screen displayed alphanumeric data.

"What's that?" she asked.

"It's the Atlantic Ocean," Blake replied, as he tapped more commands on the keyboard. Almost instantly, a chequered quilt of black and grey blotches covered the grid.

"Okay. You see down here?" he asked, pointing at the data at the foot of the screen.

"Yes."

"Well, this is the wind's direction and underneath here, these characters tell us whether we have high or low pressure. This picture is telling us that there's low pressure sweeping across the Atlantic and with it, it's bringing this," he said, pointing the mouse at grey and black blotches.

"So that means that we can expect more rain."

"Well yes, although these blotches aren't really much to worry about. In fact, there's a distinct possibility that these will burn out before they even reach us. No, there is something else much bigger than those." He turned to Sky and looked her in the eyes. "You know the showers we've had today?"

"Yes, "she said forcing a laugh. "They were hardly showers."

"Oh yes they were," he said, in a melodramatic voice as he turned his attention back to the glowing monitor. "Compared to this…" He double clicked the mouse and for the second time that evening, Sky McPherson's mouth dropped open.

It looked like a copy of satellite pictures she had seen on documentaries about tornadoes: a huge swirl of black and white cloud. As she stared at the screen, the pictures flickered slightly, giving the impression that the giant swirl was moving.

"What on earth is that?" She gasped.

"That's Mummy," Blake replied, excited.

"It looks like a tornado."

"It does, but it isn't," he reassured her.

They exchanged glances.

Then, regaining the weatherman voice he had mastered so well he said, "That's what meteorologists would describe as a bank of low pressure."

"Wow, looks like more than a bank of low pressure to me."

" It's basically a rain storm."

"A hurricane?"

"No, a rain storm. We don't often get hurricanes in Britain."

"Not very patronising, are you?" She said, sarcastically. "I didn't think that it was on a collision course with us. I just thought it was one of those tropical storms they get out there."

"Afraid not. Unless the wind changes dramatically, that mother is heading straight for us."

"So, does that mean that the best is yet to come?"

"Oh yes."

"When?"

"I don't really know. But judging by wind speed, I would say there is a good chance of it reaching us by Friday."

The room fell silent, except for the humming of the server, as both of them remained transfixed on the black and white swirl on the screen.

"You're impressed, aren't you?" Blake asked, grinning with pride.

"No, I'm just wondering what I'm going to wear to the match on Friday."

Blake's smile disappeared.

"They might even postpone," she groaned.

"So, you weren't joking then."

"About what?"

"About liking football."

"No, of course I wasn't. What makes you think that I was joking?"

"I don't know," he said, getting up from his seat. Then he added, as casually as he could, "You could come with us... That's if you haven't planned on going with anyone else."

"I thought *you* weren't that keen on football."

"I'm not but Matt is, and he's been harassing me ever since the beginning of the season. Anyway," he added, looking at his watch, "We'd better get going or we are going to be late."

They left Blake's office and made their way down the stairwell.

"You were right." Sky said, as she opened the front door. The rain had stopped, at least for now. In the still of the night, all that could be heard was the sound of the waves lapping on the nearby beach and the occasional rumble of thunder in the distance.

The scent of fresh, wet grass hung heavily in the air. Sky took in a deep breath and it was in this moment that she fully understood what had drawn Blake here.

"This place is really nice," she said with a sigh. The words were spontaneous.

"Thanks," Blake said, proudly. "Your car or mine?"

"Well, I am on call so it would make sense if I drove."

"Okay, sounds good to me."

"Hey, that doesn't give you licence to get drunk, you know," Sky warned.

"As if..." he said, smiling mischievously.

The subtle beeping sounded like a megaphone at that moment.

"Oh no. What's that?" Blake asked, even though he already knew the answer.

"Sorry," she said, pulling the pager off her belt and reading the message. "I'm so sorry."

"The phone's through there," Blake said, anticipating her next question and pointing back into the house. When Sky disappeared into the living room, he sighed deeply and leant against the doorframe.

Fourteen

B3263 Road, 21.07.

As the headlights of the BMW pushed back the heavy blanket of darkness that smothered the Cornish countryside, Sky McPherson cursed Detective Inspector Morrison for paging her at such an inopportune moment. She was actually surprised at how disappointed she was.

Okay, seeing Blake after all this time was exciting but what am I expecting? To just pick up where we left off? He might be seeing someone. Although, the look on his Mother's face would be priceless. The thought made her smile for a moment but the smile faded as the memories came flooding back and, most curiously, so did the hurt.

Never, in her entire life had Sky McPherson felt as worthless as she had on that day.

It was a hot summer's day, one of the rare occasions when Alicia had invited both Blake and Sky to stay over for the weekend. It began pleasurably. They were out in the field the Hudson's called their back garden, having a barbecue.

Then they ran out of Coalite. Blake and his Father volunteered to get some from a nearby farm. Sky was only nineteen at the time and had never been alone with his Mother and would have been more than happy to accompany Mr Hudson who was much nicer, especially for a politician.

However, Blake said he would not be long and despite Sky's discreet protests, he kissed her on the head and was gone.

Alone with Blake's mother, Sky began to feel intimidated by

her. Alicia was tall, smart, and rich. Sky was tall but the similarity ended there.

"Can I help with anything?" Sky asked, hands in her denim pockets.

After looking the teenager up and down, Alicia answered, curtly, "No thank you."

It was then that Sky noticed the change of character. Alicia had never shown Sky much affection but at least in the presence of her son she had been civil to her.

There was silence between them as Sky watched the woman hurry around the veranda, placing and straightening cutlery on the dinner table.

"May I ask you something?" The woman asked suddenly, without taking her eyes of the tablecloth.

"Of course," Sky replied, delighted that the woman was dignifying her with the opportunity for conversation.

"What are your intentions toward my son?" Her tone was clipped, like that of a schoolteacher, and was still without eye contact.

Sky felt paralysed as a billion thoughts rushed through her mind but she was unable to translate any of them into words. Instead she just stared, transfixed by how Mrs Hudson's fiery red hair shone in the sunlight.

Finally she garbled, "Well, I don't really…"

"…Because he's not interested in getting serious, you know. At least, not at the moment."

"We weren't really planning on…"

"How are your parents?"

What do my parents have to do with anything? "They're fine, thank you."

"Are they still living in that lovely caravan?"

Why are you asking me this? "My parents…"

"It's not going to work, you know. You both come from completely different worlds. It's about time you realised that."

Sky was stunned by the women's sudden attack. Her intentions were obvious and she found herself squeaking, "Mrs Hudson I love your son…"

"That's nonsense!" the women retorted, "you don't even know him."

"I've known him for over a year..."

"...And you still haven't realised?" She stopped fiddling with the napkins and turned to Sky, eyes burning with resentment. Alicia had not really said much but her glare was enough to make Sky want to flee from the house and never return.

Instead, she found herself asking, "Realised what?"

Alicia Hudson smiled a patronising smile and said, "He doesn't love you. He's just having a bit of fun." She laughed, " Do you honestly think that he could ever marry someone like you?"

"Someone... Someone like me?" Sky stuttered.

"Come on child," her smile was wolf like, "surely, even you must realise that you two just," she paused as she tried to find the words, "...are not for each other." Then she shrugged, "Think about it, what do you have in common?"

Tears were streaming down Sky's face. Although everything Mrs Hudson had said in the last five minutes was spiteful, Sky was realistic enough to know that it was true. What could she give Blake? This was no fairy tale, the prince wasn't going to marry the pauper and live happily ever after. Moreover, if he did, in years to come, would he wonder if he could have done better?

When Mrs Hudson realised how distressed Sky had become, she turned on the charm and before Blake returned Sky had freshened up and, although she still looked a bit peaked, there was no sign of her heart wrenching tears.

The rest of the day went by as if their conversation had never taken place. When they left his parents home, Blake commented on how quiet Sky had been. Her answer was to burst into tears. She explained her mood away as a heavy period and Blake accepted the pathetic excuse.

Sky could not tell him what his mother had said. She would not be the cause of a row between mother and son. After all, what difference would it make? What Alicia Hudson had said was true. Sky and Blake were not made for each other.

Ever since that day, things changed between them both and, eventually, something happened that gave her the excuse she needed to end their relationship.

Five months later, she won her scholarship and left Blake and the Hudson family behind her until today.

It was nine thirty when the BMW swung onto the gravelled drive leading to Greenacres farm. Sky squinted at the flashing blue lights of police cars as she drew nearer.

An ambulance was parked outside the house, flanked by two patrol cars with their full beams on and shining toward the front door. The farm courtyard was a hive of police activity. She wondered what could have happened here that warranted so much police presence.

She pulled up alongside the Ford Mondeo she recognised as belonging to D.I. Morrison.

She retrieved a sterile white jump suit from the car boot, slipped into it, grabbed her briefcase and made for the entrance.

She passed the ambulance; the back doors were open and she saw a plump middle-aged woman, with long wispy white hair, sitting on the back step. She looked shaken. A paramedic was fussing around her as she chattered agitatedly to two police officers.

Inside, the house was very dark. Flashlights of the investigating officers danced around the house like an army of fireflies.

She squinted up the stairs directly in front of her. Someone shone a torch in her face and she held up a hand to fend off the glare, and then snapped, "D I Morrison?"

The beam of light left her and pointed up the stairs. "Thank you." She said with irritation clear in her voice.

Without a smile or indeed checking who she was, the police officer ushered her by.

"Dr McPherson!" a voice called.

Sky looked up. Morrison was leaning over the banister, clutching a torch in his right hand.

"Detective Inspector?" she asked, unable to make him out in the dim light.

"Yes! Up here!" he shouted, illuminating her flight up the stairs.

"Sorry to drag you out here at this time," he said as she reached the landing.

"Its not problem, inspector. Although, I must say, you seem to be making a habit of it." Her smile was lost in the darkness. "What happened to the lights?" she asked.

"Storm knocked the power out. We have been onto the electricity people and they are trying to fix it as we speak. In the meantime, I've made arrangements for a mobile generator."

"So, what have we got?"

"Well," Morrison began, training his beam on a door across the landing "Unfortunately, what appears to be a homicide."

"Really? I thought you said not much happened around here?"

"Looks like I was wrong," Morrison replied pensively. With that, he snatched a flashlight out of the hand of a passing officer and handed it to Sky.

"After you," he said.

The gloom was diluted and shadows peeked out from behind the scantily furnished bedroom as their torches probed the interior. Sky squinted in an effort to discern her surroundings. The room smelt of a damp musk with traces of ammonia.

"We're getting some light up here now," Morrison reiterated with an impatient sigh and looking back down the stairs.

"Thanks," she replied, not looking at him but advancing into the room.

"She's on the bed," Morrison said, glumly.

Sky aimed her torch and revealed a mound of cloth lying on the bed. She opened her briefcase and pulled on a pair of surgical gloves.

"Coming through!" a voice shouted.

"Bloody hell Harris, I asked for that light bloody half an hour ago," Morrison barked.

"Sorry Sir, I had to…" the young officer began.

"Don't bother with explanations, just get the bloody thing over there." Morrison shone a path to the bed with his torch.

"Yes Sir." The young officer moved forward, carrying the floodlight and trailing a long electrical lead. After fumbling about for a minute or so, he finally managed to plug it in and switch it on.

The dazzling light of the halogen lamp transformed the darkness into daylight, revealing a grubby looking room approximately eight by ten feet wide, with sloping wooden beams. What little furniture inhabited the shell was scuffed. A pink bedspread covered the double bed.

Sky moved over to it, dictaphone in hand. The scene was something she had never seen before. The old women lay on top of the bed, dressed in a generously fitting cream coloured nightdress. She was on her back with her arms crossed over her chest. Her eyes were closed and her wrinkled skin was no longer translucent pink but a yellow waxy hue, and her lips, *Oh my God what have they done to her lips*, were sewn together in a cross stitch fashion, resembling the groundwork for a macabre roasted dinner.

"Is this exactly how you found her?" she asked as casually as she could.

"Of course," Morrison replied, joining her by the bed and cringing at the sight and the stench of stale urine that lingered heavily over here.

A police officer with all the enthusiasm of a photojournalist on the trail of a hot story entered the room and began snapping pictures of the death scene. The flashes from the camera were like searing lightening, branding images of the dead women onto Sky's brain.

Sky made a conscious effort to ignore the happy snapper, and speaking as professionally as she could into her Dictaphone, she began her preliminary examination. "Elderly female, in her seventies, malnourished." She paused a few seconds and then continued, "The victim's lips appear to be stitched together by what resembles tapestry thread. There is a large amount of in the chest area, soaked into the nightdress, which would indicate that the victim might still have been alive when the sewing took place. There is bruising to the temple." She gently prodded the discoloration. "This would indicate that the victim was struck by a blunt object, probably in an effort to subdue her and facilitate the stitching."

Sky broke off here. Her imagination beamed images of the events that must have taken place.

She wanted to run, screaming, from the house.

Morrison must have noticed the look in her eyes for he asked, "Are you alright, Doc?"

Sky did not reply. Instead, she spoke into her Dictaphone and continued, "There is no sign of rigor, indicting that death could not have occurred more than six hours ago."

"I need to turn her over," she said to no one in particular.

Morrison and the young police officer moved in to help her.

"After three," Morrison said. "Two…three…"

They turned the old women over. The task was an easy one for she could not have weighed more than eight stone.

The nightdress had moved up, revealing part of the woman's left buttock. The flesh was blue, grey and covered in what looked like burst boils. The young officer baulked.

Sky continued her dictation. "There are pressure sores present in the region of the buttocks indicating that the victim may have been bed ridden." Sky pulled the flimsy cloth down, as if to protect the dead woman's dignity. Then, she delicately unbuttoned the back of the nightdress and looked up. She did not have to ask; Morrison flicked on his flashlight and handed it to her. She shone it over the corpse's back, highlighting a series of dark discolorations about the size of five pence pieces. She examined the marks closely and when she was satisfied, she handed the flashlight back to its owner and continued, "There are dark blotches to the back suggesting lack of blood circulation. These coupled with the absence of rigor mortis would lead me to believe that death occurred over three but no longer than six hours ago. Establishing the time of death at approximately, she looked at her watch, " 7:00pm."

At this point, the young officer, known as Harris, fled the room. In complete contrast, the photographer seemed to be showing an unhealthy interest in this victim and squeezed off four more photographs in quick succession.

Morrison felt obliged to say something, "He's not used to this."

"Neither are you Inspector," Sky replied in a matter of fact tone.

Morrison shrugged his shoulders and stood up straight in an effort to deny Sky's comment but in reality, she was right. He had not dealt with anything like this before. Homicides yes, but mutilation such as this, no.

Sky rebuttoned the gown and, as if aided by telepathy, Morrison helped her roll the women onto her back once more. She wondered if somewhere, someone was oblivious to the bad news heading their way.

Sky stood up from her position next to the bed and removed her gloves.

"What do you think killed her?" Morrison asked.

"It's hard so say really. It could be anything from the blow to the head to heart failure."

"Heart failure?"

"Yes." Sky met the inspector's gaze "Inspector, whoever did this did so out of pure cruelty. This woman was still alive when they sutured her lips. Can you imagine how horrifying that must have been?"

She did not wait for a reply. Instead, she returned the dictaphone to her briefcase. Then, with one final look at the inspector, she said, "I will know more after the post mortem."

Blinking as the camera flashed more pictures, She hurriedly left the room.

Morrison joined her as she was descending the stairs. He flashed the beam of his torch on the steps in front of them.

"You mentioned that she's probably been bed ridden. You deduced that just from the marks on her back?" he asked, trying to keep up with her.

"She was also particularly under nourished which would suggest that she had some kind of illness that stopped her gaining weight. I doubt if anyone as emaciated as her would be capable of walking around unaided. Then there was the ammonia; either she needed a bed pan or was incontinent."

"What do you think was wrong with her?"

"Hard to say, really. Could have been any kind of debilitating disease."

Sky stopped as they reached the foot of the stairs and, for the second time this evening, looked him in the eyes. "But then you already know that, don't you inspector?" she asked with a faint smile.

A few seconds ticked by, he returned the smile.

Sky walked away from him toward the front door. Raising her voice, she threw back, "Not just a pretty face, inspector," and walked out of the building.

"Oh, I have no doubts about that, Doctor," Morrison grinned, following her.

Outside, She sucked in the fresh evening air. It was such a relief to get out of that bedroom.

"Did she live alone?" Sky asked as they reached her car and she began to wriggle out of the white jump suit.

"No. According to the neighbour," Morrison nodded toward the ambulance, where the woman with the wispy white hair was still chattering on at the two police officers, "She lived with her daughter."

"Where's she?"

"We don't know. She seems to have disappeared."

"Do you think she did this?"

"Who knows. According to the neighbour, the daughter hardly ever left the house since she moved back. They had all their groceries delivered. The neighbour came round after the power cut to ask if they needed anything and found the mother. By the way, you were right about her. She has been bed-ridden for over two years now. That's why the daughter moved out here to live with her. Apparently, she used to be some big shot at a Japanese electronics firm."

"Inspector!" someone shouted.

"What?" Morrison shouted back in the direction of a bobbing flashlight that appeared out of the darkness.

"I think we've found something," the voice said.

"What is it?"

"Another body, Sir. On the beeeeeeeech"! The voice trailed off as the officer slipped over. All that could be seen was the light of the torch flailing, followed by a loud thud and the word *"SHIT!"*

Morrison sighed impatiently as Sky suppressed a chuckle.

"Jesus Christ," Morrison mumbled. Then, without any further word to Sky, he was off, walking toward the fallen officer.

Sky looked on, still smiling until her mind replayed the snapshots of what she had witnessed inside that bedroom and now more than ever she longed for her mother's embrace.

The bloated body on the beach turned out to be that of Joyce Masters, the forty-year-old daughter of Judith Masters.

Sky had followed Morrison and his officer down to the beach where the body lay wedged in between two rocks.

Joyce Masters had drowned. There were no signs indicating that she had been forced into the water by anything or anyone. Sky's preliminary examination concluded that Joyce had walked voluntarily into the cold Atlantic Ocean and drowned herself.

Fifteen

The drive back to Stony Point was a long one. Sky felt drained. The image of the old woman still haunted her in the darkness of the car.

The only effective distraction was Blake. She could not explain it but the thought of snuggling up to him just felt so right but she knew that was not going to happen.

She pulled up outside the majestic lighthouse and sat for a few seconds, unmoving and clutching the steering wheel as her heart hammered loudly. Eventually, she gathered her emotions and stepped out into the night.

The air was fresh, heavily impregnated with the scent of rain. Nearby the odd rumble of thunder could still be heard.

When she reached the door, she knocked and shortly afterwards heard muffled footsteps on the stone floor. Then the door opened and Sky was, momentarily, struck dumb.

Blake was breathtaking: he looked slightly dishevelled, his dark brown eyes were glazed and his hair was ruffled, indicating that he had been lying down, watching TV or maybe sleeping.

"Hi," he said in a soft tone and smiling warmly. "All sorted?"

It took Sky a few seconds to reply, although it seemed hours. "Yeah. Yes, thanks." Regaining her composure, she added, "I am so sorry about this evening, Blake"

"It's okay."

"We could still go somewhere, I don't know a late…"

"It's okay."

"God, I feel so awful. You've been stuck in all night."

"I don't mind, honestly. I understand."

"I'm really am sorry. "She was rambling and repeating herself but she couldn't help it.

"Will you stop apologising?"

"I'm sorry" Sky laughed when she realised what she had just said.

There was an awkward moment.

"Look, are you coming in or are you going to stand there all night?" Blake asked.

"I well, I should really be getting back." *What? Don't say that!*

"You must be kidding! Drive home now? You may as well stay the night."

"Oh no. I couldn't."

"Don't be silly. Of course you can. Besides, I've made dinner"

"You've made what?" she blurted out.

"Don't get excited. It's only pasta. The water's on and I've already made the sauce, straight from the jar," he added proudly.

"Wow. I didn't know you cooked."

"I don't."

She laughed.

"So?" Blake stood, expectantly, with his hand still resting on the door. "It's all right you know. I won't molest you in the middle of the night. Or at least I'll try not to," he added, grinning.

"You always were a spoil sport," Sky said, in mock

disappointment as she stepped inside.

"Here, let me take that," he said, gesturing to her coat as she tried to shake it off.

"Thanks."

He hooked the coat over the door and ushered her through to the living room.

"So, would you like a drink?" he asked, moving over to the cabinet.

"Why not."

"What would you like?"

"Actually, I think I could use a Brandy."

"Ooh," he said. "Is that to warm you up or steady your nerves?"

"Both. So bring the bottle."

He smiled warmly as they moved into the kitchen.

An hour and a plate of spaghetti Bolognese later they were both seated on the sofa, sipping coffee.

"You still haven't told me anything about this emergency that forced you to cancel our dinner date, or would it be unethical of you to discuss it?" Blake was sitting back in an armchair with his leg cocked over one of the armrests, nurturing a cup of coffee.

"You're right. I can't discuss it with you but suffice to say that there are some really sick individuals out there."

"Yeah I know. We vote for them all the time," Blake said, smiling. He did not know what Sky had witnessed this evening but he did know that it had affected her. "So, do you want to sleep in my bed tonight?" he asked, changing the subject.

"Oh no, the sofa will be fine thanks," she said, patting the cushion next to her.

"No, I insist."

"Blake, really…I don't wont to put you out."

"You won't be putting me out at all."

"So where will you sleep?"

"Well, same place as you."

Sky smiled broadly. "I don't think so."

"Why not?"

"Well, because…. I, "Sky fumbled but the words wouldn't come to her and she felt her face blushing.

"Don't worry, I was only teasing," Blake said, grinning. "I've got the spare toothbrush out, it's by the sink," he said, as he swung his legs down, in one swift motion and stood up.

"What?"

"You never know when old friends are going to drop by," he added, taking the empty coffee cup out of Sky's hands and disappearing into the kitchen.

The rain came back during the night and the sound of its hammering woke Sky. Although she felt exhausted, she could not rest.

She slipped out of the bed. Blake's shirt, that she had borrowed to use as a nightgown, flapped loosely across her bare legs as she crossed the round room and descended the stairs. The stone steps were cold under her feet.

The living room door was open and Sky's heart started pounding as she approached it. Blake was in there, and by the sound of his deep breathing, he was fast asleep.

She could feel a thick knot form in her throat. Her head felt giddy and her palms started to sweat. *Get a grip!* But she could not help it. Beyond that door, Blake could be lying naked and she wanted him, she knew she did.

She paused, by the doorway; Blake had left the kitchen light on and this cast a warm glow over his body. The quilt lay in a heap on the floor whilst he lay sprawled, wearing nothing but his boxers, over the sofa. She drank in his long, powerful legs and muscular body.

She wasn't yearning to have Blake at all, there must be another perfectly valid reason why she was crossing the room toward the sofa with only one thought in mind: to touch him, if only for a few seconds.

Once there, within touching distance, she stood motionless, holding her hand over her heart in an effort to silence the pounding. Her mouth was dry but she dared not swallow. Then, in that moment, his right had moved! It travelled from his chest to settle at the back of his head. However, Sky had not seen this, for, at the first sign of movement she had darted into the safe haven that was the kitchen. There, like some love stricken teenager, she leaned heavily against the wall.

She moved over to the sink, filled a glass with water and drank with a desperate thirst.

The sound of the rain pelting the kitchen window drew her attention to the open blinds. She watched her reflection and then allowed her mind to drift through the glass to the blackness beyond. There, she saw the image of Judith Masters, her lips stitched together.

With that, she fled the kitchen, climbed the stairs two at a time, and dove under the safety of her quilt. She replayed images of Blake in her mind, never before had she wanted someone so badly.

These were her last thoughts as she drifted off into a deep sleep, completely oblivious to the dark skies overhead.

Sixteen

Morning came too soon with the sound of Blake's voice calling to her many times before Sky actually awoke from her blissful sleep. He entered the room, carrying a tray of hot coffee and warm croissants. "Fresh from the bakery," he grinned proudly, depositing the tray on the bedside table whilst Sky, conscious of what her hair must look like first thing in the morning, sat up, frantically tucking the loose strands behind her ears.

"Did you sleep well?" he asked.

"Great thanks," She replied, still composing herself.

"It's going to be a fairly sunny day today but we can expect more of those stormy showers tonight."

"Have you been consulting your computer again?" She asked, discreetly admiring the black suit he was wearing.

"No, I watched the weather forecast this morning," he smiled. There was a pause as he looked at her, then he said, "I've got to go now but I'll leave the key in the door. You can take it with you. I have a spare one."

"Are you sure?"

"Yes. I'll see you later?"

Sky did not have time to think about it, she just said, "Sure."

With that, Blake disappeared out of the door.

The Discovery revved up a few times then the engine noise faded into the distance. Sky looked up at the window: the early morning sunlight streamed through the large expanse of glass, casting a hazy golden glow over the bed.

She slipped out from under the quilt and walked across the room to be greeted with one of the most breathtaking views she had ever seen: white, foamy waves lapping the shore of a coastline that stretched for miles. She wanted to stay here, forever gazing at the aquamarine sea and the swooping seagulls.

The shrill of the phone brought Sky back to the present, where she found herself sitting in her small office in the Coroner's building.

She snatched the phone up, "Dr McPherson."

"Sky?"

"Yes, who is this?"

"It's Blake."

"Oh hi." Instantly, a smile spread across her face, although her voice remained cool and casual.

"I was just ringing to see if you got into the office okay."

"Oh, yes, fine, no problem"

"I know what the traffic can be like from my place first thing in the morning."

"Yes, I encountered the one tractor and a man on a bike."

"You're were lucky then. It can get bad sometimes."

There was a long pause.

Sky was desperately trying to find something to say to sustain the conversation but she could not. She had suddenly lost the ability to articulate. "You were right, "she stuttered, "about the weather." God, she felt so pathetic.

"You must be pretty busy today," Blake offered.

He was referring to the early morning news bulletins. They had reported random acts of violence and vandalism throughout the region. Ten people had died and thirty more had been injured in seemingly unprovoked attacks.

"It's all over the news. What do you think is going on?"

"I haven't got a clue and nor do the police by the looks of it. All I know is that my office has been inundated with new clients."

"Clients?"

"That's an affectionate name we have for them here at the morgue."

"Nice," Blake said, in a slightly squeamish tone.

"Yes, that is what I thought when I first got here," she replied, eyeing the dozen or so manila folders piled up on her desk. One, in particular, caught her attention. She reached over and pulled it from the pile. A label attached to it read, '*McElvoy, Arthur.*'

"So, when are you going to make it up to me?"

"Make what up to you?" She asked, distractedly, thumbing through the sheets inside the folder.

"Dinner."

"Oh dinner. Well…. " She read some of the text. "Whenever you like"

"Like tonight?"

"Yeah sure," she replied.

"There's no need to sound so excited about it. Look, if you don't want to…"

"Oh my God," she gasped.

"What's wrong?"

There was silence as Sky read on.

"Sky?" Blake called insistently.

"Arthur McElvoy's toxicology results."

"Arthur…?" It took Blake a few seconds to register the name. "McElvoy. What about him?"

"Well, they found a large quantity of an unknown substance in his blood."

"Unknown substance," Blake echoed. "Like?"

"I don't know. Whatever this thing is, it attacked his haemoglobin with the ferocity of a virus."

"Could it be contagious?" Blake asked.

"I don't know, but I am going to find out," she said with determination.

"Right, okay, well…" Blake stuttered. He was out of his league. "So, I'll leave you to it then."

"Yeah, okay."

"I'll see you later." There was dejection in his voice but Sky was oblivious to this, much more intrigued by the science laid out on the paper before her.

"Okay, bye." He was about to disconnect but heard her say something, "What was that?" he asked.

"I said, I'll see you tonight."

Blake smiled broadly. "See you then." With that he pressed the disconnect button on his mobile phone and slipped it back into his coat pocket.

Around him, the Cornish countryside was a canvas of lush green trees and sprawling fields. To the south, the sun shone warmly whilst, in stark contrast, the eastern sky was a shroud of blackness.

"Looks like more rain," the farmer said.

Blake followed the elderly man's gaze and, right on cue, deep guttural thunder rumbled in the distance.

"I think you're right," Blake said, pausing on the approaching gloom. Then, slowly, his gaze drifted back, like a director's camera, panning over the distant hills, the surrounding valley and then at the quarry. Here, the crater was roughly the size of a small football pitch, filled with water.

"So, when did you discover them?" Blake asked, stepping cautiously down the embankment toward the pool.

"This morning. Those darn cows won't drink anywhere else."

"What time this morning?"

The old man pondered for a few seconds and then said, "Oh, about 06:30."

"And they definitely weren't here yesterday?"

"Nope. As I said, they wont drink anywhere else and as soon as you let them out, they come trotting here. Must be something in the water. Alcohol or something," the farmer chuckled. Blake smiled respectfully.

They were at the water's edge now and Blake could see them very clearly: hundreds maybe thousands of dead fish floated on the surface.

He scanned the immediate area around the pit, looking for tyre marks or anything else that would indicate any human intervention with the quarry but he could see nothing. He made a mental note to check the rest of the surrounding area.

"And you haven't seen anyone around here? No trucks or Vans?" Blake asked.

"No, nothing."

"What about people? Any anglers?"

"No. Nobody ever bothers to come down here. A lot of people don't even know it exists."

"Any unusual smells?"

"Smells?" The old man frowned, "No, no smells."

"So, nothing out of the ordinary?"

"No."

"But you can't see this place from your farm, is that correct?"

"That's right."

"So, it is possible that someone could have come here and dumped something in the water without you seeing them?"

"I only live a few miles down the road."

"But you aren't here all the time."

"Not all the time, no, but they come here every day," the farmer motioned to a herd of black and white cows, grazing nearby. "And where they go, I go."

"Okay." Blake produced a black, numbered, notebook from the inside pocket of his jacket and scribbled down notes. "Sorry, and your full name, again?"

"Trevor, Trevor Wilson."

"And where do you live Mr Wilson? Just in case we need to contact you."

"Trevassy farm, only a few miles down the road."

"And Mr Wilson, you wouldn't happen to know who this quarry belongs to?"

Farmer Wilson moved closer and said in a hushed tone, "Well, I heard it belonged to the M.O.D"

"The Ministry of Defence?"

"Yeah."

"How do you know that?"

"That's what I heard."

"Do you know how long the fish have been in this quarry?"

"I think it's a couple of years now."

"And you have never seen anything like this before?"

"No, but there's no knowing what that lot have left behind. They could have conducted experiments in here for all we know."

"What kind of experiments?"

"I don't know. You are from the government, you know more than I do."

"Actually, the Environment Agency is an independent body."

" What, they privatising you as well now?"

Blake smiled, "You could say that."

"I've gotta' get me a pair of those," the farmer remarked, eyeing Blake's green waders. "Come in handy in the dipping season."

"You dip cows?"

"No. I would have a bit of a job doin' that," the farmer chuckled. "Nah, dipping sheep."

"You have sheep on your farm as well as cows?"

"No, I don't but Vince does."

"Right," Blake smiled, crouching down, and picking up a deflated life jacket and slipping it over his head.

"Planning on doing some swimming?"

"Regulation."

"More rules. I don't know how you people know whether you are coming or going. Every day they bring out different rules."

Blake flipped the locks on the hard case he had brought with him. He removed, what looked like, a small milk bottle and then slowly and cautiously stepped into the water.

"You wanna' be careful where you put your feet. It's deep in there," the farmer offered.

"Thanks," Blake replied. He slipped a rubber glove onto his right hand and then used it to collect a water sample inside the plastic bottle. Once he was satisfied with the quantity taken, he snapped the lid down and then held the liquid up to the sun.

"See anything in there?" the farmer asked, gazing into the bottle as if it were a crystal ball.

The water had a verdant tinge to it but that was nothing unusual. Blake signed, dated and noted the location on a sticky back label and affixed it to the bottle.

"No, not really. But the lab will tell us more."

A gale blew up around them.

"You can smell it," the farmer said, sniffing the air.

"Smell what?" Blake asked.

"The rain. Oh yes, this is gonna' be some storm."

"How do you know?"

"The cows," he said, looking down the valley. "They're headin' back. Always do when it's bad weather."

"Right." Blake nodded, following Wilson's gaze down the valley. Sure enough, the herd of cows were trotting off in a disciplined single file.

"Probably just had enough grass for one day," Blake smiled, but the farmer wasn't looking at him, he seemed much more interested in the gathering gloom.

"Would you mind?" Blake asked, gesturing to a fishing net he had left on the embankment.

"Oh yeah." Wilson hurried over to the net and passed it across.

Blake used it to fish out one of the dead corpses. He examined it closely; the fish's dead eyes stared back. Its gills were open, indicating that it had struggled to breathe moments before death.

"What do you think caused this then?"

"I don't know," Blake shrugged, looking across the water. "It's unlikely to be a disease of any kind."

"Why's that?"

"Well, if you are sure that the dead fish were not here yesterday then it's highly unlikely that it was a disease. Diseases are slow acting and are normally particular to a certain species. The dead fish here vary in species. Therefore, whatever killed them was potent and indiscriminate. It really could be a anything from a rise in water temperature to a pollutant in the water which, at this moment in time, seems most likely."

"Must have been something strong to kill off this amount of fish."

"Yes, and until we've discovered exactly what it is, I would suggest you keep your cows away from here. Do you know if this quarry has an outlet of any kind, like a stream or something?"

"Not that I know of. Why, do you think it could harm my cows?"

"We'll know more when we get the results back. I would most certainly have your vet take a look at the herd as soon as possible."

Wilson nodded in compliance. "I've never seen anything like this before," the farmer said, leaning forward so that he could get a better look at the dead fish but snapped his head away, cringing. "Phew... what's that smell?" he complained.

"Well this is it," Blake pondered, staring at the fish as if his gaze would revive it. "The smell could be decomposition but they haven't been here long enough for that. Could be BOD, yet there isn't much discolouration in the water."

"B O what?" The farmer asked still wiping his nose. The odour was similar to that of rotten eggs.

"Biochemical Oxygen Demand," Blake explained. "Lack of oxygen can kill fish and cause the water to smell."

"You mean stink!"

Blake smiled.

"So, what would suddenly cause this lack of oxygen?"

"Again, in such short a period of time, I don't know," he replied distractedly as he surveyed the surrounding area. Then, he shook the dead fish into a plastic sample bag, sealed it and deposited it into his hard case. From there, he retrieved a small electronic device, about the size of a large remote control with an LCD display and a flexible probe protruding from one end.

"What…" Wilson began.

"It's a D.O. metre," Blake anticipated. "It's used to measure the dissolved oxygen in the water. It's what the fish need to breathe." Blake immersed the probe into the water and watched as the LCD screen returned the data; it was normal.

He deposited the D. O. metre back into the case and pulled out another specimen bag. Treading carefully, he began overturning stones and grunted with satisfaction when he finally came across a small grub. He examined it closely, concluded that it was dead and placed it inside the specimen bag.

Lightening flashed in the distance, closely followed by a rumble of thunder.

"Just to reiterate what I said earlier. I would keep your cows away from here."

"That serious?"

"Just a precaution."

"Right," The old man agreed, eyeing him suspiciously.

With the help of the farmer, Blake gathered his equipment and made his way back to the Land Rover. There, he removed his boots and waders and dumped them in the back.

"So, what now?" the old man asked.

"Well, as I said, we'll run a mass scan on that sample and keep you informed." Blake paused and then said, "Just one more thing. Do you know how the water in here is replenished?"

"Rainfall."

"Just rainfall?"

"As far as I know, why?"

"Just wondering," Blake said, pensively, getting into the Land Rover.

The dark sky moaned as Blake drove away.

Seventeen

Trevassy Farm , Cornwall. 19:30

The rain hammered down on the old farm, flooding the yard and bubbling over the clogged up guttering. It was as if it was searching the whole structure of the building, seeking an entrance, a hole, a crack in the wall, somewhere it could gain access to reach the old man inside.

Farmer Wilson was preparing his dinner when one long drop of water fell onto his loaf of bread and was absorbed into the yeast compound.

"Blast!" he cussed. "Damn rain!"

The house was very gloomy and it seemed that the 60-watt bulb was on its way out as it kept flickering. The rattling of the glass in the peeling window frames drew his attention and that is when he noticed them.

"What the hell…" His mouth fell open in astonishment. All fifteen of his cows were in the yard. They stood, unmoving, as rain scurried down their coats and dripped off their ears. Their eyes watched Wilson as he peered out into the watery haze.

How the hell did they manage to get out? He had, personally, herded them into their pen and locked the gate. *I know I did.* However, now, as real as his leaky roof the cows were bundled together, filling up the farmyard with a sea of steaming bodies.

"Bloody cows, got a mind of their own," he grumbled, loudly.

Thunder roared in sympathy. Now the roof began to creak with the weight of the pummelling rain. The drone was loud, like that of jet engines thundering overhead. It was unlike anything he had heard before.

The drip over the table had become a steady stream and Wilson hurried over to the sink, fetched a saucepan and replaced the loaf of bread with it.

He looked up to the roof and the question of whether this old building could sustain this massive onslaught did cross his mind.

IT, the rain, was here and it was hunting him down, streaming over the roof, seeping into the walls, trickling under the door.

Then they began: in unison, the whole herd of cows began mooing.

"Serve you bleedin' right, that'll teach ya' to leave your pen and go out walking. Now you can stay out there for all I care."

Wilson may have spoken the words but he was thinking something completely different. The best and most expensive pedigree bull had successfully inseminated many of those cows. If they stayed out in this rain and caught cold, there would be no telling how many of them could lose their calves.

No, there was only one thing for it, he would have to go out there and herd them back into their pens. He muttered to himself as he made his way to the door and pulled his coat off the peg. As he stood there, his boots squelched in the pool of rain that seeped under the door. The liquid enveloped the soles of his boots but failed to penetrate the rubber tread.

"Damn!" He looked down to see that the water was oozing like a poisonous snake toward the table.   More thunder sounded overhead.

He pulled on his coat.

Meanwhile, the mooing continued but Wilson was going to sort them out. He would take a stick to them if needs be, that would get them back into their pens. "Blasted things! Blasted rain!"

He hauled the door open to the mooing crowd. The torrent was heavy catapulted forward by the strong winds that snatched at his raincoat, blowing off his hood.

Lightening flashed.

Green lightening? The rain stung his eyes, hissing and spluttering as it drenched his nearly baldhead, driving into his skin and infiltrating his pores.

The mooing continued louder and louder…

More thunder.

Wilson pulled his coat around him, battling against the gale as he launched forth.

Lightening flashed

"Come on!" he shouted over the din.

They did not move. They simply watched and mooed at him.

"Get in there! Go on!" He shouted, waving his hands around. His coat fell open and the rain began to attack his exposed midriff, seeping into his vest and into his skin.

"I am going to get that bleedin' stick. That'll move ya, huh?" Go on! Get in there!" "Go on!" He screamed in frustration but still nothing, the cows would not budge, instead they stopped mooing.

Then Wilson noticed her; Betty, his black and white pride and joy, was standing at the front.

"Go on Betty, love. Go on!" he said in a calmer voice, pushing the cow's head round. However, the cow was anchored in place and instead of moving, she swung her head back, butting Wilson in the chest, sending him stumbling backward. As much as he tried to sustain his balance, Wilson slipped in the mud and fell heavily into a pool of rainwater.

It engulfed him, seeping into his eyes and ears, making him drowsy. A strange warming sensation travelled the length of his body spreading from his toes, through his groin and into his head. Hot tentacles of fire reached, probed deep into the darkest side of his mind.

Meanwhile, Betty and her friends moved forward towards his fallen body.

He looked up, squinting into the precipitation and smiling at the looming bulk of the cow's body. Betty observed him as if he were a fallen animal and she the rescuing human, her brown eyes now stared black and cold.

"That's it... That's my girl.... Come and help me up... Come on."

With that, the cow threw her head up to the sky and mooed loudly. In unison, the other cows joined in. The sound was loud and frightening. Wilson wanted to block his ears but instead he attempted to scramble to his feet, but slipped in the water.

Then, suddenly, Betty jumped forward and tossed her head in the air, mooing like a newborn calf. Wilson tried to roll out of her path but he was too late. The cow's two tons thundered down into his groin in the form of a hoof.

Pain engulfed the lower part of his body and Wilson had trouble breathing, so much was the agony of the first blow that he hardly noticed the second, stamping into his chest and crushing his breastbone.

Hyperventilating and coughing blood, he crawled onto his side. The warm tingle inside his skull was his only comfort as he dragged his body through the water.

Thunder roared and lightening flashed.

The cows watched for a few seconds as Wilson tried to slither away from them but Betty danced forward and with her the whole herd moved, jumping with the excitement and trampling over their owner's body until he was nothing more than a mangled mess of blood and bone.

Eighteen

Stony Point / 20:45

Blake looked out of the window; the rain was still falling heavily, and had been doing so for the past hour. He wondered where Sky was and if she was okay. The radio had told of several accidents in the region, most of them due to reckless driving.

"Where is she?" He was pacing the room now, no longer irritated at the thought of being stood up again but worried that something might have happened to her.

He climbed the stairs to his study; he needed to occupy his mind. He sat at his computer and switched it on. He clicked on the telephone icon and the modem sprang to life.

Lightening flashed outside.

Along with a myriad of other thoughts racing through Blake's mind was the conversation he had with farmer Wilson.

Blake had checked the plans at the town council. The quarry had no other water source and therefore relied on rainfall alone to replenish its evaporated loss. However, if this were the case, then it would mean that whatever poisoned the fish came from precipitation alone. The same rain that was now deluging the west coast.

As if to confirm this, an eerie green flash of lightning illuminated the room but Blake was too busy scanning low-pressure trajectories to notice it.

Could there be a link between the rainfall and the poisoning of the quarry? Of course there could be. He lectured this very thing in college every week, Acid Rain. But how the hell did this rain become toxic enough to poison over a thousand fish? Moreover, why were these the only casualties? Or were they?

This was such a wild theory and absurd. There had never been such a dramatic and obvious case of acid rain poisoning. Yes, it had affected animals and vegetation but over a period, not over one night!

Despite this, Blake's fingers worked the keyboard and before long the spinning globe appeared. He zoomed into the map of the UK and clicked to magnify, displaying a blanket of cloud. It looked like a black cancer, starting from the southwest and spreading its way northwest.

The data at the foot of the screen indicated a low wind current; the rain was here to stay.

After punching a few buttons on the keyboard, several black wavy lines with numeric data, indicating wind speed and direction appeared over the whole of England.

Working fast, Blake right clicked. Instantly, the map of England dissolved into that of Europe.

Now the black wavy lines streaked north, from Cornwall to the Hebrides and beyond. He paused as his brain worked overtime.

In that moment, a pair of headlights flashed through the window and even over the hum of the pouring rain, Blake could hear a car engine. It was Sky!

Within seconds, he had left his study and was descending the stairs two at a time.

He snatched the front door open just as she was about to knock.

"Late again," She said, cheerfully as she stood, holding her handbag over her head.

Blake stood aside and ushered her in.

"I tried to call you," Sky said, shaking her handbag, violently, trying to disperse the water that had collected on it.

"It's this weather. It's driving me mad, you know."

Blake noticed nervousness to Sky's chatter.

"I got out of work and it was fine. Then, I drove out here and all hell broke loose. I mean, I'm surprised I got here at all. Did you hear about all those accidents? My God, it was bad! I couldn't see three feet in front of me and then," she swallowed, "This lorry nearly rammed me, Oh God." Her eyes were wide with fear for a few seconds and then she forced a smile, "I did try to call you..."

"It's okay."

"No, I really did, you know."

"I know."

"I'm not just saying that."

"I know... look..."

"We can still go out."

"Sky..."

"It's on me. That's the least I can do."

"Sky..."

"I mean, you must have been waiting here all evening..."

"Sky!" Blake interrupted forcefully.

She stopped. Blake had reached something inside of her. *Oh God, I nearly died tonight!* Blake was standing there: baggy knit jumper, jeans, and wearing the warmest smile, she had ever seen. She needed him.

Tears started to well in her violet eyes.

"Sky? Are you okay?"

That was it, the sounds of Blake's concerned voice was the drop that broke the damn. She fell into his arms and sobbed.

"Hey, Hey," he cooed. "What's the matter?"

Sky could not answer. She was a shipwreck of emotions and Blake was the tropical island.

He sensed her needs and asked no questions. For several minutes, the sound of her heart wrenching sobs upstaged the storm outside.

Eventually, she emerged from her nest in Blake's chest. He looked into her tear-stained eyes, slowly he leaned forward and kissed the bittersweet tears from her cheek.

She could smell his aftershave and it soothed her; in fact, his whole presence soothed her. She wanted him. She needed him now.

She angled her face so that they were rubbing cheek to cheek; their mouths open wide, both of them seeking, yearning for each other's lips.

Thunder rumbled loudly overhead as the rain pummelled the lighthouse. It sought an entrance wherever it could. A crack in the wall, an open window, under the door, anywhere it could find an entrance and be absorbed into a host.

As the green lightening flashed furiously at the watertight building, their mouths met in a desperate kiss. Each of them sucking air loudly through their noses as their mouths hungrily devoured each other.

Blake's masculine aroma fuelled Sky's needs as the scent from her damp hair aroused him. He was ready for her.

Their mouths remained adhered to each other, neither of them wishing to let go as they fumbled to undress. Blake slipped Sky out of her raincoat as she pulled off his jumper. Her hands searched his hair as he unbuttoned her trousers and allowed them to slip down her legs.

Pushing Blake backwards, against the front door, she stepped out of her trousers, kicked off her shoes and battled with his jeans.

As they did so, the rain washed the front step and merged into swelling pool outside the door. Slowly, it gathered form and began to trickle under the crack, heading for Blake's shoes and Sky's naked feet.

She slipped him out of his shirt and began to nip his neck delicately, her senses heightened by the thought of savouring him. She kissed him all over and then, slowly, her tongue snail trailed up his chest to his neck until it found his mouth once more.

Slowly, the rain sluiced into the house, engulfing Blake's shoes and leaking forward towards Sky's beckoning toes. It was as if it could sense the human flesh and it yearned to be absorbed into it. It grew closer and closer and was now inches away.

Sky had unbuckled Blake's belt and her hand had disappeared into his jeans. There she probed the warmth. Aroused by his readiness, she threw her head back as her juices flowed in anticipation.

It was Blake's turn to kiss and nibble her neck. He slid down into her blouse and into her bra and, frantically, pulled apart the buttons that constricted his access and then dived in. Easing her right breast free, he suckled on her nipple as she gasped with pleasure.

The water was now an inch away from Sky's feet.

Her hands searched the whole of him; from his chest to his hair, as her body quivered with desire. Blake sensed this and responded. His finger travelled deep into her panties and slipped between her legs where he discovered that she was ready. She held his hand steady and squirmed in a rocking motion, gasping aloud.

Finally, the water reached Sky's toes and began to infiltrate the pores of her skin just as Blake scooped her up into his arms. She wrapped her legs around him as he slammed her, roughly, against the door.

Squelching in the pool of rain water, Blake ripped Sky's panties off and entered her again and again as their mouths met once more, each of them grunting loudly, their desires finally fulfilled.

Outside, the pounding rain and thundering skies drowned the thumping on the door as the whole scene was intermittently flashed green.

Nineteen

Exeter, Devonshire. 21:30

"You can't light that up in here," the taxi driver barked at the boys in the backseat. They had not been in his car for more than seven minutes and were already starting to irritate him.

Alan had been enjoying the news on the radio when this lot flagged him down. They had obviously had a skin full already and were going to finish themselves off at this club. He had heard all kinds of stories about the place.

"Why not?" asked the skinnier of the lads, who could not have been older than nineteen.

"Because I say so," Alan replied, watching them in the rear view mirror. He heard the sound of sniggering but chose to ignore it.

As his passengers planned their pulling strategy for the evening, Alan found himself wondering what was wrong with world today. Earlier, the news had told of a bunch of layabouts who had raped and then doused an old woman in petrol and set her alight. He felt a surge of anger; how he would like to get his hands on those responsible.

He stopped the taxi at a red traffic light. There were hardly any people on the streets. Those that were, seemed to be revelling in the rain: some dancing, some running, others chasing each other.

Peering through the windscreen, he caught sight of a threesome on the opposite side of the junction. The party consisted of two men and a female. The light was dim and they were mostly in shadow and he could barely see what was going on, but it seemed that the girl had her back to a lamppost. One of the men was holding her arms, whilst the other rummaged under her skirt. A flicker of concern registered but Alan soon dismissed it when the girl arched her head and the glow of the streetlight revealed a deranged grin on her face. Whatever the men were doing to her, she seemed to be enjoying it.

The lights changed green and he swung right, relieved that his passengers had noticed the ménage a trios across the road.

"How long to the club?" Luke asked. He was the eldest and better looking of the three, being 26, with spiky blond hair and a healthy complexion.

"Shouldn't be long now," Alan replied, "Providing we get there in one piece." They were driving down a long, rain-drenched road. In the streetlights, a bunch of youths shoved a rubbish bin through the window of a jewellers, setting off the alarm and an orange flashing light. Then, they jumped about, roaring with laughter and congratulating each other on their deed.

Suddenly, as if they had just beamed down, a team of policemen pounced on the hooligans, grappling to overpower them.

Luke craned his neck in an effort to see as much as he could of the incident.

"Fucking hell, man, did you see that?" His skinny companion cried, excitedly, as he buzzed down the window, stuck his head out and cheered at the scuffle.

"Yeah," Luke replied, perplexed. He had never seen such blatant vandalism in the town before. In fact, he was quite perturbed by the whole scene. He had witnessed a few of these episodes this evening and it was making him feel uneasy.

"We'll have less of that, if you don't mind," Alan said in a raised voice so that the youth could hear him.

Tristan reeled his head back in, shaking the raindrops that clung to it over his two friends who both groaned and playfully thumped him.

"The problem is that the majority of them can't handle their drink and they get out of control. It's the police I feel sorry for," Alan offered, deliberately loading his words as he watched his passengers in the rear view mirror.

"You're having a laugh," was the third lad's contribution. The stocky guy with a crew cut had been busy for most of the ride, surreptitiously rolling up a joint. "If you ask me. I reckon the majority of those cops abuse their power."

"And what exactly are you basing that opinion on?" Alan asked.

"Well…" the youth struggled temporarily to find the words. "You hear about it every day in the papers."

" Oh well, if it was in the papers it must be true," Alan replied, dismissively.

"What's that supposed to mean?" Jason leant forward in a

threatening gesture.

"Nothing. I was just agreeing with you," Alan's reply was indifferent. This youth was obviously drunk and looking for trouble.

Luke opened his mouth with the intention of diffusing the situation but he decided against it. His head was feeling giddy and the motion of the taxi was making him want to puke. He knew he should not have mixed his drinks despite his friends' insistence.

"Here we are," Alan said, as he drove into a pool of blue light.

The sound of thumping music vibrated through the car. Jason and Tristan sprung out, leaving the door ajar. They joined a long queue of people who seemed oblivious to the pouring rain.

"Oi, you two!" Luke cried.

Neither of them answered for they were both busy eyeing the girl in front of them. She was wearing tight leather trousers and a jacket open at the front that revealed a well-filled bra.

As if by some extrasensory perception, the girl turned and smiled at them both, running her fingers through her rain drenched hair and then licking them. Both men looked at each other unable to comprehend their luck.

Meanwhile, Luke was handing over a ten-pound note to the taxi driver.

"Do you come here often?" Alan asked, as he took the money and then rummaged around in a small plastic container.

"Don't worry about the change," Luke said quickly, holding up a dismissive hand. "No, I don't. What's it like?" he asked, trying to suppress a grin for he knew perfectly well that this would be the last place an old taxi driver would frequent.

"It depends."

"On what?"

"On what kind of person you are."

Both men looked up as two police cars, sirens wailing, sped by.

"They seem pretty busy tonight, don't they?" Luke asked.

"Too busy," Alan replied, without taking his eyes of the flashing blue lights of the vehicles.

"Oh well, best get in there," Luke said, with one leg already hanging out the car door.

"Yeah," Alan nodded.

With that, Luke stepped out, into the rain and Alan drove away. Luke looked up at the building. It was old and needing a serious lick of fresh paint. Otherwise it was quite elegant, a gothic structure with two protruding balconies.   Blue neon lettering over the door read, *'The Pit.'*

"Come on!" Jason shouted from his place in the queue.

Snapping out of his daze, Luke ran over but instead of standing with his friends, at the mercy of the pouring rain, he took shelter under one of the balconies.

"These clothes cost me a fortune," he joked but the real reason was because he felt as if he were going to heave at any moment. Meanwhile, his friends queued patiently as the rain came tumbling down, soaking them all.

Twenty

Mrs Tennyson waved her hand in the air, trying to attract the attention of passing waiters but they seemed oblivious to her as they buzzed to and from other tables. Eventually, she caught the attention of a tall, suited, middle-aged man.

"Yes Madam?" he asked.

Another one of these, please," she said, holding up her empty tumbler.

"And what would that be, Madam?" the man asked, collecting two more empty tumblers from the table.

"Scotch, double. Oh, and could you bring the wine list too?"

"Of course," the man smiled courteously and left.

Barbara Tennyson glanced at her watch. It was ten fifteen and still no sign of him. So, what else was new? She wondered what he would have to say if she were late arriving at one of his precious dinners. *See how that would impress his fucking clients! Well, I am going to show him. I have played the fool long enough, but not anymore.*

That is why she had asked him to meet her here tonight. It would be their chance to talk, away from the office, the clients, the friends and everything else Jeff put before her, including that little harlot he took on so called business trips with him.

She looked around the room, it was late but the restaurant was still very busy.

'The Seasons' was Barbara Tennyson's favourite restaurant. It was the pioneer of a new breed of eateries and specialised solely in vegetarian dishes.

That was probably why Jeff was late again tonight. He had groaned earlier today when she had told him about the reservations and that they needed to talk.

Jeffrey Tennyson was a carnivore, one of the noisiest meat eaters Barbara had ever met. She sneered inwardly as she replayed a mental image of him sitting at the dinner table, slobbering over the roasted flesh of a dead chicken. Sometimes, he was so busy wolfing down the dead meat that he would not even stop for air, thus exacerbating that nasal breathing sound she hated so much.

The suited man arrived carrying her Scotch refill.

"Thank you," she said, taking the glass off the tray and downing its contents, wincing as it burned her throat.

"And the wine list, Madam," the man said, casually, handing her the card. "Would madam care to see the menu?"

"No thank you. I'm still waiting for someone."

Suddenly the sound from the street became louder and they both looked up. A reptilian smile spread over Barbara Tennyson's face as her husband entered the restaurant and scanned the room for her.

"He's here," she said, smirking.

"Does that mean that madam would like to see the menu now?"

"About time."

The waiter looked down at the women, confused. However, following her gaze he realised that she was not talking to him. He watched as the man with grey hair and goatee to match, took a seat at the table.

"Why you wanted to have dinner here is beyond me," the man said, shaking his overcoat off and revealing an over-stretched designer suit.

"Because I like it here."

"I gathered that," her husband replied, looking around the room and then at the man in the suit who was hovering nearby.

"Martini, dry, and hold the bloody olive."

"Straight away, Sir. Would you care to see the menu, Sir? Madam?"

"So what was it this time, dear?" Barbara asked, "Entertaining clients, call from abroad, last minute crisis?" There was sarcasm in her tone.

"Jesus, Barbara, we haven't even had dinner yet and you're already drunk."

"I haven't even started drinking yet. Look," she said, holding up her glass, "My glass is empty and you haven't brought me my Scotch yet, have you?"

She looked up, "What's your name? Or should I call you Mr Waiter?" She chuckled, "I like that, Mr Waiter."

The man smiled with her. "Actually, madam, I am the manager and my name is Anthony."

"Anthony, I'm Jeffrey Tennyson and this is my drunken wife."

With a smile, Barbara retorted, "Oh, seeing that we are introducing ourselves, I am Barbara Tennyson and this is my adulterous husband."

Anthony smiled, uncomfortably, and just wished they would make their minds up about the menu so he could be on his way.

"Are you still here?" Jeffrey Tennyson barked. "How long does it take to get a drink in this vegetable parlour, for Christ sake?"

"I was just wondering if…"

"And bring me that Scotch, Anthony, there's a good boy. Oh, and could you bring us a bottle of Dom Perignon as well?"

"I don't want Dom Perignon," Jeffrey Tennyson said, in a

hushed voice.

"Who said it was for you?" Barbara replied in an equally hushed tone.

Anthony, no longer caring whether the couple ate at all, headed for the kitchen. He had enough of his own problems tonight and the last thing he needed was to get involved in a marital row.

As soon as he entered the kitchen, two young men in white overalls, Mark and Robert, intercepted him. Mark, the skinner of the two, asked agitatedly, "Anthony, what the hell are we going to do?"

"I told you, Mark, I have tried to call chef but he's not answering the phone."

"Well, where the fuck is he?" cried Robert, Mark's much heavier colleague.

"I don't bloody know," Anthony answered, controlling his tone, well aware of the rest of the kitchen staff. "Look, I have got to get this drinks order to the bar. As soon as I've done that I'll make some phone calls, see if I can find someone."

Robert sneered, "What if you don't?"

"Then you are just going to have to manage."

"What?" They both squealed, in unison.

"I have got a full house out there tonight. I haven't got time for this." Anthony's voice was low but assertive and after staring intensely at the two men, he turned and made for the swing doors.

Robert shifted his weight from one leg to the other as if building himself up to something. He turned to Mark who spoke up, "Look Anthony, we're not paid to take on this responsibility, you know."

"No we're not, " Robert added.

The manager was just about to push the doors open but stopped and turned around. "What are you saying? That you…"

Suddenly, the swing doors burst open. The impact launched Anthony into the arms of the two young men.

A waiter popped his head around the door and bellowed, "I am still waiting on my order for table 10. Am I getting it tonight or should I order veggie burgers from McDonalds!"

"See what I mean?" Mark asked, nodding his head at the doors.

"Look," Anthony began, re-composing himself and

straightening his tie. "I am just as upset by chef's desertion as you are. However, I have a room full of people out there, all waiting for their food and I am relying on you two to do your best and more." Then, holding up a finger he added, "I don't want to hear anymore about it."

The apprentices looked at each and then turned to say something to the restaurant manager but it was too late, he had disappeared through the swinging doors.

Back at the Tennyson table, Jeffrey snapped, "I don't know what the hell you were thinking of, making a reservation at this place. You know I hate this vegetarian crap."

"You know how much I hate meat but it doesn't stop you," Barbara Tennyson retorted.

"Why should I suffer just because you've discovered the latest fad?"

"It isn't the latest fad, Jeffrey. I have been a vegetarian ever since we met, or have you conveniently forgotten seven years of marriage?"

"How could I possibly forget?"

There was a long pause as both of them looked around the room, feigning interest in what everyone else was doing and saying.

There was a couple in the corner, a young girl with an older man. Jeffrey wondered if he was her father or her lover.

"I called you at the hotel," Barbara interrupted the thought process.

"Did you?" he asked, disinterested.

"You weren't there. You'd only just finished telling me that you had tons of paperwork to plough through before your next meeting."

"Did I?"

"Yes, you did!" Barbara shrieked, thumping her fist on the table.

"Barbara, will you get a grip of yourself and stop making a scene," Jeff said. The words were spoken through clenched teeth as he smiled at those people who had looked up from their meal.

"Ha!" Barbara released a short cackle. "If you think this is a scene, you haven't seen anything yet."

The venom in his wife's eyes took Jeffrey aback. Something was very wrong. She obviously knew more than she was letting on. Had she found out about his assistant, Margaret? A flicker of fear ran up his spine. He wanted rid of Barbara but not this way. After all, she was the one with the money. She was the one who owned the business. If she divorced him now, naming Margaret, it could have serious consequences on his financial future.

"For Christ sake, Barbara. You are like this every time I get back from a business trip." He shook his head and then lit up a cigarette.

"There's no smoking in here," Barbara hissed, pointing to a 'No Smoking' sign.

"So what? He's taking his time with my drink and I need something to occupy me whilst I indulge you in your neurotic episode."

"So, you think I am just having an episode, do you?"

"Yes, I do. Moreover, before you start on Margaret can I just tell you that she has been nothing more than a pillar of strength. Without her, I would never have got this new account. Because, you see, Barbara, business is not only about selling a decent product but it is also about service. Give a customer a warm, friendly service and they will come back to you again and again."

"How dare you talk down to me!" she snapped. "If it wasn't for my money, you wouldn't have *any* business."

Barbara was a drunk but she was not stupid and Jeffrey realised that he had to calm her down before she did or said something that *he* would regret.

"I just want to know one thing, Jeffrey…"

Anthony arrived at the table, carrying a small tray with their drinks."

"…How much more of a better fuck is she?"

Anthony swallowed and blushed.

Conscious of the man's presence, Jeffrey made no response.

Barbara smiled, enjoying his discomfort. "Well, come on, on a scale from 1 to 10?"

"I don't think this is the time or the place to be having this conversation," Jeffrey blurted in his hushed tone.

"I think it's a perfect time. Then, looking up at the manager, she asked, " What do you think, Anthony?"

"Well I…"

"What in Christ's name are you waiting for man? Leave the drinks and go!" Jeffrey bellowed, his tone slightly louder than he had intended.

For the second time that evening, the people at a nearby table stopped chatting and turned to see what the noise was.

"You can't take him anywhere," Barbara said to them with a giggle.

Anthony hastily placed the Martini in front of Jeffrey, deposited the bottle in front of Barbara and, in his mind, cursed chef and ever getting up this morning!

"Would Madam care to…"

"No she wouldn't! Get lost!" Jeffrey hissed.

Anthony left the table feeling a strong sense of empathy for the waiters he employed.

"What's the matter, darling? Your Martini not dry enough?"

She was toying with him that was what she was doing. She knew about his affair with Margaret but she just would not come out with it. She was going to torture him with hints and innuendo.

"You didn't answer my question."

"What was your question?" He asked, absent minded, as his brain processed a whirlpool of, 'what ifs.'

"I asked you how good is she in bed and wondered if she was worth losing your business over?"

Barbara Tennyson smiled; she was enjoying herself. Jeffrey Tennyson downed his Martini in one; it was going to be a long night

Nobody noticed the small, tubby man enter the kitchen and exchange his rain soaked jacket for a dry white smock.

However, as chef slipped his hat on and moved over to the giant oven in the corner of the kitchen, his two young apprentices met him.

"Where the hell have you been, Chef?" asked Robert.

Chef made no reply instead he dialled the oven to gas mark 9 and began peeling a head of garlic.

"Chef!" It was Mark now, "we've been rushed off our feet, Anthony is out of his pram and it's all because you didn't bother to let anyone know you were going to be late."

Still no answer as the peeling continued.

Robert set off to find Anthony as Mark continued his reprimand. "It's not fair on us you know," he said, trying to lock eyes with his mentor.

However, chef was busy; he had a meal to prepare and he was late.

Ever since that maniac had rammed him at the traffic lights and moulded his Rover around a lamppost, Chef had been thinking of the kitchen. At first, he had been concerned about how late he was going to be but then, as he stood in the pouring rain, his concern turned into a pleasant urgency. That same urgency was on his mind right now. The guests in the dining area were waiting for their meal and tonight Chef had something very special on the menu, very special indeed.

Anthony stormed through the swing doors and watched as the young lad followed the busy chef around the kitchen.

"What the hell is going on here?" Anthony demanded.

"He won't talk to me!" Mark whined like a child who had been denied his toy.

"Chef?" Anthony called.

He received no reply, just the machine gun chopping of vegetables.

Anthony walked up to the tubby man and repeated in a stern voice, "Chef?"

This time the man turned around and looked him straight in the eyes. He smiled a cold, empty smile that chilled Anthony to the bone. Something about that smile frightened him and he knew better than to pursue this argument right now.

After several seconds, Chef turned his gaze back to the job in hand and resumed chopping the green pepper.

Anthony straightened his tie and his composure, then made his way to the swinging doors, closely followed by the two puppies.

"Well?" Mark demanded.

"Well what?" Anthony asked, conscious of the other three kitchen staff who had stopped working and were trying to hear what was being said.

"Is that it?"

"Is what it?" Anthony asked, in his favourite hushed tone. "He's here now and that is all that counts.   I shall talk to him later."   He straightened his tie again and then glanced at the others who were watching, mouths open. "Haven't you got any work to do?" He snapped.

The trio instantly went about their duties.

"And I suggest you do the same," Anthony added to the two boys.

With that, he left the kitchen.

It was getting late and most of the diners had paid for their meal and left the building. Only a few lingered on, including the couple who still hadn't ordered anything to eat but were busy shaking accusatory fingers at each other and talking in tense, hushed tones.

Anthony watched them from across the room and wondered whether he should bother going over and asking whether they intended to order tonight or if they were just going to use his restaurant as a domestic battlefield.

Then, as if they had read his thoughts, Mrs Tennyson beckoned him over.

Taking a deep breath, Anthony walked over to the table and smiled politely.

"Yes, Madam?"

"Could I have another bottle of this please? She asked, holding up the half empty bottle of Dom Perignon.

"Of course, Madam."

"Don't you think you've had enough?" Jeffery Tennyson asked.

"No, I don't," she replied in a slurred tone.

"Take no notice of her, she's too pissed to know what she's saying. In fact, bring us the bill, we're leaving," Mr Tennyson added, searching the inside of his suit jacket for his wallet.

"I am not ready to leave. I haven't had dinner yet," his wife said, defiantly.

"Barbara, darling your memory is failing you, you don't eat dinner. Your diet consists of a bottle of gin in the morning followed by a bottle of scotch in the afternoon."

Barbara cackled, holding up a wavy finger. "Oh yes, very droll," she said. Then she looked up at Anthony and continued, "I didn't tell you, did I, what's your name?"

"Anthony."

"Anthony. I didn't tell you that my husband lost his true vocation in life: comedian."

"The bill please." Jeffrey seethed.

"I told you I haven't finished yet," Barbara retorted, eyes wide.

"You've had more than enough, Barbara. It is time to go."

Anthony turned to fetch their bill. The sooner he saw the back of these two, the better he was going to feel, custom or no custom.

"Anthony! Don't forget that bottle, will you!" Barbara shouted after him.

The manager turned to Mr Tennyson who shook his head in disagreement.

"Don't ask him for permission. I am my own person you know. I do have a mind of my own!" Barbara's voice was loud.

Now, one of the remaining couples hurried over to the cashier's desk and after speedily signing a credit card slip, left the building.

"Oops," Barbara giggled, holding a hand to her mouth.

"Have you quite finished making a spectacle of yourself?" Jeffrey Tennyson asked his wife in an indignant tone.

"What's the matter, darling, can't handle the competition? You'd know all about making a spectacle of yourself, wouldn't you?"

She poured herself more drink and as she did so, Jeffrey tried to steal the bottle away from her but Barbara was having none of this and reacted violently. A battle for the bottle ensued.

Anthony watched from across the room. The sight would have been comical had it not been so tragic. This was getting out of hand. Clasping the Tennyson's receipt, Anthony hurried across the room to the battling duo.

In that moment, Barbara lashed out at her husband with her left hand, scratching his face with red painted nails.

"You bitch!" he shrieked.

Barbara cackled manically, "Serves you right."

"What is wrong with you?" Jeffrey asked incredulously, frowning with pain and holding a napkin to the stinging wounds on his cheek.

Barbara just smirked and took another swig from the bottle.

Anthony was appalled by the couple's behaviour and had concluded decisively, that he wanted both of them to leave.

"Maybe if you'd spent just a little more time at home with me, instead of jet setting across the world with that bean pole, half your age, you would know what was wrong with me," she said with tears in her eyes.

"Madam, " Anthony began, tentatively, "Perhaps it would be beneficial to the both of you if you took this discussion home."

"I gave you the best years of my life and how do you repay me?" Tears and mascara streamed down Barbara Tennyson's face, "You pass me over for that whore!"

Jeffrey Tennyson's suspicions were accurate. His wife did know about him and his assistant and at this moment, all he wanted to do was hide behind the napkin he was holding to his face. He willed himself to say something but the words just would not come to him.

"You thought I'd never find out, didn't you?" she said through tears. "But I know, I've known for ages but I just hoped that it wasn't true!" She sobbed heavily and then, as if to console herself, took yet another swig from the bottle.

Then, a blood-curdling scream and a loud crashing sound from the kitchen froze the whole scene. Before Anthony had a chance to turn around, the swinging doors flew open and out of them spewed most of his staff, screaming and waving their hands in the air as they fled out of the building and into the rain.

"Dear lord, what now?"

Without thinking, Anthony raced toward the kitchen. He stopped momentarily outside the swinging doors and listened hard: nothing, but a loud thumping sound.

Taking a deep breath, he pushed the doors open with both hands and stared in amazement at the scene before him. The normally bleached white floor was awash in a tide of red fluid. Blood spatters decorated the walls and worktops, whilst a flurry of skid marks and bloody footprints led in all directions.

Anthony's mouth hung open as more thumping came from out of sight, beneath one of the worktops. Driven by an irrational investigative urge, he slowly inched his way through the gooey liquid, toward the sound.

His heart hammered and a queasy feeling swept over him as he neared the unit. He peered around it and froze in horror. On the floor, in a pool of blood, lay a skinny, headless corpse; it was Mark and his legs were still kicking.

Anthony choked on the bile slithering up his throat and turned to run from this nightmare but slipped on the bloody secretion on the floor and fell, smacking his face against the cold tiles. He retched as he lay there.

A minute or so transpired, as he remained motionless, bathing in blood, his mind numb with shock. He was still trying to comprehend what he had just seen when he heard footsteps and then, a shadow loomed over him. It paused for a few seconds and then moved on.

Barbara and Jeffrey Tennyson were too busy squabbling to notice chef walk over to them. They stopped and looked up at him only when he dumped the serving platter on the table.

His eyes were black, his pupils dilated and there was blood, in spatters, over his face. His smock was soaked in it.

Neither of the Tennysons uttered a sound as he grinned excitedly and, after removing the lid from the serving platter, announced, grandiosely, "Dinner is served."

Twenty One

22:10. Stony Point

The intruder light had come on and was casting a warm glow into Blake's circular bedroom. The rain had slowed but it had not stopped.

Blake and Sky lay naked in his bed. They had twice made love since their early encounter at the front door, and each time the urgency to climax diminished as they enjoyed each other's bodies.

Neither of them spoke for a long while as they processed a conglomeration of thoughts about what had happened between them tonight.

"Sky?" Blake's voice sounded like an alarm bell in the still of the bedroom.

She swallowed in an effort to moisten her parched vocal cords, "Yes?" she croaked

"Are you awake?"

She heard a laugh as Blake realised that the question was redundant. "Do you feel like talking?"

"What about?"

"I don't know, just talking."

"It was good, wasn't it?"

A big smile of satisfaction spread over his face. "Yes, it was."

Although Sky could not see Blake's face, she knew that he had enjoyed their lovemaking as much as she had and this excited her. He excited her, with his clean smell, his lean body and his passion. Everything about Blake Hudson aroused her just as it had many years before.

"So now what?" Blake asked.

There was a long pause.

Then, smiling warmly, Sky replied, "Now you let me build my

strength, ready for the next round."

Blake laughed. "You always did have the best ideas," he said, looking across at her.   He admired the outline of her naked shoulders and felt compelled to roll over and kiss them but he refrained from doing so.

"Does it always rain this much around here?" Sky asked, changing the subject for she knew too well what Blake was driving at but she did not feel like discussing it now.

"No, not usually this much," he replied.

They listened to the rain for several seconds and then Blake rolled over so that he was leaning on one arm and said, "Sky?"

"Yes?"

"About tonight..."

He was not going to let it go. "What about it?" she asked, turning to face him.

He wished she hadn't done that because now he felt all his strength drain away. "Well.. Err…" he began. "I was… well I…"

Damn, he could not get the words out.

Sky smiled encouragingly.

The smile helped. "I think we should talk."

"It's all right, Blake. I know you'll still respect me in the morning."

He smiled. "No, Sky. There are other things…"

"Not tonight." she interrupted. Her voice was soft and seductive. Then, she leaned over and kissed him on the mouth.

Blake, much to his own amazement, felt himself blushing and was grateful that the room was in shadow. He so desperately wanted to talk to her but Sky was right, they would not talk tonight, but soon.

"So, any ideas on how long this rain is going to last?" She was lying back against her pillow. Her black hair was fanned out as if arranged by a makeup artist. Blake noticed her breasts peaking out from underneath the sheet and the thought of her complete nakedness aroused him once more. However, he repressed the urge and lay back with her. "Well it seems…" He began an impersonation of weather presenter, Michael Fish."…That this low-pressure front that has swept in from the Atlantic Ocean is going to be with us for quite a while. We can expect heavy downpours overnight and maybe well into the early hours of Saturday morning. There may even be the odd rumble of thunder."

"Odd rumble of thunder. That's an understatement."

They laughed.

"Are you hungry?" he asked.

"Thirsty, and I am a bit peckish."

"Then allow me to satisfy you." Blake left the bed, pulled on his shorts and flipped the switch on the stereo system. The sounds of a hip-hop song reverberated around the room. Blake mimed the words and actions of the sexy song and pointed at her.

She launched a pillow at him. He ducked, shrugged and danced out of the room.

Sky laughed and stretched her body. She felt so good.

Blake sang along as he descended the stairs but yelped when he reached the front door. He looked down to see that he had stepped into pool of freezing water.

He pushed the door shut and disappeared into the living room on his journey to the kitchen. In his happy state, he neglected to ask himself why the door was open.

Twenty Two

The Pit Night-club - Exeter

The Pit's entrance lobby was small, the walls decorated with red graffiti and illuminated by ultraviolet light.

Two bouncers, built like American football players, stood guard in front of double doors. One of them pointed to the reception desk behind which stood a slim girl with long greasy hair and a ring through her nose. She took Luke's money and handed him a ticket.

Then, as one, the bouncers pulled open the double doors and the raw, electric sounds of Depeche Mode's *Barrel of a Gun* smacked Luke with force. The volume was so loud that it vibrated through the whole of his body.

He descended several steps and found himself on a balcony overlooking a circular dance floor. It was packed and undulated with bodies. It was very dark in here, except for the occasional flash of strobe and coloured lights.

He smiled to himself. The atmosphere was electric with sexual tension and he felt invigorated by it. "Come on, Luke!" Jason called to him as he descended more stairs and disappeared into the crowd.

Luke pushed his way through the throng. At the bar, he ordered lager and scanned the masses for his two friends but they were nowhere in sight. He took long drafts from his drink and watched the dancing gathering in front of him. The place was alive with sexual encounters. To his right, a couple shared a barstool. Their silhouettes appeared to be that of a man and women but as the laser beam of lights zapped them, he realised it was two girls.

Directly in front of him, a man slid his hand under his partner's skirt. The girl, who was holding a cigarette to her lips, sucked down a cloud of tar and released it abruptly as her partner's fingers probed deeper into her crotch.

Luke struck up a cigarette and puffed as he watched; he enjoyed watching. Everything about this place was intoxicating: the flashing lights, the sex, and the anonymity that the darkness provided. His senses were heightened and he was no longer human but an animal, a being of prowess hunting through the crowds for its prey.

Then he saw her, intermittently, through the heaving bodies and the flashing lights. She was on the opposite side of the dance floor.

Her hair was jet-black and iron straight. She was wearing leather trousers and a white bra that shone purple under the ultraviolet glow.

It was as if the room had slipped into slow motion. The lights flashed, the bodies moved, but none of them like this creature; she swayed her curves like no other.

Now, their eyes met. Without even thinking, Luke dropped his cigarette and pushed forward, into the crowd, descending the few steps to the dance floor.

She was wild, an untamed animal, thrashing her head from side to side and humping the loud pulsating rhythm that was the very air around them. Now, her hands were moving, searching her breasts, her thighs and then, her crotch as she watched him through the curtain of hair that hung in front of her face.

Luke was closer now, no more than ten feet away. He felt aroused at the thought of her and was oblivious to the masses around him. He was a homing missile and nothing and no one could stop him from hitting his target.

That is when they stepped in front of him, blocking out his view and wearing manic grins on their faces. It was Jason and Tristan. They winked at him and then joined the girl.

Jason pressed his, six-foot, muscular frame against her rear. Then, sliding his hands down to her thighs, he tugged her to him and began rubbing himself against her. He rolled his eyes and licked his lips.

Luke watched through the swaying crowd as Tristan sniggered and fell to his knees beside the rocking couple. Luke wondered what game his friends were playing. In all the time he had known these two men, he had never seen them behave like this, at least not in a nightclub! He smiled disarmingly at them both.

However, neither of the men returned the smile. Instead, Jason began a thrusting motion with the girl who bent over, sticking her tongue out at Tristan who mimicked her performance. Both of them laughed as Jason's thrusting motion kept pushing them to and from each other.

Watching two men indulge in sexual enticement, especially when those two men happened to be his friends, had never turned Luke on, but tonight things were different.

He found watching the threesome, the thrusting, the music, and the darkness of the club, sexually stimulating. The men were actually turning him on and he found himself wanting more.

And more is exactly what he got.

The girl, never taking her eyes of him, rubbed her breasts and then slowly offered them to Tristan, teasing him by bringing her nipple to within inches of his face and then drawing it back again. She carried on this torment for a few minutes as Jason continued the thrusting motion.

Luke looked around the room, conscious of the other people there. However, nobody seemed to care. They were either too busy dancing or engaging in some form of sexual stimulation themselves. It was like a dream. He looked down into the golden depths of the pint of lager in his hands and wondered, for a moment, if somebody had spiked it. He drank generously from the glass, blinked and looked around. Nothing had changed. The music still throbbed, the lights still flashed and the bodies still heaved. He was not dreaming, this was all happening for real and it was happening now.

He moved closer to the trio, climbing the few steps off the dance floor. He was aroused now and he wanted to join them but despite his friends' stimulation, he could not help wishing they would leave her to him.

The trio reacted to his arrival by smiling and pouting at him. Luke shook his head, incredulously; he could not believe that his friends, both of them happily engaged, were behaving like this so publicly. They were seriously jeopardising their future. Nevertheless, none of that mattered now.

From the floor, Tristan searched between Luke's legs, feeling his erection, he began to unbuckle his friend's belt but Luke slapped his hand away, smiling. Watching his friends was one thing but having them undress him was another.

Jason stopped his humping motion and pushed the girl toward Luke in an offering gesture. The girl, who was still fondling her breasts, willed Luke to touch her.

After hesitating a few moments and taking one last look at the mad house around him, Luke sunk his face into the girl's soft mounds. She smelt and felt good. He kissed and licked her exposed flesh. Then, spurred on by the chanting of his friends and the ecstatic moaning of the girl before him, he ripped off her bra and suckled for a few seconds. Then, he emptied the last of his lager over her breasts, tossed the glass aside and licked the excess. Tristan joined him and they growled at each other like dogs fighting over a rump of meat.

He felt tugging at his belt and, for a moment, Luke suspected it was Tristan but when he looked down, he saw that the girl had started to unbuckle him. He was on such a high now and grunted with pleasure as her hand travelled into his boxers and began to handle him. He closed his eyes, enjoying her touch.

Slowly, Jason unbuttoned the girl's trousers. He unzipped her, caught Luke's hand and pushed it toward her navel. Luke complied, determined to give her as much pleasure as she was giving him. His fingers slipped into her panties and he began to probe her with a hungry lust.

Tristan had stopped suckling now and his mouth had moved over the girl's shoulder, seeking and finding Jason's mouth. They kissed, eagerly.

Luke smiled, thinking the two men were just caught up in the heat of the moment, but he soon learned that it was more than that as their arms entwined and their tongues united. Jason released the girl completely and devoted his full attention to searching under Tristan's shirt and trousers.

The girl pulled Luke's jeans down slightly so that he was hanging out of his boxers fully ready for her. Then, with hands low on his rear, she pulled him to her. It was obvious what the girl wanted and he was ready.

Through the corner of his eye, Luke could see that Tristan had unzipped Jason and was now slipping to his knees once more.

The girl threw her head back and allowed Luke to bite her neck.

Tristan's hands were inside Jason's boxer shorts.

The girl had backed up against a column, Luke slid her leather trousers down and, without wasting anymore time, he lifted her leg and entered her roughly, grunting as he did so.

His two friends had disappeared into the shadows but as the lights flashed, they illuminated an incredible scene: Tristan, back in his kneeling position was fondling Jason and his mouth was wide open.

Luke could not help monitoring his two friends through the corner of his eye and revulsion began to swell up his spine. His face was sweating, his heart pounding and the music throbbing. The girl was moaning in ecstasy and normally that would have aroused him even more but he could not concentrate.

In the blur, Tristan took Jason in his mouth.

Luke rammed into the girl, harder.

Jason held Tristan's head as it travelled the length of him.

Luke pumped but stopped kissing and biting the girl. He was going through the motions but he could still catch glimpses of his companions and this was disturbing him.

Jason was laughing. He was delirious with pleasure. The warm tentacles that pricked beyond his psyche were tripling, amplifying the pleasure of Tristan's warm mouth around him. The act was something he had never experienced before and he relished it as his temple throbbed, his heart pumped and the music hammered. Then, he helped Tristan to his feet, the two men exchanged glances and smiled with anticipation.

Luke, drenched in sweat, was thrusting harder and harder and the girl screamed with pleasure, urging him not to stop but he did! He withdrew but she pulled him back. He tried to free himself but vice-like hands, low on his back, forced him to stay inside her.

"No!" he said through clenched teeth and unclamped himself from her grip.

The girl eyed him angrily, but said nothing.

Dragging his jeans up, Luke gulped in the smoky air, trying to recover his breath. He looked across at his friends. He could almost hear Jason laughing above the pounding of the music. The flickering of the lights was highlighting the sickening scene.

The gay sexual act was something Luke could not stomach. Two men, one bending over whilst the other… He shuddered as the image of his two friends played repeatedly in his mind. He wanted to retch. The thought was incomprehensible to him.

In that moment, the girl hissed at him and for the first time Luke noticed the dark cavities that were her eyes. He watched her incredulously as the hissing continued, loudly. She held up a bony finger and pointed at him as if he were an intruder in the cult's den.

What the fuck is she on?

Had she enticed him into having sex with her just to accuse him of rape? He had heard about this before and the thought was horrifying.

Panicked, he looked around. The crowds were still oblivious to what was happening. Only now, the sexual enticement had turned into the act itself.

Could he hear, above the pounding music, terrified screams for help? Or was that his own voice inside his head?

He watched, aghast. The whole place was just a mass of heaving bodies. Everything had seemed so normal earlier and now, in a matter of minutes, it had metamorphosed into a sexual orgy. People were on the dance floor, up against walls, masturbating or engaged in a frenzy of heterosexual and homosexual intercourse.

He was dreaming. This could not be happening

He looked across at his friends. Tristan was standing now and Jason had pulled up his trousers. They both fixed icy stares on him.

Luke shook his head in disgust and, buttoning his jeans, moved to leave. The sooner he got out of this hellhole the better.

However, as he passed her, the girl grabbed him by the hair and yanked him back. Luke cried out in pain and taking advantage of the momentum, he swung around and punched her.

He saw the girl's mouth open but the music drowned her scream as she fell, sprawling, backwards. The whole scene was the essence of a black and white movie as it flickered in the lights.

The thought of whether or not he should stay and check if she was okay did cross Luke's mind but he decided against it. He no longer cared that she might bring charges against him, he wanted out of this place, now. He elbowed his way through the crowd, heedless of the sexual spectacle that was taking place around him.

As he was half way across the dance floor, the music changed to a slow pulsating rhythm and the red lights flashed slowly on and off, making it difficult to pick his way through the writhing naked bodies around him.

He misjudged the step that led off the dance floor to the bar and tripped but a pair of hands broke his fall, and when the lights flicked on, he saw that it was Jason.

Luke shrugged his friend's hands off him and continued on his journey. He climbed both steps in one go and hurried to the next flight of stairs. Jason's hands gripped him again, pulling him back. As he tried to shake him off another pair of hands appeared out of the smoky gloom and grabbed his arm. It was Tristan.

"Get off me, man!" Luke warned.

He felt hands on his groin and slapped them away.

More hands tugged at him, he stumbled forward causing the grip on him to release temporarily, and he scrambled up the stairs.

Before long, the hands surrounded him once more and, like a thick forest, they clawed at his face and clothes.

"No! Get off me!" he yelled. "Get off me!" He kicked and punched all around him. Some hands relented as others anchored themselves. They tugged and he crashed to the floor, smacking his face on the steps as they dragged him back down into the darkness.

"No.! No!" He screamed and wriggled to free himself but it was to no avail. For every hand he shook off, another five took hold, ripping his T-shirt and pulling at his jeans.

Within minutes, Luke was naked and the hands searched every inch of his body. They grabbed, scratched, caressed and tugged at his chest and his groin. They probed, groped and licked him.

"No!" he cried in terror as they carried him a few feet and then dropped him violently onto the floor once more.

The air was forced out of him as a huge weight pressed on his back. Boots, heels, arms and bodies pinned his face to the carpet where he breathed in the smell of fibre, cigarette ash, rubber and leather.

Vicious hands held his arms and legs apart and a searing pain shot up his back as someone entered him from behind.

"Help!" He opened his mouth to scream but gagged as something hard and fleshy was stuffed in. Then, the huge weight was on him again. He involuntarily bit down on the foreign object and the copper taste of blood filled his mouth.

The music pumped and Luke could just about discern the manic cries of his aggressors over the rhythm. His mind began to drift and, like a torrent of fresh water, a whirlpool of images came flooding through. Within the swirl, he saw his parents, himself and a multitude of ghosts he could not recognise. Then, the music faded and the whirlpool dissolved into darkness.

Twenty Three

The drumming of the rain replaced the thumping of the CD. Sky stretched, she felt invigorated. She rolled over, rubbing her face on Blake's pillow where there were still traces of his aftershave.

Clutching the blade in its hand, the presence crept up the stairs. It took in the room: the balcony doors, the furniture and the bare shoulders of the figure in the bed. It wanted this person. It had yearned for a moment with her and that moment was now.

Blake whistled to himself. He rinsed out the two champagne flutes and placed them on a tray with a bottle of Moet & Chandon champagne; a moving in present from Matt Allen. He sliced a couple of Mango fruits and arranged them, decoratively, on a plate. As he did so, he found himself staring out of the kitchen window and thinking, once again, about the beautiful women upstairs.

His reflection came back into focus and the darkness beyond the window gave him the creeps. He turned away and rummaged in a cupboard for the Kettle chips and the chocolate.

What prompted Sky McPherson to turn around in that moment

131

is unknown, but she did, and that was when a hand clamped over her mouth, silencing her scream. She struggled to free herself but froze when she felt the cold blade of a knife against her throat.

The shadow loomed over her with all the deathly grace of the grim reaper. Sky's eyes darted at the stairwell door, which had been left open, and then back at her attacker. The light from the security lamp outside spilled through the windows, silhouetting a slim figure with shoulder length hair, a woman.

Sky held her breath as her heart raced like an express train. She struggled to comprehend what was happening to her. *Who are you? What do you want?*

Suddenly, the blade eased its presence and then a hand yanked her, by her hair, out of the bed. She fell, striking her face on the hard parquet floor. And, before she could gather her senses, the presence had knelt on the floor beside her, pulled her head back and was prodding her throat with the blade once more.

Their angle had changed and the light spilling in from the window highlighted one side of her aggressor's face. Sky could just about distinguish the small jaw and the straggly brown her. She had seen this profile before. She knew this person.

Then, the voice hissed, "Don't say a fucking word!"

"What... what do you want?" Sky breathed.

"I want you," the voice replied in a gleeful whispered tone.

"Who are you?"

"Have you forgotten me already, doctor?"

In her panicked state, Sky searched her memory but she could not place this voice. She recognised it but could not associate it with anyone.

"But then you've had other things on your mind, haven't you?" The intruder paused as thunder rumbled, "What was he like?"

"What was who like?" Sky asked, although she felt as if she knew exactly who *he* was.

A slap cracked across her face and blinded her, momentarily, "Don't fuck with me, doctor," the voice hissed.

Blinking her eyes rapidly, Sky stuttered, "You mean, you mean Blake?"

"Mr Hudson," the voice corrected. "He doesn't like strangers calling him by his first name. Only close friends are allowed to do that."

It was then that Sky realised who this person was, "and are you one of those friends, Clare?"

"Of course I am," the girl sniggered; almost embarrassed that she had been identified.

Sky licked her lips and tasted blood. She did not know whether it was the blow to her face or the impact from falling to the floor but her nose was bleeding.

"Blake will be up soon," Sky said quickly.

"I know," the girl replied, confidently. "But you'll be gone by then so it won't make any difference."

What do you want? For some obscure reason, the girl felt strongly that Sky had wronged her. *Stay calm. Try to reason with her until Blake gets here. What the hell is he doing anyway? Oh God.* Sky McPherson had never felt this scared in her whole life.

"Now I know why," Clare said.

Sky noticed that the girl was looking admiringly at her naked breasts and it repulsed her.

"He likes them big," the girl smiled.

"Clare, I don't know what I am supposed to have done but if you…"

Another blinding slap silenced her.

"Shut up!" The girl hissed. "You fucking whore. With your flash car and your expensive suits. You think you can take him from me. But you can't!" She yanked Sky's hair back. "You can't! He's mine!" Then, much more calmly, she added, "You didn't answer my question, doctor?"

Sky trembled, "What was your question?"

"You didn't tell me what he was like."

Thunder rumbled. *Where was Blake?*

"Answer me, you whore!" The girl demanded through clenched teeth.

"You tell me, you've had him a lot more times than I have," Sky replied defiantly, half expecting another slap.

However, the girl seemed to take this as a compliment and began to snigger. She pointed a finger, knowingly, "You're testing me, aren't you?" she asked, nodding her head. "You want me to tell you what it was like so you can compare and see if I'm telling the truth. Well, here's one for you, doctor." She leant forward and whispered in Sky's ear, "How do you think I got in here tonight if he hadn't given me a key? He said I could let myself in whenever I needed to or should I say, whenever he needed me to." She chuckled.

These last words stung Sky more than the blows to her face, more than the blade that was etching into her neck. *Was Blake really having a relationship with this girl?* Suddenly, she felt cold and dirty and she wanted nothing more than to kick this bitch away from her, drag some clothes on and escape from this house, never to return.

However, Sky knew that she would not stand a chance. The slightest movement from her and that blade would slice through her vocal cords. Her only chance was to try to talk to the mad creature and hope that Blake would hurry back up the stairs.

Blake, be okay, please be okay.

"So, what was he like?" Sky asked.

"The best I've ever had. Nothing like those skinny idiots I used to hang around with," she sneered and then added appreciatively, "Blake's got it and he knows what to do with it, all right." If there was a smile on Clare's face, it disappeared instantly when she spat, venomously, "but then, you would know that, wouldn't you?" Then, in an astonishing move, the girl left Sky cowering in the corner of the room and crawled up to the bed. There, she breathed in the scent of the sheets, "Hmmm... I can smell his cum," she said, appreciatively.

Sky was too shocked to be disgusted.

"Hmmm yes... I can smell him... yes," Clare was lying on the bed now, knife still clutched in her right hand, she began to rub herself on the sheets.

It was time. Sky McPherson summoned all her strength and, with the speed of a panther, pounced up from her seat on the floor, and launched her way to the door. However, Clare had anticipated this move and with mirrored speed the teenager was up from the bed and standing in her path.

Sky opened her mouth to scream but the sound never left her lips. The blow to her face was powerful and unexpected. The next thing she knew she was reeling backwards, thumping her head against the balcony door. She was dazed but conscious enough to see Clare McElvoy lunging at her, bread knife raised to strike. Sky screamed in horror and shot a hand out to defend herself. She grabbed McElvoy's arm with both hands, holding the menacing knife away from her but the girl was blessed with inhuman strength and, aided by gravity, she bore down on her.

Lightening flashed outside, revealing the deranged look on Clare's face. This girl was not just upset that Sky had slept with her alleged boyfriend. It was much more than that; she was murderous.

The blade was inches away from Sky's face.

Clare was sniggering. It was clear that she possessed enough strength to break Sky's defences but she was simply enjoying the terror in her victim's eyes.

Sky's arm was aching, her muscles buckling under the strain. She knew she would not be able to hold out much longer. She had to do something and she did. With all the strength she could muster, Sky McPherson lodged a kick in the girl's stomach. Clare groaned and the vice grip released momentarily, long enough for Sky to deliver a right hand hook into the girl's jaw, propelling her backward.

Sky wasted no time, and scrambled forward toward the door but Clare was up in hot pursuit, slashing at the air behind her.

Just as Sky reached the door, she felt the clamp of hands around her bare ankles and crashed to the floor. "No!" She scrambled to free herself and kicked viscously but the hands would not let go. "Help! Blake!" she screamed as, nails scraping on the floor, she was dragged back.

The grip relinquished and as Sky turned, she saw the blade plunge straight for her right leg. She snatched it away and the lethal metal sank into the wooden floor.

Lightening flashed and, in a scene out of her worst horror flick, she saw Clare McElvoy cackle with glee and stab at the floor around her feet. Sky was in a sitting position now, kicking and scrambling her way to do the door but her reserves of strength were fast dissolving. She knew she was no match for this killing machine and as she watched the girl jump to her feet and tower over her with that same evil leer on her face, she knew there was nothing she could do to stop the inevitable.

Then, the door flung open as thunder clapped loudly.

Sky did not turn around. She did not need to. The surprised look on Clare's face said it all.

The tray Blake was carrying clattered to the floor. "What the fuck..." He did not finish his sentence but froze as he took in the scene before him: Clare towering over Sky's naked body with a demented look and gripping a bread knife was enough to tell him that all was not well between the two women.

However, his arrival did not deter the killing machine. With one swift movement, Clare raised the blade to finish her murderous mission.

Sky screamed.

That broke Blake's trance and he hurled himself forward, roaring "Noooo!" Grasping Clare's hands, he crashed forth, careering the demented girl backward and propelling her through the balcony doors.

Sky ducked as shattered glass showered her and a gale force wind swept around the room. Blake stared in disbelief, as Clare lay sprawled against the balcony railing as blood oozed from a gash in her head.

Sky's murmuring brought him back. She was shivering; he snatched the quilt from the bed and wrapped it around her.

"Are you okay?" he asked, shouting over the howling wind.

Sky did not reply. Instead, her head remained bowed against the elements.

"Sky?" Blake repeated, kneeling down next to her.

Finally, she looked up. Her eyes were wide and tears welled in them as the wind tossed her beautiful black hair about her face. She did not need to say anything; the horror in her eyes said it all. Overwhelmed, he pulled her to his chest and caressed her hair. "It's over now, darling. It's all over," he repeated, soothingly, as the rain invaded the house. Gliding on the carrier wind, it searched for a new host but in such a small spray, it was harmless and had no power.

A few minutes went by while Sky sobbed in Blake's arms, and then she looked up into his face and her icy stare perturbed him.

"What?" he asked.

Sky said nothing. Instead, she pulled herself from his embrace and stood up. She was cold, wet and still incredulous as to what had just taken place here. None of this could be true. She must be having a nightmare. It was impossible for her to comprehend that one of Blake's pupils had broken into his home. *Not broken in, she had a key,* and then tried to slit her throat with a bread knife.

Dazed, she searched through the debris for her clothes, not remembering that Blake had ripped them off her, downstairs, earlier in the evening.

"Sky?" Blake was standing up also. His hair was damp from the mist that was whizzing around the room.

She looked across at him, eyes wide and wild, and then at the twisted body of Clare McElvoy. She pulled the quilt around her and then inexplicably began to laugh aloud.

Blake realised that she was in shock. He needed to get her out of this room and downstairs, where he would fix her a strong drink and then call the police.

Sky moved toward the door and, suddenly, yelped and hopped about on one foot only to lose her balance and fall against the door, slamming it shut. She slithered to down to the floor and grimaced with pain as she inspected her right foot and found that a shard of broken glass had incised a nasty gash in the sole of her foot.

"Fuck"! The blood seeped out and oozed to the tip of her toes where it dripped onto the floor, joining the cocktail of rain and champagne.

"Who left that glass there?" she joked. She was hysterical.

"Come on," Blake said, moving toward her, " Let's get you downstairs."

"Don't touch me!" she said, holding up both her hands.

"What's the matter with you?"

"Just stay away."

"Sky."

"Just get away from me!"

The tone in Sky's voice told Blake to back off and he did. "Look, Sky I'm just as…"

She held up her hands to silence him. Then, she slid back up the door, clutching the quilt and trying not to put pressure on her injured foot.

"Okay." he said. "Let's just calm down and get out of here, okay?" His tone was low and reassuring.

Sky said nothing. Instead, she turned the handle and pulled the door open. Instantly, a stream of turbulence rushed through the room, tugging it shut again.

Blake moved to assist and it was then that they heard the piercing scream. He turned just in time to see the girl, with a blood-smeared face and rain drenched hair, hurtling towards him, blade raised, screeching like a wild animal.

"Blake!" Sky screamed.

He clasped Clare's hand, temporarily controlling her slashing arm but the momentum knocked him back, pinning him against the door. They fought for control of the knife but Clare was terrifyingly strong and Blake had no other option, he head butted her, hard. With the shock of the impact, Clare released her clasp. Taking advantage of this, Blake brought his knee up into her stomach. The girl buckled forward and he brought his fist up with all his might, shattering her nose and sending her reeling backwards.

She fell and slid on the wet floor. Then, with the agility of an acrobat, sprang up again and charged Blake with the knife once more.

He delivered another right hand blow to her jaw.

She went back.

A left hook.

Back further.

Another kick, another right hook and finally, she fell back out onto the balcony.

Seconds whirled by and then, to their utter disbelief; they saw her rise slowly from the floor once more! Dripping blood and rainwater, Clare McElvoy stood, wearing the same maniacal grin.

This was just too much for Sky. Something snapped inside her head and before she knew it, she felt her legs rushing her forward. Arms outstretched and screaming with rage, she collided with the girl and propelled her over the railing, to her death on the protruding rocks below.

Sky looked down: Clare McElvoy lay, back broken, over the rocks, as the waves washed over her.

Twenty Four

An hour had gone by since the episode in Blake's bedroom and neither of them had spoken a word during that time. Blake nursed Sky's wounds and bandaged her foot. She did not move or speak throughout. He was worried about her.

He kissed her forehead and whispered, "It's going to be okay." He did not know why he said it or even if Sky could hear him but it did not matter; all that mattered was that they got through this, together.

He nestled a glass of brandy in her hands and wrapped her in the quilt once more. He needed to think.

He pulled his clothes on and made coffee whilst trying to understand what exactly had happened to them tonight. The bottom line was that Clare McElvoy, blessed with inhuman strength, had tried to kill them both but had failed and had been, in turn killed by Sky!

The thundering rain that had not desisted since that afternoon had stopped now. Although black clouds still hung low, the rain had granted a reprieve. Calm had settled in as if to facilitate Blake's thought processing.

He made himself a strong black coffee and sat at the breakfast bar. He gulped down the hot liquid and forced himself to breathe deep and slowly. He rubbed the pulsating ache in his temples as the images kept replaying in his mind. The girl acted as if she was possessed. *By what?*

His headache got worse as he pondered the endless possibilities. Ultimately, Blake was analysing everything because he could not explain what the hell had gone on in his bedroom tonight. *Maybe she was possessed by some unknown entity. Fine, but how will it stick with the police?*

"Blake?"

"Jesus!" He startled, spilling his coffee, scalding his hand.

He whirled around. Sky was standing in the kitchen doorway. She was dressed now. Her once immaculately groomed hair was in matted strands around her face. Her eyes had dark rings around them and there was a red swelling on her neck where Clare had prodded her with the blade.

"Sorry," she said, flatly. "I didn't mean to startle you."

"No, it's fine." Blake said, sighing. He was pleased to see that some life had returned to her eyes. He jumped out of his chair and went over to her. "How are you feeling?"

"Fine, considering I've just killed someone," she said in an impassive tone.

Blake's heart sank. He knew that no matter what happened, Sky would remember tonight for the rest of her life.

He went over to her and held her tight. She did not respond to the embrace and Blake felt this. He remembered how she had reacted in his room earlier. *Does she blame me for what happened?*

He pulled away from her. "Sky, I am worried about you."

She moved past him to the breakfast bar and drank from his coffee cup.

"Sky, I know this is hard for you but we need to talk about it."

"Why?"

"Because it's not going to do you any good bottling the whole thing up inside."

"Oh please… spare me the psychology routine."

He blurted out, "You blame me for what happened, don't you?"

There was a long pause. *She does blame me.* His eyes welled with tears.

Sky knew that her silence had hurt him more than words. She wanted to run to him, fall into his arms and listen to him telling her that this nightmare was exactly that, a horrifying dream from which she would wake. However, she knew it was not. No matter what Blake or anyone else might say, she had killed someone tonight. She was a murderer. That was a fact and no amount of hugging and kissing could change it.

"Neither of us is responsible for what happened," Blake said seriously.

"Do you really believe that?" she asked, peering into the depths of her coffee cup.

"Yes, I do."

"Then why haven't you called the police?" she was looking at him, expectantly.

There was a long pause.

Sky shook her head in a hopeless gesture and forced a laugh. "Well, that just proves…"

"It isn't that."

"What then?"

"I tried."

"And?"

"I got no answer."

"What?"

"Something strange is happening."

She let out a short laugh, "Strange? You mean like pushing that girl off the balcony? Yeah, I would say that's pretty strange."

"No, I mean there's something strange going on around here at the moment," he said, pensively.

"Blake, what the hell are you talking about?"

"I'm talking about Clare and Arthur McElvoy."

"What about them?"

"Well, don't you think there's a connection here?"

"What sort of a connection? They were related. So?"

Sky was intrigued and Blake was grateful for her attention.

"What does that tell you?"

She shrugged her shoulders "What are you getting at?"

"You told me about what happened to Arthur McElvoy."

"Yes, so?"

"What did the Police say was so unusual about him before he died?"

"You mean besides him reeking of sea weed."

"Be serious."

"I am being serious. I just don't know where you are ..." She stopped in mid sentence. It was clear to her now. "Oh my God," she breathed. "Do you think that it's hereditary?"

"I would say that there is a distinct possibility," Blake replied with a weary smile on his face.

"But he had no history of mental illness."

"So what does that prove?"

"Not much really. But I would have expected to see something in his medical file."

"Maybe there was. You just missed it."

Sky frowned. She was very thorough in her work and she would have noticed something that obvious. "Even if your theory is correct what does it prove?" she asked.

"It proves that both of them were loopy and that what happened tonight was just another consequence of the McElvoy's family illness. Christ, the police witnessed Arthur's outburst first hand."

"We've still got to prove that both of them were mentally ill, Blake."

"Well the autopsy will reveal that, won't it?"

"Not necessarily. I examined Arthur, I didn't find anything unusual. Besides, psychology and pathology are two completely different things. I'm hardly going to be able to submit them both for psychoanalysis, am I? If there isn't any physical evidence then we have nothing."

"Except what the police saw, and look what he did to his crew members on the boat." A flicker of brightness has returned to his eyes.

"That hasn't been proved," Sky threw in.

Blake went over to her and put his hands on her shoulders. He felt encouraged; there was hope. If they could prove that both uncle and niece were a few sandwiches short of a picnic then they would be most certainly exonerated. "Can't you see it, Sky? Clare was just as unstable as her uncle was. She broke in here and attacked us both. It was self-defence. Christ!"

Blake left Sky and was pacing around the small kitchen now. He laughed aloud with relief. "I've spent most of the past hour worrying about what the hell we were going to do when the police got here. You know, feeling guilty, feeling like a fucking criminal. What for? I haven't done anything, WE haven't done anything wrong, Sky!" He was euphoric now. His handsomely chiselled face was beaming once more. "Sky, you don't know what a relief this is…"

"Blake…"

" Okay, We'll have to get through all the questions and…"

"Blake…"

"All the…"

"Blake"!

"What?"

"Aren't you forgetting something?"

He looked at her, perplexed. She was still very serious. For some obscure reason, she was not sharing his newfound optimism.

"What's wrong?"

"Clare didn't break in here."

"What do you mean?"

"What do you think I mean?" she replied, raising her voice. "There's no sign of forced entry. That would indicate that Clare did not break in but that she let herself in." Sky let Blake absorb the words and then added, "With a key. The one you gave her."

"What?"

" She told me, Blake"

"Told you what?"

"That you were having a relationship with her and that you gave her a key." After delivering the words, Sky leant back against the breakfast bar, as if to steady herself.

"And you believed her?"

"Well, yes."

He frowned. "Thanks very much."

"Well, what am I supposed to believe, Blake?" She stood up straight and held a hand to the red bruise on her neck. "The girl was holding a knife to my throat why the hell would she lie?"

"I thought that was obvious by now. The girl was a fucking fruit cake!"

"That's your theory, Blake. Do you want to know what the police's theory is going to be? Clare McElvoy, your student, was having a sexual relationship with you. Then you decide to have a fling with an old flame. Clare, obviously unstable for whatever reason, comes around here, lets herself in with YOUR key and decides to get her revenge by slashing my throat! Only it all goes horribly wrong. We ambush the poor cow and knock her over the fucking balcony!"

Sky's eyes welled with tears and Blake moved to go to her but she waved him away.

"I didn't give her that key, Sky"

"Then how did she get in?"

"I don't know. She must have got in through the front door. We left the door open after you got here tonight, remember?"

She remembered but she could not think straight, everything was such a blur now. She said nothing. Instead, she stared into his brown eyes, as if searching for the truth in there.

Blake spoke calmly and clearly, "I've already told you about her, Clare had a crush on me and I did not encourage her in any way."

"But did you report this crush?"

"No. You know I didn't."

"Why not?"

"I told you, because I didn't think I needed to. Look, Sky, I am not a cradle snatcher, no matter what you may think of me."

"You don't know what I think of you."

"Then tell me," he said, frustrated. "Sky, ever since we met again I have been trying to understand how you feel but you just keep playing it cool."

"Well, now you know what it feels like, don't you?"

"Is that what this is all about?" Blake asked, incredulously "Getting even? Christ, Sky that was over twenty years ago!"

She swallowed hard and then said, through gritted teeth, "I am not that shallow."

There was silence as they both thought about the words that had just been exchanged.

"Look, I think we should try and stay focused on the problem at hand."

"Fine by me," she replied, petulantly. "So, why didn't you call the police?"

"I did."

"And?"

"I couldn't get through."

"What do you mean, you couldn't get through?"

"Exactly that. I dialled 999 and I got a message saying that the demand for that number was high and to try again later."

"Yeah right," she sneered.

He snatched the cordless phone from the nearby wall and handed it to her.

Sky looked at the phone and then at Blake. His face was a mask of seriousness. She dialled 999. The phone rang twice and then a recording of a female voice repeated, *"Sorry, current demand for this network is high, please try again later."*

Sky hung up and then tried a few more times but got the same recording. "My God," she whispered. "There must be a fault."

"There isn't. I called the operator and she confirmed the lines are just genuinely busy."

"But how's that possible?"

"That's what I asked her and even she was baffled."

"What's going on?"

"I wish I knew."

"So now what?"

"So now we go down to police station and tell them everything."

"What if they don't believe us?" Sky asked with wide eyes as if she had only just realised what telling the police would entail.

"Of course they'll believe us."

"I could call Morrison," she suggested pensively.

"Who's Morrison?" he asked.

"I'll tell you on the way, " she said. "Come on."

Twenty Five

"*...this special bulletin once again. Over five thousand police officers, from around the country, have been drafted into Exeter to help contain the sudden outbreak of violence in the city. More than a hundred people have been killed and many more have been injured in tonight's riots. Steven Scofield is on the line, once again, live from Exeter police station. Steven, What's the latest?*"

"*Yes Jackie I cannot describe to you just how serious the situation really is down here. You would have to see it to believe it. I don't know if you can hear them, but behind me there are literally thousands of people fighting to get through the doors of the police station. It is believed that many of these people are terrified for their lives. Many of them have witnessed murders,*" *rape and a whole medley of other indecent crimes, many of them committed by members of their own families.*

"Are the police any closer to finding out what is the cause of all these riots, Steven?"

"Well, earlier I managed to get a very brief statement from detective inspector Morrison in which he could only speculate the involvement of alcohol and drugs. Many of the people here do not share that opinion.

"Are they clutching at straws, do you think?"

"Well, that does seem to be the case. The authorities are calling for calm. They are asking people not to leave their homes and for those who persistently put themselves in the line of danger they are considering the implementation of a curfew which I believe is going to be introduced and policed by the army."

"How will they actually implement such a radical remedy? Will the curfew be on a national scale?"

"Well no, not really. You see, this is the part that is baffling the authorities. It seems that these riots have limited themselves to the West Country. No other part of the nation has reported any outbreaks of violence. So, in answer to your question, Jackie, the curfew will only apply to most of this region."

"And finally, Steven. What is the word from the public?

"Panic, mainly. I have never seen such mass hysteria in my whole life. Many blamed contaminants in the water whilst others have even gone as far as blaming the recent deluge of rain."

"Steven Scofield, thank you very much."

"Thank you."

"We will be bringing you updates on the riots as they…"

Sky switched off the radio.

They were driving down the narrow road that led away from Stony Point and toward the main road to Exeter; to their left a muddy, vertical wall from which this road had been carved out years before and to their right, a steep embankment that sloped down to a shimmering lake.

The rain had stopped and the moon attempted an appearance from behind big black clouds that still dominated the sky. Thunder rumbled a few miles away, promising that the rain would come back.

"What are we going to do?" Sky asked, realising just how silent the Discovery had become without the news babble of the radio.

"I'm not sure," Blake replied, pensively.

"I could try ringing Morrison again," Sky suggested.

"And tell him what?"

"What do you think?"

"You've been trying him ever since we left the house. The man obviously has more important on his mind than switching on his mobile phone. I don't know why we're even bothering to go down," he said, squinting, as a pair of headlamps appeared in the rear view mirror, dazzling him.

"What do you mean?" she asked, pulling at her seatbelt that felt as if it had etched a groove in her chest.

"Why are we bothering to go down to the station? We won't even be able to get into the place. You heard what was said on the radio."

"It doesn't mean we shouldn't try."

"What for?"

"Because I have killed someone, that's what for"

"It was self defence and it was either her or us," he replied, adjusting the rear view mirror in an attempt to deflect the glare from the headlights of the following vehicle.

"Whatever. I should still report it."

"Do you think the police are going to be interested in what you have to say with all that is going on tonight?"

"Correct me if I'm wrong, but were you not the one who said that we should drive down there?"

"Yes, but I have changed my mind. I think we should turn around and go home."

"What are you suddenly afraid of?"

"I'm not afraid of anything. I just think that there's no point in…"

The jolt cut Blake's sentence short.

"What the hell…?"

In unison, they turned to see that a white van had bumped into the Discovery's rear.

"What does he think he's doing?" Sky cried.

"I don't know. His bloody insane!"

"Slow down, Blake. Let him overtake us."

"I have!" Blake snapped, monitoring the van in his wing mirror and decreasing his speed further, to 40 miles per hour.

The van hesitated and then, without indicating, began to overtake them.

As the vehicle drew level with the Discovery, Sky turned to yell at the driver but failed to lock eyes with him for it was too dark inside the cabin.

"Bloody maniac!" Blake shouted.

In that moment, there was a tremendous jolt as the van veered into the side of the Discovery. Sky screamed as the impact sent them, tyres screeching, toward the edge of the road. They fishtailed a few times before Blake managed to straighten up.

"Blake..." Sky murmured, horrified, as she shrank back into her seat

"I know," he replied, accelerating again, in an effort to out run the van.

They rounded another of the many bends that dominated the road. The van's lights flashed and its horn sounded angrily.

There was a loud scraping sound as it collided into their side once more. This time, Blake was ready for the attack. "Hold on!" he shouted over the revving engines and steered to compensate. Despite his counter attack, the van was much bigger and managed to push them further toward the edge of the road.

"Bastard," Blake seethed through clenched teeth as he fought to maintain control.

"Oh my God!" Sky screamed as the odds of ending up in the lake grew higher and higher.

The vehicles flanked each other as they stormed down the single carriageway, swerving around another bend and then slamming into each other, battling to retain their position on the road. Then, the van veered away from them, to the left, for a few seconds, only to return at full throttle, shunting the Discovery closer to the edge.

Again...

And again…

Blake felt the steering wheel lock and fought frantically to regain control but to no avail. The vehicle swerved away again, preparing for another attack. It was as if the demented driver sensed Blake's predicament and was preparing to strike the killer blow.

The seatbelt that had been irritating Sky moments earlier, now felt comforting.

As Blake fought on to regain control, the van delivered another blow, shunting them towards the edge, sandwiching the Discovery between it and the metal parapet, spraying the night with a shower of sparks.

Sky squeezed her eyes shut and threw her head to the right and down as the door window shattered into millions of pieces showering her with glass. Rain scented air and the growling of the two engines flooded the vehicle.

"Sky!" Blake cried. Enraged, he tugged at the steering wheel with all his might and felt it give slightly. He yanked it left. This counter strike was not expected and the van was forced sideways, into the rock face, dragging down a mudslide as it sped forth.

It was then that the car appeared from around the bend in front of them. It flashed its lights in protestation at the two oncoming vehicles.

Sky opened her eyes and the next few seconds seemed to last hours as the scene played out in the glare of flashing headlamps and to the soundtrack of blasting horns and labouring engines.

The steering wheel locked once again and no matter what Blake did, it would not budge as they sped on a collision course with the oncoming vehicle.

"Oh My…" Sky breathed with terror, as the vehicle hurtled, tyres screeching, towards them.

Blake slammed on the brakes but momentum had seized control and was dragging them onwards

Five feet…

Blake threw himself over Sky.

The van struck, shoving them sideways, through the parapet and down the embankment toward the foreboding lake.

The crash was loud as the transit van clipped the bumper of the oncoming car, launched itself over the bonnet, somersaulted several times down the road and stopped only when it hit the muddy wall opposite.

Meanwhile, the Discovery leapt relentlessly down the hill, it flipped over a boulder and dove; nose first, into the lake.

It was a matter of seconds before the freezing water began to flood through Sky's broken window. Blake reacted immediately and unbuckled his seatbelt.

"Oh God!" Sky cried, as the icy water washed over her.

"Stay calm, Sky, unbuckle your belt." Blake said, soothingly. He knew the car was sinking fast; the bonnet was already under water. They had to get out before the whole thing went under.

Sky fumbled to release her belt but she could not disengage the lock.

"I can't do it! Blake, I can't do it!"

"Let me try," he said, leaning toward her.

The car was filling rapidly, and the water was at waist level. Blake, his footing on the clutch and brake of the vehicle, was finding it hard to keep his balance as he battled to release Sky's seatbelt.

"Blake…" She whimpered, reading the frustration on his face.

"Don't worry."

"Get me out of here! Get me out of here!" she screamed, tugging at the belt that was restraining her.

"Sky!"

"Let me out!"

"Sky!" Blake cupped her head in his hands. "Baby," he cooed, locking eyes with her. "I'll get you out of here." There were tears of frustration in her eyes. He smiled at her reassuringly, kissed her quickly and said, "I'll be back." After that, he climbed upward, through the front passenger seats and into the rear of the car.

"Blake." Sky strained to look after him but she couldn't. The car was on a vertical dive and she was dangling forward, strapped in like an astronaut. She began to shiver violently and did not know whether this was because she was terrified or merely due to the water temperature.

The water was a shoulder level now.

"Oh ….my Go…d… Bla…ke…." She coughed as bitter lake water made her gag. Choking and spluttering, she cranked her head as high as she could above the rapidly rising water.

There was a loud groan as the Discovery submerged deeper beneath the water. In a panic, Sky tugged at the belt once more, clawing at it as the gelid water began freezing the blood in her limbs. Then, she took one last deep breath and closed her eyes as the water rose over her head. Never before, had Sky McPherson felt so alone and afraid. Now, as she sank towards her watery grave, she longed for her mother. She longed for the warmth of her parent's embrace.

Sky did not want to die like this, strapped into this car like a prisoner on death row. This was not how she had pictured her demise. She had positively dreamed of herself slipping away in the middle of the night at the ripe old age of ninety. Not like this, not when she had all her life still ahead of her and maybe the chance to rediscover happiness with the one man she truly loved.

The last of the air was forced out of the Discovery as it was sucked deep into the murky abyss in a cloak of gurgling bubbles.

Sky's lungs were bursting and her head felt as if it was going to explode as she battled to hold her breath. However, as the seconds flowed by, she knew that she could not last much longer. It was then that a peculiar calm swept over her. She no longer feared death but loneliness. She thought of Blake somewhere in the back of the Discovery. *Is he thinking the same thoughts? Is he thinking of me? Is he afraid?*

Sky was not aware of it but she was crying. Her sorrow was not for her own demise in this watery tomb but for the life of Blake. In her mind's eye she saw the man who once was a paragon of health and whose smile was the sun itself, turn into a twisted, shrivelled corpse in the back seat. His hand outstretched, reaching out for a touch that never was. His face; eyes bulging, lips swelled, was a mask of terror.

That is when her peacefulness turned to rage and she kicked and struggled to free herself of the ties that strapped her into her metallic coffin. She pushed and pressed against her seatbelt, hoping, as unlikely as it was, that it would snap and that she would break free.

Instead, the exertion of her movements forced what air was left out of her lungs. Tiny bubbles escaped from her lips and raced to join the universe above the surface and she began to gag. Then, she was falling, drifting to the bottom of the lake, banging her head against a rock. *Or was it the dashboard?*

It was all a whirlpool of images to Sky as she felt herself being dragged heavenwards. *Is this what it is like?*

Seconds seemed like hours as she drifted upward and even when she broke the surface, it took her some time to adjust. She coughed and spluttered as the same air that had abandoned her moments ago was forcing its way back into her lungs, oxygenating her blood and feeding her starving brain.

As she drifted back to consciousness, she became aware of strong hands supporting her waist and the soft kicking motion that was propelling her back to shore.

There was a fresh, rain-washed scent to the air around her. It was warm in stark contrast to the arctic conditions inside the lake.

Thunder rumbled over her as if it were protesting against her salvation.

"Blake!" "Blake!" She cried, pointing toward the lake.

"I'm here!"

"Blake!"

"I'm here, Sky. I'm here."

She felt his strong arms around her and suddenly the nightmare was over. She looked up into his face, and it was Blake. He was here and she was not dreaming. Blake Hudson was smiling down at her.

"Thank god," she breathed, "Thank God."

Blake had used the Stanley knife from the case in his boot to cut her free and now, after all this time, she realised just how close she felt to him. Something about their relationship had eluded Sky all these years. Yes, she had loved him in the conventional way that everyone loves. However, tonight Sky had discovered something different. She had discovered closeness to Blake that she had never felt with anyone else before, not even her parents. It was as if they had merged. Sky McPherson had become Blake Hudson, the two of them had become one soul and she knew that from now on they would never be parted, never.

"We better get back. You're shaking," he said.

"So are you."

"Then, I'd better get back too," he said, smiling.

He helped her to her feet.

Thunder groaned directly overhead and they both looked up.

"Do you think it's going to pour down with rain now, just to finish us off?" she asked, smiling.

"I don't know." he replied, gravely. "I hope not."

They climbed the embankment toward the road.

"Hey, we've been at the bottom of a lake. What difference is a bit of rain going to make now?" she asked, casually.

Blake did not reply. Instead, he hurried Sky up the slippery slope, toward the road.

At the top, they both watched the mangled remains of the van and the wreckage of the car.

"I better go and see if there are any survivors." she said, starting forward.

"No!" Blake said, clasping her arm.

"Blake," she moaned in protestation, looking at his hand on her arm.

"Let's get back to the house," he said flatly.

"Blake, they may need our help."

"It's more than our help that they need. Come on, lets go," he said, leading her away from the road and up the hill, toward Stony Point, often checking to see if they were being following.

Twenty Six

They had been walking for over 30 minutes. The shortcuts they had taken through fields and over brooks had led them to Tresea, a tiny village *on* a cliff top location.

The *place* was silent, as if the rain had brought with it a muting drug. Nothing could be heard except for rainwater gushing down a nearby drain and *their* rasping breaths.

"Where is everyone?" Sky asked through gulps of air.

"I don't know," Blake replied, looking around him. An uneasy feeling had crept up his spine and was dancing on his mind. There was something unsettling about the darkness. He felt as if someone or something was watching them.

"Come on, let's go," he said, breaking into a run.

"Hang on, Blake. Where to?" Sky asked, not following.

He stopped, looked back at her and said, nervously, "I don't know but we can't stay on this road, it's too dangerous."

They were on a bridge. In front and behind them the shiny, rain drenched, road was empty.

"Blake, as much as it grieves me to say it, I need a rest." Her voice was loud in the emptiness of the night.

"We might be able to catch a lift with someone from there." He pointed to a clump of small cottages further down the road. He was not surprised to see that there were no lights on.

"It doesn't look like anyone's home."

"Oh there's someone home all right," he said, knowingly, under his breath.

Then, they both heard it. From behind the ridge in the road came the sound of an approaching lorry.

"Great, we can ask him for a lift out of here," Sky said happily. Blake said nothing.

"Can't we Blake?" she asked, losing her smile.

The headlights were a glowing haze behind the ridge.

"Blake?"

"Let's wait and see," he replied, not taking his eyes off the oncoming headlights.

The sound of the truck's engine was getting closer and then, suddenly, it appeared over the rim of the road. The horn roared loudly, echoing around the valley.

"Get off the road!" Blake yelled, grabbing her hand.

They ran off the road, onto the embankment, slipping on the wet grass, they both fell in a heap on the ground.

The lorry sped by where they had been standing only seconds before. It blasted its horn as it charged past.

"Phew… That was close," Sky said, tossing her matted hair behind her ears.

"Well, I think we can safely count him out for a lift," Blake replied, staggering to his feet and then extended a hand to Sky.

He looked further down the embankment. A sloping field in front of them led to another row of cottages.

"We'll head down there. See if we can get help, find a car or something," he said, starting forward. After taking a few strides, he stopped to realise that Sky was not following. He turned around to see her standing where he had left her. "Sky?"

She said nothing.

"Sky?" He followed her gaze and saw that the lorry had skidded to a halt about thirty yards down the road, and was idling.

"Come on!" Sky squeaked excitedly. Before Blake could say anything, she was off, scrambling back up the embankment, onto the road.

"No, wait!" Blake shouted after her as the lorry's engine revved louder. Sky!" He started up the embankment, in pursuit.

In that moment, the truck began to reverse back up the road. Now, Blake knew. He could not explain how but he just knew. "Sky! Wait! Wait!"

However, Sky was back on the road. She turned, put her hands on her hips and looked down at him, her face creased into a frown. "What's your problem?" she asked, as the lorry reversed loudly toward her.

"Get out of the road!" Blake shouted.

"What?" Sky said, not comprehending the hysteria in his voice.

The lorry was only a few feet away and it did not look like it was going to stop.

"Oh my…" The jolt snatched the rest of the words from her mouth as Blake grabbed her and dragged her back down the embankment.

Once again, the articulated missed them by seconds. It screeched to a halt a few yards up the road.

"What's going on?" Sky complained, picking herself up from the ground. Blake did not reply. Instead, he caught her hand and, before she knew it, they were both running down the hill toward the nest of houses.

Behind them, the lorry trumpeted angrily, veered off the main road and plunged down the embankment after them.

"Keep running!" Blake shouted. Up ahead, he could see the houses. The hamlet was deserted and very dark; the only light available came from a few weak street lamps.

The lorry's growl was gaining fast, picking up speed as it ploughed down the field, after them.

"Through there!" Blake shouted, pointing at a tiny alley that sliced between two cottages.

The truck was about thirty metres behind them, never slowing, and still picking up speed. It was obvious that the driver was of an unfriendly nature and in his mind's eye; Blake could see the burly man sniggering behind the windshield.

They had reached the alley now, and their first instinct was to hide inside one of the houses but Blake knew better than that. It would take more than a thin layer of bricks and mortar to stop an articulated lorry of this weight and speed.

They entered the alley. Up ahead, a streetlight shone, casting a glow into the gloom of the cavity. Suddenly, that light dimmed as the shadow of two people appeared up ahead, blocking their exit.

However, the articulated vehicle was slowing for nobody and nothing. They had no choice; they had to move forward, now!

The two men, their faces unseen in the gloom, were standing as if bolted to the ground as the roar of the engine drew closer.

"Blake…" Sky groaned.

He clutched her hand tightly "Run! As fast as you can, and

don't let go. We're going to have to ram them!"

"What?" She cried.

Blake still could not see their faces and was not prepared to take any chances. It was a case of attack now and ask questions later. "When I say jump, jump!" he shouted.

The two men kept their ground even as Blake & Sky stormed toward them.

"Jump!" Blake shouted. In unison, they both leapt into the air, legs outstretched. There was a faint grunt from one of the men as Blake's boots thundered into his jaw, knocking some of his teeth to the back of his throat.

All four people crashed into a heap on the ground. Behind them, the HGV struck the cottages with the force of a giant meteorite. Metal screeched, glass shattered, wood splintered and bricks crumbled, spraying dust into the air.

As per Blake's prediction, the lorry was not stopping and was still, half its speed, bulldozing its way toward them, bringing with it a cloud of rubble. However, despite the bull bars, the crash had shattered one of the headlights, leaving the other to flicker in an eerie supernatural fashion.

It did not take long for Sky to regain control of her senses. She had twisted her arm in the fall but she did not feel the pain for her mind was concentrating on one thing, and that was to get up and away from here.

She slapped and kicked herself free and before long, she was on her feet and running for her salvation. That was until she noticed that Blake was not running with her. She turned back to see him grappling on the floor with one of the men whilst the other one writhed around, nearby, not knowing whether to nurse his broken teeth or stem the flow of blood from his nose.

Behind them, she saw the evil eye of the metal monster blink as it continued on its destructive course toward the trio. It was gaining fast, no more then ten metres away.

Blake was, once again, face to face with the madness of the rain. Like a laser beam, the demented look in his assailant's eyes burned deep into his soul. He winced as spatters of saliva dribbled onto his face. His head thumped as he clawed at the fingers gripping his throat. He kicked and kneed but to no avail. The man felt no pain, no emotion. He was a robot, a terminator sent by the rain to kill Blake and nothing could stop it, except…

The huge rock that came thundering down onto his skull. The cracking sound was sickening but, instantly, the man's grip slackened, his body went limp and he fell heavily onto Blake, forcing out the air left in his lungs.

"Come on!" Sky screamed," No time to kiss and make up." She dragged Blake to his feet.

The lorry was less than five metres away; dust and mortar was already showering them. Blake choked, trying to catch his breath as Sky hauled him away.

Behind them, the man who was nursing his wounds only had time to emit a grunt before the truck drove over his already damaged body, crushing his bones and grinding him into an omelette of flesh and blood.

They emerged from the alley. Ahead of them was enormous grassland that sloped, steeply into a dark valley. Beyond that, the moon, momentarily escaping the huge veil of dark clouds, shone brightly onto the sea. It was no more than half a mile away. They could even hear the sounds of the surf.

They exchanged looks.

"We'll never make it," she said, answering his telepathic question.

"We've … have... no choice," he breathed.

The lorry was gaining fast; it was seconds away.

"I suppose it's worth a try," Sky said, instantly grabbing Blake's hand and breaking into a run.

Five seconds later, the articulated lorry emerged from the alley, knocking aside what was left of the matchstick cottages. It trumpeted loudly in celebration of its freedom. No more restraints, it was going to crush them.

The grass was wet beneath their feet. Several times they each, in turn, threatened to slip and crash to the floor. They were running into complete darkness toward the sound of the ocean.

More trumpeting!

"Blake… It's gaining!" Sky shouted. Her lungs were bursting;

she was going to pass out.

"Keep going!"

The lorry was almost upon them.

"Run faster!" Blake yelled over the sound of the engine.

"I aaaaaaaaam!" she screamed as she slipped but Blake held her upright.

The clouds parted briefly and it was then that reality struck. They both had expected to reach a sandy beach from which they could wade out to sea and swim away from the sinking lorry, but this was not to be.

The cliff's edge got closer. It was no more than ten metres in front of them and they could only imagine how far the drop was from here.

They were speeding forward now, both afraid that the momentum they had built up was going to drive them over the precipice.

"Blake!"

"Look out!" He shouted and, shoved her, violently, to the right with the back of his arm. The impact was sudden and Sky lost her balance. She tripped and fell onto her side, cracking her ribs on a protruding stone. The shock and the pain twisted up her gut and into her brain. She could not steady herself and just let go, allowing the momentum of her fall to tumble her forward, over the edge of the cliff.

Before the lorry driver realised what was happening it was too late. The targets he had pursued for the last five minutes had rolled out of his path. Reacting to this, the diver slammed on the brakes. They screeched and the wheels locked but the thrust was too much. The lorry glided gracefully on the wet grass toward the beckoning cliff edge.

In a desperate attempt to cheat an icy death at the bottom of the Atlantic Ocean, the driver swerved right. The metal beast groaned under the strain of its head pointing one way as gravity dragged it the other. It growled loudly as the front right wheel lifted into the air, followed shortly by the next wheel and the next. There was a deafening crashing sound as the lorry slammed onto its side. Wheels spinning, engine roaring and glass shattering, the metal beast slid helplessly toward and over the edge of the cliff.

The foaming ocean muted the thundering impact of the articulated lorry as it broke its back on the protruding rocks below. The water bathed its new victim until it sank slowly into its Cimmerian depths.

It took a few seconds for Blake to digest what had actually happened to them, and it was then that he noticed that Sky was nowhere in sight.

As a gale tore around him, Blake scrambled to his feet. It was hard to think straight. He searched around, calling her name, "Sky! Sky!" but he received no reply. As much as he did not want to accept it, there was only one answer; he looked toward the cliff's edge.

Her head was thumping and her right rib cage and arm were both causing pain. The wind that was tugging at her clothes stung her eyes and made it hard for her to gain her bearings.

Squinting into the night, she waited for the next cycle of moonlight. Sure enough, it came, bringing with it a dreadful realisation. She had fallen almost fifteen feet to a narrow ledge on the side of the cliff face. However, she was alive, racked with pain, perhaps, but alive. She performed a quick examination of herself; at least she did not have any broken bones. It could be worse; she could be down there with that lorry driver. The one she could swear had smiled at her through the shattered glass of the lorry's cabin as it narrowly missed colliding with her saviour ledge and plunged 200ft to the rocks below.

Blake ran, walked and slipped his way to the edge of the cliff, calling out Sky's name. *This cannot be happening!*

Before Blake's brain had even processed the dreaded thought, his eyes welled with tears. Sky!" he screamed, blindly, into the darkness but there was no reply.

Twenty Seven

At first, Blake thought he was hallucinating but he was not. Like fireflies, the flashlights were bobbing toward him through the darkness. There were two of them and they were approaching fast. *Where can I go? Where can I hide? What about Sky?* He was not going to run away and leave her here, wherever here was.

Thunder clapped directly overhead and he ducked instinctively. Then, glancing at the nearing flashlights, he fell to his knees and groped in the grass for a stone or anything else that could be used as a weapon; if he was going to be taken down it wouldn't be without a fight.

Lightening flashed and he could just about discern two figures. They were men and they were coming to get him. Blake bit his lip in frustration. *Where the fuck is everybody anyway? How the hell can a lorry plough its way through a whole village and nobody notice?*

The lights homed in on him and he shielded his eyes from the glare. He felt pathetic, kneeling on the ground like a wounded animal with a rock in his hands.

They were about ten feet away when Blake heard the police sirens in the distance. The question was, where they coming to save him or were they rushing to some other emergency on this night of madness?

He looked beyond the two men and he saw the flashing blue lights. It was the police and they were coming to save him. All he had to do was hold out until they got here. Therefore, still shielding his eyes from the flashlight glare, he stood and threateningly waved the rock at his attackers. The bobbing lights stopped their approach and a low voice with a Cornish accent warned, " No, you don't want to do that lad."

"Get away!" Blake screamed, almost as demented as the rest of them. His heart was racing and the adrenaline pumping around his body. He was prepared to do anything to knock these two down.

Another Cornish voice suggested, "Put the rock down, you don't stand a chance."

Blake glanced behind them. The police cars had come to a halt, blue lights still flashing. He could see more flashlights approaching in the distance; this gave him courage, "Don't come any closer or I'll smash your fucking heads in!"

"You're not going to do anything," one of the voices said, moving toward him.

This startled Blake and he promptly lifted the rock to strike but the sudden movement caused him to slip on the wet grass and, no matter how much he tried, he lost his balance and fell, arms flailing, to the ground.

This was it, it was over and Blake knew it. The fall had knocked the weapon out of his hands and he was lying at the mercy of these maniacs.

Lightening flashed as the duo peered down on their prisoner, shining the torch in his eyes.

"What on earth's goin' on?" one of them asked, "The whole bloody region's gone mad."

"Poor bastard," the other commented.

"Shall we cuff him?"

"I think we better 'ad. Don't want a repeat performance of what happened to Perkins."

"You're right. I can't believe he bit his ear clean off like that."

As they bent down, Blake threw his hands up in defence.

"It's all right, we're not gonna' hurt you."

"You're policemen?" Blake asked, incredulously.

"That's right. We're police and you can either come quietly or by force, the choice is yours. I have just got to warn you that with the night I've had I'm not going to take any shit from you."

They hauled Blake to his feet.

One of the officers, known as Ginger, spoke into his radio whilst the other attempted to snap a pair of handcuffs onto Blake's wrists. "This is PC Baxter, reporting from the lorry incident at Tresea. We can confirm apprehension of one number suspect, over."

"Two, Sky's down there!" Blake snapped, pulling away from the officer who was trying to cuff him.

"Sir, I'd calm down if I were you."

"Who's Sky?" asked Ginger.

"She's the lady that was with me."

"Okay, Sir. For your own safety, let my colleague put the cuffs on you."

"No! Not until you find Sky."

"We can't help your friend unless you co-operate with us. Now either you let the officer put the cuffs on you, willingly or we'll have to do it by force."

"The fuck you will! She could be dying down there for all we know and all you two are worried about is cuffing me!"

"It's for your own protection. Now, I am not going to tell you again."

"No!" Blake's nerves were a mess; he could not comprehend the reasoning behind the officer's attitude. *Why are they wasting time with me? They should be down there looking for Sky.*

"This is Baxter here. We've got another one of them, we're going to need backup." The officer spoke into the radio.

A tinny, crackly, reply said, "Roger Baxter, we're on our way down to you right now."

Ginger turned to look at the approaching flashlights as if seeking reassurance.

Blake noticed this and said very quickly, "You don't understand, I am not one of them!"

"Then, why won't you co-operate with us?"

"I will! But you two idiots don't seem to understand what I am saying."

"We understand what you are saying, Sir, but resisting arrest..."

"Spare me the fucking sermon! Why don't you just..."

Blake's sentence was cut short by a low whirring sound and then, suddenly, the helicopter sprung up from behind the cliff's face, drenching the trio in a pool of fluorescent light. Taking advantage of Blake's surprise, the second officer tripped him up and pushed him, face down, to the ground, smacking his head against the rock Blake had been holding moments earlier. Not realising this, the police officer proceeded to cuff his prisoner regardless.

"No..." Blake murmured. "No, Please..."

Ginger spoke into his mouthpiece again as the police helicopter circled overhead, "Thanks, Eagle 1. Any survivors down there?"

"That's an affirmative, one female, no obvious injury, stranded on the Cliff's ledge. I repeat one female, no obvious injuries stranded on cliff's ledge. Search and rescue have been advised, ETA 30 minutes, over."

Blake could barely hear what was being said for his mind was drifting. Although, he thought he heard the words *female* and *no obvious injury.*

More officers arrived on the scene, speaking in loud tones over the whirring blades of the hovering helicopter. It was over; they were saved, then everything went black.

Twenty Eight

23, Parkview/ Exeter, England 15:03

The subdued babble of the TV brought Blake out of an exhausted sleep. He was lying in a double bed in a spacious, tastefully furnished, square room that he did not recognise. He looked out of a glass balcony door at huge grey clouds, drifting across a blue sky.

As he stirred, he felt an agonising stiffness in most of his joints and groaned as he rolled over. He glanced at the TV: some unknown female newscaster in a tawny trouser suit was reading the headlines.

He took in the bedroom. The wallpaper was a warm rusty colour with subtle triangular patterns. The carpet was beige with a bed quilt to match. There was a pine wardrobe and, in the corner, a clump of dried flowers sat auspiciously in a large cylindrical vase.

To his left, seated on a chair, was Sky. She was dressed in jeans and a blue sweater. Her arm was in a sling and she had a nasty bruise below her right cheek, other than that, she looked okay.

She turned from the TV screen and smiled at him, "Welcome back."

He smiled back and then winced as a twinge of pain shot up his chest. He glanced under the covers and groaned at the large purple bruise on his abdomen. He also realised that he was naked and could not help but smile.

"All you had to do was ask," he grinned but it was flat and held none of the cheekiness that was so attractive about him. He had been through a lot and it showed.

Sky smiled, encouragingly.

"What happened?" he asked, gingerly sitting up.

"You lost consciousness. They had to airlift you out."

"You're joking."

"You've been drifting in and out for hours. Do you remember anything?"

"Not a thing."

"Well, you were taken to the hospital where you should have been kept in for observation but things are so mad down there, they just couldn't afford the extra bed."

"Charming."

"The doctor was happy to leave you in my capable hands."

"You've been watching over me all this time?"

"Like your fairy god mother."

"What about you?"

"Oh, you mean besides nearly drowning, getting chased by an articulated lorry and falling over a cliff, not bad. Actually, I was lucky to get away with a fractured arm and rib. I don't really need this sling; I just thought it'd look good on me."

"Damn, you get all the fun," he said, sighing. *Thank God, she is okay.*

"Please try not to be too jealous. You are lucky, you were out most of the time. You missed all the commotion down at the hospital. I have never seen anything like it. Lack of spare beds would have been a luxury. They were running out of hallways."

"Bloody hell, I feel so stupid."

"You mustn't. A head injury is a serious thing. At the hospital, you came round; rambling on about how you thought the rain was responsible for what happened last night. Then you vomited on the doctor's feet, which may I add is not a good sign with head injuries, and were spark out most of the remaining time."

"Great, I feel much better now that I know I made a complete idiot of myself."

"I'm just glad we're home."

"Oh, so is that where I am?"

"Indeed. I washed your clothes."

There was a pause as they both caught a segment of the news report: a camera was drifting around the war zone that was Exeter City centre.

Then Sky continued, "I told Morrison everything about the girl at your place. Obviously, they want to talk to you.

"What did you tell him?"

"The truth. She came around with a knife and tried to kill me. I did not get the impression that he found my recount so extraordinary after everything he and his men have witnessed in the past few days. To be honest with you, I think some girl with a history of mental illness is the last thing on his mind."

"Clare had a history of mental illness?"

"Yes, she's been seeing a psychologist ever since she was thirteen. Her records were made available to the police once her death had been officially registered."

"Why was she seeing a psychologist?"

"I don't know the details but something to do with the death of her father."

"So…"

"Yes, your theory was right."

"Bloody hell."

"Anyway, her prints will be on the knife and your injuries will be consistent with the blade." Sky paused to watch more of the televised news report and then added, absent mindedly," Did you know that the army has been drafted in to maintain order? There hasn't been an uprising like this in years. It's incomprehensible that such minor legislation could instigate such a revolt.

"Is that want they think it is?"

"That's what she's been saying." Sky nodded toward the TV."

"And you believe her?"

She turned to him and asked, "Why shouldn't I?"

"I don't think it was the new legislation that caused those riots. I think something else is responsible for what has been happening.

"Such as?"

" At the hospital, last night, I wasn't rambling. I meant what I was saying."

"What, about you're mother being upset that you'd got mud all over your clothes?"

Blake smiled, "No, about the rain."

Sky frowned.

Blake shifted, carefully. "Look, I know it may sound ludicrous but I think there is something in the rain. I don't know what. I would have to get the water analysed. But I seriously think that there is something in the precipitation, some kind of chemical. There is the distinct possibility that this particular band of rain is carrying in it a concentrated strain of pollutant, something we have never seen before. However, I would need to check it out, do some tests. And I would need to see the toxicology reports on Clare McElvoy, her uncle and anyone else that may have come into contact with it."

He stopped talking, Sky was staring at him but said nothing. "Look Sky…"

"I think I am going to need to call the doctor after all." She stood up.

"Sky…"

"No, Blake, just as a precaution."

She picked up her address book from the bedside table and started thumbing through it. She did not really want to call the doctor but she needed time to think about what Blake had just told her. Her initial thought was that he was still delirious. However, the more she vacantly turned the pages, the more it seemed to make sense. It certainly would explain the sudden influx of clients.

Then, as if Blake had been reading her mind, he said, "Come on, Sky, you told me that a foreign substance was found in Arthur McElvoy's blood stream. Now, what's easiest to believe: that an old man was experimenting with hallucinogenic drugs at the ripe old age of sixty something or that he somehow involuntarily absorbed them through his skin?"

Sky hesitated for a few seconds and then asked, "How could this have happened?"

"I don't know. I'm going to need to get back to my house and track its origin." He pushed the quilt back.

"You can't do that."

"Why not?"

"Because the place is sealed off."

"So?"

"You'd be violating a crime scene."

"It's my home."

"You're a prime suspect for God's sake."

"Sky, if I am right, I think Her Majesty's Government is going to have more to worry about than whether or not I have violated a crime scene."

"I know that. Don't talk down to me."

"I wasn't."

"You were."

"I wasn't."

"Whatever. Just do whatever you bloody want." With that, Sky stormed out of the room, leaving Blake staring after her, aghast.

Five minutes later, Blake emerged from the bedroom dressed in his clean jeans and sweater. Sky was in the living room. She was standing with her back to him, staring out of the window. "I've made you some tea," she said, without turning around. "It's on the table."

Blake glanced at the tray and then at her. There was silence and then he said, "Thanks for washing my clothes."

"You're welcome," she replied, flatly.

Blake shook his head, incredulously, for as much as he tried he could not explain Sky's sudden outburst. Walking over to the coffee table, he asked, "Sky, you've got to help me out here. Have

I said or done something to upset you because if I have..."

"It's just never going to end, is it?" she interrupted.

"What isn't?"

"This. Christ, we could have died last night, three times! Instead of thanking God, that you are still alive, you just cannot wait to get back out there. There's always something with you Blake, like this whole thing is just some big adventure." Sky's voice trembled as she suppressed tears.

"Sky, I am an environment officer. This is what I know. What would you have me do, just cower away in here and hope its all going to go away?"

She turned around, seething, "No, I don't expect you to do that but what I do expect is… is…" She stopped in mid-sentence.

"What…?"

"Never mind."

"No, say it.

"I have nothing to say," she said, obstinately.

There was another long silence, broken by Blake, who said softly, "Sky, we need to talk about us and the future but now isn't the time. There are other things that require my attention right now and I need your help."

She stared off, avoiding his gaze.

"Sky. I can't do this alone," he said, angling his head so that she would look at him.

After a few seconds, she said, almost petulantly, "What is it exactly you want me to do?"

"I need those toxicology reports."

"You're insane," she said, dismissively.

"It's the only way. Those reports may be the only thing that will prove my theory.

"I have just got off the phone, telling them I won't be in.

"Please Sky," he asked, imploringly.

She hesitated and then shaking her head in disbelief at herself, disappeared into the bedroom.

As she slipped out of her sling and into her jacket, she noticed that the TV had stopped showing scenes of last night's riots and had cut to a reporter standing outside the gates of Southampton football stadium.

"...Most anticipated sporting event is going to take place in just under ten hours. Tickets for the match between Southampton and Newcastle were sold within days. As you can see behind me, hundreds of fans are already milling around the area, eager to get in to see which team will qualify. Meticulous planning has gone into this event, right from the new design of the tickets to the staggered admittance program. Fans from both sides have been issued with different admission times to avoid any potential clashes outside the stadium.

The only thing that hasn't been pre-arranged is who exactly is going to win and, of course, what the weather conditions are going to be...."

Twenty Nine

Sky was grateful that her colleagues were too busy performing autopsies to notice her slip surreptitiously into her office, grab a handful of manila folders from her desk and hurry back out of the building.

"Have you any idea how much trouble I am going to be in if anyone finds out that I removed these from the office?" she said, handing Blake the folders and slipping behind the wheel of the BMW.

"I know, and I am eternally grateful."

"Yes, just remember that when I get sacked," she said as she started the engine and drove off at great speed, eager to put some distance between the Coroner's office and herself.

It was not long before they were out of Exeter city centre and on the A337 toward Stony Point.

"What exactly are you hoping to find in there?" she asked, glancing at Blake as he thumbed through the reports on his lap.

"I don't know; a connection," he replied pensively.

" Between what?"

"The rain and the deaths of these people."

"You don't seriously believe that they were killed by something that was in the rain, do you?" she sniggered.

Blake just threw a look at her.

Sky lost her smile. "Okay, let's just say that you are right. How was the rain contaminated in the first place? I mean, are you suggesting that somebody, maybe even the government is conducting some kind of experiment on us?"

"Does that sound impossible to you?"

"Impossible no, unlikely, yes."

"Try telling that to the thousands of Americans who, during the 60s became, through no choice of their own, human guinea pigs. The CIA administered an experimental drug, in a gas entity, through the exhausts of cars. If you had told someone back then that their government was conducting experiments on them, they would have told you that you were out of your tree. And now, all these years later, they have actually admitted to it."

"They didn't admit to it, Blake."

"No, of course they didn't because they didn't need to. The evidence spoke for itself."

"So, you think our government is doing something like that to us now? Christ, Blake, you work for the government."

"I don't work for the government. I work for an independent body which is The Environment Agency and my job is to safeguard the environment."

Sky laughed, "You'll be donning your Jesus sandals and singing Bob Dylan songs, next."

Blake did not reply. He just shook his head as he flipped through the files on his lap. "You may as well have asked me to read Egyptian. This doesn't mean anything to me."

"They're post-mortem reports, Blake. What did you expect?"

They drove in silence for a short while as Sky processed more thoughts. "Okay, let's say that you are right about the rain. That means that whoever gets wet is affected. Right?"

He nodded.

"So, if that's the case, why hasn't the whole region gone mad? Why is it that with all the rain we have had of late, only a few people have been affected? And why were most of those in Exeter City? You can't tell me that they are the only ones who got wet."

"Maybe they were."

"So, you're suggesting that this band of cloud is being selective about which town, city or village it rains on?"

"I'm not suggesting that at all. I already told you that cu-nimbus does not rain incessantly. It can travel for miles without precipitating anywhere."

"So, presumably, once someone has been affected, or rained on, or whichever way you would like me to put it, that's it, they're dead."

"Presumably, yes. I don't know, Sky. That's what I am trying to find out," he said, waving the files at her.

"Well, I can tell you now, that isn't the case."

Blake looked up "Why do you say that?"

"There are survivors, Blake. Admittedly, a lot of them do not recall what they did the night before, but there are survivors. The police picked them up as they aimlessly roamed the streets this morning."

The only sound was that of the engine as Blake took in the information and then he said, "It must have a symptomatic phase."

"What?"

"It wears off!" Blake looked at Sky, excitedly.

"Don't look at me, you're on a roll."

"It wears off, Sky. Therefore, it's not what the rain does, it's what people do whilst they are infected with it."

"Yes, but it still begs the question, what exactly are they affected with?"

"I don't know yet. But I am sure the answer is in these files and back at my place."

Thirty

Stony Point / 16:20

They were back at Stony Point within an hour.

As expected, the door was sealed by blue and white police tape with the words *'Crime Scene, Do not Cross'* emblazoned all over it. Sky read the words with trepidation. She knew that what they were about to do was illegal and, if caught, would seriously damage their case as well as her career.

Blake, on the other hand, had no reservations in marching up to the front door, stripping away the tape and entering his home.

Sky followed, tentatively. The cool of the lighthouse was no longer welcoming but chilled her. It felt as if years had gone by since the attack in Blake's bedroom. *I do not want to be here. I should know better than this.*

She paused by the front door as Blake began climbing the steps to the second floor. He noticed Sky's hesitancy and asked, "Are you all right?"

Images of Clare Hudson's blood soaked face stared into her mind's eye.

"Sky?"

"I'm fine," she replied, distractedly.

"Are you sure?" There was concern in his voice, he was not impervious to what had happened here only hours before.

"Yes, I told you, I'm fine," she said, finally snapping out of it.

"Okay," he said, smiling warmly and then disappeared up the spiral staircase.

As he passed his bedroom door, he noticed that, like the front door, it was sealed by blue and white tape. He hesitated outside for a few seconds and then hurried upward.

Sitting at the leather chair behind his desk, he booted up the computer and dialled the modem access. Once connected, he launched the meteorological program. The spinning globe appeared, and with a few clicks of the mouse so did a green map of the UK.

Then, he clicked on the *Format* menu and selected *History;* a popup screen appeared and he typed in a start date, left the end date blank and clicked *OK*. The map redrew itself; most of the highlands and parts of Cornwall disappeared under a blanket of black cloud. He clicked and zoomed into the southwest region and, sure enough, parts of Cornwall and Devon remained under a shroud of blackness.

He checked the date field at the foot of the screen; it read today's date. Then, he clicked on the scroll buttons and watched, incredulously; as the date regressed, so did the rain cloud, from inland Exeter, back out to the Atlantic Ocean.

A smile spread across his face; so far his theory had been correct. Now, all he had to do was link the rain with the recent deaths.

Sky walked into the room.

Blake looked up, "Come and look at this, quick!" he said, with all the excitement of a child.

"What am I looking at?" she asked, looking over his shoulder.

He pointed to black spots on the computer screen, "See these?"

"Yes."

"That's the rain."

"And?"

"Watch…" Blake clicked the two scroll buttons rapidly, causing the rain cloud to move back and forth, toward and away from Exeter."

"That's the rain we've been having recently."

"No one is refuting that it has been rained for the past few days. What we are trying to prove is the link between it and the deaths. And so far there is no evidence to suggest…" Sky stopped in mid-sentence.

"What is it?" Blake asked, looking up at her.

"Where is this?" She was pointing to a blue part of the screen.

Blake moved in closer to the monitor as he worked out the location, "I don't know. I may be wrong but it looks like the coast just off Bude. Why?"

Sky did not reply, instead she circled around Blake and made for the post-mortem files that he had dumped on the desk in front of him.

"What is it?" he asked.

"I'm not sure yet." She was flicking through the files at demon speed. Eventually, she grunted with satisfaction and pulled out a file marked, **McElvoy, A**. She scanned its contents as Blake looked on eagerly.

"I don't believe it," she said, glancing at him.

"What?" He asked, frustrated.

She read from the report, "The trawler was found, adrift, 25 miles west of the coast of Bude." She looked up at him.

"My God, the Sea Emperor," Blake whispered.

"Yes, and Arthur McElvoy was on that trawler. Of course this may just be a coincidence."

"Of course it isn't. What else, Sky? Can you think of anything else?"

"I don't know. I don't recognise any of the area."

"What about the place you went to last night?" he asked.

"The old women, she was found at her home which was Greenacres Farm..." She searched through the folders again and then realised with disappointment, "But the P.M. hasn't been performed yet. God it was only last night, it seems like ages ago."

"Where the hell is Greenacres Farm?" Blake asked.

"I don't know. It's on that... 36... something."

"B3623?"

"Yes, I think so."

"That must be around... here." Blake pointed to a location on the screen just east of Bude.

The two of them exchanged glances; this was another incident in the path of the rain.

"Another coincidence." Sky suggested.

"You don't really think that."

"Blake, proving that all these people could have been exposed to the rain doesn't prove that it is the rain that drove them to madness."

"Maybe not, but it certainly makes the rain a prime suspect. Who else? The quarry! All the dead fish, that was... here." Blake pointed further east.

"And the farmer," Sky added, "He was at tre-something."

"Tre-something?" Blake asked, lifting his eyebrows. "Oh well, that narrows it down."

"Hold on." Sky searched through the folders. This time she stopped at one marked: **Wilson, J**. She looked inside and finally read out, "Trevassy."

"Trevassy. That would place him more or less...here." Blake looked up at her again "Still think it's a coincidence?" he asked, grinning.

Sky did not answer.

"Next stop, Exeter. And I bet that if you look at those reports you will find that all of these people had an unidentified substance in their blood stream." He looked at her, expectantly, as she read the reports.

After a few minutes of scanning the pages, she breathed, "My God. This could be a photocopy of McElvoy's toxicology report."

Blake nodded, knowingly.

"What the hell is it, Blake?"

"I don't know. But whatever it is, you can bet your last penny it came from the rain." Blake stared into the monitor.

"Can you trace its origin with that? " she asked, nodding at the screen.

"I don't know how much history this thing keeps. They probably back up the historical data and then clear it from the system but I'll try." He selected *history* once again and filled in the dates.

"How far back are you going?"

"I don't know. I'll try two weeks." He clicked *OK*.

The digital map redrew itself and the date at the foot of the screen regressed by two weeks. Clicking on the scroll bar, they watched as the black cloud retreated out to the Atlantic Ocean.

"This is impossible," Blake muttered.

"What?"

"Well, this cloud should have evaporated way before it ever reached the British Isles."

"Are you saying that this cloud isn't a cloud after all?"

"I don't know. All I know is that I have never seen anything like this before. I wonder how far back this thing goes."

He kept on clicking the scroll button until a blue box appeared on the screen with the words *'No further detail found!'*

"That's the end of that." He pushed the mouse aside.

"How far back did it go?" Sky asked.

"Umm…" Blake stared at the screen. "Don't know. It just ends over the Atlantic Ocean, somewhere south of Ireland." He looked up at her, once more.

"What?" she asked, recognizing the twinkle in his eyes.

"Didn't that plane crash around there?"

"Hold on," Sky said, holding up a hand, "You think this cloud was responsible for that too?"

"The pilot did report that they had run in to bad weather," he offered.

There was a long silence.

"So, what do we do now?" she asked.

"Well, I think the first thing we need to do is find out where this thing is heading."

Blake right clicked the mouse and cleared the screen. The map redrew itself minus the blanket of cloud and the date at the foot of screen showed today's date.

"Okay, let's see where she's heading."

"What do you have in mind?"

"Well, I won't be able to predict exactly where it is heading but I can read wind trajectories and that will give me a rough idea as to the direction."

"And once you know that?"

"I am calling Hamilton, my boss, and telling him to put out a warning."

"Will it be that easy?"

"No. Nevertheless, you know me, ever the optimist. Okay, here we go…"

He drew a rectangular frame around Exeter city and the surrounding area, "Now, judging by its history the cloud is moving relatively slowly, we can use this to our advantage. We were lucky yesterday; it rained during the middle of the night when most people were either inside watching television or asleep.

"You call what happened lucky?" Sky asked with surprise.

"That was a shower compared to what could happen," he said, ominously.

They exchanged glances.

He clicked the detail button, the map redrew itself but this time the sky above Exeter was clear. There was no sign of the black cloud.

"Where is it?" Sky asked, baffled.

"I don't know," Blake said, "Looks like it's disappeared.

Thirty One

"You've got messages," Sky said, noticing the blinking two on Blake's answering machine.

"Yeah, I've seen them, I'll play them later," he said, distractedly as the green map redrew itself on the computer screen. He clicked the detail button and a layer of squiggly lines appeared across the length of the map.

"What are they?" Sky asked.

"It's the wind direction, looks like it's heading northeast."

From the menu, Blake selected *clear current lookup*. The map re-drew itself and they could see the whole of the UK once more. He selected *detail*, and large bands of black cloud hovered approximately forty miles northwest of Exeter.

Sky gasped, "I thought you said it was moving relatively slowly?"

"It is." He drew a frame around the band of cloud and zoomed in. It was hovering over the town of Yeovil, meaning it had crossed the county border from Devonshire to Somerset.

"My God, Blake. We have got to warn them!" She moved to snatch the phone from its cradle.

"No" Blake said, putting his hand over hers.

"Blake..."

Their eyes met.

"We can't say anything yet, Sky."

"Why not?" She asked incredulously.

"Because we have no proof."

"We've got all the proof we need in here," she replied, grabbing a handful of the folders from his desk.

"Come on, Sky. You've only just finished telling me that they don't prove a thing. We need to get that rain analysed."

"And what happens in the meantime?"

"Whatever happens is beyond our control."

"Blake, I can't believe you are saying this." She pulled her hand away.

"Sky, trust me. The Environment Agency is not going to put out a public warning without concrete evidence. If I call Hamilton and tell him all this over the phone, what do you think he is going to say?"

"Well, if he's got any sense he will praise you for the good work and authorise the warning."

"Somehow, I don't think he is going to be that sensible. After all, you didn't believe me, initially."

There was a pause.

"So, what are you going to do? Grab a receptacle and go stand out in it?"

"If I have to."

"Christ, this is insane." She turned away from him and walked over to the window. There, she ran her hands through her unkempt black hair and took in a deep breath. She watched the dark sky and listened to the whirring of Blake's answering machine as he played his messages. *How the hell is all this going to end?* She remained silent for a few minutes and as Cynthia Hudson's voice filled the room, Sky said, "You're wrong, Blake."

"About what?" he asked without turning around.

"I believed you from the moment you told me about your crazy theory."

"Then why…"

"I am a doctor, I need scientific evidence."

"Was that really it?" he asked as he turned to face her.

There was a pause as their eyes met and they both feigned interest in his mother's telephone message.

"She's worried about you," Sky said, flatly.

"Then, I'd better call her and tell her I am okay," he said. "But only after you have answered my question," he continued, seriously.

"What was your question again?"

"Come on, Sky, talk to me."

Sky sighed and was about to reply when the second message was played and a husky female voice, unfamiliar to her, echoed around the room, *"Blake, are you there? Please be there."* A few seconds silence, then, *"Baby, I heard about the riots, CNN has been talking about nothing else all morning. Please call me as soon as you get this message. I miss you, darling. If I do not hear from me soon, I am getting the next direct flight to Heathrow. Okay, goodbye baby, I love you."* Then, the sound of the receiver hanging up and the machine's robotic voice, *"You have no more messages."*

Seconds drifted into minutes. They both remained unmoving, unspeaking, as if the air around them had suddenly turned into delicate crystal.

Sky's eyes welled with tears. *Oh God, not again.. He lied to me again. Oh My God, this can't be happening. Who is she? Does he love her? How long has he been with her? Is he married? Oh God, he lied to me, he used me. The rooms caving in, I cannot breathe, help somebody help!*

Jesus, Not like this. I do not want her to know like this. "Sky, I can…" Blake stood up, arms outstretched.

It was too late. She ran out of the room and hurried down the stairwell. She wanted to scream but she suppressed it. She raced down the steps as the world began to spin like a director's camera turning 360° in a dramatic scene. The stairwell encircled her; the walls closed in. She felt cheap, dirty and betrayed. After all these years, Blake had done it to her again. The thought was incomprehensible, the pain unbearable. She needed to get into her car and away from here, away from him.

Tears streamed down her face as she reached the foot of the stairs. The faceless image of a women embracing Blake kept on replaying in her mind. She grasped the door's handle, pulled it open and stepped out into daylight.

She held her hand to her nose as she tried hard to suppress more tears leaking from her eyes. History was repeating itself. She thought that the woman she had become was untouchable by the demons that had stalked her teenage days. But now the terrifying reality hit home and she knew that she was not, and, thanks to Blake, never would be.

She climbed behind the wheel of the BMW and searched her pockets for the keys.

"Sky!"

Blake was at the front door.

She looked up at him and frantically frisked herself.

Blake left the door, hurried to the car, taking her keys with him. "Please wait."

She held up her hand, avoiding eye contact.

"Sky, we need to talk."

"Could I have my keys, please?"

"No, not until you've heard me out."

"Could I have my keys please, Blake?"

"You're being irrational, Sky. Let's talk about this."

That did it. She looked up at him with her tear soaked eyes and jumped out of the car, "I am being irrational?"

"Sky, I know how you must be feeling right now and I am…"

"You haven't got the faintest idea about how I am feeling so don't you dare presume to know how I am feeling!"

"I didn't want you to find out like this."

"Oh and how did you want me to find out? Would you have preferred me to walk in on the both of you like I did with Lisa, is that it?"

"Sky, I don't want to lose you again."

"You should have thought about that before you lied to me, again! Now, give me my fucking, car keys!" she screamed, grappling with him but he was much stronger.

"Sky, she was someone I met…"

"I don't want to hear this," she said, holding her hands over her ears.

"Sky…"

"Go to hell!"

She stormed away from the car and ran down one of the winding footpaths that led to the beach. She could not deal with this now. She needed to get away and regain her composure, fortify herself against the pain. She still loved Blake but she could not show him that, not anymore.

With all the agility of a football player, she ran down the coastal path, careful not to stumble over one of the many protruding rocks. She needed to hear the soothing, healing sounds of the lapping waves on the shore. She needed to be alone.

However, the sound of running boots told her that she was not; Blake was following her, "Leave me alone, Blake!" she shouted, and sprinted forward. He followed her, footsteps splashing loudly as they ran across the shore.

They were about quarter of a mile down from the lighthouse before Blake clasped hold of Sky's arm and spun her around.

She shrugged him off but stopped running.

The surf pounded the beach as their hearts hammered inside their chests. They stood, bent over, hands on knees, sucking in air. Minutes ticked by where the only sound was the fizzing waves and their rasping breaths.

"Sky, I'm sorry."

"She's the one you cheated on. You should be apologising to

her, not me."

"Sabrina knows the rules."

"What?"

"She knows I'm not looking for a relationship."

"I can't believe I am hearing this."

"She wants her independence as much as I do."

"My God, you are an arrogant bastard."

"There's nothing arrogant about knowing what you want."

"And you always get what you want, don't you, Blake? Doesn't matter who you hurt in the progress. Just fuck them and leave them."

"If I recall correctly, you were the one who did the leaving."

"Oh yes, you made sure of that."

" What the hell is that supposed to mean?"

" Everything, Blake! You humiliated me then and you are doing it now! You made me feel like an embarrassment. Do you think I didn't notice the way you avoided me ever socialising with your snooty friends or the way you conveniently managed not to spend much, if any, time in the company of my parents? I wasn't good enough, was I Blake? I wasn't from the correct social set, was I? Tell me, is that what attracted you to me in the first place?"

Sky paused here. Memories of her parents came flooding back to her. She was just as guilty. She had rejected her parents in her desire to please Blake and had never had the chance to make it up to them.

"I hate you Blake! I hate what you are and what you and your Mother turned me into. You made me ashamed of the only two people in the world who truly loved me and I..." She faltered, choking back tears and then continued through gritted teeth, "and I will never forgive you, never!" She turned her attention to the sea as the wind tossed her hair about her face.

Blake watched her. Stunned by what she had just said, he was temporarily unable to respond.

Then, the anger swept up his legs like a tidal wave, shaking his entire being. He wanted to roar with rage but instead he said, coolly, "Have you quite finished or is there something else of particular importance that you would like to add?

She said nothing.

"Well, who would have thought that inside such a brilliant mind lie the fantasies of a petulant eighteen year old."

She glared at him.

"What's the matter? Am I not speaking the truth? That is what you want, isn't it Sky, the truth? Okay, I have few home truths for you. I was never ashamed of you; you were ashamed of yourself. Your parents never embarrassed me. I liked them. You were the one who was embarrassed; you hated what they were and their beliefs. Moreover, I didn't ask you to mix in my circle of friends because I knew how uncomfortable you felt around them, not because you weren't good enough. All of the evils you lay at my feet are the rotten fruit of your own over-active imagination. You were so obsessed with being everyone other than yourself that you rejected everything that meant something, including your parents.

"That's a lie!" Sky spat, sobbing uncontrollably.

"The only lie is the one you have been telling yourself all these years. And you've got the audacity to make me out to be the villain in your little scenario just because you felt inadequate."

"You have no idea…"

"Oh no, I think I have a pretty good idea of what a self obsessed bitch you really are. I love you, Sky. But I love the women you are now not the petulant little girl you are behaving like. Now you have to decide if you are going to jettison this baggage of guilt once and for all and look ahead, or wallow in this resentment for the rest of your life. We can't always right our wrongs Sky but we can learn from them and in turn become better for it."

"Who the hell do you think you are?"

"I am Blake Hudson, who the hell are you?"

Sky was shuddering with sobs but Blake did not feel compelled to hold her. She needed this.

"Think about what I said. You know where to find me."

"In bed with her!"

Blake was going to reply but decided against it. "Whatever. I have urgent things that require my attention right now. Give me a call if and when you grow up."

With this, Blake turned and walked back.

As he moved closer to the lighthouse and further out of her life, Sky McPherson sank to her knees and, with her head in her hands, sobbed violently.

Thirty Two

As Blake climbed up the coastal path that led back to the lighthouse, a shadow fell over him. He looked up and in a flat tone asked, "What are you doing here?"

"Nice to see you too," Matt said as Blake moved past him and headed for the front door.

"I thought you weren't here. Where's the Land Rover?" Matt asked, following closely.

"Long story."

"Ok, I'm listening."

Blake stopped in his tracks and looked at his friend.

"Oh no, you've got that look." said Matt.

"What look?"

"That pissed off look you always get after someone's rattled your pram."

" No one has rattled my pram, Matt"

"So, what's wrong?"

"I told you, it's a long story."

"Then, tell me about it."

"Not now."

"Okay, you can tell me on the way."

"On the way where?"

Matt caught Blake's puzzled expression, "Oh don't tell you you've forgotten."

"What are you talking about?"

"The match, tonight, you know, the cup qualifier, Southampton V Newcastle..."

"Oh shit, I forgot all about it."

"Oh man, you are unreal. Not even a sad Rugger like you could forget this match. It's premier league, Blake! Have you any idea how hard it is to get tickets?"

"Sorry, Matt but I have had other things on my mind."

"I bet you have. You mean, besides seeing that doctor mate of yours," Matt grinned, knowingly.

Blake said nothing, and instead looked out to sea.

"Bloody hell, you have haven't you, you dirty sod. Does she know about Sabrina?"

Blake maintained his silence.

"You get all the luck, two gorgeous women at the same time." Matt punched Blake playfully in the chest but his friend did not react, instead he remained transfixed on the aquamarine ocean as a faint breeze ruffled around them both.

"Hello... paging doctor Hudson..." Matt said, moving in front of his friend in an effort to get his attention.

"Oh my God," Blake breathed.

"What?" Matt demanded. "What?"

"The football match."

"Yes, That's right. We're going to be late."

"They've got to call it off!"

With that, Blake sprinted off, toward the front door.

"Hang on a minute! Call it off? Blake, what are you talking about?" Matt shouted, running after his friend and pausing, momentarily, when he saw the blue and white police tape around the doorframe. "What the hell? Hey Blake, wait up!" But his friend had disappeared up the stairwell, taking the steps two at a time.

As Matt rounded the stairs to the first floor, he noticed more police tape around the doorframe of Blake's bedroom and stopped once again. "Blake, are you going to tell me what happened here?" He shouted without taking his eyes off the door.

When Matt entered the study, Blake was already busy working on his computer. "Why do I get the feeling we shouldn't be here?" He asked, walking up to the desk.

Blake made no reply.

"Blake, I think you should tell me what…" He paused, noticing the black swirl on the computer screen. "What the hell is that?"

"It's the rain. It's drifting east, towards Southampton."

"Don't worry they're not going to call the game off because of a few showers. There's going to be over fifteen thousand people at that game and we're going to be two of them." Matt said with conviction.

"Does this look like just a shower to you?" Blake asked, pointing at the black cloud on the screen.

Matt peered closely at the monitor. The huge black shroud did look rather ominous. "Okay, thunderstorm. They've played through blizzards before now."

"This isn't just any old thunder storm, Matt."

"Then what the hell is it, Blake? I keep asking but you won't tell me."

"There's something in the rain."

"What, like water?" He grinned.

"No, there's something toxic."

"Toxic. What, like radiation?"

"You could say that. There's a chemical in the rain. I don't know exactly what it is or how it works but what I do know is that it is absorbed through the skin and is lethal."

"I don't understand." Matt looked perplexed.

Blake snatched the phone off the desk and dialled the number for the Environment Agency's head office in Bristol."

After several rings, the phone was answered by a female voice, whom Blake recognised as Melissa, "Environment Agency, good afternoon."

"Melissa, hi. It's Blake. Is Hamilton there?"

"Oh hi, Blake. I'm afraid he's in a meeting right now."

"Put me through, will you?"

"I'm sorry, Blake, I can't. He's with the deputy PM and I am under strict instructions not to…"

"Melissa, I need to speak with him right now please," Blake said, suppressing the urge to raise his voice.

After pondering on Blake's tone for a few seconds she replied, "Hold on…" The line went dead but for a faint bleeping sound.

"Matt, what time is the match?" Blake asked.

"In just under two hours. What's this all about? Why have the police decorated your doors with crime scene tape? And why the hell is your doctor friend's car parked outside yet she is nowhere to be seen? Has something happened to her?"

"I can't explain right now."

" What do you mean?"

"Yes, Melissa?"

"Sorry, Blake. I spoke to him and he said that he will call you back."

"Christ, I need to talk to him now!"

"Sorry. I can't make him come to the phone."

"No, I suppose not. Can you just tell him that I need to speak to him? It's very urgent."

"Of course. Is everything okay?"

"Marvellous. Just ask him to call me, will you? In the meantime, tell him that I am going to issue a warning and stop the Southampton game this afternoon." With that, Blake hung up.

"What?" Matt cried.

Blake picked up the phone again. "I just need to make this phone call, Matt and then I'll explain everything." He was about to dial 192 when he heard a clicking sound on the line.

"Christ, that's all I need!" he swore, shaking the handset.

"What?"

"Bloody phone's on it's way out." He hung up.

"Blake, should I be worried about you?" Matt asked, casually.

Blake was about to answer but was startled by the ringing of the phone. He snatched it from its cradle. "Hudson"

"Blake?"

"Yes."

"Hamilton here. What's the urgency?"

"Thank God. We've got a major crisis on our hands, Sir"

"What kind of crisis?"

"Well," Blake swallowed, "I have reason to believe that a lethal substance has been released into the atmosphere and unless we get a warning out right now, thousands of people are going to be exposed to it."

"What kind of lethal substance?" Hamilton asked, calmly.

"I'm not sure yet."

"Well, is it a gas?"

"No Sir, It appears to be an unidentified strain of bacteria."

Blake avoided Matt's gaze. He could sense that his friend was perturbed by what he had just heard.

"What kind of bacteria?" Hamilton asked.

"It's still unknown, Sir. What I do know is that it's very dangerous. Those affected by the rain become violent and even homicidal"

"The rain?"

"That's how is spreads, through precipitation."

"Are you sure about this?"

"I am positive, Sir. I experienced its effects first hand."

"You were affected by it?"

"No, I met one of its victims." Blake allowed Hamilton a few moments to absorb the information and then continued, "Sir, there is a football match this afternoon, we need to stop it."

"On what evidence?"

Blake faltered, "Well, err, I don't have any hard evidence as of yet but I know this thing is bad."

"Come on, Hudson."

I'm losing him. "If we don't stop this game today, there is no telling how many people are going to be affected. What happened in Exeter city centre will be nothing in comparison."

"Surely, you are not suggesting that this rain was responsible for those riots as well"

"I know it was."

Hamilton laughed loudly.

Blake paused, trying to remain calm, although he was starting to lose his patience.

"Sir, we need to call off that game," he continued.

"How can I? You have not given me one shred of proof to substantiate your claims. I cannot authorise something like this just on a hunch."

"It isn't just a hunch."

"Well, it most certainly seems like it to me."

"You haven't been listening to a word I have said, have you?"

"Hudson, I know you think that…."

"For God's sake, people are going to die!"

"Hudson…"

Blake removed the phone from his ear and took in a deep breath. All his instincts were urging him to tell the pompous bastard to go to hell but he knew that would not help. He had to try to reason with this man.

So, after taking another deep breath, he put the handset to his ear and continued, "Please Sir, you have got to trust me on this. I know it doesn't sound too good right now but I can get you all the evidence you need, I just need some more time. I can assure you that you won't regret it. I have never let you down before and I am not about to start now. So, for the sake of those people out there, I am appealing to you to put out a warning and call off the game."

He glanced at Matt who was listening to the conversation, aghast. Then, he shut his eyes and strained for the answer as his heart hammered in his chest.

There was a very long silence.

"Sir?"

"No."

"What?"

"Permission denied."

Blake opened his eyes, "After everything I have told you?"

"Blake, you must believe me when I tell you that I have always considered your work at the Agency to be nothing short of exemplary. But son, when you start telling me that a killer rain is on the loose, precipitating on people and turning them into homicidal maniacs and yet, as a scientist, you cannot provide me with one shred of scientific evidence to back up your claims, I have to question your judgement. I am sorry."

"You will be when that rain hits Southampton this afternoon." Blake's words were firm and hissed out of gritted teeth.

"Whatever. In the meantime I would like to discuss this incident in more detail with a view to launching an enquiry"

"Don't bother!" Blake snapped.

"What?"

" I'll call public health and get them to make the decision you find so hard to even consider."

"Are you threatening me?"

"No Sir, just taking the responsibility out of your hands." He glanced at Matt as if seeking support but Matt was feigning interest in a nearby painting.

"Look, Hudson, I don't know what it is you think you know about the rain but whatever it is, it has clouded your judgement. Now, I am not prepared to discuss this on the phone any longer. Come to my office in the morning and we will talk about it."

"Forget it."

"Hudson..."

"Go to hell!" Blake shouted, slamming the phone down. He remained there, hand still on the receiver, quivering with rage. "Christ." he seethed.

A minute or so went by in silence and then Matt turned to Blake and said casually, "I take it, he isn't going to call the match off this afternoon then?"

"No," Blake replied. "But I am."

"Uh oh. Why do I suddenly feel worried?"

Blake lifted the receiver and dialled directory enquires, "Yes, public health, please."

Matt scratched his head as Blake scribbled down the number.

"Blake, are you sure about this?"

"As sure as I'll ever be," he said with determination.

He dialled the number and waited for a reply. That was when

the clicking sound returned.

"Public Health, good afternoon…"

"Yes, hello, this is Blake Hudson of the Environment Agency… I need to…"

He stopped when there was a loud burst of static on the line.

"Hello? Hello?"

More static and then the line went dead.

"Shit!" He slammed the phone down and then picked it up again, still nothing. "I don't believe this! The line's dead."

"Blake…"

"Can I borrow your mobile phone?" Blake Asked desperately.

"Sure, if I had one."

"Shit!" With that, Blake raced outside and groaned, "Where's my car?" Then, memories of the lake came rushing back.

Matt appeared at the front door, "Blake, I am starting to worry. Firstly, you let the police redecorate your home with tape, then you piss away your job, and now you can't even remember where you left your car."

"If it rains on that football game I am going to be the least of your worries," Blake said, climbing into the passenger seat of his friend's car. However, Matt was not moving, he just stood in the doorway with his arms crossed.

"Well, what are you waiting for?" Blake demanded.

"So you want a lift then?"

"Come on, Matt!" he shouted.

"I left the keys inside."

"Then go and get them." Blake sighed.

Matt turned to comply but stopped and said, "Does this mean that we won't be going to the match after all?"

Blake just looked at him.

"I'll take that as a no." With that, he went inside to fetch his keys.

Blake drummed his fingers on the dashboard. His mind was a twister of thoughts: the thousands of spectators, last night's events and Sky. He wondered if he had been too harsh on her. However, he decided that he had not. Okay, so she had found out about Sabrina. So what? It's not as if they had been dating for months and she had just discovered that he was seeing someone else. Christ, they had only met again a couple of days ago. He had not had the chance to tell her, although God knows he had tried, many times. But they were getting on so well that it wasn't a priority. Getting to know Sky again was much more important than telling her about a woman he dated occasionally and did not love. *Are you a womanising bastard? No, I am not. Then why do you feel like one, Hudson? I should go down there and make it up to her, tell her that I didn't mean any of that stuff.* But he did. Or did he? Christ! All these nagging thoughts were driving him crazy! Time was running out and where was Matt?

Matt had decided to rush into the downstairs toilet. He had been desperate to relieve himself ever since he arrived but, with all that commotion, did not have the chance.

As he stood over the ceramic vase, he replayed Blake's telephone conversation. *"There's something in the rain."* What exactly? Some kind of chemical. How did it get there? How did Blake know about it?

He zipped himself up and was about to leave when he heard it. It sounded as if a bulldozer was making its way up the coastal path and then it transmuted into a beating sound. Whatever it was, it was drawing closer to the building. He pressed his face to the glass of the small window but could not see anything as the beating got louder and seemed to move around the building.

He left the toilet and raced through the living room to the window near the front door. He could see Blake sitting in his car, looking skyways.

Wind turbulence swept around the building and then it became obvious. Pressing his face against the window, Matt could see the Helicopter descend slowly and land on the small forecourt, just a few feet away from his car.

"What the fuck," he gasped.

The helicopter was large and black. It looked military, a twelve-man carrier with blacked out windows.

The whirring slowed and Matt was about to rush outside when the helicopter's side door slid open; four men in black overalls and caps climbed out. Two of them headed straight for Blake.

They spoke to him through the car's passenger window and then one of them stood back, drawing something from what appeared to be a pocket in his overalls. It was a gun!

"Jesus Christ," Matt whispered.

They waited for Blake to exit the car and escorted him into the helicopter whilst two of the others stood guard. One of them spoke into a radio and then, in unison, both men looked toward the lighthouse.

Matt ducked, instantly, pressing his back against the wall. *Fuck! Fuck! They've seen me.* He held his hand to his chest as if trying to stop his heart from leaping out.

No they can't have seen me. It's dark in here and light out there. What if they did? They didn't. He argued with himself.

However, he had to check, and summing up all his will power, he slid back up the wall and peeked out: both men had produced their weapons and were running toward the house.

"Oh fuck! Fuck!" Matt breathed. Eyes wide with terror, he scanned the room for somewhere to hide. He looked up the stairs and without thinking, he mounted them two by two. He deliberated whether to try to hide in Blake's room but decided against it just as the front door clanged open. He sprinted, as quietly as possible, up the rest of the stairwell and entered Blake's office. He took in the room: the desk, the leather divan, swivel chair, and freestanding lamp in the corner. There was nowhere to hide in here!

The sound of footsteps marched up the stairwell.

He scampered under Blake's desk and found refuge against the modesty panel, the thin piece of wood being the only thing separating him from the intruders.

He strained hard to hear over the crashing surf and the idling chopper outside. They were ripping through the police tape and were rummaging in Blake's bedroom one floor below.

They did see me and now they are searching for me! Oh God, why? Who are they? What do they want? Oh Jesus, they are going to kill me!

Beads of perspiration appeared on his forehead as he heard footsteps in the stairwell again.

"Oh no." He drew his knees up, made a tight ball of his body and pressed back against the panel in the desk.

The footsteps entered the room. Matt held his breath as tears of sweat fell and exploded onto his jeans.

Footsteps walked over to the window.

Just one of them? Where's the other one? Probably waiting by the door, making sure I don't make a run for it. Or is he still searching downstairs? Oh God, please don't let them see me. Please! He squeezed his eyes shut and swallowed the dry sand dune that was his throat.

After a few seconds, he reopened his eyes to see black boots standing by the window. The tension was building, his lungs were bursting, his blood screamed for more oxygen. He started shaking. *No, no, he might hear you trembling. You might rattle the desk.* He squeezed his eyes shut again and willed the intruder to leave.

He got his wish. After a few interminable seconds, the black boots turned and left the room, clicking fast and loud down the stairwell. Then, the mumbling of voices and shortly after that, the sound of the front door slamming shut.

The whirring of the helicopter's engine increased as Matt, slowly, peeked around the corner of the desk. There was nobody there. He was alone.

Furtively and cautiously he left his hiding place and peeked out of the window just in time to see the last of the men enter the chopper and slide the door shut. Blake was nowhere to be seen. *He must be inside. Where are they taking him?*

The beating sound returned and then laboured until the helicopter was airborne once more. It ascended until it was nearly level with the window. Matt ducked as it swooped by the glass and glided out to sea, away from the lighthouse.

However, despite the fact that the chopper was flying further out to sea, the engine sound appeared to be getting nearer until, "Christ!" Matt yelled as another helicopter appeared from underneath the lighthouse. He was temporarily confused, and then it occurred to him, it was a different one, a twin. It circled the lighthouse a few times and then dipped sideways, disappearing down the coastal path, heading toward the shingled beach.

He watched as it landed a few feet away from someone down there. He could not make out who it was but saw them being escorted, like his friend, into the craft.

A few seconds later, it too was heading away from Stony Point and out to sea.

Thirty Three

Oil Tanker – Atlantic Ocean, 30 miles west of the Cornish coast 17:00 GMT

The isolation chamber was roughly 10 square feet wide and hermetically sealed. Its design was a customised version of those used by America's Centre for Research into Contagious Diseases. Linked to the chamber was a small cubicle the size of a telephone box, called DETOX. Anyone who worked inside the chamber was required to DETOX for a minimum of five minutes to allow their suits to undergo a cleansing process that was, in effect, a shower of an acid solution.

Inside his white space suit and with thick-gloved hands, Dr Harket injected the green contents of the syringe into the test tube, snapped a plastic lid over it and placed the phial inside a metal container, next to a dozen more.

"Is it true, doctor?" Peter, his young assistant asked, holding the box steady.

"Is what true?"

"That there's enough toxin in that small test tube to poison a whole city?"

"Alex, have you been teasing our new recruit again?" The doctor reproached without taking his eyes off the phial in front of him.

Peter looked up at a group of people who were watching the whole process from behind a wall of glass. At the centre of these was a gaunt looking twenty-year-old man with piercing blue eyes and a blonde ponytail who suppressed a laugh and said, "Me, Doctor? I would never do a thing like that."

"Oh no, of course not," The doctor smiled, turned to the young man and said, "You'll get used to him after a while. Alex is our resident joker. Besides, he lied to you. There is not enough in one of these measures to infect a whole city but there is enough to infect the whole of the British Isles."

The junior swallowed hard.

"But don't worry, you are perfectly safe inside that suit. Astronauts wear similar costumes to walk the surface of the moon. Now, could you put this," the doctor handed him a test tube containing newly transferred toxin, "into the decoder over there and start the analysis?"

The decoder was a machine used to analyse toxin samples. It resembled a photocopier, only it had a hollow interior designed to accommodate phials of all sizes. Once programmed it would begin a breakdown of the specimen and print out a list of components.

" Ok," Peter said apprehensively as sweat dampened his forehead. The helmet he was wearing was heavy and he was starting to feel claustrophobic.

Doctor Harket touched his arm, "It's alright. You are doing fine." He turned to the observers behind the glass, "Leave him alone."

Peter forced a smile and moved to leave but felt himself being pulled back as if someone had grabbed him by the back of his neck. It was his airline; a flexible hose connected to his helmet and to runners in the ceiling that provided constant, breathable air.

Instead of rolling freely, the airline was jammed. Peter leaned forward in an effort to free himself but could not. He tugged again in frustration for he knew he was being watched.

"Hey," It was Dr Harket tapping him on the shoulder, "Steady with that thing. You wouldn't want to rip a hole in your suit," he said, pulling gently on the hose to free it. "Alex, I thought you had the runners on these things checked."

"I did."

"Well, they obviously didn't do a good job as they keep sticking."

"Maybe he tugged too suddenly. They do tend to lock like seat belts if you pull too hard."

"Whatever. Just get the things looked at, will you? Mine did the same thing earlier."

"Yes, Doctor."

Harket tugged on the hose a couple of times and freed it, allowing Peter to lumber across the room with his airline trailing behind him like a giant umbilical cord.

Once on the other side, he lifted the analyser's lid, placed the measure inside a slot no bigger than a cutlery strainer and snapped the guards in place. He dialled in the sequence on the keypad and the analyser sprung to life. The whirring sound, not unlike that of a photocopier, was the sample being spun at high speed, ensuring that the final analysis was of the complete mixture and not just one of its components. However, after only a few seconds into the process, the monotonous drone shifted pitch and then stopped.

Peter looked at the display; all the lights were blinking. *Oh no. What's wrong with it? Don't ask them, they'll think you're incompetent.*

Nonetheless, he heard himself call, "Doctor Harket?"

"Yes?" The doctor replied without looking around.

"I think there is something wrong with the analyser."

"Such as?"

"All the lights are flashing," Peter replied calmly. He could have quite cheerfully banged the sides of the damn thing as one would a television but he reasoned that this was not a good idea given its deadly contents.

Dr Harket looked across at him as sniggering could be heard

over the intercom. Peter felt a burning sensation in his cheeks. The heat inside his helmet was already unbearable and he could now taste the salty flavour of sweat as it dribbled down from his forehead. God, he wanted so desperately to wipe his face.

"Hold on, I will be right over," Harket said, snapping the lid down on another phial. He looked up to see that the rest of the team were finding the whole thing very amusing. He also smiled inwardly and then turned to leave but was tugged back. "Alex," he said with irritation.

"Try moving forward slowly."

"I was."

"Try again, it should come free."

The doctor complied; it did not.

"Alex, I am going to suspend this session and bill the time to your target until you get these things fixed properly."

Alex lost his smile and barked," Hey Peter, since you can't get that thing to work, you may as well help the Doc free himself."

" Don't worry, I think I have it," Harket said, leaning forward on the airline, doing exactly what he had advised Peter not to do moments before.

Peter moved to aid the stricken man.

However, the doctor's patience was wearing thin. He reached up and tried to grab the airline at the back of his helmet but could not reach. Instead, he leaned harder and harder until it gave. However, the momentum that had built up was much more than expected and he stumbled forward, lost his balance and fell, smashing his visor on the corner of the table and knocking over a container of phials. Glass from the shattered helmet stabbed at his face, temporarily blinding him.

"Christ, Doctor! Are you okay?" Alex shouted over the intercom.

It took Harket a few minutes to get his bearings. He blinked back the blood from his eyes and tasted the coppery flavour as it dribbling over his lips.

It was Peter's turn to ask, "Doctor, are you all right?"

"Yes, I think so." Harket felt dizzy but he attributed it to the fall.

"Doctor?" It was Alex again. He and his colleagues were all

leaning forward into the glass window, trying to get a glimpse of the man. However, he had fallen behind the bench and all they could see was the back of his white space suit and Peter who was now standing over him.

Alex glanced at the black and white monitor bracketed to the wall above the glass but that did not offer a much better view. "You'd better decontaminate and get the hell out of there, doctor. Your suit could be breached."

"Here, let me help you to your feet," Peter said, extending a helping hand.

"Thank you," Harket replied, hauling himself into a kneeling position like a pregnant women.

"Hurry up, you moron!" Alex barked.

Peter was about to comply but stopped when he caught site of the overturned container on the desk. "Where's the phial?"

Some lay strewn on the desk but there were ten to a container and one was missing. "Oh my God." He brushed by the doctor's outstretched hand and began the search for it, leaving bloody footprints on the floor behind him.

Harket watched, incredulously, as the boy walked past him and began searching under desks and behind waste disposal units. "Peter. Peter, help me up," he asked, as he struggled to get to his feet. The suit was cumbersome and it was proving difficult.

"Peter, what the hell are you doing, you idiot!" Alex shouted. Then he added, calmly, "It's okay, Doctor, we're coming in." He reached for the red button that opened the chamber door.

"NO!"

All heads turned, it was Peter. He was in the corner of the chamber, crouching down with his back to them, staring at something on the floor.

Doctor Harket was now kneeling in a pool of his own blood, clutching the side of the table. It was then that Alex noticed his shattered visor, "Jesus Christ, Doctor. Are you okay?"

"I think so. Bit drowsy and hot, " Harket replied, blowing air out of his mouth as if to expel the heat.

"Get him out of there," Alex ordered.

"NO! You can't do that!" Peter cried, turning around. His visor was all steamed up, he was shaking and his face was wet with tears and perspiration. He watched as the doctor clumsily attempted to pull himself up from the floor.

Harket's face was burning, his hands and arms were itching and he felt that if he did not get out of this suit, he was going to spontaneously combust! "Help me here, Peter," he said, forcing an embarrassed laugh and grunting with the effort of trying to get to his feet. "I feel like a beached whale!"

" Help the doctor!" Alex ordered.

That was when the siren started and A looped recording announced, *"Warning, chamber contamination detected. Warning, chamber contamination detected."*

The computer in front of Alex bleeped and data levels on a digital graph rose, indicating a high level of contamination inside the chamber. "Oh fuck! Oh Christ!" He moaned, holding his hands helplessly over the keyboard like a witch doctor about to cast a spell. He looked at the black and white image on the monitor. Doctor Harket, his mentor, the scientist he aspired to be, was still struggling to get up off the floor whilst Peter just stood in the background holding a shattered test tube in his hands. He watched in horror.

Harket could feel it, the toxin was inside him, racing around his body, destroying and assimilating his antibodies, rotting his brilliant mind.

The lights dimmed as the voice announcement changed, *"Warning... contamination.... Initiating detoxification sequence in T minus 20 seconds... 19..."*

"Let him out!" Alex shouted.

"We can't let him out!" someone else retorted. "He is contaminated with the virus. The phial has been ruptured, the room is full of it!"

"These readings are off the scale!"

"15 seconds..."

"If we don't get them out of there, the detox is going to kill them both!"

"What about Peter? We've got to get Peter out!"

"He's safe in his suit!"

"No, he isn't. It will eat through it. Prolonged exposure is corrosive. Exposure time in the chamber is double the norm!"

"Don't tell me about my job! I know my job!" Alex screamed hysterically.

"10 seconds…"

"We've got to get Peter out!"

The room was a dissonance of shrilling alarms and screaming people. They were helpless as the computer counted down the inevitable.

Peter's face was dripping with perspiration. The blended images of his life flashed before him at supersonic speed. He pictured his family standing over his grave. His mother, white and dishevelled with a black headscarf tied around her head and his siblings weeping quietly.

There had to be a solution. He could live through this thing. In training there had seemed to be so many safety procedures. *Where were they all now?* There had to be a way.

" *5 seconds…*"

He looked at the broken test tube in his hand and dropped it. Maybe this was all a mistake. After all, he could not see or smell anything.

"3 seconds…"

Doctor Harket crashed to the floor once more. It felt as if his face was on fire, his lips were shrivelled dry and it felt as if an army of ants were marching under his skin. The world slowed down and all the voices came to him like the incantations of ancient demons. He could hear, over the sound of the buzzing alarms, Alex's voice calling to him but he could not understand what he was saying. All he could think about was water; cool sparkling drinking water for his parched lips.

The lights dimmed further and a red beacon flashed. Then there was a hissing sound from the ceiling above and a blanket of mist fell down, enveloping him and filling the chamber.

With astronaut footsteps, Peter walked forward through the detoxifying mist. After what seemed like an eternity, he reached the body on the floor. He believed he was dreaming. Surely what he saw was something that existed only in his darkest nightmares or in the most gruesome of horror stories. Alas, this was reality and he knew well what effect the mist had on human flesh.

He felt the vomit rise; deep from within his stomach and in a matter of seconds it was a lump in his throat and then a splatter on his visor. He stood, motionless, over the body of Doctor Harket who was on his back, screaming in agony and clawing at his bloody face that bubbled and blistered.

Outside, behind the protection of the glass wall, his team wept helplessly.

The nightmare scenario continued for over five minutes, until the body stopped twitching. The mist cleared and a rain of clear liquid washed over the chamber, pelting Peter's helmet and bathing the bloody corpse. Even now, as the solution rinsed the blood from the stump of flesh that was once the doctor's face, Peter could not move.

He stood motionless for the next ten minutes, oblivious to the other spacemen who entered the chamber to help him.

Thirty Four

Fifteen minutes had gone by since their abduction from Stony Point when the whirring of the helicopter decreased and the sickly butterfly feeling of a fairground ride gripped the passengers and the craft began to descend.

The journey had been a silent one. Blake had bombarded them with questions but his abductors remained tight-lipped with eyes of stone. Whoever they were, they appeared to be extremely disciplined and methodical.

Maybe they are from the military. Perhaps an elite division like MI5. Maybe they are MI5. What do they want with me?

There was a jolt as they touched the ground and two of Blake's escorts stood up. One of them pressed a green button and the door swished open, dazzling them all with daylight and dousing them with the fresh scent of the sea.

The escorts stepped out of the helicopter and flanked the open door as Blake followed them out. However, nothing could have prepared him for what he saw.

The other helicopter was hovering overhead, negotiating a slow descent as Blake took in his surroundings. The copper coloured deck blended into the horizon as the ship sliced its way through the Atlantic Ocean.

The oil tanker was approximately 967 feet long and 160 feet wide, with a network of pipes running the length of the ship toward the bow and merging with two mammoth oil conduits, each the size of a small terraced house. Nearby, were two giant Electro-hydraulic anchors and two 10-ft. weather-grey winches.

Dwarfing him was a glowing white T shaped control tower. Set astern of the two large helipads, it loomed 32 feet high with giant portholes.

Blake was in awe of the magnitude of the vessel. "Where are we?" he gasped as the wind snatched the words from his mouth. If Blake was expecting a reply from his escorts, none came.

The men stood legs apart, steadying themselves against the wild Atlantic gale and the turbulence of the second helicopter as it touched down nearby. It was not long before its doors swished open and a confused Sky stepped out, squinting at the light and snatching her arm away from her escort.

"Sky!" Blake shouted, running over to meet her.

"Blake!"

"Are you alright?" he asked, as she dove into his arms.

"Yes, I think so." She remained buried for a few seconds and then, sensing the swaying motion of the ship, she emerged to scan her surroundings. "Where are we?"

"I don't know, some kind of oil tanker."

"This way, please," one of the men piped up.

"Oh, so you can speak then." Blake said.

"Where are we?" Sky demanded. "Why have you brought us here?"

"This way," the man repeated, taking her arm.

Blake boiled over, slapped the man's hand off her, and squared up for a confrontation as a trio of crewmembers rushed over to assist. The men in black did not need to say a word as their threatening demeanour said it all but Blake Hudson wasn't going to back down.

Sky knew this and tugged, fretfully, at his arm. "Blake…"

He looked at her; the wind was tossing her black hair about her face. Blake relaxed his stance.

"This way, please," the man repeated.

Sky threw him a look of utter contempt and stepped forward.

They were escorted across the ship, passing giant pulleys, thick ropes, pipes, and more men in black jump suits and caps.

"Why do I get the feeling that these people aren't fishermen?" she said.

"Maybe because they aren't," Blake replied loudly, hoping for a reaction from one of them but none came. The man walked in silence with military discipline.

They descended a flight of steps.

The ship was not very well maintained. Paint was peeling off some of the doors and railings and the upper deck was weather worn and in desperate need of refurbishment.

They passed through a hatch that led into a small, dingy room. There, one of the men pulled open a wooden door that revealed a set of elevator doors. He swiped what looked like a credit card through the slot provided and they swished open.

The man pointed inside the elevator and Blake and Sky entered without hesitating, followed closely by their escorts. After a few seconds, the doors shut and they descended, deep into the bowels of the ship.

The ride was short and when the doors opened again, it was as if they had travelled into the future. It was another world down here. Gone was the dilapidated grey deck and in its place was a gleaming spaceship.

They were walking down a long, clinically white, corridor. The lighting was dim and their journey aided only by low-level illumination similar to those used on aeroplanes.

Nobody uttered a word as their footsteps reverberated around them. Blake and Sky exchanged continuous glances, both incredulous of their surroundings. They passed a selection of locked doors, marked private and branded with alphanumeric codes.

After a minute or so, they came to a junction. From the ceiling hung a sign that read:

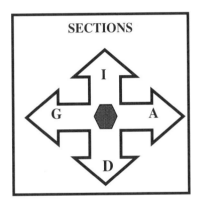

They turned right, into A Sector and stopped at a pair of large sliding doors, guarded by two armed men. The guards eyed the group suspiciously.

Blake slipped a comforting arm around Sky's shoulders as one of their escorts flashed an ID at the guards and then at the camera above the doors. Within seconds, they hummed open and a dissonant wave of bleeping sounds, phones ringing and a gentle babble of voices swept over them. They were in the ship's control centre.

In keeping with the rest of the vessel, the lighting was low, accentuated by the glow of an array of monitors set into walls and on desktops.

As the group walked into the centre of the room the first thing they noticed was a giant screen on the wall opposite. It measured approximately 10 x 20ft and displayed a digital green map similar to that of Blake's meteorological program. A bank of much smaller screens displaying endless scrolling data framed it.

"This way," their escort prompted and indicated a short flight of stairs that led up, above the control room. Blake followed but could not take his eyes off the green map. Along with the wind trajectory, cloud formation and county dividers, it showed a trail of red blobs leading from inland Exeter out to sea.

At the top of the stairs, they were ushered into a relatively small office. The walls were padded, giving the impression that they were soundproofed. A computer sat on a large desk to one side of the room whilst on the opposite side was a large tinted wall of glass overlooking the control room.

By the window, were leather divans and seated on these were two men: a burly man in a naval uniform and another in a white coat. Standing nearby, was a tall thin man who gazed at the forever changing data on the large screen as he talked on a cordless phone. He had his back to them.

"Sir," one of the men in black announced as both he and his partner stood to attention.

The man finished his telephone conversation at his leisure and then turned around. He looked well groomed and the navy blue suit he wore was obviously tailored as it hung perfectly from his thin frame. He could not have been more than fifty years of age, with slicked back grey hair and spectacles. He smiled with all the charm of a cobra and said, in a public school intonation, "Here you are. I was beginning to think you'd got lost." He tapped the tip of the cordless phone with long bony fingers.

He glanced at the two men in black and smiled. Instantly, they turned on their heels and left the room.

"Welcome aboard. I'm Williamson," the man said, extending a greeting hand.

On cue, the two men on the divans, rose from their seats, exchanged glances with Williamson and left the room without saying a word.

Williamson nodded after the two men. "Doctors and officers, geniuses at their craft but seriously lacking in social skills. Oh no offence, Doctor McPherson," he added quickly, patting Sky on the arm.

Sky smiled disarmingly whilst wondering what this socialite was doing here.

"Why have you brought us here?" Blake asked.

Williamson's smile disappeared momentarily.

He took his time and then said, casually, "You already know why, Mr Hudson."

"I do?"

Williamson moved over to his desk and took a seat on the large leather chair behind it. He gestured to the divans next to the window, "Please, take a seat."

"We'd rather stand," Sky said. She already disliked this man, intensely. He enthused a certain smugness that made her want to slap his face. "And whilst we are standing, we'd appreciate an answer."

"You were about to make a mistake," Williamson said casually.

"Such as?"

"Mr Hudson was about to cause unnecessary panic."

Blake laughed. "I'm not sure I follow."

"Warning those people would only have caused more mayhem."

Blake frowned.

Williamson continued, "It's not the rain that kills them, Mr Hudson. They kill themselves."

So there is something in the rain. "Oh well, that's all right then."

"Your initiative was commendable, yet would have proved futile. Your goal, if you will excuse the pun, was to stop the game. However, you know as well as me that the rain is not a living entity but a meteorological phenomenon. It cannot decide where and on whom it will precipitate. You may have saved most of the lives of the spectators at the game but what about the rest of the population? You would have succeeded in saving a minority but would have caused mass panic for millions of others."

"Who exactly are you?" Sky cut in.

"Who I am is of no importance but my objectives are."

"And what are your objectives?" she asked.

"To ensure that this incident is cleared up quickly and quietly."

"And how are you proposing to do that?"

"By waiting."

"For more people to die?" Blake asked.

Williamson ignored Blake's flippant remark and said, "For the cloud to disperse." He rose from his seat and moved over to the window and with his back to them continued, "We have been tracking it ever since the accident." He gazed at the green display on the control room wall. "It wasn't until it entered British air space that we discovered its power."

"What accident?" Blake asked.

Williamson did not reply.

Then, it occurred to Blake, "You knew about this all along."

"It was meant to be a revolutionary drug for the treatment of psychological disorders," Williamson continued. "A drug that would astir the dormant side of a disabled brain or heal a scarred one. Seven years in the making, hours of tests, millions on research and nothing but then…" Williamson paused, deliberately adding drama to the moment before turning around, quivering with excitement, "It all goes up in smoke. Never in my wildest dreams could I have imagined such a Godsend!" Williamson's eyes were wide and his face held all the excitement of a mad scientist.

"So, what went wrong?" Blake asked, cynically.

Williamson ignored him. "Like most major scientific breakthroughs, it happened by accident. The drug was released into the atmosphere. It appears that alone, it is a cure but, like a variety of chemicals, when mixed it is lethal. We know that the NO_2 and the NOX are two of the most dangerous pollutants in our atmosphere. Somehow, these and our drug have amalgamated, aided by the moisture in a cumulous nimbus cloud, to produce an unprecedented toxin that returns to earth in the form of precipitation. This is then absorbed into the blood stream, through the epidermis." Williamson noticed the equivocal look on Sky's face, "You're sceptical, Dr McPherson?"

"There is no recorded bacteria capable of penetrating an intact epidermis."

"Who said it was a bacteria?"

"The toxicology reports."

"With all due respect Doctor, what you mistook for bacteria was just the remains of the victims own antibodies." Williamson had that glint of excitement in his eyes once more. "The body's antigens produce antibodies as a defence against foreign bacteria such as the common cold. In most cases, it defeats the invading cells, and every war has its casualties."

Sky suppressed a disbelieving laugh, "You're implying that the foreign cells we picked up were in fact normal antigens?"

"What else could they be?" Williamson asked, laconically.

"We couldn't identify them."

"Exactly. So, with all due respect, Doctor, how do you know if what your screening picked up wasn't just the remnant of the victim's own antibodies?"

"Because, we would have identified them as such."

"Not if they had metamorphosed."

"Into what?" *What is this lunatic talking about?*

"Into a permutation of the drug."

She stared at him. "That's impossible."

Williamson just maintained her gaze, his thin lips creased into a faint smile.

"Hang on a minute." It was Blake now. "You just implied that this thing wasn't a bacterium."

"It isn't. It starts out as a chemical. A solution conceived by the environment's corruption and our drug. When this is absorbed into the blood stream of a living animal, it triggers the defence system, antigens create antibodies and the battle begins. As the war rages on around the host's body, the toxin rushes to the brain, hitching a ride on the blood stream. There, the drug element begins to stimulate areas of the brain. Only, now it is contaminated with something else. The result is violence and homicidal tendencies. However, as I said earlier, the toxin is weak and eventually destroyed by the antibodies. Hence why most of the victims who are restrained make a perfect recovery."

"If you have all this information, why aren't you releasing it to the public?" Blake asked.

"Because this is not a matter of public interest."

"No?"

"No," Williamson said, firmly.

"Then in whose interest is it?" It was Sky asking the question.

"Why, the government's, of course."

There was silence.

Blake was incredulous, "You're saying that the government has known about this thing all along?"

"There are some things that the public are better off not knowing."

"Such as?"

"Such as matters of national security."

Blake laughed.

"The importance of national security amuses you, Mr Hudson?"

"No, but hypocrisy does. You profess to protect the public by withholding information about a drug that could kill them. Something that you created!"

" If only. If only I could take credit for such a magnificent force. Admittedly, I did head the team that developed the original drug. Alas, none of them made it out of the explosion. A gargantuan set back for the corporation. They were some of the best pharmaceutical brains in the world. It would have taken millions of pounds and years to replace them and the project was cancelled until now. Until they saw its real potential."

"You are...."

"Mad? Don't you find that old cliché rather tedious? Every time someone expresses ambition or total dedication to science they are labelled *mad*. Could it be that your average human being is intellectually incapable of comprehending the thrill of discovery, the rush of uncovering something that will change the destiny of our world?"

"By turning us on each other?" Sky asked.

"On the contrary. If we can learn to harness the power of the Nimbus cloud..."

"What for? Biological warfare?"

Williamson met her gaze. His eyes betrayed his suppressed

excitement.

As reality bit, Sky uttered, "My God, you really are insane." She was incensed but controlling her emotions, she continued, "If there is one thing that history has taught us, it's that man is incapable of controlling nature."

Williamson did not respond immediately and looked out over the control room once more.

Then, without looking at them, he said, "As much as the concept is abhorrent to you, from a scientific point of view, you must be able to appreciate the brilliance of the concept."

"You mean the fact that once you unleash it, you can't do a thing to control it. Oh yes, brilliant." Blake sneered.

"Even nature is indiscriminate."

"I'm sorry, I didn't realise you were trying to mimic nature here."

"No, Doctor, we are just trying to safeguard the future of nature and the world."

"By developing another deadly biological weapon. I'm sorry but haven't most governments been down this road and failed? And where exactly were you when we agreed to ban the biological option?" Blake asked.

"We?" Williamson turned to face them. "We didn't decide on anything. It was decided by a bunch of weak-minded bureaucrats who believed that peace could be achieved by rhetoric alone. What they failed to realise is that the best foundation for peace is the fear of war."

"Try telling that to people like Sadham Hussein," Sky snapped.

"That is precisely my point," Williamson said.

"What exactly is your point?" Blake asked. "Instead of trying to disarm Hussein, we create bigger?"

"Not bigger, Mr. Hudson, more efficient. Can't you see that something like this could be the solution in dealing with extremist such as Hussein? An invisible force that infiltrates enemy lines and turns them on each other."

"But you have no control over it," Sky said in astonishment.

"With time, we will develop more control."

"You mean you still haven't learned your lesson with this

disaster?"

"Let's not be naïve, Mr Hudson. You know as well as me that if we don't continue this research, our enemies will. Deterrents are the best...."

"... Defence. So you keep saying," Sky interrupted. "Correct me if I am wrong, but wasn't that the theory of the two super powers not so long ago? And what are we left with now? One of them in such economical and political disarray that there is no telling whose hands those...those..." Sky faltered, bristling with frustration. "Weapons of mass destruction are going to end up in. The whole world is sitting on a political time bomb and...." Sky paused here. Suddenly, she was seeing images of her parents. *How horrified they would be if they could hear this fanatic*. It was now, in this very moment that she realised that they were not aimless campaigners but prophets. They had seen the future. They had seen the world that future generations would inherit, a world of ecological uncertainty where nature and man battle for domination.

"Sky?"

...Surely we could do better for ourselves.

"Sky?"

...Surely we could learn from our mistakes.

"Sky!"

The mist cleared from her mind and she could see Blake now. He was standing in front of her, shaking her back into the room.

"Are you all right?"

"Yes, of course," she said, dazed.

"You're trembling, are you sure?"

"Yes. I told you, I'm fine," she said, forcing a faint smile. Then, turning to Williamson, she said, "The world has a right to know what you are doing here."

"Dr McPherson, you are mistaken if you think that this is the only project your government has undertaken without the people's knowledge. I can tell you stories about your everyday existence that would make your hair stand on end but, for your own safety, you are denied this information."

Williamson walked over to them. Take the B.S.E scandal. This was a public relations disaster for Great Britain but someone, like me for example, had to make the decision whether or not to inform you."

"What? With all due respect, that statement is arrogant to say the least. You had no choice in the matter. People were dying just as they are now. You had no choice, you had to release the information then just like you have to release it now."

Williamson laughed and Sky could have followed through with her urge to slap him.

"And affording you the same respect, Doctor, you are naïve if you think the facts were made available to you as soon as they emerged."

"What are you saying?"

"I am not saying anything that you don't already know but choose to ignore because it suits you to. By voting for your government you are agreeing to charge them with the burden of running your nation and they can only do this by making decisions that you may not always agree with but, as leaders, feel are necessary.

"Like manufacturing a deadly virus that you have no control over?" Blake asked.

Williamson was about to reply but stopped in mid sentence when he noticed a presence in the doorway. Peter was standing there. His face was pale, his hair mottled and drenched with perspiration.

Williamson forced a smile. "Peter, good of you to join us. We have been looking for you everywhere."

"I needed some time to think," Peter replied, his face expressionless. "I need to talk to you."

"Of course. I will come over to see you as soon as I have finished here," he said, motioning to his guests.

"Now," Peter said forcefully, taking a step further into the room.

Williamson was calm. "As I said, as soon as I am…"

"NOW! I need to see you now. Dr Harket is dead!"

Williamson smiled apologetically at his guests and moved to the back of his desk. "Very well."

Behind his desk, Williamson pretended to fumble in one of his drawers and whilst he did so, pressed a red button concealed under the desktop.

"I just need to take this down with me," he said, producing a white folder full of printed documents.

"I tried to save him, but I couldn't," Peter continued as Williamson made his way toward him.

"I know, Peter. And there was nothing you or anyone could have done to save him."

"But I was there. I was right next to him I could have…" he broke off to wipe his forehead with the sleeve of his white jacket.

That was when Blake noticed the black rim around the young man's sunken eyes.

The two armed guards rushed Peter from behind but he was ready for them and in one swift motion he swung around with his right hand, snatched the automatic revolver out of the first guard's hand, pushing the man back with his left. Guard number two stopped in his tracks as he saw the revolver training its aim between him and his colleague.

Peter chuckled. "Pretty impressive, huh?" he said, aiming at Williamson for fun. The sweat was pouring down the young man's face and it seemed that his appearance worsened by the second. He wiped his brow with his left sleeve. He did not feel well. He felt hot and his flesh was tingling. There was an itching sensation under his skin as if his blood was throbbing, boiling, and he felt energised, so energised he could run a marathon or scale Everest. He was ready; ready for anything the world could throw at him. If only he could get rid of the dull ache in his temple and this desire for revenge.

"Put the gun down, Peter," Williamson coaxed.

"Why should I?" he asked, swinging the weapon around at each individual present in the room. When he came across Sky he asked, "What are you doing here?" as if he knew her of old.

Sky was momentarily startled but said, "Ask him." She nodded at Williamson.

"They are my guests," Williamson replied.

"Really? Are you going to carry out your experiments on them too?" Peter asked.

Williamson said nothing.

"What, you have nothing to say?"

"Only that you should put down the weapon and let us treat you, Peter. You are unwell."

"Really?"

"Yes, you are."

Peter laughed. "I know and it feels so good. Hmm…" He moaned with pleasure. "You wanted to know what it's like, Doctor? I'll tell you what it's like. It's like taking a thousand speed tablets all at once. What a rush! I feel I can take on the world now. I feel like I could put a bullet in your head and not even flinch."

That was where Blake had seen that look before. He recalled that stormy night at the lighthouse; Clare Harrison was there, with her hands around his throat, her eyes wide and full of hatred for him. The rain had infected this man, as it had her. *Oh God, Sky.* He glanced across at her.

"Your toxin killed the one man who truly believed in me," Peter continued.

"I believe in you, Peter. The program believes in you. We need your help to carry on where Harket left off," Williamson cooed.

"Really?"

"Of course."

Peter laughed and wiped his brow again. "You must think I am stupid," he hissed, thrusting the gun in Williamson's direction. "You don't need me. You've got Alex."

"Alex did not work as closely with Dr Harket as you did. He could never know as much as you do."

Peter liked that. He smiled.

"Yes, no more bullying, Peter. You will be the one in charge. You'll be the one with the power."

"Exactly."

"So, are you going to put that gun down and let us treat you before the toxin takes a hold."

Peter threw his head back and laughed.

By this time, the whole control room could hear him and many stopped what they were doing to watch events as they unfolded.

The balcony bars and the panelling on the wall obscured the view from the control room floor. The only thing that could be seen were the backs of the guards as they stood in the doorway.

Peter's laughter was infectious and some of the staff began to smile along, a group of them hovered at the foot of the stairs, all of them unable to see exactly what was taking place in the office above them.

The laughing continued for about twenty seconds and then Peter suddenly stopped, looked at Williamson and solemnly said, "Do you want to know something, doctor?"

"What?"

"It already has."

With that, he took aim and casually shot guard number one in the head. The bullet pierced the man's forehead and emerged from the back of his skull, bringing with it fragments of bone and brain spraying the crowd below.

There was screams from the control room, Sky held her hand to her mouth as Blake stared incredulously.

The guard went down as Peter squeezed off two more shots at guard number two. The first bullet hit him in the face and the second in the chest. The impact propelled the man over the railing.

It was now or never. As Peter was busy surveying his deed, Blake ran at him, slamming him against the wall and knocking the gun out of his hand, momentarily dazing him.

Then, he grabbed Sky's hand and they ran for the stairs and descended rapidly as another duo of guards climbed to meet them. Again, Blake's only thought was to protect Sky and if he had to kill someone, he would.

He kicked the oncoming guard in the face, sending the man reeling backward down the stairs, toppling his colleagues like bowling pins.

They stepped over the fallen men and ran for the door.

Meanwhile, Williamson, slightly shaken by recent events, was back behind his desk, frantically pressing the intercom on his phone.

"Get help in here, now!"

Then he fumbled under his desk, within seconds, produced a small revolver, and held it up in defence. He scanned the whole room, holding the gun with outstretched arms but there was nobody there. The sound of footsteps was heard running up the stairs, he took aim but relaxed when he saw a group of puzzled guards staring at him.

Williamson sat back in his chair and smiled. He had come face to face with the madness of the rain and its power was awesome.

Thirty Five

They emerged from the control room, still hand in hand. "Where to now?" Sky asked, breathlessly.

"I don't know," Blake replied, looking around.

To their right, were two sealed hanger-like doors and to their left, a long, dimly lit corridor that led into darkness. Ahead seemed the only option.

"This way!" he said, breaking into a run but voices and running footsteps could be heard up ahead, "Shit! Maybe not."

They stopped abruptly, turned on their heels, and ran down the corridor that led into darkness.

After running for about 30 seconds, they approached another pair of doors outside of which stood two armed guards. They skidded to a halt once more. "Jesus," Blake mumbled under his breath as he watched. One of guards was talking into a radio.

In that moment, both sentries looked up and began running towards them.

"What are we going to do?" Sky asked, through clenched teeth, glancing toward the approaching men and then back up the corridor from whence they had come.

Blake weighed up the chances of overpowering them but dismissed the idea. Both men were armed and he could not afford to take any risks with Sky. No, they would have to turn themselves in. Therefore, as the two men neared, he held up his hands in a peaceful gesture. However, much to his astonishment, the two men ran straight past them and it was not long before they had disappeared up the corridor, toward the control room.

"What…?"

"They must be heading for Williamson's office."

"Couldn't have created a better diversion if I had tried," Blake joked.

Sky said nothing. She was still shocked by the massacre she had just witnessed.

"Come on," Blake said, moving forward.

They stepped through the now unguarded doors and were not surprised to when they emerged into another long corridor. They ran for a minute or so and the monotonous architecture continued. Blake opened a few doors but they revealed nothing more than storage rooms.

"There must be a way out of here," he muttered, trying yet another door.

"Yes Blake, but what do we do when we get there? We are on a ship!" Sky said, through gasps.

"We'll worry about that at the time."

They reached another fire door with a glass panel in it. They had come across a few of these, dividing the corridors into small train-like compartments. A swipe card panel, mounted on the wall nearby, controlled each door. Luckily, the spy lights had all glowed green, including this one. Blake pulled it open.

"Blake," Sky caught his arm. "What are we doing?"

"Well," he began, checking back down the corridor. "Last time I looked we were running for our lives."

"Yes, but running where? It seems to me that we are just moving deeper and deeper into the ship."

"So, What's your prognosis, Doc?"

"Maybe we should turn back. At least we know where we came from."

"Oh right. So, you fancy meeting up with one of those trigger-happy psychos, do you? Who knows, we might even bump into that Peter guy. Yeah, he certainly looked like he was game for a laugh."

Sky sighed, frustrated at Blake's flippant tone."

Blake noticed this. "Look, I am sorry. I don't mean to sound sarcastic. It's just, well, what happened back there sort of freaked me out."

Sky looked up. "Me too. I don't think I will ever forget the look on that man's face. You seemed to cope well. Must be all those Bond films you keep watching."

Blake smiled. "Well, they say that films are educational. Now, can we move on? I am starting to feel just a tad exposed standing in the middle of the corridor." Blake moved through the door.

"Just tell me one thing."

He stopped.

"How do you know that we aren't walking into even more trouble?" she asked.

Blake was pensive for a few seconds. "Well, uh... I don't."

"Great." Sky nodded. "Thanks, I feel much better now."

She followed him through into the next corridor. This section was much smaller. At the far end stood another glass-panelled door, above it, a large black sign read, *"RESTRICTED ACCESS-AUTHORISED PERSONNEL ONLY."*

"What is this, Journey to the Centre of the Earth?" Blake remarked.

"It certainly feels like it. What do you think is behind that door?" Sky asked.

"I don't know," Blake said, staring at the sign. "Why don't we find out?"

Sky caught his arm. "Do you think that's a good idea?" She asked apprehensively.

Blake sensed her mood. "I'll make a deal with you." He pointed, "If there isn't any sign of a way out beyond that door we'll turn back, okay?"

"Okay."

However, as they neared the door, the sound of talking and approaching footsteps could be heard. They were trapped.

Back in the control room, the two guards rushed forth and joined the group already huddled at the foot of the stairs. The room was a hive of activity. The bodies, now zipped into black bags, were being hauled onto stretchers.

Upstairs, in Williamson's office, were two cleaners in yellow overalls. One was cleaning the blood splatter from the office windows whilst the other was steaming the rug.

Downstairs, Williamson was deep in conversation with the colonel.

"I told you, bringing them here was a mistake," the colonel said.

"What happened was not their fault."

"No, it's yours."

"I don't answer to you," Williamson snapped.

"No, you answer to the board and they are not going to be pleased when they hear that you introduced two complete strangers to this installation."

"Would you rather they had gone to the authorities?"

"No one would have believed them."

"Perhaps. But were you prepared to take that risk?" Williamson challenged.

The colonel did not reply. Instead, he looked expectantly at the technician in front of him. The man was sitting in front of a bank of monitors, each one displaying a collection of closed circuit images from around the ship. He worked the keyboard, causing a flickering slide show on all screens.

"Besides, I was under the impression that you gave the order to have them abducted."

The colonel looked up, seething. "Yes, I did. But the plan wasn't to bring them back here."

"You may be a killer, Colonel, but I certainly am not, I am a scientist."

" I wonder if you would be so sanctimonious if you had to choose between your precious project or ordering the death of someone."

Williamson was about to reply but was interrupted by the technician.

"Sir."

"Have you found them?" he asked, looking over the man's shoulders.

"We've found Peter, Sir. But still no sign of the other two."

"Well they can't have disappeared into thin air. Keep looking!" the colonel bellowed.

"Where is Peter?" Williamson asked, ignoring the colonel's outburst.

"Here, Sir." The man pointed to one of the monitors, showing Peter swiping his card to open a door and disappearing through it and off the screen. "He is in sector G, warehousing, near the engine room."

"Mirkoff." The Colonel barked at a nearby sentry. "Take those men and as many others as you deem necessary to bring him back dead or alive. He is armed so don't take any chances."

"Have you taken leave of your senses?" Williamson scowled. "The level of toxin in that chamber was off the scale. No human has ever been exposed to such a high dose. Statistically, he should have suffered an embolism or massive thrombosis by now. It is imperative that we examine him to learn more about how his body is coping."

"Fine, once my men have apprehended him, you can carry out all the experiments you like."

"No, you don't understand." Williamson grasped the colonel's arm. "I need him alive."

"And you will get him alive, just as long as he doesn't try anything stupid with my men. If he does then they will have to protect themselves." The colonel glanced at Williamson's hand, which still clasped his arm.

Williamson let go and turned to look at the monitors. *Please Peter*, he thought, *don't make these extremists kill you.* The screen showed the man walking down a corridor, still clutching a gun in his right hand. A caption at the foot of the screen read, *"Warehouse, sector G."*

The rest of the monitors were still flipping through rooms, corridors, and the deck as if they were photos in an album.

A few minutes flickered by.

"Where the hell could they have gone?" The colonel demanded.

"They could be inside one of the storage rooms, Sir."

"Well, screen all the rooms."

"I can't, Sir."

"Why not?"

"Because the cameras only come online if there is lighting in the room," Williamson interjected, without taking his eyes off the scrolling images.

"Another one of your ideas, Doctor?" The colonel asked, sarcastically.

"As a matter of fact, yes. Not much point looking at a pitch black room now, is there." Williamson smirked.

"He's just about to move into sector H," the technician said, to no one in particular.

"The engine room?" Williamson asked.

"Yes, Sir."

Then, as realisation dawned, Williamson shouted, "Seal the door!"

The technician tapped on his keyboard. The console in front of him bleeped and the words *"Area contained"* flashed up on the monitor.

"What's going on, Williamson?" The colonel asked.

"He is heading toward the engine room.

"So?"

"So, he is loaded with the toxin. He is capable of anything."

The Colonel sighed and snatched a up his radio. "Mirkoff... Cancel previous orders. Do not attempt to apprehend. The suspect is dangerous... shoot to kill... I repeat... shoot to kill."

"Sir?" It was the technician.

"Yes," Williamson responded.

"The engine room."

"What about it?"

"Well, the gun...."

Williamson eyes widened. "Yes, oh my God, you are right."

"What?" The colonel asked.

"Call your men back."

"Why?"

"Call your men back."

"I asked you why?"

"Because if you don't, we will all be killed!"

Thirty Six

The footsteps were getting closer and Blake snatched Sky's arm and dragged her into one of the nearby rooms. The lights were out; they slipped behind the door and froze there, breathing as quietly as they could.

They heard the swish of the corridor door and then footsteps. There was the sound of two male voices, both of them talking animatedly, but Blake could not understand what was being said. He squinted in the gloom of the room and, aided by the sliver of light that flooded through the crack in the door, he could see the puzzled expression on Sky's face as she strained hard to hear what they were saying. It took a few seconds for them to realise that these people were not talking in subdued tones but in a different language! There was a guttural sound to their words. Blake was not sure but it sounded of Scandinavian origin.

In that moment, there was shouting from a third voice. The two men stopped talking and the scuff of heels was heard as they stood to attention.

The third voice barked something in an angry, foreign tone. Then, in unison, both men shouted, "Yes, Sir."

"Now, get out of here!" The third voice ordered, this time, in perfect English.

There was more scuffing of heels and footsteps, as the two men disappeared further down the corridor.

There was silence. *Where is the third man? Had he gone?* Almost a minute had gone by and Blake held his hand to his lips. He watched as Sky's shadow, nodded in acknowledgement. *Someone is out there.* She too, could sense the presence.

More seconds went by as they held their breaths, waiting for the sound of the third pair of shoes to walk away but it did not come. They stared at the light that streamed through the crack in the door. It dimmed as a shadow fell over it.

Blake was trembling with tension. *What if he's armed? How can I take him on? I have the element of surprise although Sky is standing in front of me. It's freezing in here, that's why I am shivering, or is it because I am terrified we are going to get caught?* His whole body was trembling and he could have yelped when there was sudden movement nearby. Sky was moving, as quietly as she could, from behind the door to flank his left side.

The door swung open, nearly squashing Blake's nose. The lights came on. They both stopped breathing. Their hearts hammered.

Sky squeezed her eyes shut as Blake clasped her hand.

The seconds that felt like minutes ticked by and that is when Blake noticed it, directly in front of him, like a sleeping ghost on an aluminium bed. It lay motionless as the presence hovered in the doorway.

Perspiration dampened their faces despite the cold in this room. Sky's heart felt as if it were going to erupt from her chest. The room was so quiet that they could hear the person, whoever he was, breathing as he surveyed the room. His suspicion obviously aroused by the open door.

Sky's eyes were still tightly closed and remained that way even after the lights went out and the door was pulled shut.

Blake could have wept with relief when he heard the sound of footsteps walking away and the swish of a door, somewhere, opening and closing.

In the deathly silence of the darkness, they both let out noisy breaths and hungrily sucked in the gelid air into their lungs.

After a couple of minutes Sky spoke, " My God, Blake."

"I know," he said, still trying to rationalise if what he had seen was real; if he was really standing in a freezing dark room with a corpse laid out on an aluminium bed in front of him.

"I am shaking," Sky said.

"You didn't see it, did you?" Blake asked.

"See what?"

Breathing in short shallow breaths, Blake groped his way across the wall to the light switch and flipped it on, revealing a large rectangular room with fitted cupboards, a big aluminium washbasin, and two gurneys; one was empty whilst on the other lay a body with a white sheet draped over it.

It took Sky a few moments to adjust to the light and then she saw. "What on earth..." She breathed, and without hesitating, moved over to it. Blake flinched at her casual approach, forgetting, momentarily, that this is what she did for a living.

Slipping automatically into pathologist mode, she grabbed a pair of surgical gloves out of a nearby box and slipped them on. Then, without hesitation, she pulled back the sheet from the face of the cadaver.

"My God," she breathed, looking down at the man. His jet-black hair was in stark contrast to his bleached white features. She bent closer to get a better look at his face whilst Blake tentatively joined her.

Most of the dead man's forehead was missing; instead, there was a huge crimson gash. "This man has massive laceration to the forehead and…." she trailed off peering closely. Something was glinting from within the congealed flesh wound, "It looks as if there is something in here."

She looked around the room and saw a tray full of surgical instruments. From there, she retrieved a pair of forceps and used them to pick out one of the many minuscule fragments. She held it up to the light, "Looks like glass."

She turned her attention back to the corpse before her. Dr McPherson had forgotten everything that had happened minutes before and was back at work, meticulously analysing dead bodies for evidence of what had put them in this terminal state.

She probed the dark discoloration around the temple and nose with her fingers. "This level indentation here, and these fragments would suggest that this wound was inflicted by a very heavy glass object."

"Such as?"

"I don't know. It's hard to tell.

Blake looked closely but he could not see anything abnormal.

Whatever it was, it was flat and hard. See how disjointed his nose is?" Sky pointed.

"What, like a window or something?" Blake suggested.

"Could be, perhaps a glass door."

"Like the one outside?"

She looked at him, paused, "Yes, like the one outside."

"So, no evidence of foul play?" Blake said, flippantly.

"It's hard to tell."

She took one of the corpse's hands and carefully studied it, looking under the nails.

"What are you doing?" Blake asked, glancing around them.

"Looking at…"

"Don't tell me, if he was assaulted and defended himself, there would be bruises and such like on his hands. Along with traces of his assailant's skin under his finger nails."

"Actually, I was checking his manicured nails. Whatever this man did for a living, it wasn't hard labour." Then, looking up at him, she added, "And, you're right. I cannot see any obvious signs of a struggle. But what is this man doing here, Blake?"

"I don't know. But what I do know is that we shouldn't be in here performing autopsies."

"Yes, I agree." She pulled off the glove and threw it into a nearby waste bin. "What do you think this is all about?"

"Not sure exactly but I do think that Williamson and his cronies are responsible for all those people that died as a direct result of that contaminated rain."

"Why do you think he brought us here?"

"I don't know, maybe because we know too much. Lets face it, if I had gone to the police they would have started asking questions."

"Maybe, but then again, you don't have any evidence." Blake went to speak but Sky talked over him. "The only evidence we have is circumstantial."

"Why don't you say that a bit louder, I think the guards out there might have an opinion. Jesus Sky, after everything that has happened to us you still doubt?"

"No, of course I don't doubt what has happened. I am just wondering what we have to corroborate our story. It's all so incredible."

"No more incredible than a military installation masquerading as an oil tanker."

"Exactly or…"

"Or someone tapping my phone."

"Someone tapped your phone?"

"How do you think they knew where we were?"

Sky gasped. "Are you sure?"

"Well, I didn't think anything of it at the time but in hindsight it all seems so clear. I was calling Public Health and…" Reality dawned. "Christ, I thought it was just a faulty line but it went dead as soon as I got through. They were listening in and cut the connection before I got a chance to say anything."

"Blake…"

"No, it's true. Ask Matt, he was there too." Blake's eyes widened. "Matt!"

"What about him?"

"He was at the house."

"When they came for you?"

" Yes."

"Well, what happened to him?"

"I don't know. They searched the house."

"Did they find him?"

"I don't know."

Thirty Seven

Stony Point – 18:00

Matt stared vacantly out of his friend's office window as the waves crashed loudly onto the rocks below. It had been over ten minutes since the helicopter had disappeared into the horizon. He had spent most of this time gazing into space, trying to reconcile what had just happened to him and his friend. *It can't be true, this kind of thing only happens in movies, or does it? I have to call someone, who? Who can I trust?*

He moved over to Blake's desk and picked up the phone. The line was dead as Blake had said. *Killed by what?*

He listened hard but the only sound was that of the splashing surf outside. *What do I do?* What do you do when men in black, carrying guns, have abducted you friend and his girlfriend? *Jesus.* He remembered those boots walking into this office. *Who are they? What do they want? What would have happened if they had found me?* He wanted to scream, so many questions without answers. He was alone and there was nobody there to help him. *Call the police,* he thought.

"And then what?"

"Tell them what happened."

"Will they believe me?"

"Well, you won't know until you try."

"True. But the phone isn't working."

"Get into the car and drive there."

"Right, ok. Oh God. Blake, Sky. What are they doing to you?"

He descended the stairwell, taking care not to make too much noise as for all he knew, somebody could be waiting for him down there.

At the foot of the stairs, he poked his head around the door but there was no one there; the lounge was empty. He opened the front door and peeked outside, nobody out here either.

He climbed behind the wheel of his car. His destination would be the nearest police station.

Let the experts deal with it. The police will know what to do.

He started the engine and after checking, once again, that there was nobody hiding in the backseat, he drove away from Stony Point as fast as he could.

Dusk was approaching and a blanket of darkness had descended on the world, bringing with it the rumble of a thunderstorm. The car creaked and rattled as it sped up the tight, winding road and it was unsettling Matt, so he switched on the radio

"...South West will begin to feel the affects of the thunder storm that has swept back in from the Atlantic"

"So, not going to be that good for the match this evening?"

"I'm afraid not, James. Unfortunately, looks like the storm is heading straight for Southampton. So my advice: if you haven't already left for the game but are planning to, be sure to take your weatherproofs with you."

"Thanks, Gary, as always you have made my day."

"Well, you know what they say: I don't make the weather, I just report it."

"If only someone could. Thanks again Gary. In the meantime, we are going into a commercial break after which, the best on DIY divorces. I'll be speaking to a few of the many thousands of people who take advantage of this service every year, and to the woman who spent £30,000 of her settlement on a divorce party! Don't go away."

The thunder rumbled as Matt switched off the radio. *It is so bloody warm in this car.* He buzzed down the window and could smell the air. It was charged with electricity. The thunderstorm was far away but its effects radiated for miles around. The eastern sky was black. The rain was heading for Southampton where this year's most anticipated football game was about to take place. The same game he had tickets for and the one his friend had been so keen to stop.

"There's a chemical in the rain. I don't know exactly what it is but what I do not know is that it is absorbed through the skin and is lethal." He could hear Blake's words echoing in his mind.

Matt stopped at the first available telephone box and dialled 999. He explained everything to the operator and gave his location as one mile east of Stony Point. The operator told him to stay where he was and that a police unit would be out to him as soon as possible.

"Hurry!" he cried, "My friend is in danger!"

It just so happened that there was a police jeep nearby and they responded within minutes. They found Matt pacing the grass verge near his car and pulled up alongside him, hazard lights flashing.

"Are you Mr Allen?" The taller of the two officers asked, stepping out of the jeep and walking up to Matt.

"Yes."

"Sir. What seems to be the problem?"

"Jesus," Matt moaned. "I already explained to the girl on the phone."

The officer produced a notebook and began scribbling, "Well why don't you go through it one more time with me. Perhaps you could start by giving me your full name and address."

"Look, is this really necessary? We are running out of time. My friend has been abducted," Matt said, anxiously, his emotions spewing forth.

"By whom?"

"I don't know. They came in helicopters and took him and the doctor away. They had guns and they were threatening him. Christ!" Matt was shaking. "Do you have a cigarette?"

The officer shook his head. Matt watched a Transit van trundle by.

"Could you tell me the name of your friends?" Pause, "Sir?"

"Yes, Hudson. Blake. Blake Hudson."

"And you mentioned someone else?"

"I can't remember her surname. Sky is her first name. She is a doctor at the coroner's office in Exeter. Are you going to start a search for them?"

"Most likely, Sir. But first I need some more details."

"Christ! What else do you need to know? These people have been abducted at gunpoint, what else do you need to fucking know?" Matt bellowed. He was trembling with rage.

The police officer, unaffected by Matt's outburst, said calmly, "Maybe we should continue this conversation down at the station."

"Maybe we shouldn't," Matt said, shaking his head. Then, motioning to the jeep "Maybe you should get your mate to call in that two people have been abducted by armed men."

"Please, Sir. Try to calm down."

"Don't tell me to fucking calm down. You didn't see these people. Jesus!" Matt retorted.

The police officer nodded discreetly to his colleague who was still in the car, talking on the radio. They were checking out the number plate on Matt's car.

The second officer finished his conversation and got out of the jeep. The two cops looked at each other as if exchanging some secret code that only they understood.

Matt looked at them both. "What?"

"Just get in the jeep, please Sir," the second officer said.

"Have you been listening to me?"

"Of course we have, Sir. Just get in the car."

"Forget it!"

"Please Sir, otherwise we will have to cuff you."

"Cuff me? Fuck you!"

With that, the two police officers lunged at Matt, each grabbing one of his arms, bending it behind his back and snapping handcuffs on.

"Get off me! Get off me!" Matt struggled.

"Think we've got another one?" The first officer asked casually. His voice slightly wobbled by Matt's struggling.

"I don't know," the other one replied. "Let's get him back to the station. We'll let the others deal with it."

"No! No! You don't understand. No!"

"We understand, alright," the second officer humoured him as his colleague opened the back door of the jeep.

"You've got to help me! Help me!"

"We are helping you, Sir."

The second officer bundled Matt, arms cuffed behind his back, into the back seat of the jeep and climbed in with him whilst his friend got into the front seat and revved the engine.

"Wait! Wait!" Matt cried, as the officer indicated right and swung out, into the road.

"No! Blake! No!" Matt cried as thunder rumbled overhead.

"Looks like more bloody rain," the driver said, as he wound down his window. The scent of rain wafted on the breeze as Matt watched his car disappear from sight.

Thirty Eight

Oil Tanker – Atlantic Ocean, 30 miles west of the Cornish coast
18:00

"Who else knew we were at your house?" Sky asked.

"No one," Blake said. Then he paused, staring into space.

"What?"

More silence, then, "Actually, there was one person."

"Who?"

"Hamilton," Blake spoke slowly.

"Your boss?"

"Yes."

"You think he is involved?"

"Well he was adamant that I do nothing without talking to him first."

"So, nothing suspicious about that."

"No, normally I wouldn't have thought anything of it. I have seen Hamilton rattled by a few things in the past but never like this. He was pretty determined that I drop it." Blake was still thinking. "He was the same with Terry that day I went to Bristol."

"Same, how?"

"I don't know, angry, anxious about something. He ordered Terry off the case. Terry said he didn't know why Hamilton was pulling him off such a routine investigation. Hamilton said he wanted to deal with it personally."

"If that is the case, Blake, then this thing goes much higher than you and I could ever imagine."

"Exactly," Blake agreed, moving over to the door. "That is why we have got to get out of here. Come on."

Sky joined him by the door. Blake opened it and cautiously peeked out into the corridor, it was empty. "Okay, he said, stepping out of the room closely followed by Sky.

He looked up at the restricted access sign above the door. He was determined to see what was on the other side.

"Okay, lets go," Sky said, making her way back down the corridor but Blake was not following her. When she looked back, she saw him looking through the glass panel in the door.

"Blake!" she called in a loud whisper. However, he did not reply he was too busy peering through the glass. "Blake!" she called again, frustrated, looking around, expecting someone to pop out from behind one of the doors like an evil Jack in a box.

"There is something in here," Blake said in a low tone, pressing his nose against the glass in order to get a better look inside the room where subtle ultraviolet lighting reflected off a series of glass cubicles. He arched his head in an effort to obtain a better view but could not see through the reflected light.

"Blake! We have got out get out of here," Sky complained.

"Just want to see..." he pushed on the door but it would not open. He pulled it and still nothing and then he noticed the glowing red light on the swipe panel. His heart sank; it was locked.

Sky wanted to scream at him but she suppressed the urge for fear that someone might hear her. She rushed up to Blake, tugged at his arm and turned him around to face her.

"There is something in there, Sky."

"Blake we have got to get out of here!"

"Whatever's in there could give us proof," he said, pushing his face against the glass again

"How much more proof do you need, Blake?" she said through gritted teeth.

"If only I could. ...Damn!" He hissed loudly, moving away from the door and pressing his back against the wall flanking it.

"What?" Sky asked, perplexed.

There was no time to talk, he grabbed her by the arms, tugged her beside him and whispered, "There is someone coming from the opposite side."

Sky scanned around them. "Back in there!" She said, motioning to the morgue and moving to walk past him.

"No!" he said blocking her way with his arm. "He'll see you

through the door window. In there, quick!" he said, motioning to a door opposite the morgue.

They darted inside just as there was a low bleep and the red light on the locked door flashed green. From inside the storage cupboard, Blake and Sky held their breaths as hurried footsteps echoed down the empty corridor.

Then, to Sky's astonishment, Blake was exiting the room and the desire to punch him was overwhelming. *What are you doing, you idiot?*

Blake peeped out and saw the back of a man in a white coat disappear further down the corridor. Then, he turned to see that the door to the restricted area was slowly being pulled shut by the closing piston. There was a clicking sound and with one giant leap, Blake left the threshold of the storage room and was pushing on it, eyes tightly shut in the effort. He waited for the click of the lock, but it never came.

He tentatively opened his eyes again. The green light was still glowing. He had got there just in time and sighed deeply, resting his forehead on the cool glass.

Sky emerged from the storage room and tugged at his arm, startling him, "Are you totally out of your mind or are you deliberately trying to get us caught?" She hissed, angrily.

"I am out of my mind," he said smiling, making an obvious display of opening the door for her benefit.

Sky sighed, "Blake…"

"I want to know what other dark secrets Williamson is hiding."

"It's locked for a reason. And to be honest with you, I have no desire to discover anything else Blake."

"It might be a way out." He pushed the door open.

As much as she wanted to turn away, she resisted the urge and, with one final look around, followed him into the ultraviolet glow.

The room was large. What little light there was, came from overhead spotlights but was barely enough to pierce the darkness. Each side of the room was sectioned into four glass-fronted cubicles approximately eight by six feet wide. Outside of each glass door glowed a red spy light.

"What is this place?" Sky gasped.

Her voice was a fire alarm in the deathly quiet of the room. Nothing could be heard but the low hum of the ship's engines. They separated; Blake moving over to inspect the left of the room as Sky moved to the right, each heading for a cubicle.

The darkness beyond the glass was thick and Sky moved in closer, cupping her hands around her face and pressing it against the cool surface in an attempt to see beyond her reflection. However, she could see nothing but blackness.

"Sky?" Blake called in a loud whisper.

"What?" she asked, turning to him to see that he too was peering into one of the cubicles.

"I think I have found something." He said.

She moved to go to him and then it came: the scream was high and drilled through Sky's nervous system like a jackhammer. She whirled around as her heart pounded against her rib cage.

The ghostly features loomed out of the darkness of the cubicle, banging and thumping against the glass wall. Sky backed away to the centre of the room where Blake joined her, slipping his arms around her waist and pulling her to him just as another scream from the opposite side of the room shattered the tomblike silence.

"Blake," she spoke, hyperventilating.

"I know," he looked to the exits on either side of the room. Both spy lights glowed red; the doors were locked.

Still staring at the ghostly features behind the glass, Sky whispered, "What is it?"

"I don't know," Blake replied, following her gaze.

He could feel her trembling against him and now he wished he had taken her advice and left when she asked him to.

Within seconds, the slide show of horror films clicked by in his mind; images of monsters, demons, and creatures that nobody ever knew existed. They were all here, hiding in the darkness of this room and the only thing that kept them from him and the women he loved was a sheet of glass.

However, it was not going to happen. He scanned the room again. There had to be a light switch or something that would illuminate their enemy and, low and behold, he saw a panel, next to the exit on the opposite side of the room.

Slowly, and without taking his eyes of the shadowy figure behind the glass, they edged backwards.

At the door, Blake fumbled for the panel until he could feel the buttons beneath his fingers. Without hesitating, he pushed. There was a hissing sound, the door light changed green and, to Blake's amazement, it clicked open. This door, unlike the one they had just come through, was not swipe card operated.

His first instinct was to grab Sky and escape to the next room but then he heard it, another terrifying scream, like that of wounded animal.

Sky pressed into his chest and he embraced her, the scent of her hair sweet and innocent. He did not hesitate and, eyes still in the direction of the scream, he groped for the next button and pressed it. This time the light on the door turned red and locked.

"Shit," he cussed.

He pressed another button and finally the overhead neon strip flickered on, illuminating the room and the horror on their faces.

The man stared out at them from behind the glass. He was naked with an emaciated body, large dark circles around his eyes, mottled blonde hair and anaemic looking skin. He could not have been more than thirty years of age. He stood with his face and one hand pressed against the glass, whilst the other disappeared between his legs. He locked eyes with the two visitors as his pink tongue slithered across his lips indicating the pleasure he was deriving from self-stimulation. He groaned loudly, white eyes bulging, legs apart.

The man transfixed Sky as Blake took in the rest of the room. The cubicles that lined the walls were identical and each contained a male or female occupant. Some lay on the floor, asleep, others were sitting in corners, staring vacantly into space. Thick rubber straps shackled each one. Blake felt nauseous. "What is this place?" He breathed.

Sky shook her head "I don't know. Some kind of lab," she replied, noticing an empty cubicle without a window front. Blake had noticed it also and flinched as he envisioned the man in the morgue smashing his head into the glass wall, knocking himself into oblivion.

"So this is Williamson's idea of research for the benefit of mankind."

"He was developing a cure all right, against the toxin that he and his company created."

"My God. Let's get out of here, Blake. Please," Sky said, in a shaky voice.

There was moaning from one of the cubicles opposite. It came from a plump, middle-aged female, dressed only in her underwear. She was strapped to a bed with an intravenous drip in her arm. Her head lolled from side to side and she opened and closed her legs in spasmodic fashion. She moaned loudly and squinted against the harsh neon lights. Then, abruptly, she sat up, pulling against her restraints and panting like a dog. Then, she rocked back and forth, making croaking sounds as transparent spittle dribbled from her mouth. The croaking sounds became incoherent ramblings. They got louder, slowly changing into the words, "H...E.... L... P   M...E... H.... E...L...P   M...E...." Her eyes were wide open now, pleading, calling to these strangers to release her from the hellish turmoil of her mind, the pulsations in her brain and the heat searing through her blood stream. "P...l.... e...a...s...e," she continued, "H..e...l...p M...e." She coughed, and more spittle dribbled forth.

"Christ..." Blake seethed. He could not bear to watch anymore of this and he released his grip on Sky and stepped forward but she clutched his arm, "Where are you going?" She asked in a panic.

"I'm going to let her out Sky, I can't take anymore of this."

"You can't!"

"Let go."

"Blake! You can't!"

"I am not going to stand here and watch."

"Blake, these people are isolated for a reason. We have no idea what they have been exposed to, if you breach those compartments we could be infected."

"I can't just stand by and watch as they..." He stopped in mid sentence as he saw movement through the corridor door. "Fuck!"

"What?"

"I think someone's coming!"

Sky followed his gaze and saw one of the security men, looking at them through the door window and frantically swiping his card to open it. There was hissing and a clicking sound as the red spy light turned green.

"Quick! Through here!" Blake slammed his hand against the glowing door panel and it clicked open. They scrambled through as fast as they could as a group of security men launched in pursuit.

On the other side, Blake kicked at the panel with all his strength.

"What are you doing?" Sky asked incredulously.

"I am trying to disable the door locking mechanism so that their cards won't work."

"There's no time for that, Blake! Come on!" she screamed, tugging at his arm.

He gave the glowing panel one more blow and it gave way, spewing sparks from its cavity.

Then, taking Sky's extended hand they ran down another corridor. It resembled a large warehouse with shelves on either side. Behind the shelves were what looked like large diesel tanks. The area was scattered with hanging signs reading:

"DANGER CORROSIVE CHEMICALS"   "AUTHORISED PERSONNEL ONLY"

At the end of the corridor, they came to another sealed door. Blake yanked it open and ushered Sky through. Glancing behind them, he saw that the guards were still hot on their heels. Only now, they were advancing at a very slow, almost cautious pace. Blake frowned but without thinking further, he stepped through the opening and crashed into Sky's back. She was just standing directly in front of him, staring in bewilderment.

They were in the laboratory; a large room packed with glowing monitors, gauges and other scientific equipment. At the far end of the room were two men in what looked like white space suits. They ambled around, one of them holding a bleeping gadget whilst the other keyed information into a portable computer.

To their left, stood a control desk, beyond that, was another glass window looking into a hexagonal chamber where there were more spacemen taking readings. They stopped what they were doing and looked up at their visitors.

"What the...?" Blake did not finish his sentence."

"My God, this is a contaminated area, Blake."

"What?"

"The doctor is right, Mr Hudson. You have breached a sealed area and you have no protection." The voice was Williamson's and it was booming out of the paging system.

Blake scanned the room for a way out.

"There is no way out Mr Hudson. We have had to seal off the area."

Looking behind them, Blake noticed that the guards had retreated.

There was a door at the far end of the room. Blake homed in on the glowing red light and clutching onto Sky's hand they ran through an aisle of transparent receptacles and glowing monitors.

"Mr Hudson, please," Williamson boomed.

At the door, Blake pummelled the control panel but the red light remained constant. He turned to the spacemen who were just watching them as if they were trapped animals.

Blake knew Williamson was right; they were trapped in a contaminated zone and there was nothing he could do about it. He held Sky tightly. *Is this what the toxin was like? Is it invisible, odourless and tasteless? Does it sneak up on you and, before you know it, you have metamorphosed into a homicidal freak?*

"I am concerned for your safety. You could be contaminated," Williamson continued.

" Really?" Blake shouted, sarcastically.

"Yes."

"You mean you are as concerned for us as you are for the guinea pigs you have got locked up in there."

"We normally refer to them as patients."

"Do you always tie down your patients?"

There was a short pause. "Yes, I do when they are a danger to themselves."

"You are carrying out experiments on these people," Sky shouted at the ceiling as if Williamson were some mythical god.

"You are mistaken; we are trying to help them. They are infected with the rain. We brought them here for treatment and we are learning. However, you do not have time to discuss this right now. Please, for your own safety you must leave the laboratory."

"And go where?"

"Return to the room you were just in and enter one of the isolation compartments."

Blake laughed. "Oh yeah, sure," he said, facetiously.

"The compartments can scan your anatomy for the toxin. Once we have established whether or not you are infected, we can decide on your treatment."

"Well we'd much rather take our chances here, if you don't mind."

"Don't be foolish, Mr Hudson. The more time you spend in that room, the more you are being exposed to the toxin and the less chance we have of treating you."

The room fell silent.

Thirty Nine

Bodmin Police Station 18:30

"How many times do I have to go over the same thing?" Matt shouted in frustration. He was sitting behind a scuffed brown desk, upon which, an audiotape whirred inside a state of the art recording system. They had been in this room for over an hour going over the same thing.

"Until you tell us exactly what you were doing at Mr Hudson's residence. A murder scene sealed off by us and breached by you and your friends. What was your relationship with Clare McElvoy?" Ginger asked.

"I told you, she was a pupil," Matt replied, running his hands through his hair in exasperation.

"And her relationship with Mr Hudson?"

"He was her tutor too. Look, if this is going to take much longer I would like a cigarette."

"This room is non smoking."

Matt looked around, taking in the small rectangular room; the plain walls were of the same drab décor found in most government buildings. He looked at his watch; the time had just passed 6:30pm. The game would be starting in half an hour unless he found some way to stop it.

"Look, I have told you everything I know. Now will you please start a search for my friends?"

"We already have Mr Allen, simply because we'd be interesting in hearing what Mr Hudson has to say about the death of Miss McElvoy and why exactly he returned to a sealed crime scene."

"Because he lived there," Matt threw in.

"Breaking and entering, trespassing, contaminating evidence are all very serious crimes, Mr Allen."

"He didn't break and enter. That's his home."

"Not when we are investigating a murder in which he and his girlfriend were involved."

"Look, I told you. Clare had been stalking him for a long time."

"So, why didn't he report it to the police?"

"Because he didn't think it was that serious."

"Must have been pretty serious for him to smash her face in and throw her over the balcony."

The officer squared up with Matt and locked eyes with him. "Now, I am going to ask you one more time, Mr Allen. What do you know about Mr Hudson and Miss McElvoy's relationship?"

"Bollocks!"

"You do realise we can keep you up to 48 hours for questioning?"

Matt's eyes widened. "As long as you find something to charge me with other than stupidly ringing you for help from a public call box. If you can do that then I would be more than happy to spend the night."

"You violated a crime scene."

Matt pointed to the recorder on the desk, its tape still whirring, "Maybe you should rewind that, I thought I distinctly heard you say that Blake had violated the crime scene, not me. You have no evidence whatsoever that places me there."

"Don't try to get clever, Mr Allen."

"Oh I assure you I am not trying." There was a pause. "Now, either you call my lawyer, get your superior who obviously knows much more about the law than you do or let me the fuck out of here!" He yelled in frustration.

It was Matt's turn to lock eyes with his interviewer.

There was a long pause, after which, Ginger spoke to no one in particular, "Interview suspended at 18:40, PC Baxter is leaving the room." He glanced at his colleague who had sat by his side throughout the interview and then stood up and left the room, leaving Matt tapping his feet anxiously.

Matt did not know what had brought on that outburst but whatever it was, it worked. He new nothing of the law but his brother, who practiced it, did.

Outside the interview room, Ginger called to a man walking down the corridor "Inspector!"

Morrison stopped and turned to meet him.

"Yes Baxter."

"Sir, just thought you might be interested, the suspect we brought in regarding the murder at the lighthouse the other night. The one involving Doctor McPherson."

"Yes, what about it?"

"Well he does have information regarding Hudson."

"What kind of information?"

"Well, it appears that the suspect has left the county."

"Left, do we know where to?"

"Well he seems to think that the suspect was abducted by armed men in what appears to be a black army helicopter that disappeared out to sea."

"Any particular reason why he thinks that?"

"Well, he claims he was there, Sir."

"When did this happen?"

"Earlier this evening."

"Okay, I will have a word."

"There's more, Sir. About Doctor McPherson, he says that she was abducted too."

Morrison eyes widened.

"He says that he saw her escorted on board one of the helicopters by armed men."

"One of the helicopters?"

Ginger smiled. "Yes, Sir. Apparently there were two choppers."

"I see."

Morrison did not seem to share Ginger's amusement.

"What else?"

"Well…" Ginger scoffed.

"What is it?"

"He says that we should call a halt to the game this afternoon."

"What game?" Morrison asked, casually.

Ginger smirked again. "Well, the main match this evening in Southampton. Cup final."

"Really?"

"Yes Sir. It's going to be…"

"Yes, all right. Spare me the details, Baxter. Just tell me why he thinks we should stop the game." Ginger was just about to scoff again, when Morrison intervened, "And try explaining without the school boy scoffing will you."

Ginger's smile vanished. "Well, he says there is something in the rain. A toxin or something which could be harmful when absorbed into the skin."

"And what made him privy to this information?"

"Blake Hudson, Sir."

"The same man who allegedly…"

"Killed that girl the other night, yes."

"I see."

Morrison pondered.

"Do you want us to let the crank go?"

"Yes."

"Will do, Sir."

"But not until I have spoken to him. Presumably, you aren't any closer to apprehending Hudson."

"No nothing yet, Sir."

"Well hop to it, Baxter. The man is a suspect after all."

With that, the young officer turned on his heels and moved to walk down the corridor.

"Oh and Baxter!" Morrison shouted after him.

"Yes, Sir?"

"Did you say he saw them disappear out to sea?"

"Yes, Sir."

"Don't forget to alert the coast guard."

"No, Sir."

Morrison was pensive, for a few seconds and then made his way down the corridor to *Interview room 2*. He entered the room and smiled warmly at Matt, "I am Detective Inspector Morrison."

"Have you actually come to help or are you going to ask me the same questions they already have?" Matt said, flatly.

"It's important for us to establish the facts in any investigation, Mr Allen," Morrison said as he sat to the left of the officer who had remained impassive throughout these interviews.

"I have given you the facts. I have also stressed the urgency of this information and you don't seem to be interested in what I am saying only in your own agenda."

"I can assure you, Mr Allen, we have no other agenda than that of discovering the truth and apprehending your friend who is a murder suspect."

Matt sneered." Blake isn't a murderer and if you did your job properly you would know that."

"How can you be so sure Mr Hudson didn't murder his pupil?"

"Because I know Blake and I know what Clare was like. Jesus, I can't believe this," Matt said, running his hands through his hair for about the tenth time since arriving here.

"Believe it, Mr Allen. Your friend, possibly with the help of Dr McPherson pushed that poor girl off the balcony."

Matt shook his head. "No, that's impossible. I don't believe it. If

Blake did do anything to her then it must have been self-defence."

"Really? What makes you say that?"

"I just know. She must have been infected with this rain thing that Blake was talking about," *She had probably walked in and found Blake in bed with the doctor and gone berserk. God knows, she was mad enough.*

"You think that she was infected with the rain, Mr Allen? What exactly is she infected with?"

"I don't know. Blake thinks there is something in the rain that is causing all these riots. The same rain that is going to fall on that football match in half an hour if you don't do anything to stop it!"

"You want me to stop the game," Morrison said, intrigued.

Blake saw hope. "Yes, as a precaution."

"A precaution against what? Infection?"

"Yes," Matt responded, excitedly.

"But you can't tell me what kind of infection?"

There was a pause as he realised where this was going. Morrison was the psychiatrist and Matt the patient, and he exploded, "The kind that is going to get you sacked for not doing something when you had the chance. Now, whether or not you save those people this evening is of no importance to me whatsoever. It's your career. But, as for my friend, if you don't try and find him right now I am going to kick up such a stink…"

"Spare us the idle threats, Mr Allen. I have already ordered a search for Mr Hudson and Doctor McPherson. I did this simply because they are both prime suspects in a murder enquiry. As for the game this evening, I don't have the power to call off a football match simply because you and your friend believe…" Morrison paused, " Well, whatever you believe."

A smile spread across the officer's face.

Matt glanced at him with contempt but said nothing.

"As for you, Mr Allen, you are free to go on the understanding that you make yourself available for further interviews."

"Is that it? Is that all you are going to do?"

"I am sorry but there is not much else I can do. We are searching for your friend and as I say, unless something major happens like, for example…" Morrison paused, looking Matt straight in the eyes, "a bomb scare, my hands are tied. Now, I suggest you leave before I have you charged with wasting police time."

With that, Morrison stood up and left the room, leaving Matt feeling very inadequate. He had not achieved anything other than wasting time. There was no way he could stop the match without police help, although he was still going to try.

Forty

Control Room, Oil Tanker – Atlantic Ocean, 30 miles west of the Cornish coast

"Sir, the rain is continuing north, toward the city of Southampton," the operator said, looking at the radar in front of him.

"Damn, Hudson was right," Williamson said looking at the monitor beaming the black and white image of Blake and Sky still inside the laboratory.

"About what?" the colonel asked.

"There is a football match in Southampton. There are going to be thousands of people at that game. The majority of them will be infected before it even starts."

"And?" the colonel asked.

Williamson glanced at him and then at the radar screen.

"Oh I see, the doctor disapproves of my apathetic attitude," the colonel said, knowingly. "Tell me, Doctor, is that because I am genuinely a bad person or is it because you have suddenly developed a conscience?"

"Everything I have done has been for the benefit of the project."

"Yes, that is true. And you will carry on with the project at any cost, is that right?"

"Sir, Peter is approaching the T1 area," the operator spoke as if he were oblivious to the squabbling.

"Where the hell are your men?" Williamson demanded.

"They are approaching the engine room now," the operator replied, pointing at one of the monitors; it showed five armed men in black.

One and two flanked the door; three and four aimed their weapons at it whilst number five swiped it open.

"Why are they carrying firearms?" Williamson asked, calmly.

"How else do you expect them to stop him?"

"You haven't been listening to a word I have said."

"Even if my men drop their weapons it isn't going to stop your laboratory assistant from using his. At least if they are armed they have more of a chance of taking him out before he can cause any damage."

"Oh yes, they will stop him all right. By causing a chain reaction in the Turbine that will blow us all sky high."

"My men are professionals. They know what they are doing. I can guarantee your safety."

"Well, you won't be offended when I say that your guarantee means nothing to me. My work has suffered for the stupidity of others once before."

"Correct me if I am wrong, Doctor. But were you not responsible for that project too?"

Williamson threw the colonel a look of utter contempt.

The colonel just smirked. "So, what are you going to do with your guests?" He asked.

"What I do with them is none of your concern." He motioned to the monitor beaming an image of Peter skulking amongst giant petroleum tanks. "That man is the only thing you and your men should worry about. Along with the fact that those tanks are loaded with fuel that drives the T1. If you do not rupture the core of the turbine itself I would say they stand a good chance of sparking off one of them. The blast would tear a hole in this ship large enough to sink us before you even get the chance to haul your bulk out of here!"

The smirk on the Colonel's face was replaced with a scowl. It was Williamson's turn to smile with his usual subtle demeanour, like everything in his manner, never too big, never too obvious.

The colonel snatched up his radio.

Turbine 1000 was, effectively, the small power plant that drove the tanker forward through the waters of the Atlantic Ocean. Like its elder siblings situated at various ChemiCo sights throughout the world, it boasted a revolutionary process of maximising power generation whilst minimising fuel consumption.

The lighting inside the hanger-like section was as subdued as in most parts of the ship. Small overhead floodlights illuminated a landscape of giant fuel tankers the size of houses. A loud humming originated from the T1 whilst a deeper grinding sound came from the engine itself, situated at the opposite side of the hangar.

Peter moved cautiously through the giant fuel mountains as he noticed a whirring sound overhead. He looked up, giant fans rotated like helicopter blades, sucking up fumes in the air.

Swapping his gun between hands, Peter scratched maniacally. It felt as if there were a myriad of bugs crawling under his skin. They were all over his body. It was as if he no longer had veins but a network of termite tunnels. His head hurt, his face felt hot, he was dripping with perspiration and his lips were parched. He wiped his forehead with the back of his sleeve, he felt energised, ready to cause havoc. Thus, he smiled mischievously and, clutching his gun, moved forward.

Ten feet behind him, the colonel's men had achieved visual contact and were cautiously following the target's movements. Their orders were to subdue and apprehend without using firepower.

The Colonel controlled their advance by speaking through the earpiece inside the team leader's ear whilst monitoring their progress through images beamed back by state of the art micro cameras mounted on the men's shoulders.

It was not long before Peter arrived at the clearing in the heart of the engine room. A bank of six-foot high cabinets formed a square, inside of which were four desks with obligatory computer consoles.

Peter was about to step forward but stopped, something was not right. There was nobody here. He had only been in this room once but he had seen a hive of operators buzzing to and from the computer screens and glowing cabinets. Now, the area was completely deserted. Why? He could not think straight, his head was pounding and the pressure was building. He looked around, the corridors between the fuel tanks were empty, he was alone. Or was he?

Another wipe from the back of his sleeve dried up the sweat that was dripping from his face. He smiled.

From the control room, the colonel watched a wobbly image of the engine room as his men progressed.

"He is heading straight for the computer consoles. What do you think he is up to?" The colonel asked.

"I have no idea, other than the fact that he knows how volatile it is in there. He is probably betting on you sending your men in after him. And you have played right into his hands."

"What, you mean that he…"

"Wants you to open fire, yes. After all, he has nothing to lose. He has worked on this project ever since its transfer to this ship. He knows the effects of the toxin and probably is aware of the fact that he has been exposed to an amount that is incurable. Ultimately, the toxin will kill him. Right now, he is probably feeling the effects of it building up in his blood stream. Eventually it will clog his arteries, cut off his blood supply. If he can kill all those responsible for the death of his mentor before that happens, then so much the better."

"You mean we've got a human time bomb on our hands?"

"You could say that."

"And you were spurting all that rubbish about suppressing gun fire and apprehending him alive."

"Do you still not get it? That is exactly what he wants you to do. He does not intend to shoot it out with your men. He just wants them to open fire on him and make sure that they hit one of those tanks in the process. He had no other reason to enter the engine room other than that of luring your men there. That is why you must call them out immediately."

"What? And leave him to go on the rampage?"

"I've already explained what his body is going through right now."

"How long before all that happens?"

The operator interrupted. "Sir. We've lost visual."

"What? Patch in all cameras," Williamson ordered and then, turning to the Colonel, he asked, "What about your men?"

A wavy image from the shoulder-mounted cameras showed that the men were on the move.

"It looks like they have lost him too. It is imperative that we monitor his movements. We must find him," Williamson insisted.

The operator tapped keys and the album of images recommenced but none returned the location of Peter. The engine room appeared to be empty except for the Colonel's men who could be seen skulking through the fuel tank corridors of section M.

Peter was gone.

Forty One

Back in the laboratory, Sky looked up at the intercom speaker mounted on a nearby wall. It had been over five minutes now and Williamson hadn't spoken. The silence was unnerving.

"What do you think he's up to?" she asked in a subdued tone, averting her face from the gaze of the prying camera.

"I don't know but whatever it is, it won't be good. We've got to find a way out of here," Blake replied in the same hushed tone. He looked around the room, the space men had grown tired with their visitors and had returned to their investigation once more. To Blake, their indifference was surreal but he did not care, he had a mission of his own right now and that was to get both him and Sky off this ship.

Unfolding her arms from him he said, " Okay, time to go."

"Where?" Sky asked.

"I don't know," he said, distractedly, scanning the room for an exit.

"What about the toxin?"

"What about it?"

"Well…" Sky did not finish the sentence and this got Blake's attention.

He looked at her and noticed the fear in her eyes and said, reassuringly, "We don't even know if we are infected, Sky. For all we know Williamson could have lied to get us to succumb to joining his guinea pigs in there. How are you feeling?"

She took a few moments to check herself. "I think I am ok. How about you?"

"Never felt better," he smiled. "Come on, I want to get back for that meal we never had."

He looked across at the space men who were surveying the area on the opposite side of the room, oblivious to them. His eyes roamed over a network of benches, scientific paraphernalia and electronic gauges, but there was nothing of interest. Then he saw it, standing on the floor nearby; a large stainless steel dustbin.

He took Sky's hand and pulled her away from the door. He picked the bin up and tried it for weight; it was perfect. Then, with both hands and with a minute amount of exertion in his voice said, "Remember when we were running down that corridor and I stopped to kick that door panel in?"

Sky was perplexed, "What about it?"

Blake nodded at the red glow of the swipe card panel on the door, "Remember how I thought that by kicking the panel, I would engage the lock permanently but instead I just broke the mechanism?"

He locked eyes with her and grinned in his trademark way.

"Watch yourself," he said. With that, he swung the bin at the door panel. The blow was powerful and succeeded in snapping the cover off, exposing its inner circuitry.

On the other side of the room, the spacemen stopped what they were doing, attracted by the fracas of the bin and pointed at the two intruders. If they were yelling at the vandal across the room, it was muted by their visors.

They men lumbered to intercept.

Meanwhile, Blake was swinging a second blow at the door. This time, a shower of sparks spat at him and a small cloud of acrid smoke billowed out into the air. He glanced behind him and noticed that, despite the hindrance of their suits, the space men were gaining on them. Therefore, holding his breath, he launched his full weight against the door; it gave and swung open, slamming against the outer wall.

An alarm shrilled loudly and the spacemen skidded to a halt, their distress clearly visible.

Back in the control room, a buzzer sounded and a red light flashed on the computer screen in front of the operator.

"What the hell is that?" the colonel asked.

"They've broken out of the laboratory door," Williamson whispered. His face was impassive but, for the first time, the colonel thought he saw fear in his colleague's eyes.

"Don't worry about it, I'll have my men pick them up," he said, in a dismissive tone.

"They have breached the sealed sector. The toxin is airborne now in…" he looked at the computer monitor. "In the whole of the F sector corridor."

"Can't you contain it?"

"Of course we can contain it," Williamson snapped. "As long as no more seals are broken." Then he said to the operator, "Bring up a map of the ship."

The operator tapped on the keyboard in front of him and, instantly, a digital map of the ship appeared.

"Superimpose possible contamination areas."

More keys clicked and then a red glow coloured in various sectors of the map.

Williamson sighed. "Sectors Da, J, and now corridor F have been exposed."

"What the hell does that mean in English?" the Colonel asked, frustrated by all the computer imagery that meant absolutely nothing to him.

"It means that there are only another three more doors separating us from the toxin. If Hudson continues violating the doors between them and us we'll be eating the toxin for supper."

"Another scenario you didn't take into consideration, Doctor?"

Williamson took in a deep breath and calmly spoke, "Of course I did, what I didn't predict was that I was going to have a pair of hooligans vandalising the locks on the doors."

"I see. And whose fault is that?" the colonel asked in a condescending tone. He spoke into his radio once more. "This is the Colonel, proceed to intercept in corridor Fa, two intruders, one male, one female and shoot to kill. I repeat, shoot to kill."

Forty Two

A38 road, eastbound toward Plymouth.

Matt had been driving on the dual carriageway no more than five minutes. Kick off was in ten and he did not hold much hope of making it in time. He did not have a clue about what to do

when got there. The police were not going to help him; Morrison had made that very clear.

"Get out of my bloody way," he moaned. The lorry in front was driving irritatingly slow and it had been doing so ever since he joined this road.

Overtake him, Matt.

Despite the incline in the road, he dropped from fourth into second gear, gunned the engine and swung out to overtake.

However, when he drew level with the truck's cabin, he noticed that he was no longer gaining on the vehicle and looked down at the speedometer, it read 75mph.

Then why am I slowing...

It occurred to him and he looked up into the steely grey eyes of the overweight trucker who grinned back maniacally.

"What the fuck?" *The bastard is accelerating.* "Are you out of your fucking mind?" He shouted at the passenger door window but the lorry driver maintained his speed.

"HEY!" Matt protested as they sped, side by side, toward the crest of the hill. He pushed the pedal to the metal and very slowly began to gain on the truck just as both vehicles hurtled over the ridge.

As soon as they were on the other side, Matt was dazzled by the flashing blue lights. About two hundred yards ahead, a long queue of traffic sat bumper-to-bumper, taillights blazing as, in front of them, police and ambulance services dealt with an earlier pile up.

Paramedics were treating casualties laid out on the tarmac whilst the police attempted to clear the road with the help of a local breakdown truck but there was no way through.

"Noooo!" Matt screamed, stamping on the brake pedal.

100 yards...

An old man in a rusty Ford Escort, glanced in his rear view mirror and saw the two sets of headlamps, one slightly higher than the other, gaining rapidly. "Good lord, slow down!" he muttered as he switched on his hazard lights.

"What's wrong dear?" his wife asked.

The old man opened his mouth to speak but no words came, it

just gaped open as he froze in horror.

50 yards...

The Vauxhall Astra slid, tyres screeching, toward the back of the Escort. Matt attempted to avoid collision and over-steered, leaving a cloud of burning rubber behind him.

The car fish tailed several times, slamming him against and bouncing off the central reservation as a cloud of burning rubber fogged the vision of the following truck.

25 yards...

The lorry's screeching brakes resounded around the valley as the world slid into slow motion: the ambulance men, the couple squabbling over directions, the boy and the girl on holiday, the young woman fiddling with her radio, all turned around to watch the vehicles hurtling towards them.

"Fuck..." was all an officer could gasp, glued to the tarmac in horror.

15 yards...

The Astra bounced off the central reservation once more, flipping into a 360 degree spin and crashing sideways through the steel barrier, into the opposite lane where it span twice more and skidded to a halt in the middle of the road.

Matt froze, eyes shut, hyperventilating, clutching the steering wheel as if it were life itself.

5 yards...

The police officer barely had time to shout, "Get off..." as the lorry ploughed into the Ford escort, mashing the old couple into the metal of their car and flinging it up into the truck's windscreen, crushing the driver, squeezing his insides up out of his mouth.

It careered forth, flipping some cars like skittles and shunting others forward, toward the flashing blue lights of the emergency services.

Ambulance crew members, who were tending to victims from the earlier pile up, just about had time to look up as a convoy of cars was pushed over them, steam-rollering their flesh and bones into the tarmac.

The metal landslide slid forward, smashing into ambulances,

thrusting them onto their sides, all to the soundtrack of bending metal and smashing glass.

However, The debris did slow the lorry's progress and eventually, after ploughing through more than 20 cars, two ambulances and one police car, it skidded to a stop.

It had only been a matter of seconds since the scraping, crashing sound of the lorry had ceased when Matt heard the sound of yet another engine and it was growing louder.

Oh God, Please no. He peeped over his hands on the steering wheel: the bus's lights flashed and it's horn sounded with hostility as it sped on a collision course but Matt's strength had dissipated. He squeezed his eyes shut and prepared himself for the inevitable.

Forty Three

Blake and Sky escaped from the laboratory, only to find themselves inside yet another corridor within the labyrinth of the tanker. Directly in front of them was a locked door

"Where to?" Blake asked, frantically looking from left to right. He noticed a sign suspended from the ceiling that read:

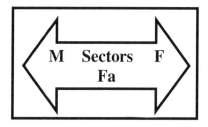

"What? You're asking me?" Sky panicked.

"Just thought I'd get a second opinion."

"Blake."

"Only kidding. Let me think."

Sky looked behind them. The space men were closing in.

"Whatever you are going to decide Blake, hurry!"

"This way!" he shouted, running to his left. Sky crashed into the back of him. "No! No! That way!" He changed his mind, pointing in the opposite direction.

"Are you sure?"

"No, but call it male intuition."

Hand in hand they ran down the corridor, leaving the space men, watching them at the door. Meanwhile, their movements were being tracked through the monitors in the control room.

"They are progressing down the F corridor. How long until your men intercept them?" Williamson asked.

"Don't concern yourself. They'll be stopped when they get to the junction."

"Sir, something is happening," the operator spoke up.

"What's wrong?"

"I am losing visual in Sector I"

"What's happening?" The colonel asked.

"The screen is just blanking out."

The colonel paused and then looked at Williamson, their exchange was telepathic.

"It's him! Bastard!" The colonel screamed.

"Clever boy," Williamson said, smiling.

"Oh you find this amusing, do you Doctor?"

"He has managed to elude five of your trained men and make his way up here whilst intoxicated."

The colonel scoffed. "There's no way out. Where does the fool think he is going?"

"Don't quote me on this but I would have thought his intentions were obvious. He wants to get off the ship."

"And go where?"

"Who knows, maybe he is trying to get home."

"We'll be waiting for him."

He spoke into the radio. "Marcus, suspect is in Section I and is now making his way to the lift and Section L. I want him cornered there. Send as many men as possible, I don't want him leaving this ship alive!"

"You won't get there in time," Williamson said, challengingly.

The colonel glared at him and then barked at the operator, "Seal off access to the elevator at section L."

"It won't help," Williamson interjected.

"Do as I say!"

"It won't help," he repeated. "He has a swipe card with Level 5 access rights and is able to override any command we give the computer from here."

"Do it anyway!"

The operator complied.

The colonel sneered. "So much for your safety protocols."

"This is one of the protocols approved by your security branch and the board; the ability to allow high ranking-personnel to override the computer."

The colonel shook his head in a hopeless gesture and then ordered, "Revoke those rights!"

"I'm picking up gun fire in Section L, Sir."

"He's reached the elevator."

The colonel smiled. "I told you he wouldn't escape."

If Williamson was disappointed, he did not show it.

"Elevator is on the move, Sir."

The colonel spoke into his radio. "L Team, report."

Silence.

"L Team, report your status."

Silence.

Then the radio burst into life "Sir, this is Marcus. Haven't been able to get through to I Team ever since they intercepted target, over."

The colonel frowned. "But…. my men were…"

"Your men are dead, colonel," Williamson said with icy casualness.

"What do you mean? That's impossible."

"They're dead."

"Scan the area!"

"They're dead," Williamson repeated.

"On screen, now!"

"I'm sorry, Sir. I can't."

The colonel was trembling with rage. "Do as I say or…"

"The cameras are malfunctioning, Sir."

"Jesus Christ." He muttered as beads of perspiration glistened on his forehead.

Williamson could not have been more delighted. Fuelled by the toxin, Peter was able to evade capture by cunning or perhaps even by brute force.

The radio crackled into life. "Sir? Sir, this is Marcus." His voice was a shaking and he sounded distressed.

"Marcus Status report."

"They're dead, Sir. All three men are dead!"

"Can someone confirm that?"

"Sir, this is Kraus, I can confirm three dead, Sir. Blood everywhere."

The colonel was incredulous. "How in God's name is that possible?"

"I told you, it's the toxin." Williamson said.

"Three of them opened fire." Marcus continued.

"And they probably hit him but Peter is infected with the toxin. At this moment he is on a high and his body will take almost anything, including several gunshot wounds."

"Are you reciting this from your medical journal?" The colonel asked, disgusted.

"As a matter of fact, I am."

The coolness in Williamson's tone irked the colonel and he could have quite cheerfully put his gun to the man's head and pulled the trigger.

"Marcus, get up on deck and use whatever force you deem necessary to bring that bastard down!"

"Yes, Sir," came the scratchy reply. "Oh Sir?"

"What is it?"

"What about the two at Junction F?"

"Don't worry about them." The colonel pulled out his gun. "I am going to take care of them, personally.

Williamson looked into the monitor. The caption below it read: *Sector F* and it showed the black and white image of Blake and Sky running down a corridor.

The wind tore at Peter's hair as the elevator doors opened.

He stood for a few seconds, training the gun on the area in front of him but there was nobody there. They were going to let him go home after all.

He looked down and grimaced at the pool of blood at his feet. Most of it had seeped into his clothes. He had taken two gun shot wounds: one to his chest and the other to his stomach, but he did not feel any pain. In addition, although he felt light-headed from the loss of blood, he was still buzzing. He knew he could still make it.

He stepped out of the elevator, climbed through the porthole and squinted. The sky above the Atlantic was its usual grim but, nonetheless, reassuring blanket of grey. He breathed in the cool sea air and felt a small boost. If only the pounding in his head and the itching in his veins would stop.

He crouched down behind a pulley and glanced out. Up ahead, he could see the two large helipads and both black helicopters were anchored there. He looked right, across the ship. As expected, he saw a cluster of men waiting outside the lift shaft, and he smiled to himself.

Then he stood up, clasping onto the pulley for support. The ship was swaying and his head was spinning. He could feel the energy ebbing from his body as he lost blood and, consequently, the boost that the toxin provided. But he could make it, he had to make it home to his family, back to the farm where he had been raised, where he had led a happy childhood, albeit an extremely impoverished one. His mother had made so many sacrifices for him and now he had to provide for her.

Gun in hand, the colonel left the control room. However, as he was about to run forward he noticed something glistening on the floor in front of him. He bent down, took a closer look at the small droplets and noticed that the trail led from the right, sector I, past the control room, to the left, Sector D.

He touched the substance with his finger and looked at it closely. It was blood. *It is his blood!*

He spoke into the walkie-talkie he was carrying.

"Marcus!" There was a pause.

"Marcus here."

"Have you got anyone posted to the elevator at D deck?"

"No, Sir."

"Get some of your men over there immediately! The bastard sneaked right by us and used the other lift!"

He stared at the trail of blood. He was quivering with anger and someone had to pay. With that thought, he ran straight ahead. The sign hanging overhead, read:

Sector A
**Leading to
Junction F**

That is where he would find Blake and Sky.

Back on deck, Peter ignored the queasiness that swept over him. He left his hiding place and ran toward the helipads. In that moment, he heard shouting from behind him and looked across to see that the group huddled around the elevator had split up and some of them were crossing to the opposite deck. Then someone spotted him and shouted.

Instantly, they gave chase.

By this time, he had reached the helicopter on Helipad 1 and startled two men, one in greasy overalls and the other in a pilot's

jump suit.

Before he had time to react, the mechanic took a bullet between his eyes and keeled backward, slamming his head against the deck.

The pilot held his hands up.

"Get in!" Peter ordered, motioning to the helicopter.

The man paused and Peter aimed the gun at his head and ordered, "NOW!"

The pilot climbed in and Peter jumped in after him, steadying himself by clinging onto the U shaped handgrip provided.

There was shouting from his pursuers, someone ordering him to stop but he ignored them. They opened fire and bullets rang and danced off the helicopter's shell.

"Get us out of here…" Peter pressed the gun against the pilot's temple and screamed "NOW! NOW! NOW!"

The terrified pilot flicked various switches in quick succession.

Peter's vision dimmed slightly, like the lights on a car with a flat battery.

The engine turned and the blades slowly began to spin as Peter, in his daze, leant out of the helicopter and squeezed off a few rounds, hitting one of the guards in the chest, propelling him backward. The others took cover behind nearby pipes and winches and responded with gunfire, showering the helicopter with miniature meteorites.

"GET US OUT OF HERE!" Peter ordered once more.

"But…" the pilot stuttered.

"NOW!" Peter yelled, his vision was blurring but he was not going to stop.

The beating of the blades increased as the pilot eased the cloche and the helicopter lifted tentatively off the helipad.

Another shower of bullets pierced the interior of the craft. One of them sliced through Peter's arm, another burned its way into his leg but he felt nothing. His senses weakened, his energy drained. His body was slowly shutting down.

Then, the helicopter started to sway from side to side.

To Peter it felt as if he was back in his mother's arms and she was gently rocking him to sleep, stroking his hair and caring for him in the same way she always had.

"I'm coming home, Mama," he murmured. "I am coming home."

The men below watched as the whirring machine hovered fifteen feet above the deck, pulling at the steal safety harness attached to its feet and straining to get away.

The mounting tension in the cable swung it from side to side and, like an enraged dog, it struggled to break free. It whined, spluttered, and smoke billowed out of the over revved engine, but the pilot continued gunning the power as he lay slumped over the controls with a bullet in his lungs.

Then, there was a twanging sound as the cable began to fray, this was followed by a loud bang and then the engine cut out.

The men on deck ran for cover as, in slow motion, the flying machine dropped out of the sky and fell just missing the deck and crashing in a ball of fire into the north side of the vessel, puncturing in it, a hole the size of a small car.

The damage was above water level but as the tanker dipped into the Atlantic basin; it took in large gulps of water that washed into section N of the ship, between the storage area and the oil reservoir containing over a thousand gallons of crude oil.

It was all part of Williamson's project to cruise the waters of the world under the guise of an oil tanker.

However, the explosion had fractured the isolating wall and cistern thus leaking oil into the corridor. Ignited by the burning fuel from the crash, it poured, like lava, into the corridor on its way to Section M, the home of Turbine 1000; the power station that drove the ship.

"What was that?" Sky asked as she steadied herself from the quake.

"I don't know. Felt like an explosion," Blake replied.

"Should we be concerned?"

"I would have thought so. Explosions are rarely good. Perhaps we should increase our rate of escape."

They had reached Junction F, the centre of the ship. The light on the panel was a steady red. Beyond the door, was the central cubicle that branched out to the four sides of the vessel, one of them leading to the elevator that would take them up and out.

"Shit!" Blake swore, "It's locked."

"Well, just kick it in." Sky said, casually.

"Ok, stand back," he said.

Then, after sizing up the swipe panel, he took a run and kicked it fiercely.

Nothing.

"Shit!" he yelped.

Sky looked at him, and rolled her eyes heavenwards.

"Oh, why don't you try?"

"Who's the man here? Actually, don't answer that."

"Thank you," he said smiling as he prepared to launch another assault on the door. "There are only so many of these you can kick in any one day."

"Come on!"

He kicked the unit repeatedly until, eventually, it fell off, spitting sparks in protestation. He looked at her and pulled a smug, superior expression as he tugged at it, but it did not open.

His smile faded. "What's going on?"

"Is it still locked?"

Tugging at the door and using his foot against the wall as leverage, he said, "It certainly feels like it."

"I don't understand."

"Nor do I," he said, examining it closely. He checked the seal around the edges and tried to locate a bolt or something of that ilk but saw nothing. He scanned it from top to bottom and back again but as he reached the glass panel, he was startled to see a face staring back at him from the other side. "Jesus!" he shouted, ducking down and pulling Sky with him.

There was a loud bang and shattered glass showered them both.

Sky screamed.

"What the hell was that?"

"My God, Blake. He is shooting at us!"

"What?"

"Get away from the door!" Sky screamed, pushing him sideways as more shots rung out, punching holes in the doorframe.

"He's trying to kill us!" she shouted, screwing her eyes shut and bracing herself for the next spray of bullets.

"Still think that these people are just egomaniacs?" he asked, casually.

" We've got to get out of here!"

"I agree! On my mark." He counted to three, "GO!"

In unison, they sprang up from their squatting positions and ran forward, back up the corridor from whence they came.

More shots exploded after them, pinging off nearby walls.

"Where to? Where to?" Sky asked, frantically.

"Ahead!" There is nowhere else to go.

The few minutes it took them to reach the end of the corridor felt like hours. They passed the door to the laboratory; which was shut now.

"This way! It's open!" Blake shouted with relief, pointing at a door ahead of them. He yanked it open but nothing could have prepared them for what they saw next.

The heat and the smell of burning oil hit with force, funnelled by the corridor, it was as if someone has just blasted a giant hair dryer at their faces.

"What the…." Blake could not finish his words; the scene was too incredulous.

There was a steady stream of water and burning oil, flowing down the corridor. The flames were low but constant. It was something neither of them had seen before outside of a Hollywood disaster movie.

Tears pricked at Sky's eyes. "My God, Blake. What are we going to do?"

"I don't know." Blake tried to mask the dread in his voice. "But it looks like we won't be going this way."

From the control room, Williamson watched the scenes unfold with horror.

"What does that imbecile think he is doing?" He snarled as he saw the colonel shoot out of the cubicle door, thus breaching the contained area. If the toxin was airborne, nothing could stop it reaching the control room now. However, that was the least of his worries.

"Sir, the burning oil is running the length of corridors N through to L."

"But that's the whole width of the ship."

"We also have a fire in the storage area of sector N," the operator added, seemingly immune to their ordeal.

"Why hasn't the fire system kicked in?" Williamson demanded, staring at the monitors.

"They work on a snuff system, Sir."

The snuff system worked by containing the fire in a sealed area and then depriving it of oxygen, regular sprinklers were not advisable on ships simply because the idea was to keep the water out not pump it in. In addition, because of their oil cargo the ship required a fire system that could smother the fire as it is not possible to extinguish burning oil with water.

"Yes, I know how it works," Williamson snapped. "Why has it not engaged?"

"We can't seal off the area, Sir. The explosion has ripped a hole in the north side."

"Are we taking in water?"

"Some."

"Some? What in God's name does that mean? Are we or aren't we?"

The operator tapped on his keyboard. A map of the ship appeared on the monitor with alpha coded grids. "The amount we are taking on can be contained by sealing off," he pointed to the screen, "all junctions in sections I through to D."

"Do it," Williamson ordered, clutching the operator's chair.

In that moment, a red light began flashing, an alarm shrilled and gauges on a nearby console began to flicker.

"Oh no," the operator said, flicking switches and working the keyboard in front of him. "No, no, no... wait a minute," he said with dreadful realisation.

"What?"

The young man did not answer. He keyed in commands, checked the information yielded on the monitor and re-keyed again.

"What's happening?" Williamson demanded with frustration.

"The fire in N sector," the operator began, checking more information on his computer. "It neighbours the T1000 and is pushing the temperature up inside there."

"What?"

"Also the flow of oil, look!"

He tapped on the keyboard. The image on the monitor changed, displaying the inside of the Turbine 1000 engine room. It showed a steady stream of dancing fire flowing into the room and engulfing the steel stands of the fuel tanks. If the scene were not so tragic, it would have been beautiful.

Williamson closed his eyes and murmured, "God save us." However, he still was not scared, he was petrified.

The sounds of running footsteps alerted Sky and they turned to see the colonel running up the corridor.

Both of them clawed at the laboratory door but it was sealed from the inside.

The colonel took aim.

Blake frantically looked for somewhere to run but Sky beat him to it, "In here, Blake! In here!" she shouted, pointing to a room opposite.

She ran in and Blake was just about to join her when there was another blast of the gun and a scraping whizzing sound as the bullet bounced of the wall. Blake clutched his shoulder, winced and grunted with pain.

Sky screamed, "Blake!"

She ran to him and, slipping her arms under his, she dragged him back to the far side of the room where she knelt next to him, "Oh my God, Blake, You've been hit!"

" You always did state the obvious."

She battled to suppress the tears, "Blake."

"I'm okay. Honestly, I feel ahhhhh!" He wailed as she prodded his wound.

She lost the battle and tears welled in her eyes as she opened his shirt and examined him.

"Hey now. You stop that."

Their eyes met and in the intensity of the moment she blurted out, "I love you, Blake."

"Wow, took your time, didn't you?" He smiled.

She smiled with him but it was short lived; the colonel appeared at the door with the gun in his hand and a deranged grin on his face.

Forty Four

The sound of screeching tyres came and went and it took Matt Allen a long time before he dared look up and check if he was still alive. However, when he did, he realised that the bus had swerved and screeched passed him, missing the car by inches. Now, as the rumble of thunder crashed overhead and a gale tore around the car, he subconsciously pulled at the door handle and stepped out.

The carnage on the opposite side of the road was devastating. The wind brought with it the smell of leaking fuel, the groans of the injured and the cries of those coming around to find their loved ones dead in the seat next to them.

Matt staggered, mouth open, away from his car, transfixed by the wreckage. A few more cars pulled over by the bus that was now spewing its passengers.

There was a babble of voices and gasps as the sightseers rushed over to get a good look at the pile up in the opposite lane. The crashing of thunder and another dash of lightening added a more chilling dimension to the horrifying picture.

Then Matt noticed it, the smoke billowing out of one of the cars. It started as a small smouldering mass and then turned into a bomb fire and he could not work out if the screaming he could hear was the sound of melting tyres or that of a child being roasted in the blaze.

More people congregated by the central reservation, almost shunting and pushing each other in order to get a better view. Before he knew he was doing it, Matt was shouting at the top of his voice. "Get away!" he yelled. "Get away from there!"

It was too late. There was a sighing sound and then a massive explosion that catapulted one of the cars into the air like a rocket. It crashed back down on top of another car.

There was more screaming, this time from a member of the newly formed crowd of spectators. A women was screaming in agony, clutching a piece of metal that was wedged in her eye as blood seeped into her yellow T shirt, forming a dark patch over her breasts.

Lightening flashed.

Matt staggered back toward his car where another group of onlookers had gathered at a much safer viewpoint. Then he heard her talking on her mobile phone; the girl could not have been more than 18 years of age

"Yeah, it's great!" she said, excitedly. "I was just in the coach thinking about how boring the bloody trip had been. I mean, I just thought some idiot had decided to park his car in the middle of the road and do a runner. I didn't even see what had happened on the other side of the road until I heard talking behind me. It was like something out of a film. I turned my head and all hell was breaking loose. I tell you, there are people crying, screaming and some woman just got a piece of metal stuck in her eye with blood dripping all over her! It is excellent. I tell you, you should be...."

She broke off as Matt snatched the mobile phone from her.

"Hey!" she protested. "What are you doing? That's my phone!"

Matt smacked her with an icy stare and the girl backed off.

"It ain't mine, it's my boyfriend's and he won't be happy...."

The girl's babbling protests were unheard as Matt walked away from the crackling blaze and the chatting of voyeuristic onlookers.

He could hear the stranger on the other end of the phone call. Whoever it was, was tucked up at home, and probably sprawled out on the sofa, supping tea as her friend recounted the grizzly details of the shattering of somebody else's life.

He pressed disconnect.

Matt's mind was a blank. He could not really digest anything that had just happened here. All he could remember was the flash of the explosion and the words of Inspector Morrison *"Unless something happens such as a bomb scare..."*

There was the answer! Morrison had supplied him with the answer and he had not seen in. That is when the autopilot kicked in and he dialled 999.

"Emergency, which service?"

"Police, please." He was talking but he did not recognise himself. It was as if he was possessed. Matt Allen, the person he had lived with for 29 years was busy recovering somewhere from shock. He had nearly died in a car crash and it was going to take him some time to recover from that.

"Police, What's your emergency?"

Pause

"Hello?"

"Yes, I would like to report a bomb, please."

"I'm sorry, Sir. Could you repeat that?"

"Yes, I said that I would like to report a bomb."

Forty Five

Police control room – Southampton football stadium

Chief Superintendent Paul Connor, immaculate in his dark blue uniform, stood on the balcony of the control room and was startled by thunder as it boomed overhead.

It looked like the heavens were going to open. *Why they don't just call this whole thing off is beyond me. Hopefully, the pitch will get water logged.*

He did not like football very much and with all these riots, he could do without redirecting precious manpower here to curtail the movements of a bunch of lager swilling troublemakers.

However, there was nothing to worry about; Paul Connor had taken zero tolerance beyond its original intentions. He had extended it from the housing estate and into the stadium where, with the help of new technology, he was stamping out the ringleaders and soon all of football hooliganism. The sport would only be accessible to those who genuinely loved the game and did not see it as an opportunity to release their frustration at their mediocre existence.

His revolutionary strategy worked by recording known offenders onto a computerised register. Each record included a scanned image of the individual. State of the art cameras were installed at the turnstiles and linked to a computer database. The spectator's features were scanned and, in seconds, the computer would search for a match. Positive matches were identified and thus refused entry.

The scheme had been in operation for nearly a year and had proved highly successful. The papers had praised it and the Home Secretary himself was hailing it as a milestone in the combat against hooliganism.

Paul smiled; he was pleased with himself.

"Sir?" An officer called from inside the control room behind him.

"Yes. What is it?" he asked, without turning around.

"Five more minutes until kick off, Sir."

"Very well. How are the turnstiles looking?"

"Good, Sir. Nearly all of them are in and in their seats."

Paul said nothing but smiled again as he surveyed the sea of multicoloured bodies, there were thousands of people here and their chants echoed loudly around the stadium as a giant screen beamed pictures of the players.

"Sir…"

"What is it now constable?"

"I think you should see this."

There was a pause. Nothing Paul Connor ever did was in haste; everything had to be meticulously planned.

He turned and walked back into the control room. It was small but packed with monitors and computers, all aiding the surveillance of the crowds and communication with the officers amongst them.

"Yes?"

The young PC handed Paul a slip of paper, which he read. His reaction was minimal, just a furrowing of the eyebrows.

*** URGENT*** BOMB ALERT ***URGENT***

WARNING RECEIVED VIA: Telephone @ **18:50 hrs**

CODE: **Unknown**

CONTACT: **Unknown**

SOURCE: **Cellnet mobile phone. 0856 201269**

LOCATION OF BOMB: **Unknown, Somewhere inside the Southampton Stadium.**

At the end of the document was a transcript of everything Matt had said during his telephone call to the police.

Paul took a long time to digest the information but he said nothing.

"Sir?" The PC attempted, masking his nervousness.

"How many minutes until kick off?"

"Ten minutes, Sir."

Paul glanced out of the balcony as a gust of wind blew in, tugging at the paper in his hand.

Lightening flashed shortly followed by thunder.

"Alert all officers to report anything suspicious. Oh and tell them to be discreet."

"Yes, Sir."

A cordless phone rang; it was a direct line, used only for communication between commanding officers.

Paul calmly lifted the handset, "Chief Superintendent Paul Connor.

Pause

"Yes, Sir. I have the communication in my hand right now."

Pause

"Yes Sir, it's unconfirmed. It is hard to say. The lack of a pass code would suggest a hoax, yes. It wouldn't be the first time."

Pause

"Yes Sir, thank you Sir. I will keep you informed. Good bye."

He replaced the handset, was pensive for a few seconds and then snapped into action.

"Call administration and tell them that the game is halted until further notice. Then notify all officers. I want the stadium searched." He pointed out to the balcony, "and I don't want that lot knowing about it."

"What are we going to tell them?"

"Tell administration the truth but not a bloody word gets out! Make that clear."

"Yes, Sir."

"And get Garrison and Parker up here right now!"

The operator and his colleague busied themselves on the phone and radio respectively as Paul stepped out on the balcony once more.

The air was thick with electricity. The gale was stronger and it blasted him with the scent of rain, the storm was drawing closer.

The masses started chanting, *"Why are we waiting?"*

What are you going to do? Think Paul. The call could be a hoax but what if it isn't? What if there really is a bomb hidden somewhere in the stadium? For all you know it could be in the control room behind you. These could be your last minutes on this planet. Any second now you could see part of the stadium light up in a detonation.

The sudden explosion of thunder startled him as the announcement was made:

"Ladies and gentlemen. We are sorry to inform you that the match will be delayed due technical difficulties. Therefore, please bear with us."

There was a roar of protest. It was like telling a pack of hungry animals not to feed on the keeper now as dinner would be served later.

If only they knew. If only they knew that the breath they were drawing could be their last.

"Sir?"

"Yes?" Paul answered with obvious irritation.

"Administration want to know how long the delay will be?"

"As long as I deem necessary!" he barked. "Christ, these people have no idea."

You have to make a decision.

He turned and shouted, "Where the hell are…" and stopped in mid sentence as the door opened and two officers walked in.

"At last."

The officers, both sergeants, joined Paul on the balcony.

"Sir?"

He handed the sheet of paper to one of the men who read it and passed it over.

"No code, Sir?" asked Parker, the elder of the two.

"No."

"Hoax?" Garrison asked.

"Possibly. But can we take the risk?"

"Evacuating everyone would be a logistical nightmare," Parker shouted above the roar of the impatient crowd.

"Army?" Garrison suggested.

"We would never be able to get them here on time."

"He's right."

"When is *on time* anyway?"

"True. We don't know who or what their motives are."

"If *they* exist at all."

All three men took time to mull over the situation.

The chanting from the stalls grew louder.

"The only way would be to tell them." It was Garrison who broke the concentrated thought processing.

"Surely that is not an option."

"It's the only way we are going to get them out of here."

"As a stampede," Parker retorted.

They both waited for Paul to comment.

"I don't think evacuation is an option right now. We do not even know if the bomb exists. I say step up the search and then decide. Do we have access to additional manpower?"

"Only if we decrease the police presence imposed after the riots."

"I think it's a case of needs must. Make the call, Garrison."

"Yes Sir."

Garrison stepped back into the control room.

Paul turned to face the chanting crowds once more.

A minute went by.

Parker joined him.

Lightening blinked.

"You don't believe it, do you?" Parker asked, casually, without taking his eyes off the swaying mass of people.

"Not really. Just all seems too far-fetched. There is no motive. Why would someone want to bomb a football game? They certainly aren't known as common terrorist targets."

"No, but if you think about it, they would be the most obvious one."

"What, even with all the gate security?"

"Presumably, it was planted well before the match."

"At the risk of it being discovered?"

They paused, lightening flashed.

Parker looked heavenwards, " It keeps threatening, I wish it would just get on with it."

"Ironic, isn't it, matches get postponed due to bad weather and water logging but today the rain appears to be the least of our worries?"

The gathering gloom disagreed and spat a raindrop as thunder reverberated around the stadium.

Forty Six

The Colonel stood in the doorway, looking down at Blake and Sky as they huddled on the floor at the far end of the room.

"Have you any idea how much trouble you have caused?" he asked in low demanding tone.

"What do you want from us?" Sky screamed.

"I just want you do die!" With that, the Colonel took aim.

"NOOO!" Blake shouted and threw himself in front of Sky.

However, the blast was much louder than Blake had expected, it was more like an explosion.

It was. One of the fuel tanks had exploded, blasting through the walls of the engine room and punching out the door that careered into the Colonel, hurtling him 10 ft down the corridor. He lay in a heap, his face melted by the blast.

Then came the loud groaning sound of bending metal.

Blake looked up. It was as though he had been beamed into a war zone; the doorframe was no longer there, what was left, was a ripped piece of wall surrounded by charred debris.

"Jesus."

Sky looked up. "What happened to him?"

"I shudder to think."

Rising to his feet, he extending a hand to her and said, "We need to get out of here. Fast! Come on! Come on!"

There was another loud groaning and a low rumbling sound.

They stepped through what had been the door's threshold into the devastation of the corridor. Hot oil smothered most of the wreckage like syrup over ice cream. They tentatively stepped over it.

"Hurry! Hurry!" Blake shouted. He helped her over twisted metal as more hot oil leaked into the corridor.

They ran, dodging chunks of steel girder, as the rumbling sound grew louder until the corridor began to shake and there was a loud hissing sound like water on hot coal.

"Oh No. Oh No," Blake groaned as they reached what was left of the Colonel; he lay there, with part of the door lying across his chest, his face was charred black and glittered with glass particles.

Sky held her hand to her mouth.

The noise grew closer and then, like something out of the Poseidon Adventure, it appeared. A four-foot wall of water rushed down the corridor, hissing as it mixed with the hot oil and heading straight towards them.

"Oh my God!"

"Run!"

"I am!"

"Faster!

The opaque water chased them like a slithering creature from the black lagoon. They were a few feet from the door but it was gaining

Closer…

And closer…

Williamson watched the drama unfold on the monitor. "Seal the door," he ordered, quickly. Then, as if justifying himself he added, "Otherwise we'll all drown."

"I can't, Sir," the operator said apologetically.

"What do you mean you can't?"

"It seems the Colonel damaged the mechanism."

It took a few seconds for Williamson to absorb the information. Then he slowly shook his head, incredulously, "The fascist bastard. He wanted this all along." He stared at the monitor and watched as the water enveloped the two people on the monitor.

Blake and Sky gasped as the Atlantic's icy cloak wrapped around their legs and the oil residue clung like leeches.

"Through here, quick!" Blake shouted, ushering her through the junction door. He followed her and pulled it shut, leaving the water to rapidly fill the corridor behind them.

They were at Junction F, inside a glass cubical about the size of a small portacabin. Four doors led off in various directions throughout the ship.

They stayed, doubled over, for a few seconds, gulping in air.

The whole tanker shuddered as another blast came, knocking them both off their feet. There was a loud groan, like that of a prehistoric dinosaur, and they felt themselves tilt forward.

The water in the corridor had risen to glass level, filling it with the blackness of the oil. It pressed on the door making it creak under the pressure.

"We've got to go!"

Blake caught Sky's hand and the next thing she knew she was stepping through a door, out of the Junction and into yet another corridor. She slammed it shut behind her.

They ran down G sector now, next stop would be the control room and off there, Blake remembered, would be the elevator out of here."

They were about five feet from the door when there was a loud thumping sound and the junction filled with water.

More creaking and then the door exploded outward, giving way to a wall of water. Sky screamed in terror as she looked back to see the black liquid creature chasing her.

"Don't look, just run!" Blake ordered over the rushing sound but he knew they were not going to make it. The tidal wave was gaining fast and the end of the corridor was too far away. It was only a matter of seconds before it engulfed them and washed them down the rest of the corridor, slamming them both against the doors and pinning them against the glass.

The corridor began to fill and the pressure of the rushing tide was so great that neither of them could move. The green light on the door went black as it shorted out and the water crept up to shoulder level.

Suddenly, there was relief, as the doors to the storage rooms on either side of the corridor began to burst inward, temporarily releasing the pressure.

Sky seized the moment and kicked the handle on the door. It slammed open and they washed into Junction A, outside the control room.

The water rushed and swirled around their feet, ready to fill the area.

Both of them panted with exertion but there was no time to recover.

"Which way?" She screamed.

"Hold on." Blake staggered around in the wash, trying to get his bearings. "We came that way, didn't we?" he said, pointing at a sign that read, "*Section I*"

"That way?"

"Yes, that way!" He paused for thought and then added, "I think."

There was another groan as the ship listed further. The sound of bending metal was loud and terrifying. It felt as if they were in a submarine at the bottom of the ocean and it was slowly imploding around them.

They staggered through the water, toward the elevator, leaving the control room behind.

Inside, Williamson sat alone; he had ordered the evacuation as soon as he learned that the fuel tanks in the Turbine 1000 area were exploding and ripping holes in the ship's hull. Therefore, it was only a matter of time before the tanker, years of research and millions of dollars of investment, sank like many ships before it, to the bottom of the Atlantic Ocean.

The control room doors shook as the water gathered outside and the pressure built. Williamson stood in his office waiting for the contents of the injection to take hold. Soon, he would experience the effects of the toxin first hand.

Outside the elevator, Blake frantically pressed the down arrow button as the slant of the ship became more obvious and the water pooled around their feet.

"Come on… come on…" Blake chanted, as the elevator slowly descended from the deck.

Eventually, the lift arrived; the doors opened and, like an anxious puppy, the water rushed in first.

"In you go," Blake said, almost pushing Sky inside and then following her. He pressed the blue button, marked "*D Deck*" and only after a dramatic pause did the doors close and the lift climb upward.

As they rose, the water slowly drained away. Seconds seemed like minutes and minutes like hours as they travelled.

The ship groaned and shook violently, forcing them both to steady themselves by holding onto the walls around them. They both stared upward, as if the triangular shaped hatch on the ceiling were a work of art.

Blake clenched his fists, willing the ride to speed up as the light went out and the humming stopped.

Sky screamed at the blackness. Her voice reverberated around the compartment, echoed by the roaring of the sinking vessel. "Oh My God… Oh My God…." she murmured repeatedly like an insane person.

"Don't worry," Blake said, seeking her out in the gloom and holding her to him. "It's just the power. It'll probably come back soon."

However, the seconds drifted and the blackness remained. They both breathed in sharply as the icy shroud of the water seeped into the lift and wrapped around their feet.

"Oh Shit!" Blake shouted.

The water was rising much faster than he had thought. They had to act fast.

"Sky, climb onto my shoulders."

"What?"

"Climb onto my shoulders."

"Blake," She protested, "I can't even see where you are!"

"Then feel me!" he shouted. He laughed, "Bet you don't get an offer like that ever day."

"Hysteria, finally settling in then?" Sky said, flippantly. Anything to keep her mind off what was actually happening to her. She felt his shoulders, his muscles, his wrists and then the stirrup he had made with his hands.

"Did you see that trap door in the ceiling?"

"Yes, I saw it."

"Well, we need to use it."

The water was at knee height now. "Hurry! This water's cold." She knew his haphazard wit was for her benefit but she was immune to anything other than terror right now.

"Can you feel anything?" he asked through grunts as she stood in his hands.

"No, not yet," she gasped as she frantically groped for the latch.

The water was at Blake's waist and rising fast, gurgling in like something out of his worse nightmare. There was a snapping sound; a hollow whale-like groan and both of them felt a swaying giddy feeling as the ship sank further.

Sky lost her balance and screamed as she fell but Blake stumbled through the water and held her up. "You're okay. You're okay." he said through gritted teeth.

"I can't find it! I can't find it, Blake!" she yelled into the darkness.

"Yes you can, Sky and hurry up because judging by the position we are in, I am going to be the first one to drown!"

"Why don't you get up here and try this?" she screamed in frustration.

"Because you are already doing an excellent job!"

"I see, even as we drown you still haven't lost that patronising streak."

"Never."

"I really hate you some times." She grunted as she flipped the catch and a slither of light fell onto them, dazzling Blake's eyes.

"At last," he said, full of satisfaction.

The water was now above his chest and freezing his limbs. "Can you climb up there?"

"I think…. so," she said, hauling herself up and out of Blake's hands.

There was another snapping sound and the ship shuddered violently. Blake lost his balance and fell, splashing loudly into the water.

Sky heard the sound but could see nothing.

"Blake?"

There was no answer, just the cracking and bending of the tanker and the sloshing of water against the hollow walls of the lift.

"Blake?" Sky attempted again, straining to see in the darkness. "BLAKE!" she yelled, panicked by the silence. Then she heard loud splashing and the sound of him sucking in air. "BLAKE? BLAKE?" she screamed.

"I'm… I'm … okay." He had to force the words out. His body had gone rigid with cold. He could just about balance himself on his feet. The water had reached his neck now and it was hard to stand up.

"Take my hand!" Sky cried, "Take it!"

He held his hand up to nowhere in particular and searched for Sky's but he could not find it nor could she find his. "Where are you?" she shouted in frustration.

"I'm here!"

"Where?"

"HERE!"

"Move, reach for the ray of light, Blake! Into the light!"

He complied and she caught his hand, gripping it so tight, she could have crushed his bones. "After three! One, two and three!"

He jumped, she pulled, and aided by his buoyancy in the rising water, he climbed through the escape hatch with relative simplicity.

"Now where?" she asked. "Have we got to climb?"

"Yes, It shouldn't be..." he stopped and examined the slither of light that was coming through a crack in the wall. "What's this?" He pressed his eye to the crack and laughed with relief. "We're there, Sky! We're there!"

"Where?"

"On deck!" Blake exclaimed, excitedly. "The lift has stopped just feet away from the deck!" Then, sticking his fingers inside the crack between the two doors, he tried to prize them apart and grunted, "Help me."

Sky fell to her knees with a splash. The water had filled the elevator shaft and was rising.

They both strained to pull the doors apart, but their efforts were very slow and the wear on their fingers severe.

Sky clawed at the door in frustration as her fingers began to bleed from the effort. Blake groaned angrily, ignoring the gun shot ache in his arm and, mercifully, their efforts were rewarded; the doors slid apart, expanding the ray of light to a centimetre in width. However, their progress was not fast enough; the water was now level with Sky's chest and growing upward.

"Come on," Blake winced through gritted teeth and the doors inched open, "Agaaaaain!" He strained.

A few more inches.

"WE can do it, Blake! We can do it!" Sky cried, neck deep in water, her hair floating around her. Then, with one final heave, the doors gave way, the water poured out and into the box room beyond.

"Get out Sky! Blake shouted, still pushing on the doors as she crawled through.

"Come on!" she shouted, once she was safe on the other side. "Come on, baby!"

Blake eased himself through, breathing in as much as he could, thanking himself for rigorously sticking to his morning press-ups.

Once they were together again, they hugged as the water swirled into a pool at their feet. Their eyes met and they caressed one another's faces, thrilled to still be alive and together. They lingered for a few more seconds then the sickly swaying of the ship brought them back.

"Come on!" He said, taking her hand and running out of the room, up the steps and then they were on deck once more.

But the sight that greeted them was much more terrifying then anything they had been through so far.

The sky was blanket grey and, like the swaying ocean, it went on endlessly for miles around them until it merged with the horizon.

The Atlantic gale blew cold as Blake Hudson and Sky McPherson felt the insignificance of their existence here. On this sea, a tanker was no more than a leaf on a lake, and on board a sinking oil tanker, they were no more than

The sound of someone screaming drifted to them on the breeze and they turned to see a clump of people, about twenty of them, retreating from the oncoming surf as it swallowed part of the bow. Like the tide, it stopped for nothing and no one.

Then, there was a loud squirting sound as water and air was pushed up the opposite elevator shaft. It shot upward like the spout on the back of a whale.

Sky clung onto Blake. She was shivering; the cold was biting and the wind was pulling her hair. She took in the deck: The helipads were empty, there were no lifeboats and there was no escape.

The tanker was sinking, the bow had disappeared under the water and the stern was soon to follow. As the water washed around their ankles, the other survivors huddled in the centre of the vessel, some clambering onto the giant winches whilst others scrambled up empty flag masts.

"Up there, Sky!" Blake pointed to the roof of the white control tower, the same tower that had loomed over them upon their arrival. It now seemed so close.

"No, Blake," Sky said.

Blake looked at her, bewilderment clear on his face.

"I can't do this anymore. I just don't have the strength," she said.

"Come on, Sky," Blake said, casually pulling her but she resisted.

"What's the point?" she screamed. She wanted to cry but she had no more tears left. She was totally demoralised and the adrenaline that had kept her going all this time had disappeared, washed away with the realisation that it was all for nothing.

"What's the point?" she cried again. "We're just delaying the inevitable!"

"Oh no you don't."

"I can't and I don't want to run anymore!" She shrieked angrily.

"You are not giving up now," Blake warned.

"Try me!"

"Look, I know there doesn't seem much point to you but there certainly is for me!"

"You are a fooling yourself, Blake! Look at us! Just look." She said, throwing her arms about, pointing at the infinite sea that surrounded them. "There is nowhere to go, nowhere else we can run or hide! It is over! You have to face the facts."

"I am facing facts!" Blake retorted. "Don't you think I know what has happened here? And believe me, if I was alone then, well, I would have given up right back at the point when we arrived at this damned place. But I am not alone, Sky, I have you. You are here with me and everything is different. I think of you," he choked back the lump in his throat, "I think of you… dead out here and I can't stand that! He blinked back tears. "Just the thought of you not breathing! Christ" He hammered his chest with a clenched fist, "And I want to kill myself!" He broke off and then added, through gritted teeth, "In hindsight I wish that fucking bullet had hit me in the head rather than live these last few moments thinking about how the world is going to go on without you. I cannot take that! I cannot take that." He repeated, angrily. "Twenty years Sky, twenty years it has taken us to find each other again and, after everything we have been through, you are telling me that you want to stop? That you do not have the strength to carry on, well, damn you! If we are going to die on this ship, then we will die together but in the meantime, we are going to make the most of every second that we have left.

Tears streamed down his face as the water swelled around his knees. Sky was speechless and at the same time, tears that could not come to her moments before now pricked her eyes. Suddenly there was hope. Suddenly she wanted to live!

She watched him standing there, legs apart to steady himself, his head bowed, his heart broken. She ran to him and they squeezed each other, investing as much energy as they could.

"I love you, Blake. I love you," she said, looking up kissing him, devouring him.

They stayed that way, tasting each other's tears as the tanker slipped further beneath the waves.

"Up there, quick!" She said, pointing to the control tower.

Blake smiled, taking her hand.

Together they splashed through the water and climbed the metal ladder that led up the facet of the tower. They ascended as fast as they could.

"Sky, hold on tight!"

No sooner had he finished saying the words when she slipped as the ship rocked, slanting backwards, pulling her from the metal rungs. She clung on, and smiling up at him with determination in her voice, she shouted, "Right until the end!"

Once they reached the roof of the tower, they gripped onto the railing as the vessel sank lower and lower into the abyss.

The deck was completely submersed now and the other stranded survivors abandoned their hasty hideouts and made their way to the tower.

Sky and Blake looked at each other, "Nothing else matters, Blake. As long as we are together," she said, encouragingly with one hand on the railing and the other on his.

He smiled, "Nothing but you and only you, my darling Sky."

Both of them had resigned themselves to their fate, at least they were together and right now that was all that mattered.

The groaning of the imploding tanker was so loud that neither of them heard the beating of the blades as they appeared on the horizon.

They were like tiny dragonflies in the distance, slowly metamorphosing into orange twin-bladed helicopters. As they drew closer, their distinctive colour was a florescent beacon against the dull backdrop of a grey sky. There were two of them, whirring their way toward the sinking ship.

Blake and Sky exchanged glances. Were they real or were they both hallucinating? Were they going to be saved? As they contemplated this, there was a violent shudder and the ship dipped further into the water. Sky screamed, "NO! Not now!"

They were sinking rapidly. The water reached the survivors scaling the tower and overtook them washing them away like ants.

"NOOO! NOOO!" Blake shouted in protest as if the tanker could hear him.

The helicopters buzzed closer. They were about thirty feet away but the ship was sinking fast. The deck was just a copper coloured blur. The white T of the tower was the only thing that protruded above the water.

"Should we jump?" Sky asked, hesitantly.

Blake considered the question, and then, quickly shook his head. "No, let's try and hold out as long as we can."

However, Blake was worried. He knew that the ship would leave strong, swirling currents in its wake but he was not going to discuss that with her. He just clutched her tight.

The first helicopter hovered over the survivors who were already bobbing about in the sea. It lowered its harness and began to pluck them out of the water.

The second helicopter flew over the tower and the harness was deployed and slowly whirred down.

But, the ship was sinking too fast. The air was blasted through the portholes of the tower and the turbulence from the helicopter created gale force winds that tugged at them both and willed them to let go. However, they gripped onto the railing with fierce persistence as the cacophony of imploding metal and the beating of the helicopter blades roared around them.

"NOOO!" Blake kept yelling as if his voice could stop the ship's determination to dive to the bottom of the Atlantic.

The harness was getting closer…

5 feet…

"Grab it, Sky!" Blake shouted over the whirring dissonance.

"What about you?"

"Just do it!"

"Not without you!"

"For once in your life girl, do as you are told!" He caught both her hands and thrust them upward toward the dangling cable. She complied, and held them outstretched, trying to get a grip, and, as she was busy doing so, he slipped his arms around her waist and lifted her as high as he could and strained there until she got a hold.

"BLAKE!"

"Don't let go!"

He felt the icy coldness of the water envelop his legs and then smack him in the face.

"NOOOO!" Sky screamed! "NOOOO!" as the winch hauled her up, slowly, away from Blake's outstretched arms and into the helicopter.

It felt like an eternity before she reached the safety of the chopper and once inside, she turned to see the tower disappear beneath the waves, leaving Blake bobbing on the surface.

The tanker that had taken two years to convert and millions of pounds of investor's money sank, taking with it over thirty lives and the world's last samples of the toxin. It descended rapidly, leaving a copper and white blur beneath the surface and then, gradually, it faded to grey.

"Quickly!" she shouted, as the winch was lowered once more. She watched, anxiously, as Blake spat salty water and flapped his arms to stay afloat. The turbulence of both choppers pushed him about in the water.

The harness was close, just a few feet from him and Blake held up a hand to grab the dangling cable. Then, to Sky's horror, she saw something white appear in the water, right underneath him. It was huge and rising rapidly.

The winch man's mouth dropped open and she heard him murmur. "What the…"

They both stared, wide eyed.

"Blake! Grab the cable! Grab the cable!"

But it was still too high.

Turning to the winch man, she shouted, "Hurry! Please hurry!"

"It can't go any faster," he replied, equally anxious.

When she turned back, she saw that the ghostly shroud was inches away from breaking the surface and then, before she had time to scream, she saw a gargantuan air bubble emerge and launch Blake into the air only to suck him under once more.

"NOOOOO! BLAAAAAAAKE!" Sky leaned forward, as if she could catch him but the winch man pulled her in. "NOOOOOO!"

By the time the cable pierced the water, Blake was nowhere to be seen. The helicopter hovered, drifting slowly sideways, dropping altitude in order to get a closer view of the area but nothing. Sky remained transfixed, clutching on to the handrail.

Her mind was frozen her heart constricted with dread as she stared into the water and the dancing patterns the downdraft created on the surface. Her mind drifted deep inside the hollow of her soul and a huge emptiness engulfed her, bringing with it the concept of a future without him.

The whirring of the blades echoed in the distance, as did the voices of the crew, leaving behind the rhythmic pounding of her heart and the sound of her shuddering breaths.

There was a sickly lurch as the helicopter climbed upward and as it did so she heard the echo of animated voices

Then, through the numbness of her mind, she saw him clutching on to the harness. At first, she thought it was dream, that her mind had fabricated this illusion to protect her from the damage of eternal loss.

However, slowly, as the echoes dissipated and she tuned in to reality once more, she felt the winch man pat her excitedly on the shoulder.

She laughed aloud, relief washing over her and quickly hugged and kissed the crewmember close by. Then, looking back down, she saw Blake coughing and spluttering, but he was alive and was being lifted back to her. He was wet and cold but he was grinning in the way that only her Blake could.

When he was pulled inside, he winked at her, "Not getting rid of me that easily," he said, shivering but forcing a smile.

Sky just hugged him as crewmembers wrapped blankets around them both.

All of the other survivors had been picked up, so the helicopter dipped sideways and flew on its way back to shore.

"I can't believe you held me up in your arms like that," she said, gazing into his eyes.

"Just as long as you know it was a sign of things to come. I am *never* going to let you go again."

"Is that a proposal?"

"Might be."

"Well, if it isn't…will you marry me?" she asked.

"Can I get back to you on that one?"

"YOU!" She prodded him, smiling broadly.

"Where shall we go for our honey moon, then?"

"Anywhere there isn't water!"

"Deal."

They hugged again very tightly and then Sky squealed, "Blake! Look!" She pointed to the distant horizon; the colours were dazzling and, for the first time in her life, Sky McPherson could see the beginning and the end of the most beautiful rainbow.

The End

Epilogue

"… And the headlines today.

The extraordinary riots that besieged the southwest of England appear to be over as police report a second night of calm. The damage resulting from the riots is estimated to run into millions of pounds.

Southampton Police have launched an investigation into a hoax bomb threat received minutes before the cup qualifier game yesterday. An independent enquiry is also underway to establish why the game was not cancelled.

Christopher Hamilton, head of the environment agency, has been arrested amid allegations of corruption.

Now, just before we go, a quick look at the weather with Andrew Jarvis."

"Hello there, yes well pretty good news all round, I am glad to say. Seems things are finally getting back to normal. The rainstorm that threatened to washout yesterday's cup qualifier failed to materialise. In fact, that large band of cloud has pretty much dissipated. This means, we can expect nice sunny spells over the next few days, but make the most of it because we all know how unpredictable the British weather can be. "

"Thanks Andrew. Well, that's all from us today, the next main news will be at six o-clock but in the meantime from Andrew and me, Elena Parker, for Southwest Radio, goodbye."